18

M   12/15/00
O'Shaughnessy, Perri
Move to strike

D1109767

MOVE TO STRIKE

PERRI O'SHAUGHNESSY

MOVE
TO STRIKE

WHEELER
PUBLISHING, INC.
ROCKLAND, MA

★ AN AMERICAN COMPANY ★

Published in Large Print by arrangement with Delacorte Press, a division of Random House, Inc., in the United States and Canada.

Wheeler Large Print Book Series.

Set in 16 pt Plantin.

Library of Congress Cataloging-in-Publication Data

O'Shaughnessy, Perri.
    Move to strike / Perri O'Shaughnessy.
        p. (large print) cm.(Wheeler large print book series)
    ISBN 1-56895-988-5(hardcover)
    1. Reilly, Nina (Fictitious character)—Fiction. 2. Tahoe, Lake, Region (Calif. and Nev.)—Fiction. 3. Women lawyers—Fiction. 4. Large type books. I. Title. II. Series

[PS3565.S542 M69 2000b]
813'.54—dc21   00-049961

                                                              CIP

To our sister Meg Peterson and
our brother Patrick O'Shaughnessy

And to the next generation:

Andrew, June, Connor, Corianna,
Alanna, Kristel, and Holly

and all their cousins,

on the launchpad, and getting ready to fly!

PART ONE

In his dream he is killing the murderer.

Bitter cold and the long wait numb the fingers around the knife, but he uses the strength of his shoulder to press it against the murderer's spine. They stand on the back porch of a cabin in winter. The murderer's back is turned; he has jimmied the lock and is turning the knob. All around is darkness, stars, ice, wind.

He has waited for hours for the murderer. He has made a promise to himself, that if the murderer comes to this woman's cabin on this night and tries to break in, he must die.

He presses the knife against the murderer's spine, and the murderer arches his back against the pain. The murderer reaches behind him, cursing, and swipes at the knife as if swatting a bee. His hand touches the brittle blade.

An infinitely long time goes by.

The murderer's head turns slowly to the right and he looks back. His body pivots carefully around the point of the knife. The murderer knows his center now, knows where his death lodges in his body.

He wants to see the look of terror on the murderer's face as he dies. But the murderer is not terrified. The murderer is laughing.

1

MOIST NIGHT WIND swept the skin on her arms and flicked sharp points of hair into her eyes. Pulling her sweatshirt tight against the gusts, Nikki tucked her hair inside the hood and splashed the oars into the deep black water of Lake Tahoe. A hundred years ago, under the same crescent moon, a Washoe Indian in a kayak would have known how to dip the oars silently, secretly, but no matter how she tipped them, they sucked water into the air, leaving behind a trail of sound.

Silvery snow tipped the mountain peaks that circled like clouds around the lake. She stayed close enough to the shoreline—flat black trees against a glinting navy sky—to track her progress, but far enough out to remain unidentifiable by anyone nosy enough to observe her. She could not be caught, because tonight...

Tonight, she was going on a raid! And for the first time, she was going alone.

She felt high with the strength of her arms and the tautness of her legs as she rowed, as high as she had felt on New Year's Eve when her mom had let her drink champagne, so even though she didn't like being out here all alone, floating above a deep, dark immensity she didn't want to think about, she wasn't about to turn back.

Scott would have come with her if she had told him about it, but tonight—tonight was personal. She was not just skulking and peeking in windows for a joke, or scrounging a few left-over Heinekens from an outside cooler. Not that she didn't miss having him along. She wouldn't mind a warm body beside her floating into this dark moonlit haze.

As a steady breeze blew over the lake, the water churned, pushing her farther out than she liked. But it wasn't far now.

She knew what she was doing was wrong. But a while back, being bad had stopped feeling bad. Scott had helped with that. So many rules were stupid. He had shown her a whole new way of thinking. You had to make your own way.

Tonight was about making something really wrong right again.

She stretched. Her arms ached. She wasn't used to rowing so much, but then, her original plans for the year hadn't included breaking into someone's house. She hadn't exactly trained for it. She had been forced into it. Three days before, the mail brought a letter addressed to her mother from a law office. That scared her. Her mother wasn't around, so she had opened it. A so-far nice day turned real bad right then. The letter said they were about to be evicted. The landlord wanted his money, and he wanted it right now.

When her mom came home Nikki held the letter in her face, making her read it. "What is this?"

"Don't worry, honey," Daria had said in that drifty way she had. As if everything took care of itself somehow. As if they weren't going to have to pack their things in boxes in about two weeks and go squat in a condemned building. Nikki sat her down, tried to have a practical conversation with her. Where was her last paycheck?

Gone. They had had a lot of back bills to pay.

Not worth screaming about. The bills never got paid until the third notice because they weren't Daria's priority. At least this time she hadn't gotten rooked by some guy who was off to make his mark as an artist or a musician in Vegas.

What about her job? Nikki had asked. Where were the paychecks? Oh, she had lost that job a few weeks ago. She didn't want Nikki to worry and had planned to tell her just as soon as she had another one, which would be any day now.

Nikki had decided. They would resort to the unthinkable. They would borrow money, using Grandpa Logan's land in Nevada for collateral. That was when her mom got nervous and darted around the living room rearranging trinkets.

Finally, Daria had admitted it. She had sold the land to Nikki's uncle Bill for twelve hundred stinkin' dollars.

Forty acres!

Her mom shrugged, saying what was done was done. "That land is in the middle of nowhere and it's basically worthless. He did us a favor."

"Where's the money?" Nikki had asked.

Maybe Grandpa's land would perform a heroic rescue. Maybe it would save their home. But no. Her mom had already spent that too paying a few other late bills. The money was gone, just like everything else. Like her dad. Like the security she had once had: that she would have lunch money or new shoes in the fall.

Her mom had never grown up. She trusted everybody, even Uncle Bill. He had never helped them out before and he hadn't helped them out this time. Nikki knew darn good and well that land was worth more than he had paid. All you had to do was to check out the *Reno Gazette.* Land in Nevada was going up, even scrub desert in the foothills. You couldn't buy land for thirty bucks an acre. You couldn't buy anything for thirty bucks, period. He had taken advantage of her mom's totally inept sense of business.

All of which she had told her mom.

"Oh, honey. Your uncle's a very savvy businessman. Believe me, he knows how much that land is worth."

Duh! He knew, all right, but he was smart enough not to pay it.

Her next thought was, okay, she would talk to him, maybe just ask him to pay a fairer price for Grandpa's acres. But that was dreaming. He couldn't stand her or Daria, because they were poor and he was rich. Sometimes Nikki even thought Uncle Bill was afraid of her, maybe because of her smart mouth.

But they were really in the pits this time, so

she thought, we'll ask him for a loan. But anytime she and Daria had been hurting in the past, he had made sure to joke about how stupid it was to loan money to relatives, rubbing his clean surgeon's hands together and watching to make sure they got it.

That made up her mind. She would go to his house, find money, and take it. She had studied the newspaper classifieds. She figured the land was, rock-bottom minimum, worth twice what he paid. She was sure he kept cash around the house. She would take no more than what he should have paid them in the first place. Tomorrow, before he had time to call the police or something dumb like that, she would 'fess up.

Because, let's face it. He owed them.

If he got really ugly about it, they could promise to pay him back when they could. He would just have to lump it and accept that the money was gone. Ultrarespectable Uncle Bill would never tell anyone his niece had to come and steal money from him to save herself and her mother from being evicted. He would never allow a public scandal that might reflect badly on him. His surgical practice depended too much on people admiring him and thinking he was so brilliant and such a saint. Nobody wanted a mean, stingy guy cutting them up.

Did she hear splashing? Turning her head, she looked behind her. If there was another boat or something out here, she couldn't see it. When she was young, she believed that monsters roamed this lake. Bedtime stories, she knew, but still...she was alone, shivering in a new rush of wind. The lake felt powerful and alive under her. For a moment, fear took over. She fought the urge to turn around and go home.

Tears welled in her eyes. For some reason, her dad's face, the one in the picture of him and her and her mom, appeared in her mind. Maybe it was a blessing on tonight, him coming around. She was off to fight. He would approve of that, wouldn't he? Thinking about the wrong that had been done to her and her mom allowed anger to heat her up and burn away the fear.

"Payback time," she said to the black sky. She was Mel Gibson in *Ransom*, out to get even. Her voice sounded high and scared, so she said it again, growling.

Through a clump of trees she saw a low wood cabin, classic old Tahoe, looking like something tossed together from recycled crates. Rich people had this trick of trying to look poor on the outside so thieves wouldn't rob them. Scott had taught her about that. But Nikki already knew this place was like a mansion inside and filled with expensive junk. She and her mom had visited there many times.

Letting the kayak wash in on a miniature wave, she managed to get out without swamping and pulled it behind a bush. Water sloshed around her feet on the brief beach, the wind making the leaves blow and sigh.

She moved commando-style toward the

house, keeping low behind the plants that made a privacy border. He had a swimming pool, she knew. The knotty lacework of reflections from the pool water flickered on the fence like the light from a TV. Her first problem was the gate, but it was unlocked, easy. She stopped just inside.

Nobody should be home. Aunt Beth and Chris were in LA and her mom had mentioned more than once that Saturdays were Uncle Bill's night to play poker at Caesars.

Remembering the Washoe, she moved slowly through the bushes near the pool, toward the French doors that led to his study. He would keep anything important there.

No sign of anyone around. She crouched down for a moment, intending to creep out into the open and try the door. Just as she straightened up, the door flew open. Shit! She ducked back fast behind the dense brush, stumbling, holding her hands out to keep the bushes back.

Uncle Bill stepped out onto the concrete patio, so close to her she could smell the brandy on his breath and soap on his nude skin. So much for freakin' poker.

Wow! she thought, checking him out. He was buck naked, his dick swinging like a pendulum under his belly as he moved past her. Tight buns and legs showed he worked out all the time. He looked so young, very different from the famous Doctor Bill she remembered seeing in starched white coat and glasses at his clinic. Probably it would give her a complex that her first good look at a naked man was her uncle.

Her heart stepped up the beat and anger took over again. That lying, cheating bastard! Just seeing him out here enjoying himself on a spring night, not a care in the world, made her so mad she wanted to throw something at him, slug him or something. He was too big; he'd catch her for sure. The thought of him catching her in the bushes made her sick. That would blow everything.

Holding the brandy bottle in one hand, he padded toward the steaming pool, put his feet in, and plunked his butt down on the highest step, where the water was only a few inches deep. He took a swig.

"Goddamn!" he said, shaking his head. He took another drink.

Nikki managed to sit down in the pine needles and make a little viewing place for herself through the fronds of one of those dinosaur-era ferns that grew under the trees. Just when she was getting used to the whole scene, he started to jabber. "Not like I had any choice," he said. The sound of his own voice seemed to startle him, and he looked around sharply. Like an idiot, Nikki closed her eyes. As if he wouldn't be able to see her if her eyes were closed! The fronds rustled. Had he sensed someone spying? She couldn't look, but in her mind he moved swiftly toward her, pulled her out of the bushes and...she was breathing loud enough to lead him right to her.

He mumbled something. What was that? "Nik?" so soft, she wasn't sure if he said it or if she dreamed it, but the sound was so chilling she froze.

Nothing happened. His hand didn't reach over and yank her out. She heard a splash. When she dared to open her eyes again, he was gone...no, he was swimming away from her, toward the deep end of the pool where the underwater light was.

He swam to the far wall, dove down deep and came up inhaling and coughing, then dove again. Nikki pushed open the branches so she could watch. He was doing something with his hands down in the water at the deep-end wall. Nikki had been in that pool when she was little. She knew it was nine feet deep. Here he was, most likely drunk, acting crazy at the bottom of the pool. Was he trying to drown himself? Should she make a run for the house while he was down there?

No. He might come out and see her.

Kneeling, she pushed the ferns back and stared. He stayed down almost a minute.

She was bad at waiting. Waiting gave her time to think and thinking had a way of contaminating the passing minutes with doubts. The smell of chlorine mixed like toxic gas with the smell of the fir trees, making her feel sick. None of this was supposed to happen. He shouldn't even be home, and here he was acting so stupid!

He surfaced, took a breath, and dived again.

Swallowing the acid in her mouth, Nikki

steeled herself and sneaked toward the study. He came up again, splashing, but he still had his back to her. In one hand he held a box made of metal. While he swam to the side of the pool, holding the dripping box up above the water with one hand, Nikki slipped back into the bushes.

Hauling himself out at the deep end, grunting, he set the box on the concrete deck. After he caught his breath, he sat cross-legged at the edge, twisting something on the box. The lid came off and he took something out.

What freakin' luck! So that was where he hid his money. In the freakin' pool!

The wind had finally eased. Now Nikki faced a new dread, the complete silence. Except for the pool pump and Uncle Bill's harsh breathing, there was nothing except the noise of her clacking teeth and whomping heart. Not even the crickets were singing.

He was holding something wrapped in a cloth pouch. Bills, she figured. Maybe some rare coins. Light filtering up from the pool pocked his face with ghoulish shadows. He looked like Jason in a slasher movie. The whole scene was like a nightmare, the pool with its blue light, the darkness closing in, Uncle Bill, squatting like an evil Buddha, drunk, fondling his secret stash.

After a few moments, he put the pouch back into the box, screwed the lid closed, dove into the pool, and returned it to some hiding place in the deep end. This time, he got out immediately and trotted to the study.

Shaking from the cold and scared to death he would spot her at any second, she watched him wrap a towel around himself. As he slid his feet into rubber sandals at the door to the study, the doorbell rang. Shocked by the sound, she let out a little yelp. He jerked, turning around to face her, scouring the bushes, looking directly at her! He took a step forward, scaring her so badly she practically screamed, but the doorbell rang again. Hesitating for a second, he finally went back into the house.

Tossing off her sweatshirt, Nikki ran for the pool. The water curled over her body as she dove. Toward the bottom, directly below the pool light, she finally felt a plastic ring in the wall, just big enough to slide the tip of her finger into. Twisting the ring back and forth, she discovered the hiding place worked just like a drawer. Chlorine stung her eyes as she reached through the milky light, pulled out the box, pushed the empty drawer closed, and shot to the surface, gulping air, trying to see through the strings of her hair.

She pulled herself out of the deep end. Holding the box, she started to run for the boat. A phone rang inside the house. Good, more to keep him busy. She got as far as the gate before she remembered. Her goddamn sweatshirt! She'd left it by the pool! Clutching the box under her arm, she ran back toward the house, staying close to the wall and away from the windows, really cold now, soaking wet. Where had she thrown it?

Through the glass, she saw Uncle Bill talking on the phone in the study, sounding happy in there, way different than when he had mumbled by the pool. With relief she realized he had no clue she was right outside, watching him. Unable to resist, Nikki went a little closer and peered in.

He held the cordless phone to his ear with one hand and the towel around his waist with the other. He was smiling, talking, saying, "How's it going?" and "Gee, that's great." In that instant, Nikki felt the sweet rush of victory. She had done it, stolen it from under his nose. She was certain now she had what she had come to get.

Just as she was turning away, a change in her uncle's expression brought her back to the glass. His face sagged, melting downward. His mouth dropped open and his eyes bulged. Like someone blinded by a bright light, he groped around as if hunting for some stable thing to keep him from falling down. He staggered, then fell against the desk.

"No! Please God, no!" he shouted over and over, first into the phone, then, pressing a hand against the mouthpiece, away from it.

She watched him stare into the receiver, then drop the phone to the ground. He collapsed onto the floor and curled up and cried like a baby. She could hear the heaving sobs.

A shadow ran in and bent toward him. Someone else was there! Well, of course someone else was there. The doorbell had rung, hadn't it! She caught a glimpse, gasped, and slammed herself back against the cabin. A large splinter pierced the skin of her palm, but she didn't feel it, even when blood began to flow onto the wood of the house.

Clutching her uncle's treasure, her sweatshirt forgotten, she pressed back against the wall, paralyzed.

2

THE TREES WERE TIPPED in new blue growth and a squall of rain scattered the gulls around Lake Tahoe. On the slopes of the Sierra, skiers would be skidding over thin patches through the late-season snow.

In the second week of May, in the city of South Lake Tahoe, mountain spring was in full swing. As the showers passed overhead and the sun spilled out from behind the clouds, Nina Reilly looked out her office window and watched an elderly man wait for the traffic light to change, shading his eyes with his hand. She rolled her chair a few feet and poured a glass of water into the fiddle-leaf fig in the corner, now so tall it scraped the ceiling of her small office.

Her secretary, Sandy Whitefeather, opened the door to the inner office and came in. Solid as Rodin's "Balzac" and similarly massive, Sandy had several inches on Nina in every direction, and a don't-even-think-of-messing-with-me-unless-you-want-your-ass-

15

kicked-into-the-lake attitude Nina had given up trying to reform. On the other hand, she and Sandy had passed through good and bad times together, and Sandy was a friend. Sort of.

Sandy observed her with onyx eyes that hid a private universe in their dark depths, arms folded.

"What?" Nina asked.

"We need to talk."

"Did the court call? Is it the Kathy Locke custody thing?"

"No. About Johnny Ellis. He needs more help from us."

"Sandy, it doesn't do any good to bleed all over the desk every time a client wants more than the law entitles. He strained his back. He didn't rupture a disc or something."

"He's fifty-six, too old for physical labor, and he needs a rest. He's tired."

"We're all tired. That's not what the workers' comp system was set up to fix." Nina leaned back in her chair and felt her own fatigue pulling down on her eyelids.

"That's because the workers didn't set it up. He needs a couple more months off. He can scrape by on the disability money." Sandy handed her Ellis's file. "And he thought he might drop by this morning."

"But there's nothing—okay, okay. I'll have a final look to see if I've missed anything."

Sandy acknowledged this by going to the bookshelf and poking at a dusty volume of the California Codes. "Business is booming," she said, giving the shelf full of leaning books a back-handed whap. They lined up like good soldiers and stayed in position. "Wish I could say the same for you."

"Uh oh," Nina said. "Here it comes."

Seven months ago, she had been doing well. She had had a loving husband and son, and faith that the world was a good place. Then, when she was on the verge of finishing up a murder case for an untrustworthy client, her husband had been killed in an attack meant to kill her and her son, Bob, too. She couldn't forget about it. Time might get her through the day, but it would not help her forget.

She was doing as well as she could.

"You need to move on. Find another man, maybe."

"Sandy, I lost my husband, not my mind."

"What's Paul doing these days? Still in Washington? How come he hasn't called the past few weeks?"

"I knew it. I knew you were going to bring him up." The last thing Nina needed was to get into a discussion with Sandy about Paul van Wagoner. When she had married, Paul had been three thousand miles away in Washington. Just as well. He spread chaos wherever he went. The usual rules never applied with him, and Nina's distinct certainties had a way of fogging in his presence.

Their relationship, hot and turbulent, had blown out like a match. When her mind tripped over the stub of it now and then, she reminded herself about all the reasons why things had turned to smoke in the first place. Funny and warm on the surface, Paul remained inscrutable to her. He did things she didn't expect, understand, or approve of, upsetting things, violent things. How could you be close to a man you might never know? He protected himself too well from intimacy. So she didn't need Paul in her life except professionally, as an expert investigator. She needed a long swim or a walk through the hot sand of the desert, not another man. "Can we get back to work?"

"Or a nice, meaty murder case might do the trick," Sandy said, tapping one finger to her cheek. "Keep your mind off your troubles. Of course, that won't keep you warm at night... You ran away to the desert to mope again this weekend, didn't you?"

Stung because she had done exactly that, Nina said, "I'm going to pretend I didn't hear that, Sandy, because it was—insolent." She spent many weekends there now in an old trailer on a piece of land a client had tossed her once in lieu of a more conventional bonus.

But last night she had not slept much, because of something that had happened out in the desert the night before. She had stepped outside to look at the stars. The moon was floating over the jagged peaks of the Carson Range. Suddenly, somewhere in the black sky, she had heard a rumble. A plane was approaching from the south. She watched its lights as it flew directly over her head and turned, banking toward Tahoe. The plane seemed awfully low, too close to the mountains, so she had held her breath, but the plane cleared the treetops, sailing over.

It's okay, she thought. You're always expecting a—

Then, disaster. As the sound faded, the plane had disappeared into the mountains. Anxious, she cupped her ear, listening, and watched for a last glimpse of the plane that was miles away. Had she heard a faint change in the sound of the engine?

A flash of sunflower yellow light had burst above the long desert horizon and for an instant, the mountain seemed to have caught fire. She had known it then.

There was no sanctuary in that valley or any other. Across the mountains, death had come again.

So late last night after she had arrived home, she had kept her vigil for whoever had been in the plane, as that yellow light appeared again and again when she closed her eyes, making sleep impossible.

But sleep was often impossible lately. Each night she went through the motions, brushed her teeth, locked the doors, checked on Bob. Then she curled up under the covers and shut her eyes, as if miming all the usual activities in the usual order would magically deliver her into sweet dreams. Eventually, her eyes gave up the pretense and opened. When she did doze, she slept lightly and briefly, as if rattled out of sleep's deeper realms by a preset alarm.

Bob was having trouble sleeping too. Several times during the past months he had appeared suddenly in the doorway to her room, eyes wide and startled, staring at something she couldn't see. "What's the matter?" she would ask, but he never answered, just turned around and left. She jumped up to find him in bed sound asleep only seconds later.

Mornings after these troubled nights were blurry. Today was blurry. She rubbed her eyes, which seemed to have just gone through a sandstorm. "Did you pick up a newspaper on the way in this morning?"

"Why?"

Maybe she had exaggerated what she saw. Maybe the plane had not crashed at all. Bad news could always wait. "Never mind. I'll read it when I get home."

They heard the outer door buzz. "I guess I'll take my insolent rear end out and greet that client," Sandy said.

"And watch your attitude."

"No need, when I have you to watch it for me."

Again the buzzer erupted. A muffled voice shouted, "Y'all inside there?"

They looked at each other.

"Oh, hell. Johnny Ellis." Rubbing her forehead, Nina opened the file. "Maybe I can find him a good chiropractor," she said.

Sandy nodded. " 'Monday, Monday,' " she said. " 'Can't trust that day.' "

At six-forty-five it was already getting dark. Joggers and dinner seekers clogged Lake

Tahoe Boulevard. Another Monday endured, Nina thought, tossing her briefcase into the back of the Bronco. Another successful defense of the status quo. She had crawled as many steps up as down.

Rolling down the window, she drove home to Kulow Street, trying to edit the smell of exhaust from the piney perfume of the air. Bob and Hitchcock would be waiting for her, hungry. She wondered as she drove past the Raleys', did they have food? Nothing fresh, but they could scrounge. As long as Hitchcock had his kibble, she and Bob could open a can or two of SpaghettiOs or something.

The small wood cabin surrounded by tall firs, its warm lamp-lit windows breaking through the darkness outside, was a welcome sight. She parked in the steep driveway and had her key in the door before she realized it was ajar. She stepped back, jabbed by fear.

"Bob!" she called out loudly, acting normal, because of course he was all right. "You left the front door open again." She threw her case into the closet by the door noisily. She would dig it out later when she settled down for the night and couldn't sleep.

A chair lurched upstairs. She didn't even make it into the kitchen for a sip of water before Bob, followed by Hitchcock, came running down the stairs, knocking directly into her. "Wait," Bob said, "don't take your jacket off. We've got to go over to Nikki's."

"Nikki's?" Now where had she heard that name before?

21

"Nicole Zack. You remember?" He breathed hard with excitement.

"Oh." The girl who invited him to a dance last fall. Bob had gone, but with his buddies, not with Nicole, and with the callous cool of a thirteen year old, hadn't thought to say anything to her all night. Or so he'd reported. She hadn't heard a word about Nicole Zack since.

"You two have become friends?" she went on. She reached out a hand to ruffle his hair and he shook it off lightly but definitely.

"I walk her home sometimes. She tells me things."

Which was more than Nina could say for Bob these days. This was news, and not very welcome news.

"She's in trouble. Come on!" Bob, who in the past five months had grown an equal number of inches, pulled an orange fleece jacket off the back of a chair and threw it over his head.

She stepped past him toward the kitchen. "Let me just put some dinner on and we'll talk..."

"This won't wait!" He took her by the arm. "We have to go, Mom!"

They were walking to the door, Bob half-dragging her, before she found her voice. "Wait a minute! Just quit!"

He let go of her arm.

"Don't you go strong-arming me. Tell me why we should skip dinner and rush off to Nicole's."

He looked at the door, then back at her. Realizing he had no choice, he said, "Here's what happened. She was having a rough time. Her cousin Chris just died and she felt really bad about it because they used to play together all the time when they were kids. So we were in the kitchen eating Oreos—"

"Whose kitchen?"

"At Nik's house."

"You are supposed to come straight home..."

He put up a hand. "I left you a message on your voice mail."

Which she hadn't checked. "Okay. Go on."

"Anyway, her mom's there rehearsing in the living room—"

"Rehearsing?"

"She's trying to get into a show. She has to practice, no matter how bad she feels. So she's, like, hardly dressed...when there's this knock, pounding, really loud, Mom. So Nik's mom says, 'Hold your horses. I'll be right there.' "

Hardly dressed? What had Nicole's mother been rehearsing, a strip routine?

"Anyway, she put on her slacks..."

"Honey, wait a second. What was she wearing?"

"...over her leotard while they pounded away. She finally went to answer the door. Mom, it was two policemen."

She waited while he gulped and took a deep breath.

"They came in. Her mom let them come right into the living room. They told us that some

23

doctor was dead and they started asking Nikki a bunch of questions."

"Not her mom? They started talking to your friend?" Nina tried to engage by letting the lawyer in her click into place, but she was distracted by hunger and the sudden realization that Bob was looking down at her from what appeared to be a great height.

"They zeroed right in on Nik. Her mom just stood there, scared. She tried to talk a few times but they shut her up so when she couldn't do anything, I tried."

That focused her attention. "What..." now it was her turn to gulp, "what exactly did you try?"

"I told Nik she had the right to remain silent. They were like, reading her her rights so fast she had no idea what they were saying."

Nina pulled him in closer and smelled his fear.

"One of them gave me a dirty look but by then...by then it was too late. She had already said some stuff. They told her mom they were taking Nik into temporary custody and to call the juvenile hall in an hour. They took her away!"

"For what?"

"Mom, please!" He tugged her arm again, but gently. "Please, just come. They need us. The police kept saying, 'Get it off your chest. You can tell us.' Stuff like that."

"Like what. Exactly."

"You know, like, 'Did you kill your uncle?' Like that."

So she was back on the wet road, stomach growling. Bob had a way of getting his way. So did Hitchcock, who had planted himself in the back seat and stuck his head out the window before they thought to take a stand. "Turn right. No, left. You almost hit the curb."

"Where did this...alleged incident happen, Bob? Did her uncle live here at Tahoe?"

Bob nodded. "In a big cabin on the lake near the Truckee meadows. Close to the casinos, but not over the state line. Acres, Nikki said. And a pool, too. She talked about him sometimes. She didn't like him much."

"Why?"

"I don't know. She called him a snob. He was mean to them. See, Nikki is broke..."

Oh, great, Nina thought.

"And her Uncle Bill said once that Nikki's mom Daria was like Marilyn Monroe—"

"Not necessarily an insult." Not to Nina, who had always thought the actress was underrated.

"Oh yeah? He said Daria was a good time had by all. And he told her Aunt Beth he didn't want them coming over to his house."

Uncle Bill sounded nasty, like the kind of uncle who rolls the garden hose up into a perfect circle and spends a lot of time chasing the neighborhood kids off the lawn.

"Supposedly she took a boat to his house and tried to break in. Supposedly she murdered her own uncle!" He seemed to use deliberately

25

harsh words to highlight their impossibility. Instead, they made an abstract act of violence all too tangible.

"Did you hear anything—why do they think she would do that?"

"Don't even ask that question," Bob said, getting excited. "She didn't kill anybody. Get in the left lane."

"It's hard for me to believe they would arrest a young girl like her for nothing..." The streetlight clouded as a fresh shower began to fall. Blue light leaked from behind the curtains of the silent houses.

"They did this time."

"There must be some evidence," she said, as much to herself as to Bob. "Something that implied she was involved. Is that why they arrested her, Bob? Did they say anything about what they found?"

"Just junk. Whatever."

"Could you be more specific?"

He clammed up. She continued to ask questions, but he refused outright to say anything more about the arrest. He looked straight ahead, saying, "We're almost there," while she wondered what had set him off.

"Tell me more about Nicole," she said. "How old is she?"

"Sixteen."

Nearly three years older than Bob. Holy Mary. "When did you two get to be friends?"

"After the dance. She asked me why was I such a chickenshit and I told her I wasn't."

Nina raised her eyebrows.

26

"We saw each other a few places and started to talk. She's not my girlfriend, Mom. She's got lots of guys interested in her plus a boyfriend."

Worse and worse.

"Anyway, I'm not ready for a relationship. That's what I told her."

She skidded around a corner.

"Slow down," Bob commanded. "Today is not a good day to die."

She slowed the car down, but could do nothing to steady her racing heart. He was growing up so fast. "What...what do you two have in common, do you think?"

"Not much. Nik's really smart but she doesn't give a good goddamn about grades."

"Language, Bob..."

"She doesn't care what people think about her. She plays guitar. She listens to crust bands like Destroy and X Machine. Her mother won't let her go out so sometimes she sneaks out." He turned an unnerved face toward her, no doubt surprised at himself for spilling the beans. "I know," he said before she said anything. "But what am I going to do about it? Tell? She would never trust me again! And please don't even think about telling what I just said or I won't be able to trust you."

"Where does she go when she sneaks out? To meet boys?"

"I don't know."

"Really."

"I don't!"

She could read the lie in the tensing of

muscle in his arm and hear it in the way he breathed.

"Well, then, why are you friends? You do your homework, you don't like that kind of music, and she's a lot older than you are."

"Well, she's sad underneath. She's not that tough, really, and she's kind of pretty"—Bob gave her a sideways glance—"if you like that type. I'm trying to get in this band she's in."

"You never mentioned that before."

"They haven't had a practice yet."

"What's her mother like?" Out of the corner of her eye, she watched his shoulders relax.

"Daria? Nik always says it's too bad Daria's mother is dead. She says Daria needs a mother."

"What does she mean by that?"

"Oh, you'll see right away when you meet her. Nik's the one who pays the bills. She got sick of the lights being turned off, and the heat disappearing in the dead of winter. She tried to put her mom on an allowance, if you can believe that."

Nicole Zack and her mother lived in a broken-down cabin in deep woods not far from the lake. Nina and Bob pulled into the muddy driveway, parking behind a rattletrap VW with a torn convertible roof. A bare bulb burned from the eaves. The windows appeared to be curtained with blankets. The wood in the depleted woodpile next to the dangerously fragile steps was just tossed there, not even stacked. Daria Zack answered the door almost

28

immediately. Tall, maybe a few years younger than Nina, in her early thirties, she wore a thin leotard under slacks and she had tied a tattered pink mohair sweater around her shoulders.

"Thank God!" she said. "Here you are!" She grabbed Nina and hugged her. Then she said, "Bobby," and pulled Bob in close and kissed him on the cheek, leaving behind a bright pink stain. As they moved inside, she pulled the door closed behind them with a slam. "Bob's told me everything about you. How brilliant you are, all the work you do helping people..." She took Nina's coat. "It's so awful. But I knew help would come."

Nina looked at Bob, who appeared normal except for the crimson burning of his ears.

The door opened directly into the living room. An area beside it had been designated the mud room, with a wooden bench and boots below, and pegs above for two old parkas, where Daria was hanging Nina's coat now. Candles burned along the windowsills. A wooden chair held a modest boom box with a stack of CDs. In the center of the wall at the far end, a fire burned in an iron stove. A large hooked rug cozied up to the hearth.

That was it for furniture.

Daria had noticed Nina's eyes. "Times are tough," she said. "Who needs a couch anyway? Nikki and I sit on the rug. Or on pillows." She looked around, saying absently, "Maybe Nikki has them in her room. She's got the computer on the floor in there."

"We're fine," Nina said. They gathered by

the fire. Here, the ancients made wise decisions. Here, families shared warmth and food. And here, as in ancient times, strong knees for squatting would help. Bob, who seemed accustomed to the situation, sat right down, and Nina folded her legs and hunched forward toward the fire.

"I'll just get us some tea." Daria rushed off toward the kitchen.

"No, really," Nina said. "We're okay."

"You don't want tea?" She stood in the doorway, framed by a yellow glow from the kitchen, pushing brassy gold hair back with her hand. "I may have some lemonade..."

"No," Bob said. "Daria, just tell her what's going on."

Nicole's mother threw herself down and pulled her long slender legs up into a full lotus. She was as supple as a young birch tree, and Nina thought, she's a showgirl. But her hair dye job looked lackadaisical. That and the slapdash clothes taken in conjunction with brushy, unplucked eyebrows created a surprisingly run-down effect, given her youth and natural beauty. Even her moist pink lipstick slopped haphazardly around her natural lip lines. She might have been a sexy, healthy girl once, but she had been letting things slide for a while. All clues pointed toward an unemployed showgirl.

"I don't know what to say. They've arrested my daughter. I don't understand the karma here, because I don't think we've done anything to deserve this. Is it because we're poor? Do the cops think they can just grab some innocent child and blame her? I've been chanting to stay calm, but obviously I'm going to start screaming soon." She lit a cigarette, her hand shaking. Her wrist was thin and bony.

Bob put out his hand and patted her shoulder. "We're here," he said. "Don't worry."

"But Bobby, she's scared and alone in a prison barracks and I'm scared to death about it."

"My mom'll fix it." They both turned to look at her, Daria's face as open and full of trust as Bob's. Chronological years and emotional years didn't seem to match up in her case.

"Tell me about it," Nina said.

"My nephew Chris died in a plane crash on Saturday night—I guess Bob told you about that?"

"In a plane crash?" Nina drew in breath sharply. The plane she had seen? She hadn't had time to check the paper for details.

"Yes."

"Where?"

"In the Carson Range. He was the passenger in a little Beechcraft. A charter. The pilot died, too."

"I'm so sorry." She saw the terrible light again, sunflower yellow, and could almost feel the heat sweeping across the flats toward her from the mountains where the plane went down. After her husband died, she had imagined the moment of his death many times, trying to visualize something like a soul drifting up from the earth, moving toward something like a heaven. Maybe this boy and the pilot had gone that way.

"Chris was only nineteen. Just starting out in life. We loved him. Everybody did. And then, you've probably heard my brother-in-law, Bill Sykes, died the same night, killed by some thug."

"The same night?"

Tears shiny as tree sap dribbled down Daria's cheeks. She nodded. "Saturday night. If you read the papers you know there's a bunch of people getting robbed who have houses on the lake. Bill and Beth had valuable things in that house. He was a surgeon. Wealthy. Obviously, they became targets. He was attacked with a sword he had hanging on the wall of his study for a decoration... Thank God Beth was out of town." Wiping her cheeks with a hand, she blushed all the way to her black roots. "That sounds bad, like I never cared about Bill."

"You're focusing on your sister. That's natural."

"The timing's got me completely freaked." She tossed her spent cigarette into the fire, immediately lighting another with trembling fingers. "Bill dying the same night as Chris. What's that all about?"

"What kinds of things did they keep at the house?"

"Oh, gee. I don't know." She crinkled her forehead and thought hard. "Plates, doo-dads. Some strange oil paintings of Bill's. The place was loaded full of stuff. My sister used to like antiques. Something in that house must have been very valuable. I keep thinking how glad I am Beth wasn't there that night, too, or..." The thought was so distressing she stood up and began moving around the room, still smoking, letting the ashes fall where they would. "And now the cops have gone crazy. Should we go down to Placerville tonight? Can we see Nikki? She called just before you got here, but she only had five minutes. She was calm, or I think I'd be—what should I do?"

"Has Nikki ever been in trouble before?" Nina said.

Daria pushed aside a blanket and looked outside. "No big deal," she said. "Kid stuff."

"She was arrested before, Mom," Bob said, "for vandalism."

"That was dismissed, and rightly so!" said Daria. "What kind of world doesn't make room for kids to mess with spray paint! In museums they call it *art*!"

"And picked up once for shoplifting..."

"That was an accident! She forgot to pay!" Daria turned a beseeching look on Nina. "Haven't you ever forgotten to pay? When a teenager does it, they are so dead. The way we treat our kids is a shame."

"Is that all?" Nina asked, as if the list wasn't long enough.

"Oh, there's the one time they got her fair and square for trespassing. They let her off with a warning."

"She was with a bunch of other kids and they lit a bonfire at Pope Beach. At midnight. It's illegal, it turns out," Bob said, as if they hadn't discussed it many times. There were signs all over the place. "Plus the beach was closed."

"Of course, she had no idea," said Daria. "At sixteen, who knows these details." She settled back down on the floor and looked intently at Nina. "I know what you're thinking. You're thinking I'm one of those mothers who make endless excuses for their kids. But you're wrong if you think that. Nikki's an unusual person. Sensitive. Intelligent, like her dad. Musical like him, too, but she got some of her talent from me. She could really make it but she should go to college first." She took a drag. "Use her brains, unlike me.

"Anyway. Deep down, she's very sensible. I rely on her for everything! I was just a kid myself when she was born, seventeen. Married at sixteen. I was way wilder than she is at that age. I mean, she totally organizes things around here, pays bills. Makes grocery lists. Remembers to buy the TP! She ran around with the wrong crowd for a while there. Then she met Bobby." She reached over and held his hand. To Nina's amazement, he let her.

"He's been like a brother to her, only better because they don't fight like cats and dogs! He's such a good influence." She let go. "She was straightening out..."

Nina was realizing something about Daria. She had known people like her before. Daria saw the world a certain way, her way. The rest of the world might not agree, but she would stick fast to her version. Opinion carried as much weight as fact, or perhaps more, in her book.

She was still talking in that rapid-fire way she had. "You can imagine. My sister Beth—her heart is broken! She's having a complete breakdown. I mean, oh my God, first Chris, who was only nineteen years old, and then her husband. This afternoon, she came home from LA with her friend Jan. Her house had police tape all around it and they wouldn't let her in at first.

"Then she had to go make a statement and then she went to a hotel and called me. Jan and I spent the rest of the afternoon with her. We talked her into taking a sleeping pill, and she finally went to sleep. I dropped Jan at the airport limo stop, because she needed to get back to a job down south, then I got home and Bob and Nikki were in the kitchen and we were going to go for a walk when the rain let up to try to take all this in. And now Nikki."

"Does your sister know your daughter is accused of killing her husband?"

"Not yet." Daria turned her chin up, and it was rock hard bone. "I thought about calling her, but figured I'd wait until I talked with you. But don't worry. Beth will never believe that Nikki did that to Bill. Never. And you shouldn't either. Don't entertain one single moment's doubt!"

"Your sister was in Los Angeles when her husband died?"

"Right. Visiting her friend Jan down in Hollywood. Beth and I...we don't see each other very much. It's not that we don't get along. I just love her to death! I want you to know that. She's a great person. We've just kind of drifted apart. And Bill...well, he liked to keep her close to him."

"That happens," said Nina. "You say he was a surgeon?"

"A cosmetic surgeon," Daria said. "He never liked the term plastic surgeon. He had his own clinic here in town." She jumped up again and went into the kitchen, returning with an envelope with writing on it. "This is where Nikki is. I made them write it down for me. There's supposed to be some kind of hearing tomorrow that we have to go to."

"I'm familiar with the juvenile detention center, Mrs. Zack."

"Oh, please call me Daria."

Nina read the envelope, which said, "Detention Hearing—2 P.M. Juvenile Court, Placerville." Nina thought. "Have you contacted Nikki's father?"

Daria shook her head. "We haven't seen him for six years. He left us one day. We were fighting a lot. It's so much responsibility raising a child, and he's a musician, which meant there was never any money. We got postcards from him a few times from big cities back East. Just short notes saying he hoped we were okay. That he missed us. He sent cash a few times. That was a little weird because the money always came when we were most desperate. I wondered..."

"What?"

"Oh, if maybe he was keeping an eye on us somehow. It creeped me out. But that really doesn't make sense. He had no reason to stay away from Nikki, even if he was mad at me. Anyway, after a couple of years, I guess he got tired of the game. We didn't hear anymore. I got over it and got a divorce. We had to put a notice in the paper. He never even called about that. I wonder if he knows."

"And Nikki?"

"Nikki still thinks about him quite a bit. You only have one father."

"Where is he?"

"Who knows?"

"Is there anyone else we should notify?"

"Nope," Daria said. "I've had several guys hanging around since Nikki's dad left, but none that lasted very long and none that hit it off with Nikki. I don't know what it is about me but I sure don't bring out the best in men. Nikki says I'd trust Satan if he had a nickel in his pocket and a good singing voice."

"I'm assuming you want me to represent your daughter in this matter?"

"Yes! I thought that was obvious! Will you?"

Nina sensed the tension in Bob's shoulders as she watched the eight ball heading for the pocket in her mind. Did she want to represent a teenaged girl accused of killing her uncle?

Looking into Daria Zack's red-rimmed eyes, Nina felt the tug of her desperation. She was war-torn, a single mother like Nina with a teenaged child, struggling just to get by. If what her eyes told her and Bob had said was true, Daria Zack had a lot of trouble taking care of simple, everyday needs in the best of times. Faced with this, of course she felt desperate. And Nina could help her.

As for the case, she didn't have enough information to judge it on its merits, but she knew one thing. It had fantastic elements she couldn't even begin to enumerate, the most profound being that teenaged girls did not make a practice of attacking people with swords.

And there was the plane crash. Apparently, the son had died the same night as his father, although miles away and under utterly different circumstances. Could the two deaths be connected? The idea made her shiver. Here she was being offered a chance to make sense out of events that made no sense, bring some order into the chaos of death and accusations. She couldn't bring her husband back, couldn't create meaning where there was none, but she might be able to do something useful for this girl.

"I may be able help you," she said, intentionally tamping down the strange excitement she was feeling at the prospect, "but we'll need to talk some more." There were money issues. She could not afford to take a murder case *pro bono*. "I'll talk with Nicole before the detention hearing that's scheduled tomorrow, and make a special appearance on her behalf. If I don't end up representing her, at least she'll have counsel tomorrow." She got up, trying

38

to look half as graceful as Daria. "I promise I will see you there."

"But can't you get her out now?"

"There's a process involved. She's stuck for tonight, but I'll call Juvenile Hall and make sure everything's okay over there. She'll be all right until we can straighten things out."

"I just knew you were going to fix everything," said Daria valiantly, struggling to hide her disappointment at the news. "In this kind of situation I'm worthless. We're so lucky to have someone as smart as you on our side!"

"One last thing," Nina said from the doorway. Bob had already run out to the Bronco to let Hitchcock out and was throwing a stick for him in the yard. "Bob mentioned that the police questioned Nicole after they read her her rights. Did she tell them anything?"

Daria's eyes seemed to search the room for an answer. "Bob had the balls and presence of mind to remind her she had a right to remain silent, which is more than I could do with all those uniforms and shiny badges flashing around the room like they owned it."

Nina felt a little like a cowboy rounding up a bunch of wayward cattle, trying to keep Daria on track. "Did she admit something?"

"Thank God, my poor baby had the smarts not to confess or anything. But—it's bad. There's a witness. Someone told the police they saw her there that night."

3

JUST BEFORE NOON, Nina finished her Superior Court appearances in Tahoe and drove down the mountain to see Nicole Zack. The thicker air hit as she descended the first few thousand feet and its rich earthy smells, along with the lushness of an aquamarine sky and the stretch of dry open road, tinged a cheerful pink in the spring sunshine, intoxicated her.

It took an ugly tangle of traffic to bring her mood back down to earth. She edged into a spot on the street, and walked a block to the center.

The Juvenile Detention Center in Placerville was not the horror story of B movies, but it wasn't Grandma's kitchen either. The kids milling around acted like a group of high schoolers passing in the halls between classes, joking and nudging each other. Even the security people seemed easygoing. Not for the first time, Nina reflected on how the most desperate situation carried on long enough devolves into banality.

On the TV in the day room, a blond character on a soap opera confessed tearfully to pregnancy and a married lover. From a scratchy tweed couch in the corner, two girls stared at the screen, entranced. High windows allowed a thin daylight inside. A scatter of bent aluminum chairs completed the dreary picture.

Nicole came in from the hall, and Nina got up.

"Hi, Nicole. You got my message?"

"Hi. They gave it to me this morning."

The girl sat down, back straight, feet flat on the floor, chin out. She was very slender, very pale, tiny and young-looking for sixteen. She wore black jeans and a black T-shirt with a chaotic and unreadable logo on it. Wispy brown hair hung so that it covered a lot of her face. Nina saw a glimmer of Daria's physical grace in the way Nikki languidly moved her hand, pushing hair behind one ear. She studied the girl to see what Bob found pretty about the angular little face, finally deciding it must be the heavily fringed, willful brown eyes, now focused intently on Nina, at the moment glowing almost gold with not-very-well-suppressed anger. "How are they treating you here?" she asked.

"Okay."

"Has your mother been able to see you yet?"

"She came this morning," she said. "So you're Bob's mom. I would have known right away. He looks a lot like you, except his hair's so much darker."

"Bob said to say hi."

"Uh huh. Say hi back."

Nina took a breath. The girl stared at the floor. She didn't seem to have the insistent urge to talk that so often afflicts the newly incarcerated.

"Would you like me to call you Nikki? Is that your nickname?"

"Whatever."

"Well, Nikki, your mother wants to hire

41

me to defend you. I'll be talking to her further about that this afternoon. Meanwhile, I want to know from you what you said to the police when they came to your house."

"You're younger than I thought you would be. You look like you could still be in school." She examined Nina as a botany student might inspect an unknown specimen. "Did Bob make you come over here?"

"Your mother asked me to come."

"No, she didn't. Bob made you come. Daria can't tell her ass from her earhole. She'd cry, then maybe have a beer or two, then call up her friends and everybody would get all worked up trying to figure out what to do about me being in jail. Then, later, after I'm convicted, years later, they'd figure out how I needed a lawyer." She laughed.

"Bob asked me to come, too. The first thing you need to know is, I'm not going to lie to you."

"Of course not! It's a known fact lawyers never lie."

Nina had seen that coming. Something about this girl, her attitude, felt so familiar. She smiled.

The tense edges of Nikki's lips eased, returning the ghost of a smile.

"Now tell me what happened last night."

"Well, first thing that happened was they knocked on the door. Bob and I were in the kitchen making out." She squinted for a reaction. Looking a little disappointed at finding none, she continued. "Ha ha. Joke. Actually,

42

we were eating a snack. Daria was in the living room doing the boob dance thing she does. Trying to make her boobs go in different directions. She does that when she can't remember the steps she's supposed to be learning..."

"You call your mother Daria? Why?"

"She's not much of a mother," said Nicole. "So, to continue what I was saying before I was so rudely interrupted...these cops bang on the front door. Daria answers and uh oh, dumb move number thirteen hundred and six for that day, she invites them in! Or at least they do that cop thing of coming in before you have a chance to think, and they started looking around at the hovel. She should have known better, but when you get to know her you will recognize the vast extent of her cluelessness.

"Me and Bob go into the living room to see what's going on. They're telling Daria about Uncle Bill, how some slasher wasted him. They go into all the blood spattered around, etcetera." The timbre of her voice changed imperceptibly. "They ask her things... God, she's so dumb. My theory is that she had me so young it arrested the natural development of her brain cells."

"What did your mother say?"

"Oh, Bill was such a fabulous guy! So good to us and to Aunt Beth." She was a good mimic. Nina could hear Daria in her voice. "A buncha crap, that's what."

"She lied?"

43

"If you gave her a lie detector test she would pass! You would think somewhere inside she's got to remember what a bastard he was but you'd be wrong."

"Did you say anything?"

"Not much. They started in on her, like she might know something, which of course, she didn't. She was getting really upset, crying. What did they expect!"

"Go on."

"Then they started on me. One of them took the other aside and showed him a report or something. They looked at me and then looked back at the report, like they were comparing me to some description they had. That's when the woman asked me where I was that night. I said I was here, at home.

"Then they said a neighbor saw me at Uncle Bill's that night, so I might as well admit it, otherwise I'd be perjuring myself and obstructing a police investigation, and they'd arrest me. And I got confused at that point, I admit it. I was afraid..." The chin jutted up into the air, as firm and stubborn as her mother's. "I was thinking they might arrest me if I didn't admit it, but Bob jumped in and told me to shut up, so I did. They went and arrested me anyhow. It's a miracle I didn't tell them. They were asking fast and standing close and they wore these uniforms with big guns in holsters and..."

"I know how it is," Nina said.

"Good band name," Nikki said. "Big Guns in Holsters."

44

"Did they—did you feel they were pressuring you?"

"Of course they were fuckin' pressuring me. You did say you were a lawyer, didn't you?"

"Let's get something straight, Nikki," Nina said. "You may get away talking like this to a lot of people, maybe even your mother, but you can't get away with talking like that to me. If you don't straighten up and act civil, I leave. Do you want me to leave?"

"No." A little voice. Nikki looked down at the floor again. A tear dripped down her nose, hung for a moment, and she shook her head sharply, flinging it away.

"Okay. Tell me what happened on Saturday night. Did you go to your uncle's?"

"Yes." Defiant.

"How did you get there?"

"By boat."

"Why?"

"I went there to get something of ours."

"Something that belonged to you and Daria?"

"Uh huh."

"You went there to steal?"

"Not to steal."

"Then why?"

"I went to get something."

"What?"

"None of your business. I'm being civil. I just won't answer that, okay?"

Nina paused, then went into her standard explanation about attorney-client privilege but Nikki just shook her head, so Nina called upon the same god of patience she called on in her recent dealings with Bob. "Did you take anything?"

"I'm not telling."

"If I'm going to be your attorney, you need to trust me and tell me the truth."

"Are you going to represent me?" Nikki said. "You haven't said one way or the other."

"You sure need help. I'm here to help today, but we don't have an arrangement after that."

"I sure do need help. I'm not arguing about that."

"I have to talk to your mother about money."

"She doesn't have any. So that lets you out, huh?" Nikki hugged herself.

"It may," Nina said. "I work alone, Nikki. I have a little office on Lake Tahoe Boulevard and I don't come from a wealthy family either. I have to take care of Bob. It's not just getting paid for your case that matters to me. It's that your case might take up a lot of my work hours for a long time to come."

Nikki's face worked. Nina could see she wanted to ask Nina to take the case anyway, but she didn't. "I'll trust you when you show me I can trust you. I don't exactly know a lot of adults worth trusting."

Nina thought of Daria, of Nikki's father who had abandoned her, of the poverty of Nikki's home, and of a girl she had known a long time ago and decided not to press the point. "Okay. Go on with the story."

"Uncle Bill was home. I watched from the bushes by the pool. He was in his study. The front doorbell rang and he went to answer it."

"Did you go into the study?"

"No."

"Are you sure?"

"No, I said. I did my thing and went home."

"What's that supposed to mean, Nikki?"

"I can't elaborate on that," Nikki said with exaggerated care.

Nina thought, if she won't cooperate, I ought to leave. She took a moment to study the girl, her shabby clothes, the overall air of neglect, the proud angle of her chin, the sad droop of her hair, trying to make up her mind whether she should shoulder her bag and say good-bye and walk out of this young delinquent's life forever.

Aware of the scrutiny, Nikki veiled her eyes with hair, as if she was expecting Nina to leave and protecting herself in advance. Her hands lay quietly on her legs, the knuckles large and the fingers long and thin.

Bob had spent a good part of his life not knowing where his father was, too. She wondered if he and Nikki ever talked about that. She wondered if Bob was her only friend.

"Nikki?" she said.

The girl looked up with eyes empty of hope. Nina found herself wincing. She knew that expression.

"Did you kill your uncle?" According to her law professors, she wasn't supposed to ask that. It was the perverted courtesy of the defense attorney—don't ask so your client won't have to lie to you. Don't ask because if the rare client admits guilt, you've lost all sorts of trial options. But she often asked anyway, and she always got something from the answer that shaped her defense.

"I didn't do it."

"Do you have an idea who might have killed him?"

Had Nikki started at that question? "No," she said. She was lying.

"When's the last time before Saturday that you saw your uncle?"

"A long time. Years? We used to go over there when I was little."

Nina couldn't read the look on her face, but thought it might be nostalgia.

"Then we didn't anymore. He called us trailer trash once," she continued. "I heard him say it, even though he didn't know I was listening. We didn't want to know him either. Aunt Beth came over sometimes when he was out of town and brought Chris. Neither of us had brothers and sisters, so—when we were little I pretended Chris was my brother. Then when Chris went to private high school down in LA, we didn't see him either." Clearly, this had been a blow. "I tried writing to him a few times, but I quit doing that a while back."

"Why?" Nina said.

"Oh, it wasn't that Chris was a snob like Uncle Bill. It's just—I changed too. We were nearly three years apart in age and I didn't feel like I could live up to him. I've been busy with my downhill spiral." She smiled. "Band name. Downhill Spiral."

"Were you ever in your uncle's home?"

"Sure. When I was little. He had these really violent paintings, and always had sharp things around. He had a set of medical instruments from the sixteenth century or something. And of course, the famous sword. Some samurai owned it in ancient history. Daria told me this morning—she read it in the paper, that he was killed with that thing. He used to have a whole collection of swords. He had this one with a silver handle—no, I guess he said it was made of nickel or something like that—anyway, it had a carved eagle head on the handle. Another one he called a Japanese naval dagger—that had a kind of cut down the blade he called a blood groove. Gross. He had a bunch of these evil-looking things hanging on the wall. Aunt Beth hated them, so about five or six years ago he got rid of all of them except the samurai sword. That one he kept. Turns out, that wasn't such a brilliant idea, was it?"

"A strange collection. Sounds like those weapons fascinated you as much as they must have fascinated your uncle."

"Yeah, well, I still didn't use that sword to kill him. Believe it or not. Your choice."

"Okay," Nina said. "This is important, Nikki. Before you said anything to the police, did you understand that you had a right to an attorney?"

"They read me my rights, uh huh. Right after they looked at their report. I think they came to tell Daria about the mur—the thing with

Uncle Bill—and I fit some description they already had, 'cause man, they stared at me like they were starved and I was this juicy Big Mac."

"Your mother was present, right?"

"You might call it that. She was standing right there."

Nina rested her head on her hand for a moment, thinking.

Nikki watched her. "Bob kept saying, shut up till I get my mom. Just shut up. I finally did. I didn't say much. But just my luck, someone saw me there that night. That's really bad, isn't it?" she asked. "What will they do to me?"

"Well, you have many rights protecting you as a juvenile. We're about to go and see a very decent judge named Harold Vasquez. He'll determine whether you have to stay in custody. After that, whether or not you're allowed to go home, there may be another hearing to determine if you will be declared a ward of the juvenile court, or possibly"—she hesitated—"possibly be shunted into the adult criminal system."

"But I'm just a kid! Can they do this to a kid? I heard that when a kid gets caught, they don't get in as much trouble. Like with those kids that run drugs for older guys in the city."

"Who told you that?"

"I don't remember."

Lie number two, Nina noted. "The definition of 'kid' is changing fast."

"If I went into the adult system and got convicted—then what?"

"The death penalty is out. A juvenile can't be sentenced to death in California."

"Then—how long in prison? What's the worst that could happen?"

"Two years in a youth authority facility. Then, when you reach eighteen, state prison. Thirty years, maybe. Life, if you were convicted of first-degree murder."

Nikki's face went paper-colored.

"That's the absolute worst possibility. We'll know more about possible outcomes when they formally charge you. The system is very complex."

"The System," Nikki said, and her lips pursed as if against a bitter taste.

"Let's go to the hearing. Then I can advise you better."

"I thought they would let me get out on bail or something. I'm no risk. I'm not going to go around offing people, for Chrissake! This is so unreal."

"Nikki, you're going to have to tell me what you took from your uncle's. Was it money?"

"I've told you everything important."

She was so painfully young, too young to understand just how frightened she should be, that was the problem. Or maybe she understood and was being brave. Even the prospect of thirty years hadn't scared her enough to open up to Nina. What had she taken? Was she protecting someone? Her mother?

"Your mother is very worried about you," Nina said. "You'll see her in a few minutes."

51

She had meant to be comforting and was a little startled at the bleak look that passed over Nikki's face.

"Oh, sure, and she's working hard on this. Praying, hoping. Lighting candles. Making up dances..." Rancor mixed with resignation. "She expects me to waltz home and join her any second."

"I have the feeling that she loves you a lot."

"Too bad love can't buy you money."

"You sound pretty tough, Nikki."

"She drives me crazy," Nikki said. "And I'm worried about her. She needs me. She can't take care of herself. I always thought that's why my dad left. If only somebody had taught her to type or repair plumbing fixtures. Something practical, to bring in money. When she does get a job, she goofs up and gets fired right away. She never lets it get her down, though," she said, reluctant admiration creeping into her voice. "Goes right back to her dancing and her fantasies of fame and fortune."

"I take it that your father wasn't much good at being reliable either," Nina said.

Nikki's face darkened. "Don't badmouth my father."

"Sorry. I'm just trying to point out..."

"Look, just make sure she pays the electric bill. It's a mess if she doesn't. If I don't get out."

"Okay." Nina checked her watch. Ten minutes to go. "They'll bring you in shortly," she said. "I have to go look for your mother."

She wanted to put her hand on the prickly girl's shoulder, but knew better.

Nikki was already waiting in the Juvenile Court when Nina came in with Daria. The Probation Department had acted with due diligence in filing the paperwork and contacting Daria, and the clerk had set this rapid hearing on the detention calendar for two P.M.

The only other attendees were official: the court clerk, the bailiff, and the court reporter; the Juvenile Referee, Harold Vasquez; the Probation Department caseworker who had just been assigned to the case, Pearl Smith; and Barbara Banning, a deputy district attorney from the South Lake Tahoe office.

Barbara gave Nina a formal nod as she came in, and Nina took that nod as the first blow in the legal war that started as of today. Barbara was a smart lawyer, still somewhat inexperienced, who had been taken under the wing and, it was rumored, into the bed of the county district attorney, Henry McFarland. Her status as Henry's protégée was an early warning that Henry would try to have Nikki transferred into the adult criminal court system at the earliest opportunity.

On top of that bad news, there was Barbara herself. Barbara disliked Nina for a number of reasons. Their adversarial positions, her natural competitiveness, and her fledgling-prosecutor disgust for lawyers base enough to choose to work as criminal defense attorneys, were only part of the problem. Barbara had made a determined play for Nina's husband before he married Nina. His rejection must have hurt. Sitting down beside Nikki at the counsel table, Nina nodded back to Barbara. Daria sat down right behind them.

"In re Nicole Zack," Judge Vasquez said. Vasquez had been a juvenile probation officer before law school and had earned the trust of attorneys on both sides. First glancing at the petition in front of him, he then shot a quick, inquisitive look at Nikki over his glasses. A sixteen-year-old girl accused of a slashing murder did not come before him every day. Nina saw in that look the interest the media would also have in Nikki.

"This is a hearing to determine whether the minor present today will remain in custody or whether some other disposition should be made. I see that this young lady has spent one night at the Juvenile Hall facilities. Ms. Zack, this is an informal hearing not subject to the rules of evidence, but you have a number of rights you should know."

He made sure that Daria had received notice of the hearing and was present, and took note of Nina's appearance on Nikki's behalf.

"I see that we have been unable to locate the father," he told Nina. "I take it the parents are divorced?"

"Yes, that's correct."

"Does the minor or her mother have any information as to his whereabouts? As a parent, he should know about this."

"He—he left the area more than five years

ago," Nina said. "Other than a few notes home, he hasn't been heard from and we have no idea how to locate him. Daria Zack, the mother, has sole legal custody."

"Okay then," Vasquez said, but he shook his head. He was already forming an idea of the case, something to do with a fatherless delinquent kid. Like everybody else in the juvenile justice system, he couldn't help searching for logical reasons behind the mystifying and horrific acts of violence which brought children into his court every day.

"Ms. Banning?" he said. "Your presence here today indicates an interest on the part of the district attorney's office."

"It's a murder, Your Honor," Barbara said. Her voice was round and full and musical, fittingly, because with her, everything was as painstakingly orchestrated as a Brandenburg Concerto. Pulling a sheaf of papers from her briefcase, she said, "We are filing a petition herewith. The petition requests a hearing on May twenty-fifth to have the minor declared not amenable to assistance within the Juvenile Court system pursuant to section six zero two of the Welfare and Institutions Code. Our office intends to file a criminal complaint against the minor on a charge of murder in the first degree. We will request that this matter be transferred into the adult court, to proceed as though the minor was an adult."

"You are filing the petition today?" Vasquez said.

"As soon as this hearing is over," Barbara

said. "May I provide the Court and counsel with a copy?" Vasquez nodded, and she handed one set of papers to his clerk and then walked the few steps over to Nina and laid the papers on the table before her without so much as a glance of recognition.

Nina skimmed the paperwork. With a complaint about to be filed, Vasquez would never release Nikki.

And so it went. Barbara argued the seriousness of the offense, Nikki's previous brushes with the law, and the fact that Nina had requested that the hearing regarding a transfer to the adult court commence in less than two weeks. Nina protested hotly when Barbara said that Nikki was a flight risk, arguing that Nikki had never been convicted of any crime, but Vasquez was too conservative to take a chance when a murder was involved.

"The Court remands the minor to the Juvenile Hall for a period not to exceed fifteen days," he announced. "Counsel, the law is very plain. If that hearing doesn't occur as scheduled, she will probably be put on home supervision."

"Oh, we'll be ready, Your Honor," Barbara said.

And so will we, Nina thought.

Neutralizing her expression, Nikki went along with the bailiff. Watching her go, Daria cried without restraint.

"You can visit," Nina said as she packed her attaché at the table. "I promise you, she'll be safe." From the corner of her eye she saw

Barbara sail out, trailed by the bailiff's admiring eyes.

"She may be safe but she'll be hurting every minute in there, I promise you."

"She's strong," Nina said.

"She sure puts on a good show of it, doesn't she?" Daria said. "Anyway, I'll follow you back up the hill. Beth just couldn't manage Placerville today. It was too much. But she's going to meet us at your office at four."

"What for?"

"She called me and she really wants to come along. She wants to help us. She loves Nikki. I told you she'd never believe Nikki killed Bill."

The air inside the courtroom had been icy. When Nina went outside, warmth settled over her like a sweater. Traffic had quieted. The good folk of Placerville all appeared to have gone home for siestas this afternoon.

She pulled onto the highway, Daria following in her old VW, already a few cars back.

Nikki would be a difficult client. But she admitted it to herself—she wanted the case. She'd take it no matter what Beth Sykes offered.

She knew all about girls like Nikki.

She had been one herself.

Under Sandy's watchful eye, Beth and Daria Sykes waited in the outer reception area. The two women walked into Nina's office, Daria in the lead.

Beth introduced herself in a voice as soft as her cashmere sweater. "I understand you've seen Nikki," she said, seating herself closest to Nina. Even skin as fresh and dewy as hers had suffered under the strain of the past few days. She wore shadows under her eyes instead of makeup and when she said hello, her voice was flat and heavy, medicated sounding. Daria took her time getting comfortable in the other chair.

From far away, no one would mistake these two women for anything but sisters. Like images in a broken mirror they bore a disjunctive similarity. Daria was wider across the jaw and Beth's chin was less developed, but their clothing was a study in personal expressiveness. Daria's seriously distressed leather jacket over a wrinkled black turtleneck and black jeans fit her personality, and Beth's fitted purple bolero-style sweater and linen skirt, set off by a pair of fine leather boots, fit hers. Slightly crooked canines lent Daria's smile a guileless friendliness, while Beth's mouth opened into a smile that exposed rectangular nuggets of white, movie-star perfection, but left a personality void.

Though they both were blond, Beth's hair had the subtle streaking of natural-looking color Nina suspected was the expensive kind. She also couldn't help wondering how much magic Beth's husband, the plastic surgeon, had wrought, to keep Beth looking so young and vibrant, when she knew already Daria was four years younger. But these were trivial thoughts. This woman emanated a fresh, shocked grief.

"I'm sorry about your loss," Nina said.

"Thank you," Beth said. The sympathy shook her composure, and Nina could see her struggling for calm. Beth looked barely functional, slumping there in her chair. "I lost my own husband a few months ago," Nina heard herself say, and then stopped, surprised. She avoided personal contact with clients, but Beth Sykes's vulnerability and pain were too brutally present in the room to ignore.

Beth nodded.

Daria squeezed her sister's arm, and for a moment, except for the tapping of Sandy's fingers in the outer office, there was silence.

"Nikki's holding up pretty well," Nina said.

"Daria told me everything. We're very close."

Which wasn't exactly what Daria had said.

"What kind of papers do we sign?" asked Daria finally. "Beth's offered to loan me your retainer."

At that, Beth lifted her head. "It's not a loan, Daria."

"I'm paying every penny back."

"I want to do this for Nikki. Let me help her." Her voice trembled.

Preoccupied with her own concerns and oblivious to her sister's shaky emotional state, Daria shook her head. "No. I don't like to owe people. And ten percent interest. I insist."

"I'm not people!" Beth cried.

They argued until Beth's growing frustration exploded into tears. Through her sobs she said, "Just forget your goddamn pride for once, Daria. Take the money for her sake. For my sake. Call it whatever you want!"

Instantly contrite, Daria put an arm around her sister's shoulder. "Jeez, Beth," she said. "I'm so sorry. I can't believe I made you cry. After all you're going through! I'm a rat and an egomaniac! I hate me!"

Through her tears, Beth's shoulders shook slightly at the joke. She took the tissue Nina offered and dried her eyes.

"Don't cry, honey pie," Daria murmured. "Of course we'd be completely grateful for anything you want to do."

And so it was settled. Nina had been sitting behind her desk, hands folded, while the sisters worked out their differences. Her thoughts had been on Bill Sykes and the slashes on his face. The attack, according to the newspaper account she had read that morning, had been ferocious.

Hard as the wind ripping over the mountains on these spring mornings, the meaning of a new murder case swept over Nina. Her new obsession had arrived, bringing with it months of profound challenges, fear, stress, and humble hopes...

"You can save her. I know you can," Daria was saying to Nina now.

"I'm not a savior." Nina had learned that the hard way. "If I represent Nicole, I'll do everything I can to help her but you need to know there are no guarantees. The outcome may not be what we want. Nobody wins every case, and this one's especially tough."

"Why do you say that?"

"She may have done it. If she did, I can help her but I can't save her."

"You really don't like that word. Okay. Don't worry about saving her. Just get her off," Daria said.

"She didn't do it!" Beth said, her voice quavery. "We can't lose her too. Not after Chris. I couldn't stand it."

Daria leaned forward. "She's just sixteen. She's so f— screwy, Nina. She does things and doesn't know why. I don't know why..." her voice trailed off.

"You understand we might lose?" said Nina.

"Do I look like a moron?" asked Daria. "Of course I know we might lose! I just know we won't. We can't!" She was getting upset again.

Tapping Daria's foot with the toe of her boot, Beth said softly, "That's right, Daria. Everything will be all right." Directing herself to Nina, she said, "I wish... I wish I could believe this situation will work out. I'm afraid for Nikki. I'm afraid for all of us." She gazed out the window at Tallac. Touched by ragged white clouds, the mountain loomed. "Too many things have happened for me to imagine anything ahead but more tragedy." Reaching over, she touched her sister's hand. "Daria's an optimist. That's her charm."

"I just hate a defeatist attitude," Daria said. "If Nina doesn't think she can win..."

"I have as much hope of that as anyone could," said Nina firmly.

"Well, that's what I like to hear," said Daria.

Beth reached into a woven leather bag and pulled out her check-book. Setting it down on Nina's desk, she began to write. "R-e-i-l-l-y. Is that right?" she asked.

"Yes."

"Is fifty thousand dollars enough to start?"

"Uh, that'll be fine."

Nina realized Sandy's typing had ceased several minutes before, and at the same moment, she thought she heard furtive rustling behind the door.

The sound of Sandy jumping for joy.

"Mrs. Sykes..."

"Beth."

"All right, Beth, Daria, I know this is a very tough time for you, but there are a few things we should touch on before you leave. I'll be hiring help to put together Nikki's defense. Paul van Wagoner is the private investigator I usually work with. He's very sharp, very experienced, a former homicide detective. We need to work fast. I'm counting on your cooperation."

"You've got it," Daria said.

"Where are you staying at the moment, Beth?"

"I'm at the Embassy Suites but the police say I can return home this weekend."

"We'll want to look at the house at some point."

"Of course," she said in a low voice.

"Have the police determined whether anything was stolen the night your husband died?"

"Nothing was missing from the house. I think they are going on the premise that Bill interrupted the thief before he got anything. Then...he was scared off after what he had done. You know about the thefts around the lake?"

"Yes," Nina said. "Did the police hint at whether they thought this event might be related to that series of crimes?"

"I know they are looking at links," Beth said. "That's all they said about it."

"Good." Nina glanced at her notes. "I understand your husband was a very successful surgeon."

"He was," Beth replied. "He ran his own clinic and kept very busy."

"What will happen to his patients?"

Beth looked confused, as if she hadn't given that any thought at all. "I guess Dylan will have to hire an associate. Dylan Brett, his partner."

"I take it you aren't very involved in his business?"

"No."

Nina wrote down the partner's name and details about the clinic location. They would need to go there soon.

"Did you know your son—Christopher—was coming up to Tahoe on Saturday night?" she asked Beth.

Beth took a minute to answer, and appeared

to be deep in thought. She may have simply been giving herself time to contain her feelings. "I didn't know but we loved having Chris home. We encouraged him to visit anytime."

"Was he coming specifically to visit his father?"

"Maybe he thought he would catch both of us. He didn't know I was down there visiting a girlfriend. We were just going to shop, go to a movie, that kind of thing. It was such a quick trip, and it was getting close to his finals, so I didn't expect to see him. I hadn't spoken to him for a couple of days."

"Isn't it unusual for a boy his age..." Nina consulted her notes again, but before she could find the answer, Beth spoke again.

"Chris was only nineteen."

"Isn't it unusual," Nina continued, this time very gently, "for someone so young to charter his own plane?"

"Not really," Beth said. "No. Chris already had lived away from home for nearly two years. We always used charters so that we could keep our own schedules. He would be comfortable with that."

"What about the expense?"

"Chris is..." she swallowed, and started again, her voice choked, "...was...a full-time student. We covered all of his expenses, and he knew we could afford it. He had our permission to charge anything he needed to one of our credit cards."

Daria, whose arms were crossed lightly across her chest, sighed. She had apparently been musing about Chris. "You know, you were such a great mom, Beth. You have nothing to knock yourself about. You were able to give that boy everything he ever wanted, and you did! Nobody could have loved him more. You gave him a happy life."

Stunned by this unintentionally brutal reduction of nineteen years of motherhood, Beth said, "Oh, Daria." Putting her head into her hands, she wept again, this time inconsolably.

Stepping inside Nina's office, Sandy shut the door. Beth and Daria had gone, Beth still crying.

"I expect a passel of people are out there waiting to see me..." Nina heaved out a breath, letting the emotions of the previous meeting go.

"I need to tell you something before you find out for yourself," Sandy said. She came in and sat down in the chair next to Nina's. "It's about Linda."

"Linda?"

"Linda Littlebear. You came to my wedding. She was our minister."

"I remember. The Shoshone woman from Death Valley."

"Part Shoshone. Her mom was an Anglo park ranger originally from Virginia. Anyway, Linda sued him. Dr. Sykes."

"Really."

"Did you know people can die from plastic surgery?"

65

"It makes sense," Nina said, "but no, I don't associate that kind of surgery with death. Who are you talking about, Sandy?"

"Linda's daughter Robin hated her nose, which was too much like Linda's. Too Native looking. Too ethnic. She begged and begged for surgery. For years, Linda resisted, talked politics, talked sense. Finally, for her sixteenth birthday present, she gave in. Linda bought Robin a new nose. To make her happy, you know?"

Nina nodded.

"They went to Sykes but there were complications. Robin was in the operating room for seven hours. She died some hours later."

"How?"

"She quit breathing. Happy Birthday."

"Your friend sued for wrongful death?"

"There was an insurance settlement. I don't know how much. How much does the life of a sixteen year old go for these days?"

"How awful. What a tragedy! But, Sandy, I'm sure she was fully informed of the risks, signed papers and so forth."

"You don't go into a nose job expecting to die," said Sandy.

Unable to refute this logic, Nina asked, "Did Linda blame Dr. Sykes for her daughter's death?"

"She did, but she blamed herself more for giving in. Why couldn't Robin see how beautiful she was? Anyway, Linda would never hurt that man. She just has a big mouth. Makes her a good minister."

"Has she said something about Dr. Sykes's death, Sandy?"

"Talk to her if you want to know her side of the story."

"So she blamed him for her daughter's death," Nina said, thinking about it. "I can imagine how she must have felt."

"Maybe you can," said Sandy, and Nina felt a rare current of sympathy pass between them. Sandy knew all about her, all her foibles and fears. Her preferred lunches. How her husband had died.

For a big woman, Sandy moved lightly. Swinging the door to the office open in one movement, she motioned to a waiting client.

"Linda's been hinting that she has some information for you. I'll set it up," she said, pulling the door shut behind a man that scurried forward fast as a rabbit into one of the orange chairs in Nina's office, planted himself there and crossed his arms, as if daring them to try to displace him.

4

"MR. VAN WAGONER—may I call you Paul?"

"Please do," Paul said. The interviewer had very pretty knees, sharply outlined by the black stockings she wore. The face in its trendy specs was about fifty, with a warmly interested look he distrusted. She was a high school teacher working as a stringer for the *Monterey Herald*, the biggest paper on the central coast of California. Which wasn't saying much.

And he was the interviewee. Call me Ishmael, call me a cab, he thought. Just so you write it up so I sound experienced, charming, and brilliant.

Which should be no stretch. All he had to do was act naturally.

She had warmed up by nosing around his condo while he was in the kitchen fixing ice water. He had caught her eyeballing the bed, which was large, the better to eat you with, my dear, he had wanted to say, although he refrained. She had stopped under the paintings of mountains and a blowup of himself and his friend Jack climbing at Pinnacles many years before. "Your brother?" she asked, but Paul told her no and she lost interest. Then, drifting around the living room, putting her hand on the back of his leather chair, fingering a bowl of eucalyptus he had just picked out back to fight the dusty smells, she had stopped at a picture of his mom and pop, telling him, "You look like your dad," something you might not find so flattering when the woman is saying that you resemble a man you will always consider ancient.

"So you've just returned from Washington," she said, setting a recorder on the table between them. She wore a red AIDS ribbon and a camisole rather than a bra under her shirt.

Paul deduced that she was a former hippie whose radical politics had cooled to a tepid PC temperature. "I got back a couple of days ago. Haven't even been into my office yet. I was head of a security detail for Senator Ashford of Kentucky."

"How did you and the senator get along?"

"He plays a great game of golf."

"Is he still trying to keep the women of our country from exercising their reproductive rights?"

Ah, a trick question. And so early in the interview. "Not at all," Paul said. "I'm sure he is in favor of reproduction of all kinds." A picture formed in his mind of the senator and his current lassie in the back of the limo, exercising.

"I see. Well, you have had a very exciting career, Paul. I've been hoping to have a chance to talk with you for some time. You won a scholarship to Harvard for your undergrad studies, and have an M.S. from Northeastern University in Criminal Justice, I believe you said on the phone?"

"Right."

"You were a homicide detective when you left the San Francisco Police Department a few years ago, right?"

"Yes."

"How many murder cases would you say you worked on during the years in San Francisco?"

"Dozens. I couldn't say."

"What would you say was the most difficult case?"

"Depends on what you mean. The worst were times when we got the bad guy, but the jury let him off."

"It must be awful, arresting a killer and then having him get off in court. Does it happen often?"

"Less so these days."

The line of a woman's body always drew a man's eye to one part. Paul couldn't take his eyes off her adorable knees, which people must have been patting her whole life. "Besides," he went on, "I have found over the years that even if the legal system doesn't work right in an individual case, society tends to provide the punishment. And that's how it should be."

"What do you mean? Vigilante justice? Lynching?"

"Not exactly. Ostracism. Inability to find a job. Divorce. The wife always knows. Loneliness, depression. Guilt. That's the big one. And, face it, once in a while, citizens do have to take the law into their own hands."

"Give me an example, Paul."

"Oh, Ellie Nesler. Killing the guy who molested her son. Shooting him down in open court. He wasn't going to pay like he should pay."

"You agree with her act of violence?" Raised eyebrows.

"Definitely."

"Coming from a homicide detective, that's an unsettling statement."

Paul smiled. "Ex-homicide detective. I am now a private detective. With offices right here in Carmel." But her pen didn't move. She wasn't interested in putting in the plug for Van Wagoner Investigations yet.

"Even so. You agree that a private citizen may sometimes be justified in killing another human being? I don't mean in self-defense of course."

"Occasionally." She took off her glasses, revealing disapproving bleeding-heart-liberal eyes.

"When?" she said.

"How did we get on this topic?" Paul said. "Of course I believe in following the law. My license depends on it."

"It sounds like you're avoiding the question, Paul. Let's talk more about Ellie Nesler."

"A good mom," Paul said.

"But she was arrested and spent many years in jail. She didn't get to raise her son. How is that a good result?"

"Her son understands," Paul said, wanting to end the conversation. Why had he allowed her to stray into the militarized zone? You couldn't convince people like her. People either comprehended or they didn't. "She did what she had to do." And, not that he was about to mention it ever to anybody, he had done the same.

Seven months ago, Paul had killed a killer, not to restore honor, but simply to end a reign of terror. Nobody knew it, and nobody ever would.

Looking back now, he saw Nina's and Bob's frightened eyes superimposed over a white glaze of snow and knew he would do it again. He wasn't proud of it. Sometimes you did what you had to do.

The cold primitive place inside himself that had committed that act had always existed and might exist in everybody, but you could go whole lifetimes without exploring this place. He hadn't known he had it in him, and the knowledge of what lurked there did make the old homicide cop in him deeply uneasy. With that act, he had permanently severed his ties with simple notions and repudiated the ideals that had motivated him for most of his life.

"Do you think that it was wrong of the jury to convict her and send her to jail?" the interviewer was saying.

"Yes."

"But people can't just go around and—"

"Molest other people's children," Paul said, finishing for her, getting irritated. He wanted to talk about Van Wagoner Investigations. She seemed to be zeroing in on certain closely held opinions that he didn't want his clients reading about the next day. On the other hand, he couldn't stand weaseling around.

"It's a free country," he said. "I have some personal thoughts about these things but in my work, I follow the rules."

"Did your personal opinions lead to your leaving the SFPD? And two years later, the Monterey Police Department?"

"I preferred running my own show," Paul said. "It was a natural progression." A bumpy one, too, having to do with not accepting authority, a problem that had been solved when Paul opened his own business.

She smiled. "Well, Paul, your office is located right here in Carmel on Delores. What kind of cases do you take? Tell me about your work."

"Van Wagoner Investigations handles a lot of things," Paul said, feeling much kinder toward her now that they were getting down to it. "A lot of it is helping businesses settle bad debts. Collections. Child custody cases. Finding hidden assets. Locating missing people. Once a kid asked me to find his father. I work a lot with attorneys preparing for trial. Criminal cases, mostly."

"What's the best thing about your work?"

"Being outside in the middle of the day. I'm not the office type."

"No, you don't look like the office type. What's the worst thing about your work?"

"Hmm. Have to say, I love my work."

"There must be something. You deal with a lot of emotional people. Do the emotions rub off?"

"Not anymore." She waited, but he didn't add anything.

"Why Carmel? What brought you here?"

"The job. I like the beach. Love Big Sur, Point Lobos. Play Pebble Beach when I get the chance."

"Your family must love it too."

"My parents live in San Francisco. My ex-wives live in Reno and last I heard, San Diego."

She looked sympathetic, which surprised him. He felt that his bachelor lifestyle was enviable.

"I just find it hard to believe that the little old Monterey Peninsula would have all this drama going on," she said. "Enough to support several investigative agencies."

"We work all over the state, but there's plenty going on here."

And then she wanted details, and he wasn't going to talk about local cases, and they fenced for a while, and then they shook hands and the knees disappeared behind the door of her Chevy Suburban.

Stopping in the kitchen for a Tuborg, Paul went out to the balcony overlooking the poison-oak forest on one side of the condo building. Afternoon sun filtered through the Carmel oaks. Everything felt unfamiliar. He had only arrived back from Washington a few days before, late at night. After driving thankfully into his parking spot under the building, he had vaulted up the stairs and turned the lights on in his condo to uncover only a rough approximation of the enchanting seaside hideaway of his memory. He had used the place as a way station rather than as a home lately, and it looked sorry as a bowl of rotting fruit and smelled about as zesty.

The first thing he had done was to get his nest in order, which involved hiring cleaning and repair services at a premium for speedy work. Then he wasted time waiting while people didn't show up, spent another few hours on the phone haranguing the miscreants, and squandered more hours supervising.

Still, after six months of being empty, even

spruced-up, the place felt as empty as a sarcophagus after a grave robber's binge.

He was going to have to do some hustling, too. He would have come back with a fat bank account, except that Pop had had that little stroke, and the money he had made in D.C. and most of Paul's savings had gone to the folks up north.

Not to worry. In a few months he would be rolling again.

He leaned over the railing to watch a lizard on the deck below his. It slithered into the sun and froze, its blood warming slightly in the spring afternoon, waiting patiently for an excuse to move, eyes full of philosophical detachment but in fact attuned to any flicker of movement. It waited for prey, and when prey passed by it would strike. Paul observed the lizard for a few minutes, watching it jump into action, snapping at invisible passersby, and it grew larger in his mind, man-sized, and suddenly his wet hand slipped and he was on his toes, going over, madly gripping the railing and watching the full beer bottle fall with a crash to the concrete parking lot three stories down.

Just in time he caught himself, openmouthed and ready to scream, eyes bulging and hands gripping the railing. He fell back onto his deck, gasping.

Had he really almost killed himself there? Casually fallen over the railing like a goddamn fool in a moment of inattention? Feeling profoundly shocked, he lay propped on an arm, blinking, getting his heart back into his chest.

After a while he went back into the kitchen and popped another beer. Nothing had actually happened, except that he had to go clean up the broken glass before somebody drove over it. The fall amounted to a nonevent. But he felt very odd about it. The week before, he had slammed the limo door on his index finger. He held up his hand. Blue had turned yellow and black.

He'd have to pay more attention, that was all.

Drinking half the bottle in one long series of gulps, he set it down on the coffee table and picked up the phone. Time to roll.

"Trumbo and van Wagoner," said a voice.

Since when did Deano's name get mentioned, much less first in line? Oh, well. Deano had been substituting for six months. It was probably less confusing while Paul was gone.

"Hey, Deano," he said. "It's me."

"Hey! How you doin', buddy?"

"Great. Just arrived back a couple of days ago. This morning, I did a quickie interview for the *Herald* to drum up some business, and here I am."

"All right! How long you in town for this time?"

"I'm back. The job's over. Finished up early."

A pause. "That's just great!"

Deano sounded a little flat. Well, having Paul back meant the end of having the run of the place. Deano was an old friend from the Monterey police who had been working for Paul while figuring out what else he was going to do with the rest of his life. He had explored accounting school, then played around with the idea of opening up an Italian restaurant on Ocean Avenue. Finally, he had accepted Paul's offer as a stopgap arrangement. For months now he had been managing the business, and recently the reports hadn't been sounding too good. That had created another incentive for Paul to come back. Anyway, Deano would lay it all out at the office, and Paul would get busy pumping some new life into the old girl. Maybe Deano was disappointed that Paul was back. Tough. Paul owned the business. That was the fact, Jack.

"Let's get together," Deano said, putting on a more plausible show of enthusiasm. "Dinner? I'll fill you in."

"I thought I'd stop by the office in a half hour or so."

"Not a good plan, ol' buddy." Paul could almost hear the long hair slithering from side to side over his shoulders as Deano shook his head. He was making up for the regulation short haircuts of his cop days. The black Cossack mustache he wore these days wouldn't have gone over too well on the force either. He claimed its rakish look drove women mad.

"Why's that?"

"I wasn't expecting you. I need a chance to straighten up in here before you come waltzing in to claim the kingdom." He laughed. "At least give me a day to get someone in to do the filing."

Paul thought about it. Yeah, cut Deano some slack, if he wanted it.

"Okay. The Hog's Breath?"

"Shut down. Big deal here, Clint's restaurant closing. Surprised you didn't hear about it. Let's try Triples in Monterey. They do a mean gazpacho. Seven okay? I've got a few things to do here."

"Sure." So the Hog's Breath was gone. Nothing good lasted, baby, he knew that. Still, it was a blow. He'd rented the office specifically so he could look down at the Hog's Breath courtyard with its long-legged tourists.

"Think you can find it?"

"I can still muddle my way around Monterey, Dean."

"Ha, ha! I've missed you, dude!"

Paul hung up and started making other wake-up calls. Susan Misumi had left a message on his voice mail a month before. She was a friend, a professional contact, and a some-times-more.

Not home. She would still be at work. He left a message.

Then he called some clients to let them know he was back in town. Dennis Garcia was tied up in a meeting; Mike Tons gave him about twelve seconds of his time, sounding brusque and bothered; and Ezra Friedman, good old Ez who always had something good going for Paul, had his secretary say to call back some other time. These guys represented accounts he'd had for years. He considered Ez an old friend and couldn't help feeling deflated when he couldn't even manage a minute to touch base.

Nothing felt quite right lately. Since he had come back from Washington, he would be sitting in his car and suddenly feel the air grow quiet and still, as if time was suspended and the long parade of minutes left in his life had come to an abrupt halt. Before he thought to take another sip, the coffee in his cup would be cold.

Here he was living his own individual version of the American dream, a fit, single male, still young enough to catch the eye of a pretty girl, footloose, free to drink too much beer when he wanted, stay up all night listening to the Grateful Dead, and do sit-ups out on the deck naked as a jaybird. He ought to be flying high. Instead, he felt bothered.

Back out on the deck, regrouping, binoculars up, he watched a red-tailed hawk coasting on the wind out on the ridge. It drifted in place for a long time, like him, slightly stalled at the moment. He had arrived back at square one. Or, correction, back at minus square one, because the business obviously needed some damage control. For now, he would console himself with another beer.

The phone rang. He took the time to pour his beer into a glass this time and take a long sip before he sat down on the couch and answered it.

"Hi, Paul."

"Hello, Nina. How'd you know I was here in Carmel?"

"Called Washington. The senator's office told me you had come back. I figure you've had just enough time to take your shoes off and pop one."

"You know me too well." He propped his feet on the couch. "What's up?"

"No 'how are you?' No banter? Are you okay?"

"Still a little jet-lagged. So. How are you getting along?" Seven months had passed since her husband's death. He had called her office now and then, hearing each time that her preoccupations didn't include him. She was grieving too hard to think about anybody else. He had let her alone.

And he had worked on letting her go in his own heart.

"I've been slaving away. Hmm. What else? Well, it's spring. I can sunbathe out in the backyard even though Tallac is still covered with snow. Bob's got a yen to join a band. Matt and Andrea and their kids are growing older and wilder, every one of 'em. It's been a long time since we talked, Paul."

"There didn't seem much point in it."

"Whoa," Nina said.

"Sorry. Didn't mean to be so blunt."

"We're still friends, aren't we?"

"Sure. Friends forever. So what's up?"

"I'm calling about a case. It's a murder."

"I figured."

"I need a top investigator, Paul. The client is a girl, only sixteen. The transfer hearing is coming up in nine days, and they want to charge her as

80

an adult. I'm going over to Henry McFarland's office to try to talk him out of it this afternoon. Meantime, she's in custody, and it's a real strain on her and her mother.

"The victim was her uncle, a plastic surgeon at Tahoe who was slashed with an antique sword from his collection. They've placed her at his home about the time of the murder. But that's only half of it. There's something extraordinary about this case, and that's where you come in, I hope."

"Yeah? What's extraordinary?"

"Her cousin was killed in a small-plane crash in Nevada at the same time, Paul. I mean the very same moment, practically. A college student named Chris Sykes. The victim's son."

"So? What does the NTSB say?"

"They're hinting at pilot error. But I've talked to the pilot's widow—her name is Connie Bailey and she lives in LA—and she swears her husband was a complete stickler, highly experienced, and it just can't be."

"In my experience, coincidences like that don't happen."

"No, they don't. The El Dorado County D.A.'s office isn't making the connection, though. The crash was in another state. They know there's no way this girl could have engineered it, and they want to nail her for the uncle's murder so they aren't looking into it. I need you to see if you can find a connection."

Paul took a drink of the fine, faintly astringent beer, smelling hops and Danish summers as he did so.

"Paul?"

"I'm going to have to pass," he said.

"You're already tied up with other cases?"

He laughed shortly. "Not exactly. No other cases, and a lot of work I need to do here to get some cases."

"You can put that off. Give me a week, then you can go back and forth all you want."

"No can do."

He could hear her mutter "What the heck?" although her hand was over the receiver. Then she came back on.

"Listen, Paul, let's not let whatever personal situations we're having interfere with a successful working relationship," she said, a note of entreaty entering her voice. "It's been a long time. Months. I've missed working with you, and to get a handle on this case, I need you. I trust you, and you're the best."

"Get Tony Ramirez. He's in Reno. He can handle it."

"I want you, Paul. Please."

"Frankly, honey, I just don't want to see you."

"But why?"

"Because it would hurt too much." Because she was so dangerous, impaling him with her sharp chin and making him do things he shouldn't, like love her, and kill a man... "It hurts me just to talk to you."

"Oh," she said. After a long pause, she started in with the pressure. "Can't we put all that aside and just be..."

"Listen, Nina. I just got back, I've got problems down here, and it's not a good idea."

There was a long silence, and Paul thought, well, shit, I'm right. She's given me nothing but heartache. She won't let me love her or protect her, so I'm finished; I'm gone, and that's that. He wanted to get off the line and tailspin into a deep morose drunken stupor. Some days needed to be written off as soon as possible.

"Bye, honey," he said, and was just about to punch out when he heard her voice again.

"I can't sleep, Paul," she said. "Sometimes... I know this is ridiculous, but I'm so afraid. I worry that his killer will come back. They never caught him, you know."

"He's not coming back. I told you that."

"I tell myself that too. But then I wake up in the middle of the night, and God, it's awful..."

"I can't help with that," Paul said. He knew it had been hard for her to tell him that, and he knew how he sounded—gruff—but that was another thing he couldn't help.

"I could give you ten thousand up front."

Having failed to sway him with the straight skinny, she had sunk to bribery. Although he felt pushed and pulled in all directions by her naked maneuvering, he had to smile. She wanted him, and when he didn't jump, she wanted him more, and when he still didn't jump, and she couldn't win him back by engaging him, she pulled out all the stops to win any way she could. It was all so Nina. "I'm not for sale," he said, and finished off his glass, but then he started thinking about his checking account, which was all he had left since he cashed in the CDs and gave the money to his mother.

"Twenty," Nina said. "My retainer was fifty. I'll give you twenty. Just for some follow-up."

Paul ran his finger across his lips, wiping off the last of the foam, considering this.

"Please."

"Ah, Nina."

"What do you say?"

"I'll come up there and work my tail off for you for a week, all right? Then take some time to deal with my situation here."

"Absolutely."

"And there's one other condition."

"Anything."

"You have to sleep with me. I get so lonesome up in that big bed at Caesars."

Nina laughed. "Oh, Paul. It's going to be so good to have you back." The relief came through in her voice. All was restored to normal, her tone said, the Paul who wanted her and couldn't have her, the lusty jokes.

But all was not normal, whether she realized it or not, and he was no longer that Paul. This Paul simply wanted her money. Her pretty body was wasted on him. He was done trying to seduce Nina, done wanting her. He hereby declared his freedom from her.

Deano could wait a week. Susan had been

waiting a long time already. The money would help set everything straight. "Did I say I couldn't be bought?" he said. "I lied. Where'd this plane go down?"

5

INSIDE THE EL DORADO COUNTY District Attorney's offices, the militantly mediocre style of furnishings reminded Nina that law and law enforcement met here. The scratched gray desks, the aged government-issue copying machine, the featureless bookcases, and the overworked clerks all spoke of constraints: budgetary, philosophical, and creative.

Also a powerful symbol, Henry McFarland's sofa was as unyielding as Victorian horsehair to sit on, so uncomfortable that after squirming there for five minutes a visitor was dying to leave. It conveyed Henry's real message to the various defense lawyers, witnesses, and police officers he entertained: get to the point and get out.

But Henry himself, with the open face and affable manner of a born politician, socialized relentlessly. He was always hosting little get-togethers for the staff and jollying the judges. Nina only resolved this conflict between sofa and personality when she learned that Henry had been an actor in a TV series called *Green Pastures* before going to law school.

Like an actor, he was all style. Unfortunately,

as a lawyer he rated down there with Judge Judy. A pragmatic egotist, he had a heart as cold as a crocodile's. Nina couldn't stand him.

"I thought we should talk," she said.

"Always happy to talk to you, Nina." His high forehead, which gave such a deceptive impression of intelligence, was exaggerated by a slightly balding scalp of dark brown hair. He wore a classic navy blue Brooks Brothers-type suit with a red silk tie he had not purchased on his salary as district attorney.

"I'm not here to make a deal. My main interest right now is keeping this matter in Juvenile Court. You filed the petition to try my client as an adult. It's entirely within your discretion to withdraw that petition."

Expressing only polite interest, Henry nodded. "I assume you've read the Probation Department report. Pearl Smith dropped everything to get it done right away. Good job, I thought."

"Henry. This girl is only sixteen."

He picked up the report on his desk. "Criminal trespassing," he said. "Shoplifting. Suspicion of burglary. All in the past year. All tended to in Juvenile Court. All resulting in a short rap on the knuckles. Now this. I think she has graduated, Nina."

"No hint of any violence in any of that. She fell under the spell of a real idiot named Scott Cabano. It was a period of confusion for her."

"Even more confusing for her uncle," Henry said, smiling.

"Look. Why don't you let the court that has been set up for people her age handle this? Has Barbara described her? She's a child!"

"So were the assholes who blew away all those other children at Littleton. It's the public temper to try murders as adult crimes. Have you seen the local paper lately?"

She had. A long article over the weekend had heralded the arrival of a wave of evil young criminals right here in Tahoe, with Nicole Zack leading the crowd. Although the local newspaper had refrained from naming her, the town was hot with gossip. News traveled fast. By now, everyone knew about Nikki.

"We've had several cases of violent crime in the Sierra where the kid was tried as an adult at the age of fourteen," Henry continued. "They're growing up fast and committing adult crimes."

"This isn't Littleton and it wasn't some gruesome, random hate crime. This young girl didn't stockpile weapons or shoot strangers."

"A slashing murder doesn't do it for you?"

"If she did it—and that remains to be proven—she didn't go there with a weapon, which means she wasn't planning a murder."

"But she seems to have been attempting a burglary. And that's a felony. And when somebody gets killed in the commission of a felony, it's first-degree murder. The juvenile court system isn't set up to handle a crime this serious."

"It's set up to handle children under the age of eighteen," Nina said stubbornly.

Henry turned the pages of the report. "This young girl just turned in a very interesting paper in her World History class at school. The title of it is—let me make sure I read every word—'Violent Overthrow of the Capitalist-Consumerist System As Explained in the Writings of Che Guevara.' Well written, except for the spelling and the complete lack of objectivity. She seems to idolize Che, which, let's face it, is idiotic. Che would have her shot, because she's not a communist. She thinks once everything is burned down we should start over with complete anarchy."

"Is that really your problem with her, Henry? A paper she wrote for school? She's bright and she's unhappy, whether it's from poverty and not having a father or just from an upsurge of hormones. A certain kind of smart kid goes political. Eventually, that kid grows up and changes, and maybe she loses interest in radical idealism, maybe not, but for sure her politics are going to mature, too. Anyway, I can't believe we're sitting here arguing about a silly paper she wrote for a class."

"Silly? I would describe it as ominously unbalanced. I would agree that she's intelligent and she's unhappy. I would add that she believes in violence as a solution to her problems."

"A school paper is not evidence, for Pete's sake."

"We're not in court," Henry snapped. "I'm charged with determining whether I should ask that she be charged as an adult, and that's what she thinks she is. She thinks the world is out to get her and she thinks she's fighting back. I'll bet she doesn't feel a second's remorse for the killing. We'll find out in the postconviction sentencing report."

Nina's rear end was numb, but she refused to give up. "Henry, do you have any children?"

"Oh, please," Henry said, spreading his hands. "No, I don't. And that has nothing to do with this."

"I suppose I'd say that too, but I do have a child a couple of years younger. It's gotten very hard to be an adolescent, Henry. They've been stripped of all those comforting illusions of childhood we remember. The ugliest things Planet Earth has to offer is blown in their faces all day long. Boy Scouts, soccer teams, church, school—those old cultural mainstays are fighting a losing battle. These kids turn on the TV to witness a hundred acts of violence every night. They see friends and families loading up on legal and illegal drugs. They click around an uncensored Internet to hate sites from around the world. Their cultural icons pierce and tattoo themselves.

"A lot of kids can't handle the negativity overload. They get unhappy. They may even act out some, like Nicole Zack. But you know, Henry, in general, they do work through it in time. They find the way to a good life even without Ozzie and Harriet as models.

"It would be wrong to warehouse Nikki and give up on her, even if she did commit this crime. Please, Henry, give her the chance to move through the system that's set up to help kids, not the one that's set up to punish adults. You don't want this on your conscience."

Henry looked at her. He stood up behind his desk. He put his hands together. Clap. Clap. Clap.

Nina stood up too. "I'm going to beat you anyway."

"You're going to take whatever deal we may offer after the prelim, and like it."

"Uh huh. You know what Che says about that?"

"No. What does he say about that?"

"Nothing. He's dead. Like your case is going to be."

Henry laughed. "Let's have lunch sometime. You can't really be this wrapped up in your cases, Nina. It's a great show, though. I respect that."

Nina shook her head. She picked up her briefcase and went to the door.

"See you at the transfer hearing," Henry said, chuckling.

"Here you are," Sandy said. "Months later. Hoo ha."

"I missed you, too, Sandy," said Paul. "And yes, my work in D.C. is over. How's married life? Loosening you up some?"

The strict line of her mouth tightened. She was leaning over a file drawer. A stack of colored folders lay spread on the floor beside her.

"How about a little kiss to say hello?" Paul said and went around behind her bent-over body and gave her a squeeze.

"Hey! You stop that!" She pushed him into the secretarial chair, which rolled away, and he stumbled after it trying to keep his balance, but he went over anyway, landing on the hand with the sore finger just as the outer door opened and Nina walked in.

He sat there rubbing his hand. Sandy shrugged and flicked a file into the drawer, but her shoulders were shaking.

He saw black heels, neat legs which rose to dizzying heights before the skirt began, creamy skin with the beginnings of swelling curves below the throat of the blouse as she leaned over toward him, bright eyes and long brown hair swinging toward him, and he thought to himself, I made a big mistake. I should have stayed in Carmel.

"Welcome to Tahoe," Nina said. She held out her hand and helped him get up.

As always, Paul looked larger than life to Nina, sitting in the client chair across from her desk, rubbing his hand. He wore khakis, and one long leg extended way across the room toward her. Blond hair fell over his forehead.

She hadn't seen him for so long. Not since...but she wouldn't think about that right now. Those thoughts owned her nights, not her days.

"You look great," he said, sniffing. "Smell good, too."

She laughed. "Barbecue sauce from the

chicken at lunch. That also contributed the delicate pattern on my great-lookin' blouse."

"But you also look tired."

She shrugged. "I am tired. Sleep problems. I've been spending weekends tramping around in the high desert. I sleep fine after a long day like that. Paul, I saw the plane crash that killed the Sykes boy and the pilot. It was too far away for me to hear anything, but I saw the flash of light as it crashed."

"What were you doing in the desert?"

"Remember the land Lindy Markov gave me? I go out there."

"Alone?"

"Sometimes Bob comes." She turned back to business. "Thanks for dropping everything. I owe you, Paul. I know you didn't really want to come up."

"I'm here now. And I'm interested. I already called the NTSB office in Carson City to set up a visit to the crash site."

"That's fast work. Did you learn anything?"

"Well, it'll be a year before they come up with anything other than a 'preliminary finding,' but yeah, they're still tending toward blaming the crash on pilot error. There's no evidence of equipment failure so far. According to what they've been told, the plane was in tip-top shape. They've spoken with the mechanic who worked on it before takeoff. Apparently, he's pretty reassuring. One thing though, he let slip that old Skip Bailey, the pilot, has an error on his record."

"That's interesting. Maybe it was pilot

error then, and there's no connection to the doctor's murder."

"It needs looking into. I talked to Connie Bailey on the phone last night. She swears her husband was the most careful man on earth. I plan to fly from Reno to LA tonight after the crash-site visit and talk with her some more. What do you think?"

"Go for it. Here's your check." She took it out of the drawer and handed it to him. Without looking at it, he stuck it into his pocket. "And here's a file with all the paperwork we have on the William Sykes murder to date. Police reports, preliminary autopsy report, crime scene photos, and so on."

"I'll read it on the flight from Reno down south. I'll put together a report and make sure you have it in a couple of days, all right?"

"The hearing is next Wednesday, on May twenty-fifth. Do you want to meet Nikki?"

"No need, at this point."

"I don't think she did it."

"You never do."

"I've changed a lot in the past few months," she said.

"So have I."

She didn't like the way he was not looking at her, not trying to figure her out, or listening for the subtle tune that had always run between them.

Her brows knitted.

Sandy appeared in the doorway. "Your three o'clocks are here," she said. "Two of 'em." She closed the door behind her.

He got up to leave and Nina was aware of an old feeling streaming over her. She didn't want Paul to leave. She wanted something from him, more...

"Wait," she said. "I have something else for you to do in LA. I want to check out Beth Sykes's alibi." She kept him there a good five minutes longer. When he finally left, she felt vaguely dissatisfied. She didn't like the cooler atmosphere between them, when she should be welcoming it.

Paul drove the rental jeep up a four-wheel-drive road as far into the Carson Range as he could toward the spot where the Beechcraft had gone down. His directions proved unnecessary. The closest spot along the road was cluttered with trucks and utility vehicles. Today they would be hauling the wreckage away.

He pulled to the side, got out with his water bottle, crammed on a baseball hat the senator had given him that said "Washington Redskins" on it, and began hiking through a good mile of rugged terrain, well marked by the various agencies that had passed through in the past few days. He was glad he had changed into shorts because the sunlight burned steadily at his back.

Breaking through a thick stand of ponderosa pine, he came to the spot where two people had died.

The place looked appropriately forbidding. A long channel of charred grasses marked the area where the plane had tumbled along the ground. It had come to rest against the side of a hill. From where he stood, he could imagine the event in miniature, the plane rising and falling like the plastic toys he had crashed as a boy. Following the path of devastation, he got as close to the plane as he could before an official type tried to stop him. However, stating that he was the representative of the pilot's widow won him some respect. After a short verbal spar, which he won handily, he was allowed to get in closer.

He pulled out his old silver Nikon and began to shoot, first wide-angle shots that took in the setting, then close-ups of anything that looked even vaguely interesting, especially the engine sections. Moving in as he shot, he found himself peering into the cockpit. Blackened shreds of fabric clung to the pilot's seat. Behind it, in one of the two passenger seats, a burned blue jacket with an emblem reading "Pomona College" lay in a heap. A mangled laptop, curled from the heat and almost unrecognizable, lay next to a phone on the floor between the seats.

Wiping a bead of sweat from the top of his lip, the portly, official type returned and stood nearby. He put his hands in his pockets. "I have a son in college," he said. "How must his parents feel?"

"His father died the same night."

"Couldn't take the news? I've heard of that happening now and then."

"No." Paul didn't want to get into it. "There's no known connection."

"Eerie," said the man.

On the way to the Reno airport, Paul called his office. "Trumbo and van Wagoner," said Dean's hearty voice. "Dean's busy right now, but he'll call back real soon." He punched the cancel button and dialed Susan Misumi.

"You're back?" she asked.

"No. Just thinking of you. Sorry it took so long to get back to you, but I'm finished with Washington now and I'm busy playing catch up."

"Are you in town?"

"I'm"—he looked around for a sign, saw nothing but gray asphalt blending into the gray sky, and took a guess—"ten miles outside of Reno, on my way to the airport."

"Flying back to Carmel tonight?"

"No. Down to LA on business, unfortunately. How'd the latest film festival go?" Susan organized film series for a local group in her spare time, when she wasn't conducting autopsies as medical examiner for the county of Monterey.

"Great. We took in more money than last year. I was thinking next year maybe we'll do a series of provocative female movies, really contrasty, cutting-edge stuff."

"What movies?" he asked, so that he did not have to come up with some polite bullshit. He hated chick flicks.

"Oh, say, *Cries and Whispers*, one night. That's heavy Bergman, all dark and red. Then, something trashy and lightweight but fun like *There's Something about Mary*, or *Rich and Famous*."

"Isn't that last one the movie where Jackie Bisset does it in the airplane lavatory with some guy she meets on the plane?"

"See? There's something for everyone, even you. Or are you having these sorts of thoughts because you're about to get on an airplane?"

"I'm having these thoughts because I'm talking to you." It was true. He felt anxious to jump on some undemanding, curvy, female hips. More ignominiously, he felt anxious to line somebody up to stand between him and Nina.

"Ready to be bad?" she said, and it wasn't a question.

They made a date for the next weekend. It would have to do.

Swinging into Reno on the multi-laned freeway coming up from Carson City, he imagined what it might be like to live here in this town that grew like a staunch little tree in America's outback. He thought about Nina out in those treeless hills beyond on her weekends in the desert. Whackos found convenient hiding places in such desolation. Why didn't that scare her?

Underneath the polish of her suit and careful grooming, she had looked so sad.

But no point in dwelling on that. Nothing he could do. Wounds took a long time to heal and sometimes the scars didn't go away. They just got uglier.

On the plane, he sat next to a slick young man in a slick young suit who surreptitiously fingered an unlit cigar throughout the forty-five-minute flight. A quick glance at the other passengers assured him that if Jacqueline Bisset was anywhere nearby she was heavily disguised.

At LAX, he stood in line for a long time to claim his rental car. Avoiding the freeways, he worked out his route on the map, finding his way to Pacific Coast Highway. It didn't matter—the traffic found him, and he felt the old familiar road rage coming over him as though he'd never been away. He gritted his teeth and sat with the other drivers, feeling the heartburn firing up.

It took an hour and a half. He had rented a motel room on the beach in Hermosa, which was the town right next to Redondo, Connie Bailey's town. Why not squeeze a little pleasure out of his business?

The modest room had a view of the ocean, but at this hour, who could tell? Even with the lamp lit, the corners stayed black. He put his duffel down and for a moment poised on the brink of one of those dead times, dangerously near the tingling void that he fell into so often lately. But tonight the sea was out there to fill in the empty places. He could hear it roaring like something alive, filling the room with rhythmic pounding, calling out to him, drowning out whatever it was inside that was burning him alive.

6

SHE LIVED IN A HOUSE overlooking miles of high tension wires and sixties' ranch houses. A rusty security screen door creaked when she opened it. "You're Paul van Wagoner," Connie Bailey said. "Please come in."

The dead pilot's wife led the way past a tiny foyer into the living room. He sat down.

Everything in the room matched precisely. Teal blue walls were trimmed in a deep, almost black, purple. The couch was purple with teal and beige in a wheat pattern. On the wall, abstract drawings of tree trunks in black bore inklings of the room's primary colors in the background.

"Nice," he said, looking around. He found the compulsive coordinating soothing. She probably did, too. African American, very proper, she had black hair pulled back in a band and a broad forehead that ended in warm-looking, golden brown eyes. She was keeping herself on a tight leash, tucking her navy cotton dress neatly underneath her when she sat down.

"Thank you," she said. "I called a lawyer I know here in Los Angeles. Winston Reynolds. We went to high school together. He knows both you and Mrs. Reilly. He said I can trust you."

"Oh, yeah. Winston."

"He told me about you. He's quite the character, really exaggerates something terrible. Told me something about kayaks up on that big lake up there. Probably another one of his stories."

She didn't believe it. But it had happened, the kayaks on the lake, the explosion...

"How is Winston?"

"Still playing cat and mouse with the IRS. One of these days they're gonna get tired of chasing him and pop that man in jail."

"He's a lawyer. They don't do jail."

Liking the sound of that, she relaxed a little, smiling. "That's right. And he's a good one, too."

Paul pulled out a notebook. "What do you want to tell me about your husband, Mrs. Bailey?"

She got up and walked to the mantel, taking down a framed photograph. She studied the picture for a while, then handed it to Paul.

A round-faced, balding man smiled out from the photo. He looked a little older than Connie, probably in his late forties or more, and had darker skin, with the clean jawline of a military man.

"He was fifty-three when he died in that crash," she said. "A kind man. A loving husband. A caring father to his kids."

"You have children?"

"Two. Grown up. Working. Married. I'm so grateful he lived to see them happily married. We married when I was twenty-one and stayed married for twenty-three years. That's a long time."

"Yes."

"A long time to love somebody and get used to them. The way they comb their hair just so in the morning, or in Skip's case, search for it! The way they make coffee for you, too strong, but it's the love that goes into it, you know?"

"You miss him."

"I don't know how I'll get along now."

"I understand you were in Carson City?"

"I just got back. I flew up to identify his body. Came back last night." She was working to subdue her feelings, but the curtain of sorrow came down now over her face like heavy blue velvet. "It was very difficult. I didn't recognize him. They identified him from his teeth, all those expensive inlays he had done."

"Are you alone?"

"My sister's staying with me until after the memorial service this weekend. She's down at the Vons picking up some food. She was here when those two men came yesterday afternoon..."

"What men?"

"From the National Transportation Safety Board. They asked me a lot of questions."

"What did they want to know?"

"Was Skip depressed? Did he tend to be forgetful? Any health problems lately that might have affected his ability to fly? When they asked to search his office, my sister flew off the handle. Booted them out."

"Any idea what they were looking for?"

"Maybe they thought he went down on purpose," she said, "like they thought the Egyptair pilot did in the seven fifty-seven crash. I don't know. Maybe they want to frame him. Maybe they're lackeys of the engine manufacturer. Who can say? I tell you one thing, everybody's looking for a scapegoat, including the newspapers and at the moment, Skip's their man. Did you see the article this morning in the LA paper? They refer to the cause of the crash as pilot error without a report, without a finding, without even an investigation."

"There have been a number of small-plane crashes lately. There's a lot of interest."

"It amounts to the same thing. They're destroying a wonderful man's memory without any evidence that he did one thing wrong." She got up to make coffee in the kitchen. Paul leafed through the magazines, aviation this and pilot that, wondering why Mrs. Bailey had called a hotshot lawyer like Winston Reynolds. He smelled a wrongful death lawsuit brewing over Christopher Sykes's death right along with the coffee in the kitchen, and realized that Mrs. Bailey was going to have a lot of reasons for not wanting the crash to be a result of pilot error.

Here we go again, he thought, the legal system twisting up honest grief like an old dishrag.

"Skip never quit thinking about planes and flying," Mrs. Bailey said, coming in with a tray. "He was like a kid about that stuff, very into the technical side of things. Built model airplanes until we needed a second house to stow them in."

She poured them both cups and sat back.

"I donated most of them yesterday to a day care center. They're going to hang them from the ceiling. I couldn't have them around anymore."

"Tell me about his charter business."

"He flew for years for a commercial shuttle service between Los Angeles and Las Vegas. You're going to hear about this, so let me be the first to tell you the exact truth. He fell asleep while the plane was on autopilot. One time, for a very short period of time. Nothing happened to the plane, but he was reported. Got fired."

"I guess that looks pretty bad on a pilot's record."

"It took him years to get over the guilt. 'Course, the reason he fell asleep was he spent the whole night before that flight staying up consoling me because my father had died." She waved her hand, picked up the creamer, and poured into a cup. "Doesn't matter. You just can't do that. Even though no one was in a minute of danger. Even though most pilots probably fall asleep one time or another on a long flight when everything's going smoothly."

"So he started his own business."

"That's right. Got a business loan and bought his plane. He never had an accident. He maintained that plane like he was going to take his own child on it." She sipped. "I miss his lousy coffee. Isn't that something?"

"Did your husband keep records?"

"Of course. The NTSB people brought a

scanner and made copies of a lot of papers, but I'm keeping the originals for now."

"Can I see them?"

She showed Paul into a neat but cluttered study tucked behind the stairway. A few delicately assembled models dangled from the ceiling.

"I kept a couple for the grandkids," she said, setting one swinging. "To remember him by."

Paul had a hard time imagining Connie as a grandmother. She would be about forty-five, only about five years older than he was. In his mind, grandparents would forever remain the older generation, the generation in which he did not belong.

The records the NTSB had already been through lay on the desk, fastidiously kept, neat, revealing the pilot's obsessive concern with details. His handwriting was crabbed and tight and hard to read. "He checked and fueled the plane a couple of hours before taking off for Tahoe," Paul said, studying college-ruled notebook paper in a three-ring binder. The page had been marked with the year, the date, and the time of maintenance. "And here's his flight plan and the passenger manifest. He came up the Nevada side of the mountains."

Connie nodded, her hand on one of her husband's models.

"Passenger," said Paul. "Here it is: Mr. Sykes. The kid was young to be called mister."

She started to look at the notebook, but teared

up and wiped her eyes with a handkerchief. "Skip was formal in that way."

"Was your husband accustomed to piloting planes chartered by college boys?"

"You'd be surprised at the people who hired him. Housewives who want to run up for the weekend to Tahoe or Vegas to gamble...rich kids who need a ride back to Mom's ski condo after a few days spent visiting Dad in the Hollywood Hills."

"Yes, but wouldn't a parent reserve the plane?"

"This is LA, remember? People grow up fast in this town." She took a deep breath and exhaled. "I guess I'll be hearing from that poor boy's family now. I guess they'll be wanting something from me since Skip's not here. Revenge. Well, it wasn't Skip's fault. It plain wasn't." At last she released the model, turning eyes full of tears toward Paul. "I'll wait for you outside, okay? This room smells like him."

"Can I borrow this notebook?"

"There's a copy machine in the corner. You can make copies. Do not take anything. Anything at all." She left.

Paul spent a few minutes poking through the files on Bailey's desk. In the maintenance records, he found a file of invoices for services rendered by someone named Dave LeBlanc. He made copies of the more important paperwork.

Back in the living room, he found Mrs. Bailey drinking the last of the coffee, ankles crossed, hair perfectly smoothed, holding herself together until he was gone.

"Who's this?" he asked, showing her the invoices.

"Dave is—was—Skip's maintenance engineer." She almost smiled. "Fancy term for mechanic. But Skip thought highly of his abilities."

Paul noted the phrasing. "But that's the only way he thought highly of him?"

"Oh, you know. Dave's the same age as us, but with a whole different set of criteria."

"Objectionable lifestyle?"

"You should meet him. Form your own opinion."

"Skip didn't like him."

"Skip liked everyone," she said emphatically.

He got up. "Too late to catch LeBlanc?"

"He comes in late. I'm sure you can find him at the John Wayne Airport."

"Mrs. Bailey, I know it's hard, but I want you to look through your husband's paperwork. See if there's anything there that catches your eye. Even if you think it's completely stupid, I want you to call me immediately." He handed her a card.

"If you think it's important..." she said. "I just about can't stand to but I'll try."

Paul didn't really think she would, not anytime soon. He just hoped she would.

She saw him to the door. "You know, unless a plane explodes, it takes a long time to crash," she said. "A long time you know you're going to die. I hope he wasn't too

106

scared. I hope... I hope he had time to get over how afraid he was watching the ground get closer. I hope he thought for one second about how happy he made us."

After a quick stop for fortification from one of the thousands of fast-food restaurants along 190th, Paul hit the freeways by two P.M., heading south toward John Wayne Airport in Orange County. Rush hour in greater Los Angeles now encompassed all daylight hours. Slowed to a crawl, flipping stations in his rented car, he had plenty of time to note the differences between northern and southern California.

People here were all colors, not so different from up north, but what was different was the proportion. By his estimation, the so-called minorities outnumbered Anglos by two to one. With heat rising from the asphalt pavement and the old clunkers on the road that could only live in a climate as cordial as the one in southern Cal, he felt he was cruising the roads of Mexico, Africa, India, even the South Pacific, anyplace hot, where people wore brighter colors, where loud music ruled, and people were louder and brighter too.

In those faraway places, years ago, people chose to take their time. Now the traffic had returned them all to the pace of a burro.

Somebody cut in front of him and he sat on his horn and shouted imprecations, which got him the finger from the other car, which almost led to something, because Paul lost his temper and returned the favor. He said to himself, I've got a goddamn air bag after all, and swung around the guy in the right lane. But the guy chickened out and didn't try to tailgate him or pass him again. Paul was violently disappointed for a second.

Then sanity returned. You're in handgun central, he said to himself, take it easy.

Passing the signs for South Coast Plaza, the amusement park for prosperous adults, he searched for some jazz on the radio just long enough to miss the airport exit and waste another twenty minutes inching his way back onto the 405. Cut off half a dozen times by aggressive drivers, forced to slam on his brakes for inexplicable dead stops in the traffic flow, he felt his heart beating again in his throat and the spirit of savagery rising, rising... He steeled himself to remain calm. Thousands fought this daily battle honorably and so could he.

The airport, tucked in the corner formed by the boundaries of the densely populated towns of Costa Mesa, Newport, and Irvine, handled small planes in addition to regular flights. Bypassing the major terminals, asking questions along the way, he worked his way over to a hangar on the fringes where Connie Bailey had told him he might find Dave LeBlanc. Unable to locate a place within half a mile to park legally, he pulled up right beside the hangar and parked.

Inside the tall, unmarked, corrugated metal building, he followed the noise and advice of other workers until he located LeBlanc in an air-conditioned bay much like the ones used by auto mechanics. Wearing dark blue coveralls with a black plastic visor over his face, the mechanic looked like Darth Vader manipulating a futuristic gun that shot fire. He turned the gun off, flipped up his visor, and peered at Paul quizzically.

"I know you?"

"Connie Bailey sent me," said Paul, introducing himself.

LeBlanc took his hand out of his glove and shook. "Poor old Skip," he said.

"You too busy to talk for a minute?"

"What's this about?"

"Some loose ends. You know, the widow wants things tied up before..." He left the thought dangling.

"Oh, right," said LeBlanc hurriedly, uncomfortable, as everyone was, with the hint of death, funerals, burials, and all the other unmentionable things lingering in the unfinished thought. He tossed his gloves and helmet on a bench, ruffled his flat gray hair, and led Paul into an office that smelled of grease and chemicals.

On the shelves above a desk, a collection of weapons made Paul stiffen. He moved closer.

Hoisting himself up onto the battered metal desk, LeBlanc scratched a bulging gut. He turned to the shelf and lifted an object up, holding it out for Paul to see. "This one's an atomic pistol from *Buck Rogers*. Recognize it?"

Dimly recognizing the title of a movie he had seen as a child, Paul said, "Not really."

"Used to have a ray gun from *Forbidden Planet* but I sold it to a guy who lives in Boston. That one's bigger. Long. Maybe two feet long."

Paul took the ray gun from him and shot it out the window. Heavy. Real metal. But nothing happened, no buzzing, no red light, no disintegration. "These all from movies?"

"Yep. No point in living down here if you can't take advantage. Sometimes the studios have auctions. Sometimes, I pick 'em up in warehouse sales, collectors' markets."

"You have quite a collection."

"Over a hundred. A lot of vintage fifties."

So the Darth Vader look must have been intentional, although a little out of his preferred era. The guy was a sci-fi movie freak. "Any of them work?"

LeBlanc laughed, turning his face into the warren of lines that showed a hard-living past. "I wish."

"Ever sit up here and pick off people going by down in the yard?" asked Paul, looking out the window.

"Tempting, isn't it?" he asked. "Beats therapy."

"Mmm," said Paul, handing it back.

Setting the ray gun lovingly back on the shelf, LeBlanc reached into a drawer, and offered Paul a fruit drink in a collapsible aluminum packet.

"No, thanks. Too early for me," said Paul.

LeBlanc chuckled. "Funny man." He was in an incongruously fine mood for someone who had lost a friend. He raised his eyebrows at Paul, smiling, stuck a straw into a hole in the packet and made sucking noises. He stopped, wiped his mouth and said, "Ah. That hit the spot."

"What are you working on?" Paul asked.

LeBlanc nodded toward the room they had just left. "That's a Cessna, single engine. Needs a complete overhaul and the owner wants it yesterday. The usual horseshit."

"I've always wondered. Why would anyone choose to fly a single- engine plane? Isn't a twin-engine plane safer?"

"Now that's a typical beginner's mistake," LeBlanc said. "Actually, there are more fatal accidents in twin engines. See, with a single engine, something goes wrong, you head instantly for the nearest open stretch of land and get on down. With two engines, it fools you. You think, hey, I've got one more engine. I can make it home: increases your risk because you already took one more risk than you should have. You start with a minor mistake and end up smacking into a mountainside like old Skip."

The callous way he dismissed Connie Bailey's husband didn't sit well with Paul. "You been doing this work for long?" he said.

"Must be more 'n twenty years now. Whew. Time flies when you're having supercharged fun."

"All that time with Bailey?"

"Not at first. Skip had a regular job for a

111

while. So it's been more like the past ten with him." LeBlanc dug around in his drawer again, coming up with a fistful of airplane peanut packets. "Want some?"

"No, thanks," said Paul.

"How's Connie making out?"

"She's holding up."

"That's good," he said, breaking open the plastic on the packaging with his teeth. "I'm glad to hear it, even though I don't know her too well. She and I never really hit it off."

"Why do you think?"

"I don't know why. I like her fine."

"How about you and Bailey?"

"Skip and I got along. He treated that plane like a baby."

"So people say."

He crunched his peanuts, looking thoughtful. "Except maybe not the NTSB," he said. "I got a visit. I mean, aren't they saying he blew it up there? Me and Skip go way back. I don't like hearing them say things like that about him. Draggin' up that old business about how he fell asleep at the wheel. It isn't right. Let the dead rest in peace."

"Buddies, huh?"

"Damn right, buddies."

"Wasn't it you who told the NTSB about Skip's old problem?"

LeBlanc's face screwed up into an exaggerated expression of innocence.

Paul reached over beside him and picked up a plastic packet. Ripping it open, he asked, "How long were you in?"

"How'd you know about that? Connie tell you? Because I think maybe she holds that against me sometimes."

"Lucky guess."

LeBlanc cocked his head and a new look entered his eyes. He began shaking his head, smiling. "I shoulda known right away. You're an ex-cop, aren't you? Well, I'm an ex-con, so we're even. It's no secret. I did five years. Shot a guy in a bar fight. Didn't kill him, though I sure wanted to at the time. Bastard screwed my woman. That was a long time ago, early seventies. Right after I got out of 'Nam. Did a lot of drugs back then, lots of alcohol. I don't do that stuff no more. I'm a changed man."

"With guns that don't have bullets."

"That's right. I sublimate."

"Glad to hear it. That where you met Skip? Inside?"

He laughed raucously. "He'll be turning in his grave, hearing you suggest any such thing. No, ol' Skip was straight-arrow all the way. We were both Air Force."

"You worked with him?"

"For him, you might say. Just like here."

"He took pity on you. Hired you when no one else would."

"I'm a damn good mechanic. If ol' Skip had come to me all high and mighty I wouldn't have worked for him. He knew he had the best plane mechanic in California. What's that word that comes between sympathetic and copacetic? Both gettin' something out of the deal?"

"Symbiotic?"

"Right. I have a way with machines. Skip knew how good I was. And I needed a job. It worked out good."

"The plane he flew. A single engine Beechcraft Model 18. That's a pretty old plane, isn't it?"

He nodded. "Built in the sixties. But let me tell you a little secret. Most planes you fly in were built twenty, thirty years ago. They stuff in a coupla new seat covers, out with the orange and in with the mauve or whatever the hell else color people are painting their living room walls, and call 'em refurbished. That plane was as good as you'll find top to bottom, and I'm not talking upholstery." He crumpled the trash of four snack packets and two drinks and dropped them on the floor. "I gotta get moving," he said. "Time's money for us wage slaves."

"Tell me about the last day," Paul said. "What did the Beechcraft need done?"

"The usual checklist. Want a copy?"

"Sure."

He rustled through a pile of paperwork on the desk and pulled out a folder. "I keep good records. Skip liked that about me, praised me for it many a time."

"Tell me about that last flight. Were you here?"

"I split after we went through the check. He was a little skittish, new passenger and all. Thought she might act up, maybe."

"She? I thought the passenger was male."

Either he was holding back a laugh or was about to be sick. "Sorry," he said. "Didn't mean to confuse you. You know, we always called the plane 'she.' I know it was a boy that went down with him, of course."

"Was there anything iffy about that plane the day it came down? Anything in need of attention? Anything at all?"

"Not a damn thing. She was in perfect condition for a nice easy ride up to the mountains."

"Ever been up there yourself?" Paul said casually.

"Where?"

"Tahoe, Reno, that area."

"Nah." No more smiling, and when he wasn't smiling, you noticed the heavy-lidded eyes and the hard thin mouth.

"Ever met Christopher Sykes?"

"Who?" He had tensed. He knew they were at the heart of the discussion.

"The kid who was the passenger."

"I never saw him. Never met him. Too bad about him. Yeah." LeBlanc shook his head over Chris Sykes, and Paul thought he actually did look sorry.

On the off chance, Paul said, "I'll be talking to Jan Sapitto tomorrow."

He looked blank.

"You know, Jan. Lives here in LA. Old friend of Beth Sykes."

"In case you're wondering," LeBlanc said, "I don't know the lady. I don't know these people, and I'm just a mechanic and I don't want to be hassled because Skip took a header.

115

It's too bad, and not only because he's dead. Lawyers and cops are coming out of their holes in the ground to make my life miserable. I had enough of that a long time ago."

Paul gave him his card. "Call me if you forgot to tell me anything," he said. "I don't have anything against you. I'm just trying to find out what happened to that plane."

"Keep your card," LeBlanc said, handing it back. "I told you all I know. If I see you down there in the yard again"—he whipped a red plastic spacegun off the wall and aimed it at Paul—"I might just pick you off." He shot a dot of blue light directly into Paul's heart, threw back his head, and laughed.

7

NINA HAD READ ABOUT a plastic surgery arrest in San Jose the week before. The Vietnamese doctor, catering to a primarily Vietnamese clientele, operated out of the back room of a beauty shop. He performed liposuction, facelifts, and breast implants and apparently had only a passing acquaintance with anesthesiology. The problem was, anyone with an M.D. could do it. Plastic surgery was a tremendously lucrative specialty, and the market was growing as the baby boomers entered their fifties demanding to remain in their thirties.

William Sykes's Re-Creation Clinic on Saddle Road appeared to be on the other side of the universe from San Jose, instead of just a few hundred miles away.

Sited close to the center of town on a slope below Heavenly, from the engraved brass sign to the custom Murano glass light that hung above the doorway, the clinic was a study in discretion and class. Nina parked in a small lot secluded behind tall trees and buzzed for entry. A soft voice preceded an almost ceremonial opening of the double doors leading inside. The sleek receptionist, whose desk sat in front of one of the largest picture windows overlooking the lake Nina had ever seen, practically wall-sized, led her immediately into another room. There, a capable-looking nurse in whites expressed her sorrow at the passing of Dr. Sykes, seeming quite sincere in her praise of the dead doctor, and invited Nina to wait in a chair that faced yet another incredible view.

While she waited, she helped herself to some of the glossy albums lying around, featuring before and after shots of patients who were identified only by number. Some she recognized from the advertisements on television. Others were new. All showed spectacular improvements.

"We don't put them all in there," a young man said, and she jumped. She closed the album she had been looking at and set it down. "Believe it or not, some clients don't want their surgery shouted from the rooftops." He extended his hand and Nina took it.

"I'm Dylan Brett," said the best-looking man

Nina could remember meeting in her entire life. "Bill's partner here at the clinic."

"Nina Reilly," she said. While she was recovering from touching someone who looked like Pierce Brosnan and Gabriel Byrne rolled into one throbbing mass of maleness, she forced herself to remember who she was and why she was there. He sat down across a table from her, muscles tensed as if ready to run a race, a man who, by his mere presence, created an atmosphere as vibrant as sunlight in the room. Holy cow, she thought foolishly, observing him as she spoke. How the women must swoon.

"Bill's death is a terrible blow," he said. "He was a really special surgeon. In addition to his gift for surgery, he had a gift for dealing with people. He knew how to set them at ease. Most people come here feeling uncertain and even frightened at the prospect of surgery, but Bill could get the most panicky patients wishing they had decided to do it years ago." A memory flitted over his face and as he laughed and shook his head, an unruly lock of dark hair fell down over his forehead, just like in the movies. "Anyone who came in here less than committed left a visit with Dr. Bill ready to mortgage the house."

"Will the clinic continue without him?"

"Oh, yes. Chris...his son, showed no interest in practicing medicine, to his father's great disappointment, although I'm sure he never told Chris that. Chris was interested in graphic arts and communications, so maybe he would have ended up doing some marketing for us eventually, but Bill was grooming me to be his successor here. He was considering retirement. We had discussed how we would handle things when that time came, so I'm prepared to take over without even having to close the clinic temporarily. I've already got an associate lined up who will start next month."

"Another surgeon?"

"Yes. Board-certified, of course. He comes highly recommended. And it was my impression from meeting him that he is more like Bill than I am."

"You mean a better salesman?"

"That's right. I'm a surgeon and not much good for anything else."

Oh, Nina doubted that very much. But the sensible part of her put her tongue on hold while she consulted her notes.

"Did you know Christopher well?"

"He grew up hanging around the clinic with his dad. A great kid. Funny. Close to both his parents. Quiet and smart."

"Did he have a girlfriend?"

"He dated now and then, but no. He didn't settle on anyone. He was only nineteen. Told me once he had to sow his wild oats until he was at least twenty-two." Brett sighed. "What a waste. And, of course, I can hardly believe the police would arrest Nikki. I remember her coming into the clinic with Chris a number of years ago. The whole story—the knife wounds and so on—it just doesn't make any sense. I'd like to help any way I can."

"Thank you. I appreciate that and I'll tell

Nikki. What about Beth Sykes? How well do you know her?"

"How is she doing?"

"She's having a hard time."

"Yes, I imagine she is." He stared out the window for a minute, cleared his throat, and said, "We knew each other, of course. Got together socially. My wife and she were both active in the Friends of the Library group."

For the first time, Nina saw the gold ring around his finger. He was married. Good for him. Bad for the women of the world.

"Tell me your impressions of the marriage."

He shrugged. "We were all on good behavior when we got together."

"Did he talk about their relationship?"

"Sometimes. Bill was old-fashioned. Devoted. Protective. Of course, he was older than Beth. The role fit."

"What about signs of friction between them? Ever witness any?"

Only a slight quiver of his heavy lashes betrayed him. "No."

"Dr. Brett, your partner was murdered."

"Don't tell me you're trying to blame Beth?"

"I'm merely asking you if..."

"Look. In my business, as in yours, discretion is a religion. I don't like talking about other people."

"I understand. And you must understand that we are just trying to find out exactly what happened..."

"No, you're trying to figure out a way to save your client. And that's fine. But if I were you, I wouldn't be wasting my time looking at Beth. She was in LA, wasn't she?"

"It's not just Beth," Nina said. "It's Dr. Sykes. I need to understand him. I need to understand his relationships."

Looking disturbed, Brett stood up and put his hands in his pockets. He was wearing a white lightweight coat over an open-at-the-collar cotton dress shirt and soft olive-colored chinos. "Some years ago, they had a falling out of some kind. I don't know any details, I just know he was very upset. There was a phone call..."

"What kind of phone call?"

"He was talking with Beth. He told her he had decided not to leave her. He would forgive her anything, do anything to keep them together. Actually, it was sweet," he said firmly. "And since then, things have settled down to normal. That's all I know."

"Do you think she was having an affair?"

"No idea. I just know there was a lot of emotion tossing around for a while. I was glad when they got through that phase. It was a long time ago. Couldn't have anything to do with Bill's death."

Nina thought she was beginning to understand Brett better. Messy emotions got those long, lean muscles of his up and running. His comfort zone, she imagined, was basically sterile and predictable, and he liked his toys laid out on a tray, sharp and in order. "You had an equal business partnership?" Nina asked.

Looking relieved, Brett launched into an explanation of their business agreements which revealed a sophisticated grasp of legal matters and boiled down to an equal partnership. He would have to buy Beth out now, and the details of how that would come about were already spelled out in written agreements.

Brett had no obvious motive for wanting his partner out of the way. Apparently, these agreements had been in place for many years, and Sykes had been considering retirement. That sounded more like a good reason for Brett to hold tight and watch the clinic become his in the natural course of events.

"Tell me a little about your practice."

Now, relaxed, he flashed a smile, and she held on to the table edge to keep from melting into a puddle. "Between us, we performed about fifteen minor procedures and twenty more major procedures in a week."

"Impressive," Nina said, really impressed and not just working to keep him feeling loose. "Thirty-five patients a week?"

"Roughly," he said, holding on to his smile. "Some take only a few minutes, you know. We don't run people in and out like cattle. We want enough time to make the experience here extraordinary. We want to be available to hold our patients' hands when they need it."

She bet they enjoyed the extraordinary experience of holding Dr. Brett's large hand. "Did the two of you specialize in one type... I mean, did you do mainly faces, for example?"

She resisted the urge to run her hand over her cheek at the thought.

"No, we do everything, although Bill took on the more traditional work when he had a choice. He didn't go in for some of the newer techniques. Face and neck rejuvenation, body reshaping through liposuction, endoscopic brow lifts, breast enhancements, reductions, and reconstructions, laser skin resurfacing and chemical peels, tummy tucks, thigh lifts, batwing removal..."

"Batwing removal?"

"Sorry. Some of our patients refer to it that way. That's slang for removing excess skin from the upper arm. Rhinoplasty..."

"Do you cater mostly to wealthy people?"

"Not at all," he said emphatically. "We have clients who save for years for these procedures, or, as I said, take out loans. There's no reason everyone can't look wonderful nowadays."

Hoping he was not looking at her so intently with an eye toward improvement, she forged on. "Excuse me, but...have you...?"

"Lantern jaw," he said, touching his cleft chin. "Two miles longer than Jay Leno's. Ears that stuck out. I had those reoriented. Hooded lids... Bill did the work. The operations were difficult and he did a good job. The pain and long healing process put him high on my shit list, especially after he broke my jaw. After I finally recovered, I realized that Bill had changed my entire life. Having those experiences made me a better surgeon. I'll never be as good as Bill was with his patients, but I think I do have empathy, and my patients respond to that."

So he had not always been Bondian. Inside he was normal. "Are all your patients pleased with their results?"

"There's a lot of subjectivity in this business. Naturally, opinions vary about outcomes," he said smoothly.

"Were there any unhappy clients in particular who stand out in your mind?"

"You're suggesting one of our patients killed him?" The idea seemed to make him both outraged and nervous.

"It does happen, doesn't it, and not that infrequently in your business. I've been looking into it. Last year a plastic surgeon in Seattle was killed by a patient..."

"In that particular case, your information is incorrect," he said. "He was killed by a person who consulted him and who he deemed unsuitable for surgery, who reportedly killed him because he refused to operate."

"And I'm sure the clinic has had a few of those. Come on, Dr. Brett. Not everyone walks away happy. And I'm sure you are as concerned as I am about the slashing of Dr. Sykes's face. Pretty obvious symbolism, it seems to me."

"Yes, I did think about that. There is one man I thought about," he said grudgingly. "He got through his psychological evaluations with flying colors. It was only much later we realized he was body dysmorphic."

"Body...what?"

"It's a word used to describe people who have major delusions about the way they look. Nothing you do will satisfy them."

"Can you tell me this patient's name?"

"Stan Foster. It's in the public record. He had six major surgical procedures and several minor ones, only no matter how well things went, he was chronically displeased. Once we identified his real problem, Bill told him he couldn't in good conscience do any more surgery. The man went berserk. We had to inform the police about him after he made threats. He sued us for medical malpractice. Eventually, after we paid a lot of lawyers a lot of money, the suit was dismissed. I assume the records would be in the county clerk's office. But don't bother to write his name down there," he said, pointing to her notepad.

"Why not?" She stopped writing.

"He was killed in a car crash in March."

"Hmm." That made him an unlikely suspect for a murder that happened in May. "Any others?" she asked.

"Of course, there were occasional difficulties with patients, but we did our best to alleviate any bad situations. When a patient isn't satisfied, we generally do whatever it takes to make them happy. It isn't good for business to have a dissatisfied clientele."

"Any other surgeries that stand out in light of Dr. Sykes's murder?"

"One other that I—I regret. A young woman named Robin Littlebear who died of a previously undiagnosed lung ailment. She never recovered from the general anesthesia. Bill handled the surgery. He was very broken up about it. She was the only patient he ever lost. The family sued everybody, of course. Bill was cleared, but I believe he settled a small amount on the family anyway. All of that should be on file, too."

"Oh, yes," Nina said. "I've heard about that," thanks to Sandy, who was setting up a time for her to talk to Robin Littlebear's mother, Linda.

"What about Dr. Sykes? The autopsy report showed he had undergone extensive surgery through the years. Who performed that?"

The smile left him. His surgery was one thing. Other people's surgery he had a hardcore habit of keeping under lock and key. So intrusive, his eyes said. Not a lady at all. "I did the most recent work."

"Would you say he was abnormally concerned about his looks?" Nina asked.

"Certainly not," he said, narrowing his devastating gray eyes. "You have to see this from his point of view. Patients come in here wanting to look great. He had to look good, or he would lose patients. End of story."

She took a guess. "Was he more concerned about his looks lately, would you say? Worrying about aging?"

"I couldn't say," he snapped, clearly annoyed with her line of questioning. "What could his own surgery possibly have to do with him being murdered? You act like it was Bill that went crazy and killed somebody or something."

"It's very hard to know this early in the investigation what is important," Nina said. She ventured a second guess. "He had something done recently, didn't he?"

"A face lift. His second," Brett offered crisply. He looked at his gold Piaget watch. "I'm sorry. I have patients to see."

"Is it possible that Dr. Sykes had a compelling need to stay young looking that went beyond his professional requirements? Maybe he did it out of desperation, to keep his young wife?"

"I would never speculate about that." He crossed his arms. "Anything else?"

"Well, yes. You could tell me where you were on the night Dr. Sykes was murdered."

"Why, at home, making love to my lovely wife," he said. He strode to the door and held it open for her. She got up and walked through it. "A pleasure meeting you," he said coldly, leading her out to the reception area.

She would have Paul check his alibi, but she certainly could believe he was at home and his wife was fantastically beautiful and was making mad love to him that night, as he had said. What else would a man who looked like that do on a Saturday night?

Ginger Hirabayashi said, "God, I love this place." She stood at Nina's office window, the one that looked out over the lake. "You are so lucky to be here." She came back and leaned over the desk. "Finished reading?"

"You'll have to explain it all to me anyway," Nina said. "I know I need to become an expert on DNA testing, but the language just doesn't track for me." Ginger had come up to talk about the blood evidence in Nikki's case. A forensic physician with a nationwide reputation and an alternative lifestyle, she was linked in with experts in just about every scientific field.

"You only have to know enough to ask the right questions," Ginger said, running her hand over the soft short bristles of her black hair. She had tossed her black leather jacket on the other chair and was wearing a men's white T-shirt tucked into her jeans. "They have two areas for blood investigation in this case, the samples taken by the police from the crime scene and weapon and Nikki's blood on the outside wall of the house six inches from the French doors that led into Sykes's study."

"So there's no doubt it's Nikki's blood on the wall outside?"

"None. A ninety-nine point ninety-nine plus probability of a match there. Hey, Sandy! Bring me some coffee!"

"Get it yourself," said the voice from the outer office.

Getting coffee out of Sandy required a certain tone of voice Ginger didn't own. Nina said, "I'll get you some." She brought back the cup to Ginger, closing the door to her office behind her.

"She's thrown you off the mat," Ginger said. "She reminds me of this sumo wrestler from Samoa I used to go see in Yokohama."

"I wouldn't say that to her face," Nina said. "So. It's Nikki's blood on the wall. And the blood on the sword—"

"We have only the preliminary report, remember," Ginger warned.

"...is Dr. Sykes's blood?"

"Yes. As we can see from the crime scene photos, it's all over the floor, too. He bled to death, rather quickly due to the deep gash in his neck, which nicked the carotid."

"What about the slashes on his face? His nose...is there some way to match the blade to those cuts?" Nina said.

"They all match," Ginger said. "It's obvious that the sword was used to mutilate his face from the general circumstances and also from the autopsy photos. Whether before or after the coup de grace may be hard to establish but it sure makes sense that it happened after he was totally disabled."

"You have a funny look on your face. What's up?"

"Oh, it intrigues me that the murder weapon was a samurai sword. I know something about them."

"I wonder why he fixated on collecting swords, and why he kept this sword in particular," Nina said.

Ginger looked at the photograph. "It's an old and well-kept specimen, and weapon collecting is a huge hobby worldwide. I collect something similar myself. Flutes."

"Doesn't sound similar to me."

"But it is. Samurai had a long tradition of

converting common objects into weapons. The *katana*—the sword—wasn't always convenient to use, so they had other weapons which could be easily concealed but could be quite lethal."

Sandy pushed the door open. Seeing that they were still talking, she leaned against the doorjamb, folded her arms, and listened.

"For example, the *tessen*, an iron fan. Looked like a fan, but the ribs were iron. And the bamboo flute was the perfect marriage of art and function. According to the story, it was redesigned to be made from the bamboo root, making it longer and stouter like a club so that it worked as a deadly weapon, too."

"You have one of those?" Sandy asked.

"Several."

"You scare me, Ginger."

"And you scare me, Sandy."

"What about the blood on the sword?" Nina said.

"I'm getting to the sword," Ginger said. "There's nothing in the report you received about a trace sample that didn't match with the victim. But... I have a good friend in that lab in Sacramento that did the initial workup. And for you, Nina, I got a copy of a report your prosecutor's been holding back. Guess he's waiting to spring it on you at the prelim. How do you like that?"

"I love it." She poised a pen over her yellow pad. "What's in this purloined report?"

"There was one blood sample they got from the sword so itty-bitty they managed only one test on it. Here's the dope on that. This speck definitely does not match the victim's blood. But...and you're not going to like this...they found a similarity to Nicole Zack's blood."

"It was Nicole's blood?"

"I didn't say that."

"But usually it's a definite match or it isn't."

"Problem was, because there was such a preponderance of victim blood on the sword," Ginger said, "they only had one sample that differed, but the difference appears legitimate. The test shows an unusual third allele on the autoradiograph that matches a sequence also found in Nicole's blood. In my opinion, that's not conclusive, but it may be enough for the prosecution experts. They may not agree with me."

"Oh. I don't love that."

"Sorry."

"So you're not able to conclude that it's Nikki's blood?"

"Well, it's this allele problem."

"Ginger, talk to me like you do to a kindergartner, okay? What tests did they do?"

"Okay, a nutshell run-through of PCR, which is short for polymerase chain reaction. When we have a blood sample or biological material like hair from a crime scene, the first thing the lab does is isolate the nuclei from that material. Then they isolate and amplify the DNA found in the nuclei—that's the PCR part. They take the amplified fragments and separate them using gel electrophoresis. The DNA is transferred on to a nylon membrane, hybridized to labeled probes, washed and used to expose X-ray films, so they can see where the labeled probes ended up. What you get out of this process is an autoradiograph of patterns, kind of like a photograph with supermarket bar codes on it. That's the DNA pattern, and if you can match it up with a suspect, you are one joyful homicide detective."

"So the autoradiograph showed that the sample of blood they took from the sword might not have been Nikki's blood?"

"Not exactly..."

"Tell me about the allele they found in this one sample," said Nina, frustrated. "I never heard of an allele, but I have a bad feeling I'm going to have to become an expert."

"Each person inherits two alternative forms of a gene, one from each parent," Ginger said patiently. "Those alternative forms are called alleles.

"There are usually two alleles for simple traits, such as eye color, blood type, etcetera. In this case, there was an unusual third allele found on the sample they discovered that did not match Dr. Sykes's patterns. It did match Nikki's. The pattern is somewhat rare but doesn't specifically pinpoint her as the other person who bled on that sword. It's a suggestive but not damning finding."

"Hmph. Experts," Sandy said.

"It could well be her blood," Ginger continued. "It's likely to be her blood, since there is this uncommon similarity. But if I was a police forensic technician I wouldn't be able to testify with a reasonable degree of scientific certainty that it was her blood."

"Great!" Nina said. "They still haven't placed her inside the house, then."

"Let's make sure we get Daria's blood tested. Or maybe it will turn out to be the blood of someone the samurai killed four hundred years ago," Ginger said, eyebrow arched. "That's about how old that sword is. You know, they say the samurai sword carries the soul of the samurai in it. And sometimes the souls of those the sword killed."

"It must be crowded in there," Sandy said. They all looked at the picture of the old sword again. Handsome, with a gilt handle and hilt, it lay curved on the floor next to Dr. William Sykes's bleeding body, glinting and wicked-looking.

Still too many damn cars, Paul thought at ten o'clock as he set out on the freeway to do the alibi check. By God, he planned to charge Nina every dime she owed him for this wasted time. This environment was working on him, and he didn't like the feeling. Nina would never move to Carmel to be with him, never give up a goddamn thing for him, but she was still lodged like flak in his ass, a constant aggravation. A mile before his exit onto Santa Monica Boulevard, he found himself jockeying for position with a Caprice driven by a young man wearing a Dodgers cap and the florid, warped look of a driver who is permanently enraged.

The car attempted to zip in front of Paul twice, got blocked, dashed into the lane alongside attempting to pass, gave up and tried one last time, scraping Paul's fender very slightly. The scratch finally did it, forcing Paul to drop back. Once settled into the coveted position in front, the death driver slowed to a crawl, his middle finger prominently positioned in the rearview mirror as a victory sign, his mouth open in a laugh.

There was only so much a man could take.

Paul knew about control, knew how to impose it.

He hoped he scared this bastard Caprice.

Pulling out from behind and up beside the car, he swerved close. Good thing he had accepted the rental car insurance for a change. Something must have told him it might come in handy. The Caprice never flinched.

So, stronger measures.

He gave it a tap on the mirror. The mirror shattered. So did the one on his rental.

He watched his fellow driver's face contort, but not for long, because he was accelerating, speeding up, feeling gloriously in control of his vehicle and of the situation. With a jerk, he swung left and regained dominance.

The Caprice limped along behind.

He looked in the rearview mirror. The Caprice was dropping back. Another car took its place.

He was grinning like a baboon. He felt like

a baboon. The more intelligent, human part of him was asking, what was that all about? Because just for a second there, he hadn't cared if he hit the other car, hadn't cared if he killed himself asserting his rightful place in the line. I thought you were going to pay more attention, he told himself, and stopped grinning.

He decided to forget it and turned his thoughts to the upcoming interview. Nina just wanted to be sure that Beth Sykes wasn't part of her case. Beth had been in LA visiting a friend the night her husband and son died, fine—but Nina had instructed him to double-check at an early stage. Anyone could concoct an alibi.

She was getting more suspicious and more aggressive from case to case. When she had moved to Tahoe, she had been an appellate lawyer who had a way with words and a problem with inexperience. The hard knocks she had taken since would have sent some lawyers scurrying for a way back into appeals work, but Nina was a fighter. Now she was smart and tough, not just smart. With some wonder, Paul thought, she really is dedicated. She's in it for the long haul.

He hadn't thought she would last.

Jan Sapitto lived close to Beverly Hills in West Hollywood. Her high-rise condo would command quite a view on a day that had a view. Unfortunately, the fog had sneaked in with Paul, and her tall windows looked out upon featureless murk.

Before going up to the seventeenth floor, Paul cornered the doorman. Slipping a bill into the man's willing hand, he asked about the weekend of Bill Sykes's death. Had she had a female visitor that weekend?

The doorman remembered Beth Sykes's arrival. She had gone up with Jan late Thursday night. He didn't remember her leaving, but said high traffic in and out on weekends made it impossible to keep track of every tenant and visitor.

So far, Beth's alibi held up the way most alibis did—shakily.

A medium-size woman with bow-shaped lips painted a flamboyant fuchsia, Jan Sapitto wore a tight knit shirt with tight jeans and a snug apron with a logo in the shape of a rose that said, "Faux Foods." Long, frizzled golden hair blew down her back, except where she had tucked a silver clip in the shape of a butterfly.

Paul showed her his identification and she let him in. Sandy had called and prepared the way.

She sat him down on a stool in front of a long granite kitchen island.

"I'll be with you in a second," she said. "Sorry. I'm right in the middle of this."

"Smells good," he said, as she rushed to the stove and lifted a lid to release a steaming aroma.

"Cream of asparagus soup. Artichoke frittata. Mashed potatoes for the ice cream."

"Pardon?"

She pointed to the table through double doors, where a glistening golden turkey, carrots, pies, and other side dishes were laid out invitingly on a lace cloth beside silver candelabra on an oversized dining-room table. For the centerpiece, a cornucopia decorated with autumn leaves spilled out bright, perfect oranges, apples, bananas, and Concord grapes.

"Very nice," Paul said. "But it's only May."

"I'm a food designer, and sometimes we do setups months in advance. I have a studio, but the natural light's really nice in this room for this dining-table setup, especially since it's overcast."

He went back to it. "Ice cream?"

"Oh, mashed potatoes don't melt. It's not all done with mirrors these days."

She picked up a bottle, walked over to the table, and began to spray the carrots and the turkey. "Thanksgiving, here we come," she said. "Yum, yum, yum."

"Smells terrible."

"Looks glossier than butter." She cast a critical eye on her handiwork. "Perfect."

"Who do you work for?"

"Magazines. Local ad agencies. Anyone flashing a wad of bills. I'm a freelancer." She tasted the soup and cooed with satisfaction. "This, I plan to eat. Otherwise no need to cook it."

"Do you know a lot about photography?"

"Nope. I have a photographer on his way over in about twenty minutes. I move the food around. Make different displays, individual settings featuring different dishes. Add candles, fruit, bits of fern. Dry ice for that steamy effect. That kind of thing. I leave the f-stops to him."

"What's this particular job?"

"These guys I know are trying to get a film produced. They're putting together a series of stills in storyboard form to go along with the script to take to producers. Like a sales piece. The film's called, 'Declaration of Dependence,' and it's about this woman who has an affair with two men at the same time."

"French, huh?"

She laughed. "In fact it's written and directed by two computer geeks from Palo Alto. Anyway, one of her lovers lives in the past, somewhere around the late eighteen hundreds. I love that era, the clothes, the food, everything. I would fit right in."

Paul could picture a flouncy little bustle adding a voluptuous generosity to her narrow hips. Like so many women these days, Jan fell on the scrawny side of his taste. Well, maybe that was to be expected from someone who confused ice cream with potatoes. "Where does this food fit into the story?"

"A crucial scene takes place around a big American holiday feast. The two men duke it out over the ice cream."

"Then I have to question the frittata."

"Background in soft focus. Ambience. Also my dinner."

"A lot to do for just a storyboard, isn't it?"

"They promised to use it as the proposal cover

art with a credit printed right there on the front. And as with everything a freelancer does, you've got to believe it's going to land you big money later or you would never kill yourself for the nickel you're getting this time."

"You don't work nine to five, I guess."

"Wish I did. I could use a steady income. I spend lots of time diddling with my portfolio and going on interviews, although maybe it's time to close up that part of my life and move on. You wouldn't believe the pressure on a woman in this town. I mean, I'm almost too old for Hollywood."

She didn't look more than thirty. Since when did that become old? "What's your age got to do with how good your food looks?"

"First part of every job is getting hired."

"You're attractive. I think you know that," said Paul.

She flushed prettily. "You're going to think I was aiming for that compliment, but I wasn't. Anyway, if I do look good, credit my surgeon."

"You wouldn't be talking about Dr. William Sykes?"

"Sure. He sculpted my nose, plumped up my weak chin, and threw in a mini-lift when I turned thirty. God, it bugged him to see a woman get those character wrinkles."

At thirty?! However, Paul had to admire the guy's ability. You would never know, just by looking, how much was her real face and how much was fake. "I understand you and Beth Sykes are old friends. How did you two meet?"

"We're fellow desert rats. Grew up in Yucca Valley back when Beth and Daria were the Logan girls. You know the area?"

"No."

"East of San Berdoo, near Joshua Tree, where hot always means hot as hell. The Logan house didn't even have air-conditioning. Maybe that's why we became friends. At least we had it in one of the bedrooms. Beth and I ran around together as kids. People sometimes took us for sisters, said we looked alike, which I never could see. We went with our families up to Big Bear Lake, drove too fast and raised hell when we were teenagers, then ran away looking for greener pastures. We're both older than Daria by four years, and we stayed close. Beth grew up fast. You could say Daria never grew up."

"You see Daria?"

"Sometimes, when I visit Tahoe. Beth stays with me whenever she comes down to LA." Her tight cheeks pulled together as she pursed her lips. "Naturally, I'm flattered she chooses me over a hotel. She could afford to stay anywhere."

"Is she down here often?"

"Now and then."

"What do you do when she's visiting?"

"Everything. We hit the museums, the beach, first-run movies, plays at the Ahmanson. Tahoe's a small place, and she and Bill have lived up there for a long time. She gets stir-crazy. Of course, Chris was a big lure, too. He went to high school down here, and then to

Pomona College. He was only a freshman. God, it's terrible about Chris. I watched him grow up. He could make you laugh at anything."

"Was Chris why she came that weekend he died?"

"No. In fact, I kidded her about it. It seemed like she never came anymore unless she could see Chris, but this time she promised we'd just spend some time together doing girl things. She got here late on Thursday. We shopped all day Friday and hit the beach on Saturday. I don't think she talked to Chris while she was here. I don't think she even knew he was getting on a plane to visit his dad in Tahoe."

"Do you know if Chris ever chartered a plane before on his own?"

"I don't know, but it wouldn't surprise me if he had. He was a gutsy kid."

"So were you with Beth Sykes on the night of May eighth?"

"We went to the Hollywood Bowl to see Shania Twain. Kicked up our heels with the other cowgirls."

"You two went alone?"

"That's right."

"No men."

"Don't look so suspicious, Paul. Women do get out on their own in this century. Beth, she's—she was—married."

"How was their marriage?"

"How's any marriage? Theirs lasted a long time, longer than I ever expected."

"What do you mean by that?"

"Bill was quite a catch. Fun, ambitious,

smart. Had a lucrative practice, even then. I'm sure a lot of women were interested in him."

Paul wondered if Jan Sapitto might be among them. "You think he was unhappy with his wife?"

"Not at all. I hope I'm not giving that impression."

"Did you like Bill Sykes?"

"I did, although sometimes I think he saw himself in competition with me for Beth's attention."

"Ah, a jealous type?"

"He doted on her."

Once again, Paul wondered about the feeling behind her words. Wasn't it possible Jan resented her friend's good luck just the smallest bit? "How late did you stay out that night?"

"Not too late. Midnight or so. Then we crashed here. Most of Sunday is missing, until the phone call came late in the day about Chris. We were sitting outside on the deck having a margarita. Beth went into shock. She couldn't reach Bill, but she was in no shape to fly that night. I gave her Valium and put her to bed. Then the next morning, I was packing clothes in her suitcase, getting ready to drive to the airport. The phone rang again. This time it was about Bill. God! It's so unfair that this should happen to Beth."

She knew who he was and why he was asking the questions, and she didn't seem to mind. In fact, he thought she had already prepared her answers before he came. Her description of spending time with Beth sounded very pat and remarkably similar to the story Beth had told Nina. On the other hand, if the women had talked about it, it wouldn't be surprising they might use similar language. "You went up with her that morning?"

"I did, until Daria could take over. She needed someone with her."

"You said Beth went into shock at hearing about Christopher?"

"She fell into a million pieces. She adored that boy. They both did. Bill thought Chris was going to save the world. Chris didn't even get to live long enough to let his parents down. Do you have any kids, Paul?"

"Never got that lucky," Paul said, but he didn't mean it. He had never wanted kids. You loved them and they left you or died on you. It never came out right.

"What made the plane crash, Paul? What do you think?"

"Bad judgment, the NTSB is saying."

He tried to read her expression. She looked like she wanted to say something and was biting her tongue.

He waited for it to come out. But she got herself under control.

Paul got up to leave. "One last question," he said.

"Anything," she said, and there was a question in her eyes, a little smile there just for him.

"The woman with the two lovers. How does she do that?"

"You mean have a relationship with two men?"

"I mean with men in two different centuries."

"Doesn't matter what year it is, the same old excuses work," she said. "Doing anything for lunch? Because as you can see, I love to experiment in the kitchen. It's the place I feel most free."

"Thought you had a guy coming over. Your photographer."

"Women are so flaky, and he has a cell phone."

He imagined experimenting in the kitchen with her, then shut the thought down. Jan Sapitto would want much more than he could give her in one afternoon. " 'Fraid I can't make it," he said, truly sorry. Walking out to his car he wondered what the hell he was doing, passing up an invitation for making whoopee on a gourmet kitchen island.

He would drive back up north this afternoon. He wanted to make a stop in Carmel to see Susan, in addition to making an unscheduled visit to the business before heading back to Tahoe. Then he would look at the forensic evidence and police reports, interview an ex-patient of Sykes's who had sued him, and check in with the NTSB to see how they were doing with their investigation of the plane crash.

He got back on the freeway still smelling Jan's soup. His stomach had settled and he was definitely hungry now. Instead of messing around in Jan's kitchen, he was engaged in this war with traffic again.

This infernal, everlasting traffic jam, he thought, giving in to his annoyance. A Cutlass Supreme dashed up the on ramp beside him, too close, the bastard! He put his hand to the horn and raced to beat him. As the car came close enough to breathe on he suddenly thought, shit, what am I doing? Risking my life, and for what?

He dropped back, and in that moment of weakness, that single moment when he didn't stubbornly insist on winning, the Cutlass smelled his frailty and pressed in for the kill. He had one last thought as he tried and failed to drop out of the competition for space on the ramp, that they were in the grip of a shared insanity, this aggressive foolhardiness, barreling along at seventy miles an hour, traveling through space without regard for place or time...when he heard a crash, felt his leg crack, and heard someone howl like a baby....

PART TWO

He is in the dream, his right hand pushing the knife into the murderer's back, watching for the murderer's terror, but the murderer is laughing. The murderer is glad to die.

He's surprised and lessens the pressure for a moment. He wants the murderer to turn around and fight. But the head turns away from him, back to face the cabin door.

The cold moves over them.

The murderer leans toward the door and then pushes back against the knife, wanting to get it over with. The wind presses against them both. The murderer laughs and laughs.

He can feel the shaking of the body, the quick spasms. He reaches around with his left hand and claps his hand over the laughing mouth. The lips of the murderer are warm and his breath is like a breath of fire.

His hand burns.

8

TUESDAY NIGHT, the night before the transfer hearing, Day Thirteen in stir, always a total nothing even when Nikki was outside, and she'd just used up all her telephone time listening to Daria carry on. Somewhere in the middle of her fake good cheer and maddeningly trivial gossip, Daria had passed on one piece of real news. Aunt Beth had come out of the blue and offered to take care of the rent arrears. They weren't going to lose their home after all. "It's just like I told you, Nikki," Daria had said in that infuriating way she had, all roses and cupcakes and Girl Scouts. "Things have a way of working out." Well, they had worked out one more time, rescuing them from the gutter for now, until the next big crisis and the next bad boyfriend came along.

On the bunk, arms tucked behind her head, trying to block out the noise, Nikki fretted. The racket, the three roommates, even the clothes that were too tight across the crotch, obviously designed for some squat toad, didn't bother her as much as not having the telephone right there so she could talk to somebody. She wanted to call Bob, tell him about the people here, the things she had heard. She wanted him to tell her that his mom would get her out tomorrow, that she would be going home. She missed the Net, and her guitar. Daria had some kind of new job starting tomorrow and would be getting home exhausted and she wouldn't be there to make sure Daria ate something hot.

A shout from somewhere nearby made the hair on her arms stand straight up. She still couldn't believe she was in Juvie. She kicked off her shoes and there was something wet like beads of sweat or tears on her face that she wiped away with her hand. Until all this shit came down, she could have passed for a normal person. From now on, she was blighted.

Well, maybe she did belong here. Everything in her life had changed a long time ago. The world was just catching up to how much she had changed along with it. Up until she was ten years old, she had fit in. She joined Brownies and learned to knit with the other girls, even though Daria bought her the wrong-sized needles and yarn that was too fine.

Then came the night her father didn't come home. She was in fifth grade, Mrs. Bennett's class, the best speller, the best out-loud reader. She loved her teacher, who had black hair that came down into a low point over her forehead, forming two mirror-image question marks on the sides of her face. She liked doing well just to see Mrs. Bennett smile.

When he didn't come home after work, Daria had kept his dinner warm in the oven until it charred. Then she called everyone they knew on the phone. Then she had sat up all night on the living-room rug shivering, without even bothering to light the fire two feet away.

Nikki had waited under her bed. She had

thought that if she hid there and wasn't so obvious about waiting, he would not be too afraid of how much they needed him to come on home.

But she went to sleep. She hadn't even been able to do that right.

Another noise zigzagged her mind back to Bob. If only she could reach him. She liked him because he didn't think like the other kids. He was like an alien, never fitting in but so cool about it, like he had something special going for him or was planning to return to his home planet and just didn't give a shit about Earth. She knew he was younger; it just didn't matter. He had confidence in himself.

He was her only friend, in fact, except for the Net and the bands she listened to at night.

Not that she'd ever let him know that pathetic fact.

The lights went out, and she pulled the covers over her. Last year, she had still been trying to fit in, going to dances and stuff like that. She yawned, thinking about Scott. What a difference between a friend and a boyfriend. Scott was a boyfriend, an ex-boyfriend actually at this point since he hadn't even bothered to call and see how she was doing. A boyfriend who pushed you around and taught you things.

If she had a phone, she was so messed up tonight she might just call Scott instead. She was so bored and so scared at the same time, and the kinds of things you did with Scott put

you right there on the roller coaster, too pan-
icked about the deathfall to worry about anything else. There was something to be said for
that.

Then she wouldn't be lying here worrying
about whether Daria had remembered to pay
the water bill after the rent or that she was gonna
be locked up forever, or about the big transfer
hearing coming up.

She wouldn't be worrying that the police
would search her house and find what she'd
buried in the woods behind the house.

"Back on the record," Judge Harold Vasquez
said.

They sat in the small Juvenile Courtroom
in Placerville again as if two hard weeks hadn't
gone by: Nikki in her Gothic black to convey
her disaffection; Nina in her black lawyer
suit to lend her dignity; Harold Vasquez in his
black judicial robes for the sake of authority;
Daria in a black leotard under her fluffy skirt
because she hadn't read the rule book on
appropriate dress for court; and Beth in a
black skirt because she was in mourning. Barbara Banning's vivid red stood out, to sym-
bolize prosecutorial confidence. Also appearing
was Barbet Schroeder of the *Tahoe Mirror,* scribbling notes in back, Pearl Smith from the
Probation Department, the clerk and reporter,
and Nikki's history teacher from the high
school Nikki had attended until Bill Sykes's
death. The teacher was still in his twenties,
nervous but game.

"All right," Vasquez said. "We are very close to the fifteen-day limit specified for this minor to remain in temporary custody, so I sincerely hope you are all ready to go."

"Ready, Your Honor."

"We are ready, Your Honor."

Vasquez read from the paperwork. "I have before me a verified petition to declare Nicole Zack a ward of the court pursuant to section 602 of the Welfare and Institutions Code. The District Attorney's Office has in its discretion instituted these proceedings pursuant to subdivision (b) of section 650 and Section 26500 of the Government Code.

"Now, Ms. Zack, I'm going to speak directly to you because you are the person with the most at stake in this hearing. This petition requests that I make a finding that you are not a fit and proper subject to be dealt with under the Juvenile Court law. Before I could do that, I must conclude that you would not be amenable to the care, treatment, and training program available through the facilities of the Juvenile Court. And to decide that, I must consider five factors: the degree of criminal sophistication exhibited by you; whether you can be rehabilitated by the age when Juvenile Court jurisdiction would expire; your previous delinquent history; the success of any previous attempts by the Juvenile Court to rehabilitate you; and, last but not least, the circumstances and gravity of the offense you are alleged to have committed.

"The petition specifies that the crime

involved is a felony and it contains a statement of the facts which have brought you into this court. I also have a report from the Probation Department regarding your behavioral patterns and social history. Attached to that is a Victim Impact Statement submitted by Beth Sykes, who was the wife of the decedent. Ms. Reilly, have you and your client and your client's mother received and reviewed those reports?"

"We have."

"Any luck locating the father?" Vasquez asked Barbara.

"Not at this point," Barbara said. "He's not in the system and he doesn't have a driver's license in this state."

"Too bad. Now, Ms. Zack, what I'm going to do today is look at some factors which will help me decide whether or not I should follow the recommendation of the district attorney. I am going to pay particular attention to this report by the probation officer assigned to your case, which I have already read. Ms. Reilly, do you have any other witnesses you would like to have heard on this issue?"

Nina said, "Ms. Zack's history teacher didn't have an opportunity to speak to the probation office investigator. He's here today. Also, my client's mother would like an opportunity to speak."

"Fine. Let's start with the report."

Probation officer Pearl Smith stood up and summarized the report for the record while Nikki twitched in her chair. Pearl had tried to find some socially acceptable threads in

Nikki's life, but hadn't been very successful. She started with Nikki's eleventh-grade report card, in which Nikki had scraped by with a C-minus average, a number of detentions, enough cut classes to result in a suspension earlier in the year, and a general consensus among the teachers that Nikki could not care less about her studies.

"Anything to add?" Vasquez asked Nina when this sorry record had been summarized.

"This would be a good time for me to call Mr. Edwards in," Nina said. Nikki's history teacher came forward and sat down, clearing his throat excessively before speaking, even more nervous than before.

"I've only had Nikki this past semester," he said. "But we have talked often before and after class. I can't understand her general lack of interest or progress in school, because I know she's bright. She's a reader, with a passionate interest in history. She's read everything I've suggested to her besides doing very well on her tests. She has tremendous potential, and certainly with some help she can be rehabilitated, even if she has committed a crime. It would be a tragedy for her to be put into the adult system. If she could be allowed to be on probation or something, I would be glad to act as her independent studies coordinator. I like Nikki and I want to help any way I can."

"Thank you," the judge said. He was nodding, but Nina knew what would come next. "Ms. Banning, any questions?"

"It's nice of you to come to Nikki's aid, Mr.

Edwards," Barbara said. "The two of you share a similar political philosophy, am I correct?"

"We-ell, you might say that."

"You encouraged her to write a paper on Che Guevara advocating the violent overthrow of our system of government and you gave her an A on that paper, did you not?"

"It was a good paper," Mr. Edwards answered, fidgeting.

"Ms. Zack is—what? An anarchist? A nihilist? A Communist?"

"A student."

"How lucky for her that she fell under your guidance. Has she ever expressed an interest in assassination of public figures?"

"No, no..."

Barbara pulled out the essay Henry had been waving at Nina in his office. "Read to us from the second page of this essay by Ms. Zack, which I'm about to submit to the court. The portion I've marked."

He took the essay and read. " 'Sometimes the only way to stop the oppression is through summary execution of political oppressors who cannot be dealt with in any other way.' Let me explain..."

"Let me see that," Vasquez said.

By now, Nina had read the essay several times. She saw in it all the grandiose arrogance that masked immaturity but found nothing evil about a young girl's bumpy political awakening. She felt incensed enough by Barbara's insinuations about Nikki's work to interrupt.

"She's old enough to stick in State Prison but not old enough to be granted ordinary First Amendment rights. Is that the way it should be? Why shouldn't she have opinions? We're talking about her intelligence, her potential..."

"Exactly. Her potential to commit more murders," Barbara said.

"That's enough," Judge Vasquez said. "Let me read." He read the whole thing. When he looked up, he had a grave expression on his face. He thanked Mr. Edwards, who gave Nikki an encouraging nod as he left.

"Well, let's turn back to the report," the judge said. Pearl noted that Nikki had joined no school clubs, had no extracurricular activities, was not a member of a church, had no record of volunteer work, had few friends, and was not employed. As she discussed Nikki's contacts with law enforcement and her association with Scott Cabano, Nikki slid down farther and farther in her chair.

"I'd like to call Daria Zack," Nina said when this recitation was complete.

Daria tried to speak calmly. "Your Honor, what you're reading and what Nikki really is like are so different that—it's just that Nikki doesn't fit into a conventional mold. She doesn't join clubs or run for school president or work on the school newspaper. She'll never make homecoming queen. But does that mean you should send her into the adult court?

"As a matter of fact, Nikki has many interests and activities. She loves to go mountain biking in the forest. She's a wonderful guitar player and has a beautiful voice. And she is learning everything there is to know about computers. She writes poetry and she loves to read. She thinks about the suffering of so many people in this world and it makes her angry, Your Honor, but she'd never harm a fly. She didn't kill her uncle. Even Beth, my sister, who wrote that letter to you—you'll see that she doesn't believe Nikki had anything to do with it. Nikki has learned to cook and balance a checkbook and help me in so many ways"—Daria started to break down but pulled herself together—"and if you'll let her come home and remember that she's very young and just needs a little help, then I—I will try to take better care of her. Please, Your Honor." She wiped her eyes.

Vasquez listened seriously.

Barbara took over, making everything Daria said sound sinister, twisting Nikki again into a loner terrorist caught just in time. But Daria didn't cry anymore. She sat with her back straight and answered the scathing questions as well as she could. Vasquez himself winced a few times. Maybe he didn't care for Barbara's combative style either.

"Thank you, Mrs. Zack," the judge said, excusing Daria. "Anything else, Ms. Reilly?"

"This is a very young girl who has never been accused of a serious crime," Nina said. "The United States Supreme Court has pointed out in *Kent v. United States* that this short and informal hearing is at the same time a critically important action determining vitally important statutory rights of this child. I know the court will read between the lines of that report and see that there is every opportunity for rehabilitation for this child within the juvenile system, assuming she is found to have committed the felony, which is very much in dispute. Yes, she's a loner, a reader, a thinker. That only makes her more amenable to the help this court can give."

Vasquez nodded. "Ms. Banning?"

"She's a loner, all right, and she's been getting into deeper and deeper trouble each time. She's charged with a *vicious*—let's not forget that—a *vicious* crime. Of course Beth Sykes spoke up for her—she's Beth Sykes's niece. And who else came to speak today? One single teacher who sounds like he ought to be teaching in Cuba, and her mother! As for her being intelligent, the Unabomber is intelligent too. I fail to see how that makes her more amenable to rehabilitation. The district attorney's office doesn't decide to request that this court waive its jurisdiction lightly. Our recommendation is based on long experience which the court should weigh heavily. Thank you."

Silence. Nikki sat so still she appeared to have stopped breathing.

Vasquez set down the papers, straightened his robe, and blinked a couple of times. Finally he said, "I appreciate the hard work of all parties concerned today. This is a very difficult decision for me. I want to be very careful not to send a child into the adult criminal courts without good reason. In this case, after fully considering the report and attachments and the testimony today, I am going to grant the petition of the district attorney's office."

He went on, listing his reasons and conclusions, but Nina didn't hear him any more. Nikki knew exactly what was happening. She looked back wildly at Daria. Barbara allowed a tiny smile to play on her lips. Nikki belonged to her and Henry now.

They had lost this round.

But at the last moment Vasquez tossed the defense a bone. Over Barbara's vociferous objections, Nikki was placed on home supervision with electronic surveillance. She would be wearing a monitor on her ankle and was not allowed to leave the vicinity of her home without express permission.

So happy was Nikki that she would be imminently released from Juvie, she didn't seem to care about the rest. "I've got me a ball and chain," she said cheerfully, as her mom and Nina finally left the premises with her after she had been processed.

Nina said, "I'm depending on you to follow the rules, Nikki."

"You won't be going back to school right now," Daria said. Her mood was much more somber. "The judge said you can't leave the house."

"A long vacation. All right!"

"I'll have to get you a tutor."

"Daria, get a clue. We have no money. How you going to hire a tutor?"

"There's only one more month of school before summer. Maybe we can work with your teachers. Get you into independent studies with Mr. Edwards."

Nikki almost skipped out to the car. "Come on, Daria, let's see if the place fell down yet."

Nina got into the Bronco, took her shoes off, leaned the seat back and closed her eyes.

She had lost an important early skirmish. Now Nikki would be arraigned and a preliminary hearing date would be set. Today was May 25. The prelim would be set for mid-June...

A car door near her slammed and she jerked awake and jammed the Bronco into gear and pulled back out into the hectic world.

9

IN THE END, Paul had allowed the hospital to call his sister in San Francisco. When he had regained consciousness, they had bedeviled him for answers to a series of arcane and irrelevant questions, including next of kin, and whom to notify in case of this or that. In his drug-weakened state, he had freely divulged a number of closely guarded secrets.

He recalled a moment when they were inserting a pin in his right knee...the screaming, wrenching pain of the moment. However, raise hallelujahs for the miracles of modern medicine. He hurt but he didn't give a damn!

His sister came and moved briskly about the room, by her mere presence reminding him of things best forgotten. She, too, had questions for him, but by this time he had regained enough of his sensibility to refuse to incriminate himself. The less said about that, the better. The moment he came to his senses, he sent her back to the city. The folks needed her. He could get along.

He left a message on Nina's answering machine late at night that he wouldn't be able to report in for a few days and would have to miss the transfer hearing. He did not call Dean. He called Susan and broke his date with her, not mentioning the leg.

Truth to tell, he was ashamed about the leg. He didn't want to talk about it.

He spent five days in the hospital, the first

in surgery, the next four in extremis. They had him up and hobbling on crutches, in excruciating "discomfort," as they called it, within a day.

"We don't want any blood clots in your legs."

An alarming thought, which got him out of bed. Leaning on the railing along the hallway, passing frailer patients when he had the energy, he began getting used to his new physical state.

"You got off easy," the doctor had reported with cool interest. "A slight concussion, a simple leg fracture, a tear in the anterior cruciate ligament of the knee"—the bad knee, the one he had babied ever since he'd torn another ligament there playing high school football. He would need crutches for a while. The exact number of weeks or months involved was apparently one of the hospital's closely guarded secrets.

"Oh, I'll take a rain check on that one," the doctor had said, chuckling. "Don't try to pin me down."

As they had pinned him, oh so neatly.

On the fourth day he made more calls. He tried calling LeBlanc at work and at home and when he got no answer, spoke with LeBlanc's building manager. He told Dean he'd have to hold the fort a little longer, because he'd had a little accident. Deano seemed awfully busy for a guy running a half-dead business. Well, he'd get around to Deano later.

The man who had hit him came to visit

him, bearing a huge vase of flowers. "I'm going to make sure my insurance company doesn't give you any trouble. I'm afraid I went a little wild out there. I feel kind of guilty about all this..." In normal life, removed from the roads of horror, he was a meek supermarket cashier.

"Don't," Paul said. "I was asking for it."

He'd been cruisin' for a bruisin', as though a stranger inside him wanted to take him down. He had the dream again, and woke drenched in sweat.

And he thought, am I trying to kill myself? Is that what it's about?

On the fifth day, Dave LeBlanc's apartment manager called the hospital.

"You owe me a fifty for this," he said.

"I'll judge that when I hear what you have to say." He was lying in the hospital bed, nicely doped up, thinking about lunch. The case seemed far away.

"You better pay me."

"Speak. Or I hang up and you get nothing."

"LeBlanc's still missing. He hasn't been at his place for four days. I went in with my key to make sure he wasn't belly-up in there. No sign of him. Clothes in the closet, beer in the fridge. But gone."

"His wallet?"

"No sign of it."

"Okay. I'll be stopping by." Paul hung up. His experienced guess was that LeBlanc was back in jail. He rang the bell, and when the nurse came in, asked for a phone book.

When Nina told Bob that Nicole was back at home, he wanted to drop everything and run to see her.

"Tonight we have dinner at Matt's."

"We go there all the time. They won't miss us. This is more important."

"Nicole needs some time with her mother. They have a lot to talk about."

"She doesn't talk to her mother! She talks to her friends. She needs me, Mom."

"Not tonight."

"Why not?"

"She said she needed some time alone." Sometimes, only a lie shut the battle down. Nina found dealing with Bob more wearing than dealing with adults. She argued all day and now, all night. Bob burst with energy and intensity and a persistence few adults could equal. He was testing his intellect and the strength of his will against hers like a lion cub tussling with its parent. Home was no longer a refuge.

But once they arrived at Matt and Andrea's, Bob disappeared into Troy's bedroom with Hitchcock and his cousins and she sank down in front of the fire in blessed peace. Later, as the platters of lemony salmon and then blackberry pie circled the table and the air filled with chatter, she felt the iron band that held her together on many days loosen.

After dinner, Bob organized the cleanup. From the dining room, sipping coffee with Matt and Andrea, she watched him order his two younger cousins around. He was firm but fair in doling out the chores. Tomorrow, when he was a man, he would reenact this scenario, only from the perspective of the dining-room table watching his own child....

"You look beat," Andrea said. Her red hair was pulled back in a frizzy ponytail, and a booted foot was propped where the salmon had rested at dinner.

"Just give me one more cup," Nina said, pouring herself another. "I'll show you zip. I'll show you can-do."

Matt pushed blond hair off his forehead. It fell back down. He got up, opened a cupboard, and pulled out a bottle. "Irish whiskey," he said. "Dad's favorite, remember?"

She remembered Harlan drinking it on the night he got the news their mother had died. A drink for mourning and celebration. Irish whiskey covered all bases. "Of course." She held out her cup for a dribble.

He poured liberally into her cup, gave her a spoonful of sugar, then went to the fridge and came back with a small bowl of whipped cream.

"No, Matt, spare me. Alcohol, yes, sugar yes, but whipped cream—I'll go to hell for sure."

"Relax." He laid a big dollop on top of her drink.

"I have to drive home..." she said, taking a long drink, which fell over her like a warm blanket on a cold night.

"You can sleep here," Matt said.

Nina yawned, wishing she could sleep anywhere. "Say, Andrea, maybe you can help me with this problem I'm having."

"Sure."

"Well, I have a situation, a young girl I know..."

"Her new client, Nicole Zack," Matt interrupted. "Accused of killing her uncle, the plastic surgeon. Strange the way her cousin died in a plane crash that same night..."

"How in the world..."

"I get around. The newspapers don't give her name, but the hints make it pretty obvious. And there are no secrets in South Lake Tahoe. And then, there's Bob."

"Oh, no."

"Don't worry, I told him to shut his big mouth or he'd get a bad nickname," Matt said.

"Like what?"

"Bob the Blabbermouth."

Nina and Andrea laughed. "What were you going to ask me, Nina?" Andrea asked.

"Well, this girl doesn't seem willing to open up to me. I've tried being understanding. I've tried being tough. She knows whatever she tells me is completely confidential. Nothing works. You've studied psychology and you use it every day in your work. Any suggestions?"

Andrea said, very seriously, "She is protecting a secret with her life. Either she is protecting herself, or someone she loves very much."

"Yes. I think it's someone else."

"Note that she is being honest. She's not lying, she's just not revealing. That's good. You just have to build trust."

"I'll keep working on it."

167

"I saw Sandy at the post office today," Andrea said, shifting her boot to the floor and pulling her chair in closer to the table.

"What's she up to?"

"It's amazing. You work with her every day, yet you come to me for the scuttlebutt."

"I sometimes think she's afraid I'll try to horn in on her life or something if she tells me anything really personal. Interfere with it the way she does mine."

Matt said, grinning, "Why, she couldn't possibly think you're a control freak or anything, could she?"

"Hush," Andrea said. "She got a job for Johnny Ellis. Your client, I believe?"

"He was."

"That's the one. He's going to be the day manager at a motel in the casino district. Her niece had the job, but she's pregnant with her fourth child and decided to quit."

"Wow." So Johnny could quit the road work. The phantom pain might go away at last. And Sandy hadn't said a word. "Sandy ought to go into social work. She's got a knack."

"Not always," said Andrea.

"What do you mean?"

"She and Joe have been trying to work with some at-risk Native American teens, trying to get them on track. One of them was arrested last week."

"What for?"

"You know that series of robberies that's been happening around the lake?"

"The guys in a boat?"

"That's what for."

"Who was it?"

"A kid named Scott Cabano. His family has been through a lot of turmoil. Scott spent time in foster homes. Anyway, he's out on bail. Showed up at the ranch. He'd been staying there now and then. He got aggressive. Sandy and Joe had to disinvite him. Joe doesn't seem worried."

Great, Nina thought. Another heap of trouble Nikki didn't need. "You can't save people," Nina said. "They keep to their paths. Sometimes they decide to save themselves, though."

"I disagree," Andrea said. "Look what Sandy did for Johnny Ellis."

"Sandy gave him a chance. But he has to decide he's not sick and angry and ready to give up anymore. That'll take some kind of inner revolution, not just a change in his outer circumstances."

"We wax philosophical," Matt said. "So allow me to state that I am a self-protective, selfish son-of-a-gun who's very busy keeping me and mine together. So I'm glad there are altruistic people out there willing to do what I won't do."

"Your wife runs a women's shelter! You do your share!"

"That's Andrea."

"It affects your family every day, too, Matt. You know you sacrifice a lot."

"Hey, I could be making good money working for the Man, honey," said Andrea. "We

169

could get a big house and new clothes and go to Hawaii every winter…"

"Ha," said Nina. "You wouldn't last a day."

Matt put his arm around Andrea and stuck his nose in her neck. "So you're saying that some of the magic rubs off on me," he said to Nina. "That's good. Unearned brownie points."

"Did someone say something about brownies?" said Troy, wiping wet hands on his jeans. "Because we're still hungry." He was joined by Bob on the left, half a foot taller, and Brianna on his right, a foot shorter. And Hitchcock, nearly as big as Brianna.

"After all that pie?" asked Andrea.

The three children nodded in unison, Wynken, Blynken, and Nod. "At our age, we require more calories due to an accelerated growth rate," Bob said.

"Well, then of course you must have some," Andrea said. To Nina she whispered, "At my age, I require more alcohol."

"And I require more coffee," Nina said, "the soft stuff."

"At this hour?" Andrea asked.

"Coffee never affects my sleep."

Matt hopped up to make sure everybody got what they required.

The minute Nikki arrived home, she ran to her room, shut the door tight, and picked up the phone. Her lifeline. God, how she had missed talking to her friends.

She called Bob but there was no answer. Disappointment, big-time. His mother must have told him she was coming home! Why hadn't he come over or called her?

She was lying on her bed, phone in hand. Her room looked strange. The sheets on her mattress were fresh. The clothes she had left lying around were neatly folded in their drawers. The quartz crystals she collected on her hikes had been lined up in a corner by her mother, who had even put a coffee can full of flowers on the windowsill. She knew Daria meant well, cleaning her room, trying to show her how much she cared, but the order depressed her. This was how the world went on without her in it. Her personality drained out of her things. Bob forgot about her.

Or had his mother told him to stay away?

Outside, the sun shimmered. In the old days, she would be out there on her dad's old mountain bike, riding the trails.

She picked up the phone again, punching in some numbers. "Scott?"

"Well, well, well. Look who's back in business. When did they spring you?"

"This afternoon. This is the first chance I got to call."

"I need to see you, baby."

A thrill tickled the small of her back. He could do that, just with his voice. So handsome and so rough. Just her type, and not her type at all. The way he drove too fast and did everything for the hell of it. He just didn't care, and sometimes, when she was so mad she had to get out and do something crazy, he was just right.

Too bad she couldn't trust him. "That's just it. I can't go anywhere. I'm under house arrest. I've got this ankle thing that keeps track of where I go. I have to check in with someone every day, and be here in case they call."

"Huh. Well, lucky for you, I've got no such limitations."

"Why would you?"

"You didn't hear I was arrested?"

Was that pride in his voice? "No! Why?"

"I'm accused of ripping off those houses around the lake," he said carefully. "I'm out on bail. My mother practically had to strangle the old man to get him to cough up the money."

"Good band name," Nikki said. "Cough Up the Money."

He laughed.

"Why do they think you did it?"

"You tell me."

"But we never took anything valuable, Scott, and I never told anyone anything. Why would I?"

"Nobody I know closer to the police than you lately, Nik. But nothing to worry about. I've got a great guy defending me. A real cut-throat named Riesner. He'll get me off. Listen, if you can't leave, I'll come over."

"When?"

"I can't get there until later. Midnight."

"That's too late, Scott. Anyway, my mother's here."

"Get rid of her."

"She's really upset about all this. I don't think..."

His tone changed. "I'm coming over, so get her out of there."

He ran around like a Sierra wildfire, she had thought once. Quick, turning anything that got in his way into dust. He scorched you if you turned your back. She had thought he was everything she ever wanted. But what was this about stealing? She thought back to those nights. They had gone out two or three times...sprayed a few cans of paint, picked up throwaway things people left lying around outside. But they had never broken into anyone's house.

He could have gone back on his own. He probably had.

But Scott was going to have to be her connection to the outside. He was the only one that might know how to do what she needed done. She couldn't ask Bob. She didn't want to involve him in this. Scott could take care of himself. She would have to trust him one more time, then maybe...

Could she handle him? She would have to.

Nina and Bob stayed to watch a movie but left Matt's at midnight.

Bob fell asleep on the way home. She looked at the few long hairs jutting from his chin and cheek and realized he needed a razor. He needed instruction in how to take care of himself as a young man.

The dark rushed by. She hadn't wanted to stay at Matt's. If there was a hope of a good long rest, she felt she had a better chance of finding it at home under the soft comforter on her own pine four-poster bed. There she would fight the insomnia and win or sweep the kitchen, or get some work done, or listen to the late-night radio maniacs rail at the government. She had her choice of appealing alternatives.

She was just turning off Pioneer Trail into the neighborhood of Indian-sounding names, Minniconjou, Hunkpapa and Kulow, her street, when she saw a car she recognized reflected in the rearview mirror. She reached up, tilting the glass for a better view.

Headlight beams from a passing car illuminated the car and its driver. The old silver VW convertible she had seen in front of the Zack house, with Daria Zack driving. What in the world was she doing driving around at such an hour with her daughter under house arrest?

10

NIKKI HAD GOTTEN her mother out of the house late at night by telling her she had an earache. When she was little, an earache had always meant an ear infection. Convinced it prevented more serious trouble, Daria developed the habit of dosing her with eardrops early on. Naturally, Nikki had flushed the eardrops first, insuring the need for a trip to the pharmacy.

Before she would go, Daria fussed for a long time. She didn't want to leave Nikki alone, like she had an idea something was up. Nikki said whatever she could think of to ease her mother's suspicious mind, covered her skimpy house clothes with a jacket, and pushed her out with directions to the twenty-four-hour pharmacy.

Scott was already waiting up the street in his car, engine running, headlights out. He ran to the front door before she could even close it, grabbed Nikki and tried to kiss her.

"Don't!" She wrestled away from him.

"You called me, right? So what's the problem?"

"We're in plain view. Let's not give anyone anything to talk about, okay?"

He came in and made another grab for her, but she moved toward the kitchen. "Want a Coke?"

"You sound like your mother," he mocked. He'd shaved his head since she'd seen him last.

She didn't like it, so she didn't say anything.

She slammed the refrigerator door shut and came out, popping a can of soda. "I'm thirsty," she said. She took a long gulp, never taking her eyes off him. "I like your jacket. Mmm. It's real leather, isn't it?" she said, moving closer, touching his arm.

He liked that. "Yeah."

"Where'd you get it?"

"What's the difference?" He yanked his arm away, mad again. Settling himself onto a pillow, he propped his dirty sandals flat against her mother's favorite white cotton pillow. "I've been thinking," he said as she sat cross-legged on the floor nearby. "If you didn't rat me out, it must have been one of the other guys in the band. I mean, nobody else knows anything."

He always talked as if the band really existed outside of their own conversations, as if it was out there somewhere rehearsing, getting gigs. "Hamid or Jane? I can't believe it."

He took her Coke away from her and threw his head back, sucking it down. "Who else? Unless it was that asshole who's been hanging around. Bob."

"He's not an asshole. Anyway, it wasn't Bob."

"You sound pretty damn sure. Why's that?"

"I didn't tell him anything. Did you?"

"Not yet." Finding the remote control next to him on the floor, he flicked the television on and began to flip channels.

"What's that mean?"

"Well," he said, reaching down and touching her ankle monitor, "you're not much use to me now, are you?"

"Be serious. He's a little kid."

"Less time if he's caught." He laughed.

"So you were robbing those houses?"

"Steal from the rich. Wouldn't Che approve?"

"Why did I ever trust you? You never told me anything about this. You got me involved..."

"You loved it."

"You know what? It was stupid. I was stupid. You don't care about anyone else, do you? You haven't asked me one thing about what I'm going through..."

"Because I don't give a shit, Nikki." He ruffled her hair. "You're tough. I know you can handle it."

"You lied."

"About what?"

"About everything. About the band. There's never gonna be any rehearsal. You don't want a band. You want a gang. And you lied about how a person who is younger doesn't do as much jail time. They say they're going to try me as an adult."

"Well, gee, Nikki. It was you who got the bright idea to kill your uncle." He tossed his car keys into the air. "I don't remember advising that. I'm not going to take the blame for that. Besides, what's the longest they can hold you? Ten years?"

"Life, Scott."

He let out an impressed whistle. "Big-time convict!"

"I'm not going to jail. There's got to be a way out of this."

He shrugged and continued to flip his keys.

"Scott..."

"What?"

"You can't stay here. If Daria finds you here..."

"I'll give her a good hard rap on the jaw if she gives me any lip." He illustrated, cuffing her lightly on the chin.

"Don't talk like that!" She stood up, deciding he couldn't help her after all. Scott always followed his own agenda. She must have been nuts to think she could arrange anything through him. "Why don't you just go. Just get out."

He stood, towering over her. "I'm not through with you, Nikki." This time when he kissed her, he held her neck and pressed her toward him, not giving her the option to get away. He kept his face very close to hers, and held her hair in his hand. "You owe me."

He knew something. Or was he pretending to get her to admit something? That was his style. "What are you talking about?"

"Remember, we split everything down the middle. Don't tell me you killed him and didn't even grab a souvenir."

"Let go."

He pulled her hair.

She beat him with her fists, but he held on. "Ow! Stop!"

"Where is it, button nose? What did you take?"

"I didn't take anything. What makes you think I did?"

"The newspaper says you did. Killed him while you were burglarizing the place."

"Don't! Please, Scott, you're hurting me!"

"Said some neighbor spotted you taking something. And remember, I taught you everything you know. What was the number-one rule?" He let go of her hair.

She rubbed her scalp. "You tell me."

"Never leave empty-handed."

"There's nothing."

"You're lying."

He said it with such assurance, she shivered.

He put his lips to her ear and whispered, "You owe me, Nikki, and you'd better believe I plan to collect." He waggled a meaty finger at her.

Their heads turned to the window. They both heard it at the same time. Daria's car.

"You have to go now," Nikki said. "Use the back door." She pushed him toward the kitchen.

"What if I don't?" he said, turning suddenly, putting her off balance. She stumbled against the table. "What if I stay here? Let's discuss this whole thing with your sexy mom. She's bound to agree with me that you shouldn't hold out. She know about our adventures around the lake?"

Her fury and frustration overcame her. She couldn't hold back a second longer. "You leave," she punched his arm, "my mother," she punched it again, "out of this! Or I'll kill you, Scott! I swear I'll kill you!" She kept her voice as low as she could, hoping her mother wouldn't hear.

They struggled briefly as he tried to hit her and she fended him off. He pinned her arms to her sides. "I'm shakin' in my boots, bitch! Come and get me!"

A key scratched in the living-room door.

"Just go," she cried, wriggling. His fingers were embedded deeply into her arms. "Please, Scott!"

He shoved her so hard she fell to the floor, then ran out, leaving the screen swinging.

"Honey?" Daria called from the living room.

"Right here," Nikki said. She caught hold of a chair and hauled herself up. "Getting myself a snack." The back door slammed.

Her mother came in, looking around. "Is someone else here? What was that?"

"I had the radio on."

"Oh. I had to go to two stores to find the right kind of drops," she said. "It's a good thing just about everything stays open late on the Nevada side." She looked at Nikki with concern. "Are you all right?"

Nikki opened the refrigerator and looked inside. The door shielded her from her mother's view. "Fine. Funny thing is, my ears feel fine. After you went to all that trouble. Isn't that weird?"

Daria put the bag and her keys down on the table, yawning. "No, it's typical. Just like taking your car in for a repair. If by some miracle someone's available to work on it at all, you can bet that funny sound went away between your garage and the shop."

Nikki unwrapped a square of rubbery American cheese and stuffed it into her mouth.

"You want crackers with that? You don't eat enough."

"No, thanks," she said, waving her mother off. "Think I'll go beddy-bye. Good night."

"No kiss?" said Daria.

She pecked her mother on the cheek and fled upstairs to her room, rubbing the sore spots on her arms, her mind whirling. She couldn't leave the house for God knew how long. She was so stuck.

Scott was totally out. She could see it now. He was just another user, like the men Daria dragged home. He treated her like dirt and didn't respect her. He had led her the wrong way and worse, he pushed her around. If only she'd never met him, she might not be in this fix. She might never have gone to her uncle's that night. Then she wouldn't have seen...

A lump formed in her throat. She couldn't think about that.

So she let herself get mad at Scott again. There was never going to be a band.

She needed someone who would do something for her without demanding anything in return.

Maybe Bobby would.

The first thing Paul did when he got out of the hospital on Thursday morning was to hire a Lincoln town car so that he would have more legroom. He could drive with his left foot but the cast was a problem, and the pain when he tried to contort himself into even this large car was a bigger problem.

"You sure your doctor said you could drive like that?" the young rental car agent said, frowning, eyeing Paul's cast and crutches. He turned his head and scanned for someone, anyone, to shoulder the responsibility of rejecting this disabled driver, but there was no one else around.

"Definitely okay," Paul lied. He bought the extra insurance and drove carefully down the road toward John Wayne Airport, radio blasting out the crying cramp in his right calf.

Since he had missed the transfer hearing, and couldn't have done much good even if he'd been there, there was no immediate need to get back to Tahoe. Meanwhile, Dave LeBlanc's sudden absence from the scene bothered him and he intended to look into it.

During a slow patch in traffic, he pulled out his cell phone, which had survived the crash undamaged, and called the NTSB guy. They were still evaluating the evidence, he was told. They had found nothing new. They were going over the Beechcraft splinter by splinter. Paul made an appointment to talk to the chief investigator the following week. He ought to be back at Tahoe by then. He called Sandy at her ranch and told her to look for him then.

"What happened to you? You better have a broken leg or something."

"Nothing happened to me. Well, actually, I do have a broken leg."

"Very funny. She was worried about you."

"Were you?"

"None of your business."

"Sandy?"

"What."

"I'll see you on Monday. Will you greet me with a smile?"

"What's got into you?"

"Will you? Please?"

"I might bring you coffee, if you ask me nice."

But he thought she was smiling.

He turned the phone off. It was good to be back in action.

Arriving at John Wayne Airport by noon, he parked in his favorite spot and stumped over to the hangar, leaning heavily on his crutches, feeling decidedly uncool and worse, weak. There was something to be said for the mind-body connection. He found himself looking at flights of steps with loathing, felt the anger welling inside when he confronted even a slight unevenness in the pavement. This could definitely insert a minor chord into his spirit. He said to himself, anger got you into this spot, buddy. Take four deep breaths and take them slowly.

Heat appeared to vibrate along the miles of asphalt in the fume-soaked air. Fortunately, the hangar and LeBlanc's office were located at ground level. The door was unlocked, but there was no sign of LeBlanc inside. Even more puzzling, his office had been cleared of all the ray guns.

"They fired his ass," said a passing mechanic.

"Why was he fired?"

"He's been off his game lately. Coming in late, picking fights. Guess they decided he wasn't worth the trouble."

"Any reason you know of why he might be having a rough time?"

"Women?" the man said, taking a guess.

"Who'd he fight?"

"He got loud a few times, but the fistfight was with me. Accused me of lifting his tools. He cooled off and apologized after I punched him out."

"Where'd he go?"

The mechanic shrugged. "I don't know. It might be hard getting a job when you've been fired plus have a record."

"Anybody here a good friend of his?"

"He's a loner. Decent maintenance tech, though. He helped me out a few times. Knows his planes. I'm sure he'll land on his feet."

By the time Paul got back to the Lincoln, he was sweating from the exertion. He tossed the crutches in the back seat, turned on the air-conditioning, and leaned back. Took a deep breath. He didn't want to go to Newport. He wanted to go home. He wanted someone to tuck him into bed with a drink, turn on ESPN—he'd even watch soccer if that was all that was on—pull the blinds, and let him sink into pleasurable convalescence.

LeBlanc lived in a five-story apartment building on Westcliff Drive, a busy thoroughfare off Newport Boulevard. While located some miles from the seashore, the building sported an ersatz beach ambience, with four palm trees struggling for survival in front and impossibly round bushes below the windows of apartments with the bad fortune to back onto the noisy street. Once again, Paul lucked out. The apartment was on the first floor.

Paul knocked but there was no answer. He rang the bell of the apartment manager.

"Hello," he said. "You must be Eddie. We talked on the phone."

"Hey! I thought you were gonna stiff me," said the fellow who stood in the doorway. He looked like one of those ex-gang members who shapes up when he grows up. A tattoo on his hand had been blurred beyond recognition but he still wore his baseball cap backward. He held his hand out.

Paul reached into his pocket and pulled out his wallet but didn't open it. "I need to go in," he said.

"That'll cost another fifty."

Not too expensive. Paul nodded. Eddie came out with a set of keys and they went back to LeBlanc's apartment.

Hot, stifling air. The living room had been turned into a workshop, with white melamine cabinets lining the walls and tools and small machine parts strewn all over, what looked like an air filter here, engine parts there. On a table in a corner under a greasy sheet were smaller things, coiled bales of wire and string, nuts, bolts, wrenches, even a turkey baster. Posters from *The Phantom Menace*, with Princess Amidala prominent with her powdered face and unearthly beauty, had been tacked up on the walls, and some strange imaginary weaponry of the future was lying around. Eddie lifted a plastic tarp from the rug. "Oil spots," he said with disgust. "When I came in before, I shoulda looked the place over better. I never knew what he was up to in here. He's out, man."

Paul was already moving to the bedroom. Decorating the walls in here were posters: girls in odd getups holding ray guns, a large framed illustration from *Cat Women of the Moon* and another from *The Day the Earth Stood Still*, with Gort, the robot, lugging a blonde in a red cocktail dress. "Klaatu Barada Nikto," in black marker pen, emanated from roughly where the robot would speak. More plastic phasers. A wooden chest full of work clothes. No sign of drugs. No computer. Suitcase in the closet, toothbrush lying on the sink in the bathroom.

The kitchen. One cupboard full of Wheaties and Trix. Another cupboard cluttered with half-empty bottles of Beam and Gordon's. More tools on the counter were sprinkled between a million tiny parts, squiggly bits, unrecognizable machinery, white foam balls, and even samples of upholstery. LeBlanc loved his work, too.

"Jerkoff," said Eddie. "What's he been cookin' on the stove here? Airplane fuel? He could have blowed us up, man! I have a three-year-old!" Paul had located a drawer full of bills and correspondence next to the sink.

He sat down on a kitchen chair while Eddie poked around, complaining.

No check registers or credit card bills. Shoot. No personal letters. Our boy leads a simple life, Paul thought, or knows how to keep the complicated stuff hidden.

"How long since you've seen him now?" he said to Eddie, who was pulling the trigger of one of the toys, causing it to light up and make a buzzing noise.

"Four days, man. I should have come in here before. I'm calling the owner."

"So where is he?"

"How should I know? I don't associate with him. I got my own life."

"Has he gone away like this before?"

"He never goes anywhere."

"How long has he lived here?"

"Two years."

"Pays his rent?"

"He's been late a few times. He says he gets paid late. He's straining, man, like the rest of us. He says he likes it here. We got a nice pool and that attracts the girls. Some nice girls here, and he's got the window," said Eddie, pointing toward the beauties lolling around the courtyard pool below in the blazing sunshine.

"Any special girl?"

"They don't like him. He just looks."

Should he stump down there and try to talk to the girls? He was sweating like a pig now, and the bright sunlight out there was—face it, buddy—too much to take. Laboriously, Paul stood up. Eddie was looking at the cast.

187

"Crackup, huh?"

"How'd you know?"

"It's always a crackup in LA."

"File a missing persons report on LeBlanc, Eddie," he said. "This doesn't feel like a junket to me."

What with myriad pit stops for rests and revitalization, Paul didn't make it home to foggy Carmel in the rented Lincoln until one o'clock in the morning. Leaving his bag in the car, he humped into his frigid condo. First thing he did was to take a couple of pain pills. Then he turned up the heat and examined his stores, found a can of tuna, opened it and ate the contents while leaning on one crutch, looking out the window into a pool of light that lit the quaint village street. Nobody stirred out there, not a human being or even one of the little birds that made such a ruckus in the mornings around here. He wondered how they hung on at night. Did their little claw feet hold them to a tree limb, or did they all have nests in which to retire? Alone in the night, he dragged off to bed.

Turning the light out, he pushed his head into the pillow, adjusted himself. Pulled an extra blanket up over himself. Kicked it off. Groaned.

Wished for a glass of water but saw that one of his crutches had fallen far from the bed. He would have to crawl to get it.

Shut his eyes again. Felt sleep prowling around. Had a fleeting vision of himself creeping through snowy woods, gun in hand. "Rhapsody on a windy night..."

He flipped the lamp on, grabbed the phone and punched a long series of numbers. "Wake up, sleepyhead!" he said.

"Wha?"

"Hey, honey," he said. "What are you wearing?"

"Who... Paul?"

"Who else?"

"What's the matter?" A fumbling in the background. "It's nearly two o'clock!"

"Did I wake you?" he said meanly.

"What's going on?"

"Obviously, not a damn thing. Hence my call."

Nina's voice sounded wide awake. Could she really not have gone to bed yet? "Are you in Tahoe?" she said.

"Carmel."

"What's going on? Where have you been? I've called and called. Did you stay in LA?"

"Yep."

"I assume something major happened down there to keep you away from the phone for so long."

Yeah, something major had happened. To an *hombre muy macho.*

"Well, what happened?"

"Conversations, calumny, crashes."

"What are you talking about?"

"Say, Nina. You know what I'm thinking about while I'm lying here in my birthday suit, skin rubbing against the soft covers?" The habit of being suggestive with her clung.

"I can't imagine."

189

He had her now. "I'm wondering how the little birds stay in trees at night. Don't they just build nests in the spring? What happens the rest of the year when night descends and there's no place to lay down their tiny little bodies? Why don't they fall down?"

"Are you serious?" He heard her yawn. "Is this really what you ponder in the dead of night? Whatever happened to the old mainstays, death and ghosts? Whatever happened to nostalgic reminiscences?"

"Some, the unlucky injured, may even have lost full use of their uh...whatever. Feet, toes. Whatever they use to hang on to the branches."

"You mean 'claws'? I guess those birdies are shit out of luck, Paul."

He listened to her grouchy voice with perverse pleasure. She hardly ever used that kind of language.

"Thanks for faxing those reports, but we have a lot to talk about. Where have you been? When are you coming? I need you up here right away!"

"I didn't call you to talk about work."

"Then I'm going to sleep now."

"I just wanted to say hello."

"Grrr. Good-bye."

"I just wanted to hear you growl."

He hung up. Talking to Nina could be so relaxing. Or else the Darvocet must have kicked in, because suddenly he felt he could sleep like a baby.

11

WHEN NINA ARRIVED at the office on Tuesday morning after the long Memorial Day weekend, a courier from the D.A.'s office was loitering by the door with an envelope for her. Ripping the packet open, she went inside, not bothering to take off her jacket or her shoulder bag.

Random-sounding scientific explanations grew in meaning as she studied them. The paper showed the result of DNA tests. At the top was a reference to Daria Zack. A cover letter from Henry explained that due to an oversight the results hadn't been sent earlier.

So they had already tested Daria! The paperwork showed a comparison of Daria's blood pattern to the pattern of the sample of blood on the sword.

Daria's blood didn't match the sample. The autorad showed no sign of a third allele.

She scratched her head. She didn't want it to be Nikki's blood, but she hadn't really wanted it to be Nikki's mother's blood, either. The allele was a squiggle on a piece of paper, and she had to find some explanation for it. She would fax it to Ginger and call her later.

The day heated up and five hundred things went wrong. An obstreperous DWI client had busted the chops of an arresting officer. She claimed the police must have beaten her when taking her into custody, which explained all the bumps and bruises she had that she was too hungover to remember getting. Another client accused of car theft had allegedly made the mistake of stealing a casino owner's car. The windows of his house had been bashed in the night before and he had decided to leave town and his bail bond.

Johnny Ellis called. He had a new doctor and wanted to start fresh with his back pain claim even though he had the new job Sandy had found him. Nina multitasked frenetically until lunchtime, then shut the door to her office and sat in one of her orange chairs, taking a breather, closing her lids down over her stinging eyes.

Sandy knocked.

"She's not in," Nina said.

Sandy entered her office with a flurry of paperwork to be signed, then hung in the doorway.

"You're going to wear the paint off that spot," said Nina.

"You have an appointment with Linda this afternoon."

"At three, that's right," said Nina. "It's only one o'clock. What's the problem?"

"She wants to talk but...you're not gonna like this."

"What?"

"She's drunk. She'll be drunker by the time we get there."

"Cancel the meeting," Nina said. "I don't want to talk to her like that."

"You don't understand. She drinks. You won't catch her sober. I forgot to mention it."

Nina thought she knew why Sandy hadn't

mentioned it. She knew it from Matt's drug phase years ago, when she hoped daily for a miracle, always to be disappointed.

"Are you sure this is a good idea then? Maybe she should have an attorney present. Yes. I insist that she have an attorney present when we talk."

"What for? You're not the cops."

"I can't do it, Sandy. What if she incriminates herself? Then I have to go after her. It wouldn't be right."

"Listen. Two things. First. She didn't kill Sykes. Okay? I already told you that. When are you gonna listen to me?"

"You're her friend, Sandy. You're loyal, naturally, but..."

Sandy spread her hands. "She was passed out in a bar at Round Hill called the Thirsty Duck the night Sykes was killed."

"How do you know that?"

"She told me."

"Uh huh," Nina said. "So if you're convinced she did nothing to Sykes, why should I go and see her?"

"She knows something you ought to hear. She laid that on me too."

"And what's that?"

"She's hard to talk to these days. I didn't push it."

"She ought to be in a hospital if she's that far gone. She's dangerous to herself."

Sandy said, "We tried getting her into detox. There are some good programs in place that are geared toward Native Americans—alcohol's just one of the problems that can drag people down—but she's not ready yet. Meanwhile, she has a doctor, and Joe watches her days when I'm at work. She's gonna get through this."

The Linda she had seen at Sandy's wedding was hard to reconcile with this stranger Sandy was talking about. "You think this is a temporary breakdown caused by what happened to her daughter?"

"That, and her husband leaving. Yeah, she has to grieve before she can get on with it."

Linda was another woman riding on that cold tide Nina knew so well, grieving over someone lost. Suddenly, the world seemed full of women like them. For most, there would be macaroni to cook for hungry children, leaves to sweep from the steps, checks to write. Sex and love and hunger, all the normal drives would rear up and seize them again. Life itself would drag them back into the mainstream. But what happened to the ones that never got yanked back? What about Linda, sinking so far down she might never rise to the surface again? How did a mother recover from losing her child? What about Nikki? She floated in one place, unable to move forward. How did a child move on after being rejected by her father?

Sandy was still talking. "But you need to know what happened and I guess Linda thinks she knows something so I'm gonna take you to her. Not Paul."

"Why the insistence that she see me and not Paul?"

"She's got enough pride left not to like people seeing her like this. You're easier for her. Wish is coming back in a while. He can watch the office while we're gone." Her son, Wish, did odd jobs for them.

"All right," Nina said. "Sandy? You said 'two things' when I said it wouldn't be right to interview her when she was intoxicated. What was the second thing?"

"Second thing is, what's ethical about being nice to people when you have a little girl charged with murder? I don't care who Linda is or how messed up she is, I'd be on her like a hungry dog on a rib steak if I thought it would help the client."

Nina thought about that and thought some more. "You know, Sandy, I think you've got a point there," she said finally. "I guess I do get tangled up in the fine points of professional ethics sometimes."

"Like I always say. You lawyers think like spiders, weaving these webs that you get stuck in. Make like a cockroach. Go for it and just remember to run for cover when the bright lights come on." She dropped the set of points and authorities on Nina's desk.

At two-thirty, Sandy directed Nina to a red Chevy pickup. "It's Joe's," she said, climbing into the driver's seat. "Only breaks down on hot days."

Shifting from park to drive made the entire vehicle shudder. The day was straight out of a tourist brochure, warm and bright, the trees dropping yellow pollen like fluffy snow on cars and roofs and streets.

Nina leaned back and enjoyed the scenery while Sandy drove. She usually drove these roads automatically and it was sheer luxury to take time to look out the windows and smell the wildflowers blooming along the verges. She had driven this way with her husband to Sandy's wedding, and back from it with Paul.

Hard to remember that only a few months before, in late March, these green fields and blooming waysides had still been a dense field of white extending into eternity, or at least as far down as Placerville. The earth had renewed itself and somehow, so would she. Lulled by the back and forth motion of the car, she dozed, half in and half out of awareness.

By the time she had fully returned to her senses, they had stopped at a stout wooden gate on a dirt road. Sandy and Joe's property. "I must have drifted off," she said.

Sandy got out, lifting the gate carefully into place before giving it a push with her hip. "You could use some coffee before you talk to her."

"Yes, I could," she admitted. In addition, she was dying to see where Sandy and Joe lived. She had never seen the place. Sandy's wedding had been at a friend's home. Sandy got back into the truck and revved the engine to a lurching start. Without taking the time to close the gate, they drove down a dirt road, stopping for some ducklings following their mother toward the pond to the right. Ahead, a low ranch house with a big porch stood, and behind, a forested hill began its ascension toward the sky.

Sandy stopped the truck and got out, walking toward the house, but the truck's door wouldn't open on Nina's side. "Uh. Is there a trick to this?" she called.

Sandy came over and jiggled the handle. "Nothing to it," she said, opening the door with ease. She led the way up a path to the house.

"It's so beautiful up here, Sandy," Nina said, clutching her briefcase and following Sandy's stately sway. "You have so much sky. You must love it."

"It'll do."

The house was all Nina would have hoped for Sandy and Joe: older, comfortable, very homey and well-loved looking, with pine furniture and an orange blanket with a zigzag pattern on the couch. In the large, sun-yellow, tiled kitchen, she helped Sandy assemble a tray with coffee and sandwiches. Linda wasn't staying in the house. Sandy and Joe had a one-room studio out by the barn they had fixed up for her.

Two small windows framed Linda's door. A tiny porch in front held a rocking chair with gingham pillows. They knocked. No answer.

"It's Sandy and Nina Reilly, Linda," said Sandy firmly. "We've brought you some lunch."

The door cracked open. Linda blinked at the

sunshine. She looked disheveled, as if she had been sleeping, and her dark hair had a matted look. She didn't even look at Nina. Her eyes were fixed on the tray. "That all?" she asked.

"No booze, if that's what you're asking," said Sandy, inserting a foot in the door and giving it a rough heave.

Linda jumped back. They walked in.

Some effort had been made to make the room habitable, even pleasant. A braided oval rug filled most of the large floor. An iron bed painted white was against one wall. The walls were light blue, and navy-and-white-striped curtains fluttered in the windows. Two upholstered chairs sat opposite each other at a circular wooden table. Other than the unmade bed, the room looked reasonably tidy.

Next to the table, on the floor, stacked like wood, were the empty bottles, enough to fill a wine cellar. A glass, heavy and round, sat on the table, also empty. Several more bottles lay alongside the bed.

Sandy ignored them and put the tray on the table. "Sit down," she said to Linda. "Have a sandwich."

Linda sat. Her eyes roamed around the room for a while, trying to fix on Nina and failing. She closed them. "Hell. Hate it when you get to the dizzies."

"Food helps," Sandy said. "Eat up, now."

She handed Linda a half-sandwich and stood over her until Linda, making a face, ate it. "I'm blotto. No fooling." She spoke slowly, enunciating precisely.

"I'm Nina Reilly," said Nina, taking the chair opposite. "I met you at Sandy's wedding. Remember?" It hurt to see Linda like this, hardly able to speak. Her eloquent simplicity at Sandy's ceremony had touched Nina.

"Not—not really."

"I represent a young lady who has been accused of killing Dr. William Sykes."

Linda nodded. "Right. Right," she said, taking a bite of food, chewing a little. Sandy put a coffee cup in her hand and excused herself, then headed back to the house. Finishing her coffee, Linda put a hand on her stomach. People did not really turn green in Nina's experience, but Linda came close.

"I wish you didn't know me like I was before," Linda said to Nina. "Now let's talk about—what? What did you come here for? About Robin?"

"I'm here about Dr. Sykes."

"Not much to say. Six months ago, he killed Robin and ruined my marriage. They gave us some money but that didn't change anything. I had to give up my ministry. Lost the joy. Lost the faith."

"I'm so sorry..." Nina said.

"I took her to him. I gave her the money."

"Don't blame yourself."

Linda stared down at the table, lost in thought. "Drinking's the only thing that helps. Ever heard of Buffy Sainte-Marie? No, you probably haven't. My mom loved her songs."

She sang a few lines in a harsh voice from "Codeine."

"Well, my belly's cravin', too, only my curse is the oldest kind. I've bent to drink."

"Tell me about your daughter."

"Robin was her name. Wait," she said, getting up. Pulling a suitcase out from under the bed, she opened it, rummaging until she found something. She left the suitcase out and handed a photograph to Nina.

"There she is."

A girl with short black hair cut very stylishly smiled, showing a top row of even white teeth. She had Linda's strong, jutting nose. "She liked herself straight on, but wouldn't let you take her in profile," said Linda.

"A pretty girl," said Nina.

"She hated her nose." She took the picture back. "It was all she wanted for her sixteenth birthday, to have the surgery. She had a scholarship to go to beautician school. Loved people, talking with them, helping them look their best. She lived through the operation." Linda stopped. A tear fell down her cheek. She didn't seem to notice. "Where was I?"

"It doesn't matter."

"Oh, yeah, and she died a couple of hours later. She stopped breathing. 'A rare outcome,' he said. They blamed it on some hidden defect in her lungs, but what it comes to is that sometimes people can't take the insult of surgery. Isn't that a perfect way to describe it? The insult. That's what they told me."

"Pretty vague."

"Why my daughter? Our doctor said Sykes was careless with Robin. But his lawyer was a man named Jeffrey Riesner. You know him?"

"Yes."

"An animal has more sympathy. He bit into us like a rat in an alley. When he got done, we felt like—dirty."

"I understand you made some threats," Nina said.

"I got Sykes's number, never mind how. Late at night a few times, I called him up and told him what I thought of him. I wrote him a letter once." She shrugged. "I was drinking. Makes me meaner."

"He got a restraining order against you."

She rubbed her hands against her cup, as if wishing it into something more potent. "He was the one needed restraining."

"You attacked him." Sandy had told Nina this.

She snapped her fingers. "That's what Sandy said I should tell you. That's right. I remember now. Now listen. This was about— oh, a month ago. I went into Prize's for a nightcap. I was wanting not to be alone. I lost it. You know. Lost it."

"At Prize's."

"At Prize's. Oh, yeah. I had been"—she brushed her hair back and tried to sit up straight—"at the Horizon before that, drinking. Just beers."

"Yes."

"I came in. I saw Sykes standing up from one of the tables, smiling. Something came over

201

me, just so much hatred... I never felt like that before! Wild! Insane! I wanted to kill him! So I smashed him in the face with my fists and landed a couple of kicks before the bartender and the guy with him pulled me off. They called the cops." She shifted around in her seat and eyed the pile of bottles on the floor.

"So?" Nina asked.

"That's what I wanted to tell you. Before all this stuff, I saw him with somebody, sitting at one of the little tables. This other guy was yelling when I came in and Sykes was trying to shush him. This hairy guy was really mad."

"Why?" Nina said.

"They both stood up and they didn't even see me, and the hairy guy says something. And his fists came up and I thought, he's gonna kill him before I get to kill him." She closed her eyes and shifted from one foot to another, rocking like a boat on a wave. "What I wouldn't do for a little wine. You sure you don't have anything? Even a beer?"

"No. What did this other man look like?"

"Big and burly like a logger. Filthy dirty, matted hair. Rough. Bearded. A knitted cap on his head. Had some kind of accent."

"Did you catch anything that was said?"

"No words. They had this bag on the table in front of them. They were arguing about it." Nina had a prickling sensation. Was this what Nikki had taken?

"And Sykes died a week later," Linda said. "One week. You're a smart lady. You figure it out. What were they arguing about?"

"Linda, did you ever go to Sykes's house?" Nina asked.

"Just the one time."

"When, Linda? What happened when you went to his house?"

Although Nina persisted with her, Linda had nothing more to say. Her attention had wandered away to the thing she really cared about at the moment, and would not be shaken back. "I don't feel good. You must have something. A few beers. A bottle of wine in the groceries. Maybe out in the car?"

"I didn't bring anything."

"Your mistake," Linda said. She got up and crossed the floor. She sat on the bed. "I need a rest. Then I got to hitch to town. So you better go." Her head hit the pillow and her eyes closed.

"Linda?" Nina said, coming over to the bed and looking down. "Let us help you."

Linda just lay there, arms at her sides, eyes closed.

"Listen..."

"Go 'way," Linda said. She wasn't asleep. She opened her eyes, and what Nina saw there frightened her.

Two hundred miles away on the coast, the view from Paul's living-room window that day embodied the best of California, all floating blue sky, water, and pirouetting eucalyptus leaves. At the bottom of the landscape, like the arms of a hula dancer, the Pacific swayed to its own rhythm. Here, the sea determined the moods of the day. Not so different from Tahoe, he thought, except there, the lake ruled.

Gathering the contents of his pockets, he got himself out the door. At the rental agency, he cajoled a pretty girl into driving him back to his condo and his own car.

"That yours?" she said admiringly as he got out.

He looked. A yellow Lamborghini preened at the curb. "You like it?" he said.

She kissed her hand and blew on it toward the car. Then she looked pityingly at Paul. "But I can see why you needed a rental." She roared off.

He hoped, he really hoped, she meant because of the cast.

Parking, never easy in downtown Carmel, stunk on sunny days. Circling until he could get a place close to his office, he confronted his first major flight of stairs.

Five minutes later, huffing only a little, he landed at the door to his office, where a new sign announced "Dean Trumbo," on a tastelessly large brass plate. Below it hung his original sign which said in the more subdued, antiqued brass which Paul thought both dignified and imposing, "Van Wagoner Investigations."

He touched the handle, which was unlocked, and turned it, ever so slowly. The door pushed open, and he peeked inside.

Dean held Paul's telephone intimately close to his mouth, his loafered feet rested on Paul's desk, and he was puffing, if Paul was not mistaken, on one of Paul's prime Cuban cigars, the gift of a grateful client. Paul's coffee cup, dirtied by Dean's lips, rested lightly on the papers in front of him.

"Hello, Deano," said Paul, watching with satisfaction as the cigar fell out of Dean's mouth. The feet went down and the telephone crashed into silence.

"My man! Come on in!" said Dean, dusting ash off his shirt and crushing the cigar out in an ashtray.

Paul moved in and looked the old place over. He almost didn't recognize his own office. The color photos of Namche Bazar, Tengboche, Machupuchare, Everest—gone. In their places were posters in silver frames featuring mega-magnifications of chrome in glossy black and white. His Tibetan rugs casually strewn about—missing in action, replaced by gray industrial carpet. Where once his bendable metal lamp had sat bolted to the desk edge, a black geometrical sculpture with light coming out of its head radiated illumination. Worst of all, his treasured battered venetian blinds had been usurped by mini-blinds.

The place looked like the "artistic" loft of some pretentious rich boy. Paul felt a snarl forming.

Dean stood up, reaching out to grab Paul's hand from across the desk. Paul let the hand shake air for a few moments.

Dean took his hand casually back. "Good

to see you," he said. "What happened to your leg?"

"Work-related injury," said Paul.

"Someone come after you?"

"Sort of."

"Helluva big cast," Deano said.

"Yeah." Paul's voice had dropped almost to a whisper. "Yeah, Deano. My good friend Deano."

"Why don't you take a load off?" Dean said. "That bum leg can't feel too good."

Pushing past him, Paul sank into the ergonomic chair behind the desk, the one thing in the office which remained undeniably his. "Have a seat," he said.

Dean sat in the client chair across from the desk, while Paul pushed the papers onto the floor. "Paul, listen..."

"I don't want to listen, Dean."

"No, but..." Droplets of nervous sweat were springing up on Dean's forehead. "Those are the accounts. I was organizing them to show you." He got up again and picked up a stack. "See?" he said, putting some back onto the desk. "And see this?"

Paul knocked them off the desk, never taking his eyes off Dean. "I don't want to look at papers, Deano. I want to look at you."

"Don't you like it?" Dean said.

"You mean the office?"

"Things were slow. I was looking for some ways to get the business jump-started. I really fixed it up, didn't I?"

"You fixed it all right."

"Your rugs are safe. I put them in the store-room. I called a rug store to make sure I stowed them right."

"And the posters?"

"They were so old," Dean said. "Yellow on the backs. Torn."

"They weren't torn when I left."

"I ran into a little trouble peeling them out of the frames."

"Ah. Peeling them."

"Thought I could save us some money there by recycling."

"Even the one signed by Edmund Hillary?"

"Who?"

Paul said nothing for a moment, then, "I guess business must be booming, judging by all this redecorating."

"Well, no," said Dean. "That's what I wanted to show you."

The phone rang. Dean jerked. Paul picked it up. "Van Wagoner Investigations."

"Hey, Dean," said a voice Paul recognized. Ez, his oldest client. "About that job..."

"Hey, Ez. It's Paul."

Ez hung up.

"Why'd Ez hang up on me, Deano?" Paul said.

"Why, I haven't got the slightest idea. I suppose Ez and I have worked together for six months now and he prefers that."

"But he hung up on me."

"Must be a bad day."

"Did you tell him something about me that upset him?"

"Me? Oh, no. No, my man. I would never—you shouldn't have left for so long. Things dried up without you, Paul. The clients left. It's just too bad."

"What are you saying?"

"I'm saying that the business is going under. You have debts…"

"I have debts?"

"People that need paying," he said hurriedly. "Suppliers knocking on the door. The income just isn't there anymore, Paul. I'm really sorry I let you down like this." Once again, he picked up the folder from the floor. "Just take a look. You'll see what I mean."

Paul poked a button on the machine. After preparing a less grating message, one that mentioned his name several times and Dean's not at all, he let the machine take calls. For the next half hour, he studied the papers, while Dean sat opposite him, not daring to move.

"I see," he said at last. "Van Wagoner Investigations does appear to be going under."

Dean nodded vigorously. "Like I said. I know it's tough. You've been here for a long time, my man…but maybe it's time to start new, somewhere fresh. The old stomping grounds aren't so fertile anymore."

"Get out, huh?" Paul said, nodding, steepling his fingers. "You think I should?"

"I'll try to help out. Here's my offer. I sublet this office from you, and buy out your position with your few remaining clients here. There's just enough to make a start, as long as only one of us is drawing on the pot. I could give you five thousand. That gives you a little financial pillow, too. Maybe you're ready for a big change. I didn't see you flying back from Washington any more often than you had to, except to see Susan a couple of times. And then you spent more time up in Tahoe than here when you did come around. This is a small pond for a big guy like you."

Paul stood up. He pulled his crutches under his arms.

As if preparing to give Paul a hand, Dean rushed over. "So what do you think?" he said. He took one look at Paul's face and backed off, but too late. Paul nudged him with his crutch. Deano fell on his ass.

In about a tenth of a second, Paul was on him, thumb pressed against Deano's throat.

"Gawk. Gawk, gawk," Dean sputtered.

"I think," Paul said softly, "that you have been cheating me and slandering me and embezzling from me. But that's not important, because you'll pay back the money, every stinkin' penny. What's really important"—he pressed the thumb a little and saw Deano's terror increasing as the breath began to be cut off—"what I can't forgive"—Deano's rasping breath and bulging eyes—"is your not knowing who Sir Edmund Hillary is. You've gone too far, *my man.*"

"Don't kill me," Dean rasped.

Paul pressed a little harder, until he judged Deano would be seeing red, then leaned close and whispered, "You're the one who's leaving town. Tonight."

Dean nodded and gasped. Paul rolled off him, grabbed a crutch, and hauled himself up. Dean sat up on the floor, getting his breath back.

"Get out, Deano."

Dean went without another word, sport coat flapping. Paul flopped down at his desk again and reached behind him in the credenza for his special bottle of Scotch. Gone.

He had thought, when he had Deano on the carpet, of inflicting a little damage, pressing the point as it were. But when Deano said, "Don't kill me," all the fun had gone out of it.

Back in the car, he left a message on Susan Misumi's voice mail, making nice without a long-winded explanation of his absence. He specified a particular picnic table at Point Lobos, saying he would meet her, lunch in basket, in an hour. Stopping at a deli on the way out of town, he loaded up on his favorites, deviled eggs, barbecued chicken, sourdough bread, cold beer, a Beringer Merlot, pippin apples and Bartlett pears, tucking them into a basket with red and white napkins and crystal stemware he had remembered to stick in the trunk before he had left home. He made a second stop at a booth on the road to buy some fried artichoke hearts.

He looked forward to spending time with an uncomplicated woman and some good food.

She arrived not long after he had staked out a table with a spectacular ocean view. They talked and ate. He liked her a lot. He decided to go home with her, and she didn't mind.

Which is why Nina found him at Susan's place later that afternoon, crutches abandoned in the living room, Susan asleep beside him, her mouth open, snoring softly.

The phone rang, stirring him out of a serene trance of post-sex nothingness. When he saw that Susan was not going to answer, in fact could not, given her advanced state of unconsciousness, he picked it up.

"Paul?"

"Who else?" he said, because it was such an all-purpose retort, and the circumstances were still groggy in his mind.

"It's me. Nina."

"Hi, there," he said. Susan moved. He held the phone and his breath absolutely still. Her head sank deeper into the pillow.

"You have a minute?"

"Sure." He lifted his arm ever so gently out from under Susan's right breast. "Maybe you could hold on for a minute while I, um...just hold on..." He meant to change phones but realized suddenly that his crutches were in the living room and he was in the bedroom and never the twain would meet, short of waking Susan and asking for help or going down on all fours. All three, anyway.

"No, wait. This will just take a second. You're sure I'm not interrupting something?"

How irritating the woman could be. "Of course not."

"Nobody was at the office, and I couldn't

211

raise you, so I called Dean on his cell phone. He was kind of short with me. Said I might find you here."

Susan's arm snaked its way over to his thigh. "Umm," she moaned.

He edged away. He did not want her hand on his thigh. There was a time and a place for that sort of thing. "What's up?" he asked.

"I need you to get back to Tahoe right away," Nina said. "Can't you come first thing in the morning?"

Susan's eyes drifted open, then closed again, but lightly. Her breathing deregulated.

"Why?"

"I'm beginning to feel you aren't really committed to this case, Paul. I told you I need you. I've got a young girl's life in my hands, and so far, nothing to stop the machine from putting her in jail for the rest of her life. How's that for a reason? Now, are you with me on this, or not?"

"I am, Nina." He felt a stab of guilt and looked at the cast.

"Beth Sykes offered to give you and Wish the run of her house tomorrow, and her neighbor Louise Garibaldi is willing to be interviewed, but she says it has to be tomorrow or we have to wait another week. I can't really prepare for the prelim if my investigator hasn't seen the main witness against Nikki and the place where the murder occurred. I spoke with the mother of a girl who died after a procedure Sykes did. Linda Littlebear. Remember her?"

He remembered Sandy's wedding very well, remembered Nina focused entirely on another man, wanting to marry him. "Yes."

"She blames him for her daughter's death. She attacked him once at Prize's. She also told me about a man who was arguing with Dr. Sykes at the casino that night. A man who might be a foreigner, who looked like a logger. And there was a bag on the table in front of them. Who was he? What was that all about? What was in the bag? Sykes was a doctor. Was he doing some illegal traffic in drugs? Could the man have been Dave LeBlanc? Is that the connection?

"And I had a conversation with Daria Sykes last night. Turns out she recently sold the victim a piece of land she inherited from her grandfather some time back. Nikki was angry when she found out. She felt ripped off."

"That's interesting. She ever tell you what she took?"

"I tackled her about it again last night on the phone. I used her mother, used the threat of prison, used everything. She won't talk." Tension and anger flowed through her words.

"You'll get what you want out of her eventually, Nina. Somehow, you always do. Now, where is this land? At Tahoe?"

"No. It's in a place called Clay Hills north of Winnemucca. It's an old silver claim. Totally mined out. That's been checked from here to eternity, according to Daria. She said everybody knew it, even her Grandpa Logan, who was a real silver prospector and knew all about that kind of thing."

"Sykes bought worthless land," Paul said, drawn in in spite of the hazards of the moment. "Maybe he wasn't as bad as we're making out."

"According to some, he could be a real stinker. Sandy set up some appointments for you over the next couple of days with other associates, too. I want you to meet his partner, Dylan Brett, get a read on the man. See what you can dig up. Can you come?"

"Sure. I'll drive up first thing in the morning. Have Sandy tell Wish to pick me up at Caesars tomorrow about 11 A.M." He felt her surprise at his easy agreement, but an instant later, she had recovered and was pressing him further.

"Maybe I can fly you up out of San Jose," she suggested. "They've got direct flights running to Tahoe again."

"I'll drive," he said firmly, putting the phone back in its cradle. Nina, Nina, everywhere, even here, in another woman's bed.

"You're leaving again?" asked Susan, stretching. "You just got here."

"Be here now," he said, putting his hand back where it belonged. "Remember that old saying? Remember Baba Ram Dass? Remember when bliss was attainable by chanting and shaking rattles at airports?"

"No," she murmured. "But it doesn't matter." She started fooling around, too, and pretty soon they were traveling once more toward those distant realms.

12

BETH SYKES, now the sole owner of the house on the private court off Bayview Way, had left a key for them under a slat by the front door. She had gone to Carson City for the day.

Parking to one side of the narrow lane, Paul and Wish got out and tried to get a feel for the property. A lodge-style home, it reminded Paul of Yosemite's Ahwahnee, true to its rough mountain setting on the outside but luxurious on the inside. Running down a gently sloping hillside toward the lake, the two-story house appeared to be only a single story from the road. Afternoon sun poured down on them from between the branches of neat blue spruces. The birds had returned from their winter getaways and were taking full advantage of the beautiful day, staking out territories, making a mad racket in the surrounding pine trees.

"Only two houses with any kind of visual access," Wish said, returning after a few minutes of wandering around. "One of 'em was empty that night. The other belongs to Louise Garibaldi." In deference to the early summer day he was wearing baggy shorts with his hiking boots. Sandy's son was a gangly young man, even taller than Paul. Wish was taking courses in criminology at the community college and wanted to get involved in law enforcement.

Paul got out of the van. By pushing through

an unlocked gate and maneuvering just a short way down a path to the left of the house, he could get a decent view of the backyard and into the study where Sykes's dead body was found.

The study was the lowest point of the house. A large desk faced double doors that opened to a short stairway, and then a deck and pool. On the wall to the right of the desk there were two large bookshelves. Several feet behind the desk, an easy chair and lamp stood in a corner.

"The hardest thing for me to believe," Wish said thoughtfully, "is that she'd kill him with a sword."

"You mean, assuming Nikki did it."

"And assuming she was probably fighting him."

"The sword was a weapon, right in plain view, easy to reach," Paul said.

"It just seems like there must have been something easier to use to fend him off, if he was coming after her. A heavy bookend. A vase. A lamp, even."

"The report doesn't mention anything else broken or turned over in the room," said Paul. "Looks like whoever killed him caught him off guard."

They studied the room from the outside, as Nikki Zack presumably had.

They got a better overall view from beyond the pool. The upstairs curtains were drawn and in the stillness of the day the house had a hush around it, as if waiting for something.

Back to the front. While Wish unlocked

the door, Paul admired the intricate work-manship of the carved oak door and porch sup-ports. Money bought those details, and taste kept them subtle. The living room had the look of early Ralph Lauren, with plaid throws, plush couches, and real oils on the wall.

In the biggest painting, above the rounded river rock of the fireplace, men dappled by a pale sun stood face to face dueling violently, fencing swords tangled and glinting. The artist captured the mood so realistically, the cold morning light, the fierce faces of the duelists, Paul could almost hear the clanging of the swords. Over to the sides of the picture, shadowed by trees, their seconds waited. One raised a hand to his cheek and watched, riv-eted. The other bowed his head. A woman with long red hair cried behind a bush.

The painting belonged in a museum, not someone's home, Paul decided. It was lurid and savage. He wondered about a man who retired to his living room with a drink to study a picture like that. One of those men up there hanging above the good doc's fireplace would be dead soon after a bloody fight. That pretty dawn was doomed to be shattered. The woman would cry harder...

The doc's hobby had gone beyond col-lecting artifacts. He had collected precision cutting tools and their images, the blood and sharp silver tips of the weapons an integral part of the effect. Surgery in its most primitive form permeated his psyche. What kind of a husband had he been? What kind of a father?

While Paul pondered, Wish used Paul's camera to take photos for Nina, asking for advice on exposure settings here and there, but on the whole taking charge of that chore.

They saved the study for last. Somebody had cleaned up the blood and the place looked normal. "There are some decorative things in the shelves between all the medical books. A metal statue, looks heavy. A couple of Oriental vases, probably some dynasty," said Paul. "Get that shot."

"Yeah, why not pick up 'The Thinker,' and smash him with that when he came after her? That looks easy to grab. Or even one of those heavy books," Wish suggested, bent at the waist, focusing on the statue.

"If she was on the other side of the room, over by the chair, maybe she just couldn't reach the shelves." Paul closed his eyes, imagining the crime, the man angry, the girl frightened out of her wits at being discovered. She came in through the double doors, surprised him in...the chair reading, maybe? Maybe, slumped down, he couldn't be seen behind the big desk. It was possible, Paul thought.

"Has Nina got a lead on what Nicole wanted from him?" Wish said.

"No. The girl's not talking," said Paul. A faded spot on the wall marked where the murder weapon had been, and Wish shot the empty place. "If he'd put the sword in a locked case..."

"But it was so old," Wish interrupted. "Four hundred years old, Nina said."

"You don't see that kind of workmanship anymore. Speaking of which, you still want the van?"

Wish turned around. "Well, sure."

"It's not working too well. I think it may need a ring job."

"I have a cousin in Markleeville who's a mechanic. No problem."

"I'll sell it to you for five hundred."

Wish's face expressed a struggle. "I could give you payments," he said. "Can't write you a check."

"How about twenty-five dollars a month?"

"I can do that!"

"She's yours. As soon as I find some new wheels."

They shook hands and went back to the van so Wish could check it out.

After a half hour of looking under the hood and turning the motor over and talking about rods and rings and pistons, they went back to work. Paul sent Wish off to canvass the street and see if anyone else had been out walking a dog or stargazing that night. He took his time negotiating the path over to Louise Garibaldi's cottage.

The prosecution's star witness lived in the house opposite the Sykes house on the cheap side of the street. The lakefront probably commanded an additional five hundred thousand, Paul figured, and even a place this close to the lake didn't necessarily have easy access to a beach. Must be frustrating. Still, the house was

219

on a forested rise opposite the Sykes property and slightly offset, so that the front porch overlooked portions of the Sykes side and backyards. It hadn't been painted in a millennium, but the garden which took up the whole front yard with its deer-proof fencing all around had been loved to the point of tumultuous excess. Plants and vines on trellises ran amok competing for light and space.

Louise opened the door herself. She held a stout stick almost six feet long, a staff really. "Hi there, Mr. van Wagoner," she said. "The lawyer's office called to say you were coming just a short while ago." She had short white hair, a leathery, handsome face, intelligent eyes, and a sparkling smile. A pair of plaid shorts hung around her knees above the dirt-encrusted Van's tennis shoes, and she wore a T-shirt sporting the New Hampshire state motto, "Live free or die." Beside her, a German shepherd stood erect and as intelligent-looking, ears pricked and tail at attention. "This is Arthur. Arthur, say hello to the man."

Arthur held up his right paw and Paul bent down with some difficulty and shook it.

Paul showed his identification. "You saw us having a look at the Sykes house?"

Louise chuckled. "Big guy on crutches with a tall skinny Indian boy and a Dodge Ram van drive slowly around the block. Gotta be a simpleton not to take note."

"You spend a lot of time out here on your front porch?" One lonely Adirondack-style chair faced the driveway of the Sykes house.

"Used to. His house kinda sorta blocks my view, if you want to know the truth," said Louise. "They tore down a hundred-year-old shack to build that. But it was a shack. Nobody wanted to buy it."

"Made you mad?"

"Who doesn't want a view of the lake?" said Louise.

Without being too overt, Paul studied her.

"I usually go for my hike this time of day," she said, brandishing the walking stick. "I'd ask you to join me, but looks like you better not." Stringy, muscular legs attested to her excellent physical condition. Between the walking stick and Arthur, Louise had her security system worked out. Paul wondered if she really had been going for a hike, or if she had brought the stick to the door to let him know that.

"I'll take a rain check on the hike," Paul said. "This won't take long. I just want to ask you a few more questions about the night Dr. Sykes died."

"Come in, then," said Louise. She opened the door wide to allow Paul to pass, pulling it firmly shut behind him. They stood in a small foyer with dried plants hanging upside down from the ceiling, Paul leaning on his crutches, Louise, leaning on her stick.

"You a florist?"

"An herbalist. Naturopath. From way back." She fingered some drying flowers, lavender colored. "I've written several books on the subject."

"Ah," said Paul. "Got anything to mend a broken leg?"

Louise looked thoughtful.

"How about a broken heart?" Paul asked.

"You're a charmer, aren't you? Not the broken-heart type."

"Even charmers get charmed sometimes."

"But the leg—hurts bad, eh? Follow me." She set her stick against the wall, opened a door and started down a short flight of stairs, the dog at her heels. "Hold onto the railing," she said. "It's pretty steep but the steps are wide. You should be able to make it."

"Wait," Paul said. "No..." but Louise had disappeared, and Paul had no choice but to follow.

Fifteen minutes later, or what felt like fifteen minutes later, Paul, who eventually resorted to scooting downstairs on his bottom, found himself in a basement room with high windows and hundreds of gleaming colored bottles stopped with corks. Some sat on windowsills, reflecting sunlight, some hid in dark nooks of shelving below. He could see a large spiderweb in the corner.

All she needed was a cauldron and a pointy hat.

"My lab," Louise said. She took out a bottle, examined it, shook it, and returned it to the shelf. "I've got a number of things I could suggest to you that will aid in the healing process."

What in hell did that mean, Paul wondered, feeling a pain shoot up from his injured knee.

"Great," he said, sitting down on the bottom step and letting out a tiny groan.

"Hmm. Here's something for you. *Ulmus rubra*, otherwise known as slippery elm, an excellent dietary supplement for someone who's convalescing. It's a powder. Add it to your hot oatmeal in the morning." She handed Paul a small blue bottle. "You keep that. And here's purple sage. I'm sure you've heard of that, but maybe you don't know it's an all-purpose antioxidant that will keep the body pumping out those poisons. Also is associated with longevity. An old poem says, 'He who drinks sage in May, shall live for aye.' We all want that, don't we? I've dried and condensed it and put it into tea bags for easy ingestion." She set down an orange bottle with squiggly green things suspended in an oily liquid. "And this," she said, "is what you need the most." He took the bottle of red liquid. "If you do nothing else, take this one daily."

"What is it?"

"Don't ask. Just take a big spoon of it morning, noon, and night. It'll help you with your temper. You've got a bad one, don't you?"

Surprised, Paul said, "No worse than many."

"Oh, I can tell from your eyes. All that white eyeball showing under the iris. A yang imbalance." And she turned her own green eyes on him with a look that seemed to penetrate his skin and move on inside. "You know, we're not far removed from the animals and plants. We have lots of trained behaviors that help us get along, but the mind is really an assemblage of agents that have evolved with specific functions, such as, to feel alarmed by the sight of a predator, or to be able to recognize faces, for example. There are things that motivate us that you wouldn't believe, things we pretend don't exist. You're aggressive, yeah, but the bummer is that you mistrust your own instincts." At that, she gave a hearty laugh. "My advice is to eat more vegetables and less meat. Get back in balance. You'll calm down in due course."

"Can we talk about Dr. Sykes?" Paul said, wishing he could take a hit of the red stuff right away, although he should debate her analysis of him.

"Go ahead," she said. "Have a big drink right out of the bottle. It's clean."

He smiled. "You've tried it?"

"My, my. You're a suspicious one," she said, laughing. She poured a big serving into a glass and swallowed it down. "Oh, I feel like I'm walking through a field of golden flowers on a lovely spring afternoon," she joked. "Go ahead. Take a hit."

"Thanks," Paul said, taking the rest from her. "Thanks very much." He drank. "Ah." The syrupy liquid tasted like cherries and sugar, with richer depths hinting at chocolate. Warmth rolled over his tongue, spread down his throat, and dribbled into his chest.

"All right," Louise said, still smiling. "Let's talk."

Her consistently beatific mood communicated itself to him, making him feel more cheerful than he had in days. "Did you know Sykes well?" he said.

"Well enough to know that there was more than meets the eye." She leaned forward, speaking in a conspiratorial whisper. "He got younger every year."

"You knew he'd had cosmetic surgery?"

"He liked Tony Bennett and Andy what's his name. You know, Mr. 'Moon River.' He played Elvis records until I felt like marching over there and giving him what-for. Guess he emotionally arrested in the fifties. Your age has nothing to do with how you look. That's where plastic surgery fails. It only changes the outside. He wasn't really a good person, you know. He clung to that wife of his, but it was a sick kind of clinging. The changeable kind that's love one minute and hate the next. I think she had a hard time with him. You can never completely trust a man like that."

She looked at him and once again he got the peculiar feeling that she saw too much. "I read your statement to the police, Ms. Gari..."

"Louise. That's what everyone calls me."

"Louise. You said you can see into the Sykes backyard from your front porch."

"Don't tell me your sidekick didn't notice that. I saw him looking."

"Yes, he did."

"And I can, can't I?"

"Yes. I'm wondering if you can tell me in more detail what went on that night."

She was checking another bottle. "It was

sometime around ten. I don't sleep well at night, so I do little chores like fill the feeder with wild birdseed. There's not much else to report. He went out there to his pool like I said, naked as a newborn."

"Did you see him before he went in the pool?"

"Yes. He came out of his study with a bottle. Something good, no doubt." She looked thoughtful. "Dr. Sykes had good taste in booze. Good taste in everything, carefully cultivated. I went to a party there once. Beautiful home, except maybe for his peculiar decorations. I didn't have much use for him. I know Beth a little better. She's going to sell the place. Unhappy memories."

"Could you tell if he was drunk?" The lab reports had put Sykes's blood alcohol at .12, pleasantly lit.

"He was loose. Moved like he had fluid for bones, kind of like my husband, bless his soul, when he'd tie one on."

"Did he set the bottle down before getting into the pool?"

"No. He sat in the shallow end for a while drinking right out of it. I could only see him when he leaned back a few times. The shallow end is mostly out of sight from here, as your friend no doubt noticed."

"Then he went in?"

"Yes."

"Dove, you said."

"Yes." She hesitated. "He went under.

Then nothing for a long time. Like he was holding his breath."

"Uh huh."

"He came up once. He was really puffing then. Then down he went again for a long time. Next thing I knew, he was getting out."

"Where was the bottle? Did he pick it up again?"

"Actually, he tossed the bottle in the bushes. I remember now. He did that before he went in the pool the first time."

"So what did he have?"

"No idea," she shrugged. "Wet. Box-shaped."

"Then he went back into the study with this box?"

"No. He swam to the side of the pool. I could see him once or twice. The lights reflected up on his face. He was looking at something in his hand. Then, he dived in once more."

"And stayed down a while?"

"Yes. When he came out, his hands were empty again. Strange, isn't it?"

"Very."

"What in the world would he store in his pool?"

"What in the world," said Paul. "Then what?"

"Well, the girl came out from the bushes and went into the water herself and got the box out of the pool. I remember it all quite well. I was astonished to see that she'd been hiding there in the bushes."

"I still don't quite understand. Did you see her go into the study?"

"I made that very clear. I did not. I can't see the study doors from here."

"You must have heard something."

"Well. No, I don't hear as well as I used to. But there were sounds. Arthur heard them. He had his nose pressed right up to the screen and his ears went up and he nuzzled me and whined. I would have called them, but their number is unlisted. And I just couldn't bring myself to go over there or call the police. Dr. Sykes would have been livid." She shook her head. "I regret that. And that's it."

"That's all you saw."

"That's about it."

"At any point in the evening did you happen to glance over at their front porch?"

She thought about that. "When I went to turn out the light. Just for a second."

"Was the front door at the Sykes house open?"

"I don't remember. Sorry."

"Was the moon out?"

"I don't recall."

"Could you see far, up the street, for example?"

"No-o. Wait a minute. I saw a hawk. Late for a hawk to be flying around. Wait just a darn minute." Arthur trotted over to her, and she bent down and scratched his ruff. "Well, now. Imagine that. You got me thinking some more."

"Was there—" Paul began, but she held

228

out a hand to stop him. She closed her eyes and screwed up her forehead and nothing happened for a minute. Paul had another quick sip of the elixir. He was already feeling better. He didn't care what was in it, and he didn't want to know in case it was opium or something.

"I have just one word for you...convertible," Louise announced, her eyes still closed. Then she opened them and said, "Imagine that," again.

"Go on."

"Not much happens on this road. It's dirt. It's private. Doesn't lead anywhere. But that night, I saw a hawk, and it seems to me that there was a light-colored convertible parked up the street a ways, one of those little ones. Old. Some type of Volkswagen, I think."

"What time did it get here?"

"No idea. But it wasn't too long after I saw Dr. Sykes and the girl when I noticed it."

"How long was it parked there?"

"I have no idea."

"You didn't see a driver?"

"Sorry, no."

"Tell the police about it?"

"I'd forgotten about it. It was thinking about the hawk that helped me remember. I'm going to call that nice officer just as soon as we're finished. Could be a clue, eh? Help the little girl?"

"Maybe. What else do you remember about the convertible?" Paul tried everything he could think of to jog her memory further, but she couldn't remember anything else.

"Okay," he said at last. "Thanks again. I better get started up those stairs so you can have your walk."

"He told me once I was crazy to let the sun shine on my face all afternoon when I was working in the garden," Louise said. "He actually took my chin in his hand and turned my head back and forth and said a face-lift would make me look a lot better."

"What did you tell him?"

"I didn't say anything."

"What'd you think?"

"Honestly? It shook me," she said. "You feel pretty happy, you're healthy and getting along fine, and along comes somebody who makes a remark and then you can't stop thinking about it." She grimaced a little. "I'm still thinking about it."

"Well," Paul said, "you're a fine-looking woman, Louise."

"Am not."

"I'd be going after you if I didn't have that broken heart."

"Now, you stop that."

"You saved my life with this syrup of yours. I feel like I can get up those stairs now. I feel much better."

"Well, you better get on up, then." She helped him this time, and she may have been weathered but she was a strong support who smelled like fresh cinnamon, and Paul disliked Sykes more than ever because he had shaken Louise.

Easing himself up into the driver's seat of

his van, Paul turned the key and his engine sputtered. He tried it again and the engine sputtered again.

He waited until Wish found him, playing the radio and taking small sips of red elixir. Wish got under the hood and it took a while, but it was no problem. Paul felt very mellow about the entire incident. Very damn mellow.

13

SUPPORTED BY ROCK-FACED PILLARS and covered in a wide shingled roof that created the illusion of an unassuming one-story building, the courthouse at South Lake Tahoe sat at the top of a gentle incline. Its location, in the middle of parklike woods, lent a deceptive tranquility to the setting.

But in Department Three, the second floor Superior Court, at some time or another, the violent crimes that plagued the inner cities all put in an appearance. The wife-beaters whined excuses, the molesters lied, seeking to justify heinous transgressions. The casino muggers, the thieves, the carjackers—all faced hard time in front of the judge.

On Wednesday morning, June fifteenth, it was Nikki's turn in the courtroom. Today, during the preliminary hearing, the court would decide whether or not there was probable cause to believe that Nicole Zack murdered Dr. William Sykes. If the court found there was cause, she would go to trial. If Nina could pull a miraculous fast one, the case would be dismissed and Nikki would be home free.

"Let the record show that the defendant, Nicole Zack, is present in court. Are you ready to proceed, Counsel?" Judge Flaherty looked at Henry McFarland, who was standing.

Henry had taken over the Sykes case but retained Barbara as his cocounsel. Deeply tanned and looking refreshed after a weekend she was rumored to have spent with Henry in Palm Springs, she was busy organizing files on the table. She wore a gold bracelet that flashed even under the dull green tinge of fluorescent lights.

"Yes, Your Honor." Henry wore a meek look that complemented his respectable gray pinstripes. I am the humble instrument of the People of the State of California, his expression said. Flaherty liked him. No matter how much subjectivity the law tried to remove from the courtroom, a judge's personal likes and dislikes still played a big part in the game.

"Is Counsel for the defense ready to proceed?"

"We are, Your Honor." Nina had dumped the soft colors imposed on her by her jury consultant in a previous case and was wearing a black suit with a white shirt and a silver pin given to her by Sandy for her birthday. She wanted to look serious and be taken seriously and peach didn't cut it.

Nikki had promised to wear a dress with a jacket, but, as Daria had breathlessly explained when they finally showed up, Nikki had gone into her cell at the last minute and emerged five minutes later in a denim jacket and baggy black jeans. With her pale, thin face, jaw thrust forward and downturned eyes, she radiated teenage hostility and angst. Nina didn't need to look at her. She understood that Nikki's hard looks masked fear. Unfortunately, the judge probably wouldn't. Reaching over under the counsel table, she squeezed the girl's limp hand.

Now, face to face with the prosecution, Nina could already feel her blood pressure surging, her heart beating so furiously she thought everyone in the courtroom could hear it. She had read something in one of Paul's reports the night before that disturbed her a lot, but wasn't sure how to handle it. Closing her eyes, she counted until the quivering stopped and a calm descended.

Now she could fight.

Nina sat with Ginger and Nikki. Paul was nosing around the Re-Creation Clinic today and had some other errands. He had been so busy the day before he hadn't even been able to stop by the office.

"We'll keep it short today, Your Honor," Henry was saying. "We have probable cause to believe a crime has been committed, and after we've presented evidence today, I don't think there will be much doubt we have probable cause to assert that this defendant committed that crime." He cleared his throat. "The prosecution calls Dr. Ben Baruch."

The new medical examiner wore blue jeans and an ironed white shirt underneath a permanent five-o'clock shadow. Heavy, gold-rimmed glasses sat askew his nose. With scruffy, boyish black hair without a hint of silver, he looked young for a man in his position, but when he spoke, any doubts about his maturity fled.

He gave an abbreviated account of the

autopsy. No, there was no doubt about the cause of death. The weapon used was an ornamental sword. He talked briefly about how the cuts matched various aspects of the weapon. The doctor's throat had not been slit. The fatal blow had been one strike to the front of the neck. Another major blow to the back of the neck was noted but would not in itself have been fatal. Mutilation of the face most likely occurred shortly after death. He ruled out suicide or accident. He gave details as required, but Henry, apparently trying to minimize any troublesome complications, put on a minimum of evidence. Time of death—between eight and ten P.M.

The next witness, Lieutenant K. C. Potts, was one of the officers who had taken Nikki into custody. Medium-sized, with freckles and fair hair, his blue eyes were narrowed into permanent slits, as if to protect against the potential violence in any situation, including this one. Henry led him through the sequence of events that night, which hardly differed from what Nikki had told Nina. They had gone to the Zack house because they found some correspondence relating to land matters in Dr. William Sykes's study.

"Mrs. Zack became quite upset when we attempted to talk to her," he said. "Hysterical, you might say."

"After that, what happened?"

"Her daughter called my partner and me a few choice names. She was belligerent."

"Object to the characterization," said Nina.

"Sustained," Judge Flaherty said.

"She yelled at us. Used a lot of language. We took a good look at her. We had just been talking to the doctor's neighbor, a lady who said she saw a teenage girl at the pool behind the house at around the time of the murder. This girl fit the description. I asked the defendant if she'd gone to her uncle's house the night before. She wouldn't say. I noticed she had a bandage on her hand and some fresh-looking blood had leaked through. We had seen signs of blood on the wall outside the doctor's study, and her recent-appearing injury seemed very suggestive.

"So we Mirandized her. She signed the card with the warnings. Then I asked her if she killed her uncle."

"And what was her response?"

"She refused to answer. I took her into custody."

"Call Detective Jamie Ditmar." The diminutive evidence technician for the department was sworn. In full uniform, with a head covered in natural brown curls, she looked bright and competent. She was established to be a fingerprinting expert, a blood expert, and an expert at crime reconstruction.

"Were you called to the scene of a possible homicide on Sunday morning, May ninth this year?"

"I was. The time was eight-oh-seven when the nine one one dispatcher called it in to the main South Lake Tahoe station, where I had just arrived. Lieutenant Potts assigned me and Detective Sergeant Russ Balsam to go out there and secure the scene. We arrived at the scene at eight-eighteen. The ambulance had already arrived and the techs had gone in. The police photographer and the medical examiner, Dr. Baruch, arrived just as we were entering the house. Two women who work for a cleaning service were standing outside, and we questioned them for a minute or so before we went in."

"And what did you observe when you went in?"

Detective Ditmar outlined, with admirable conciseness, the succeeding events; the examination of the body, the photographs, and the painstaking collection of physical evidence and recording of other information that had followed. The fingerprint evidence was sparse. Other than family members and cleaning personnel, no marks were found in the study or house that seemed relevant. The only useful fingerprints were found outside the study door. They were also able to match a blood sample from the defendant to some blood found on the wall outside.

In the 8x10s that were introduced next, Bill Sykes's body lay spread in the middle of the study. Nina and Ginger had studied and discussed all of her copies of the photos. They weren't pretty. The naked, bloody corpse on his back on a beautiful spring morning was hyperreal and yet not quite convincing, like a Dali painting. The marring of his face after death added a macabre touch to an already gory scene. Flaherty examined the crime photos with an impassive expression as Ditmar described the placement of the body and the scene in detail.

Henry turned to the antique sword found lying two feet from the corpse, and everybody looked at those pictures, including more shots taken in the lab, where the long, curved sword, lying on a stainless steel table, clearly showed that the bottom two-thirds was covered in blood. "We removed blood samples for testing. On May tenth we tested the sharpness of the blade."

"How sharp was it?"

"It had been retempered. Sharpened. I couldn't say when, could have been twenty years ago. Odd for a weapon that qualified as antique, but anyway the steel blade had been honed down to extreme sharpness. I understand some collectors like to keep them that way."

"Sharp enough to have caused the wounds on the decedent's neck?"

"Sharp enough to have cut his head off, if more pressure had been applied. I would say that the pressure applied was relatively light."

"Based on all the evidence before you, have you come to a conclusion as to how the weapon was in fact wielded?"

"It's my conclusion that the assailant went to the wall at the far end of the study, withdrew the weapon, swung the weapon blindly, or wildly, however you want to put it, probably using both hands. An initial strike to the back of the neck may have slowed the victim, but it's our reading of the evidence that the victim then turned and faced his attacker and at that point, received the fatal blow to his neck. May I demonstrate this?"

"No objection," Nina said. Detective Ditmar came down from the witness box, picking up the long wooden stick used to point to evidence on the easel by the wall as she came around. "If you'd be so kind," she said to Henry, taking him by the arm and standing him in front of the judge.

Now the detective stood with her back to Henry, between him and the stick, facing Flaherty. She was almost the same height as Nikki. Suddenly she seemed to leap forward, grabbed the stick, whirled around to the left, holding it with both hands, and as she turned raised the stick chest high—

—And thumped Henry right in the chest. Not the neck.

"Ow!" Henry said, clutching his chest through the suit.

"Sorry," the detective said. "Let me run through that again. That wasn't quite right."

Nina leaned over to Nikki and whispered, "Stand up! Look at the judge!"

Nikki obeyed. She stood up.

Nikki was about the same height as Jamie Ditmar. Standing behind the defense table she looked as tiny as a ballerina in a music box. The judge stared at her, getting the message.

Henry collected his wits. "We will need to do that one more time," he said.

Nina sprang to her feet. "Oh, no. I object to any further demonstration," she said. "We've seen what we've seen. And I don't think Mr. McFarland can stand another hit."

Flaherty smiled.

"Let's do this again. The witness feels..." said Henry gamely, holding his hand to his aching chest like he was about to recite the Pledge of Allegiance.

"I don't care what the witness feels," Nina said. "I don't care if Counsel wants to keep on getting hit until his witness finally raises that pointer high enough to hit him in the neck. I think we've all seen where a person who is about the height of the defendant—excuse me, I mean the witness—would connect. Not nearly high enough."

"Okay," Flaherty said. "Enough. I get the point."

Detective Ditmar went back to the box and Henry, fuming, went back to his examination. The morning break came and went before they moved into the physical evidence. The judge had warmed to the detective, who was exhibiting both stamina and a steel-trap memory.

After explaining that the assailant must have wiped the handle of the weapon, since no fingerprints were found, she went on to tell what they had found. "There were deposits of sodium chloride, which was quite possibly dried residue from chlorinated pool water, near the pool where water had dripped, on the towel by the body, on the floor of the study, on a brandy bottle found in the bushes by the pool, on the cell phone found next to the body, and on the frames of the French doors that led to the pool," Ditmar said, reading from her notes. The preliminary hearing settled into the forensic details that make a murder case.

"Now, did you supervise the collection of fingerprints at the scene?"

"Yes, Sergeant Balsam did the actual collection under my direct supervision."

"And the collection of blood samples?"

"Yes. Sergeant Balsam again. I was present at all times and accompanied him to the lab in Sacramento where this evidence was actually analyzed. I have the reports right here."

They broke for lunch. Ginger and Nina ate together in the cafeteria, or rather, Ginger did business on her cell phone while Nina read over her notes. They both managed to gulp down a cup of coffee and eat a few bites of sandwich before returning to court.

At one-thirty they reconvened, Detective Ditmar still on the stand. The South Lake Tahoe Police Department wasn't a big one to start with, and wasn't fully staffed, so the usual chain of police officers had boiled down to one. Nina hadn't objected to the forensics work because she hadn't found much to challenge. The conclusions were what she wanted to challenge.

"Does blood on the outside door frame match the defendant's blood sample provided to your office?" Henry asked.

"Yes." Jamie Ditmar was all business.

"There was blood all around the study?"

"Yes. The victim's blood."

"And where else if anywhere did you find blood?"

"On the murder weapon."

"Did you identify that blood?"

"Yes. Almost all the blood belonged to the victim. However, while confirming that the blood on the sword belonged to the victim, instead of the expected two alleles which would match all other samples of the victim's blood, the testing lab detected a weak contaminating band in one of the PCRs. A third allele."

"Can you explain a little better for us what that means?"

"Certainly. The lab ran polymerase chain reactions, PCR, on the blood found on the sword. Basically, what they do is take a small sample of DNA and make more, essentially copying it millions of times to make analysis possible." Her description of the process was much like the one Ginger had given Nina before only in more exhaustive detail. Nina listened, but listened harder when the detective got to the results that mattered.

"During one routine," Ditmar said, "the lab was running random checks of the blood from the sword to make sure it all matched the victim's. In one of those reactions, instead of the expected two alleles on the autoradiograph which matched all the other samples, they picked up a third allele. That suggests that particular sample was contaminated with traces of a second person's blood."

"And were you able to match that blood sample against any other sample?"

"Ordinarily a single matching allele wouldn't be decisive on that point, but we had some luck in this case. The third allele we detected traces of is rare and does match the blood of the defendant in this case. Nicole Zack's."

"How unusually rare is this allele?"

"Oh, the odds are about fifteen thousand to one against encountering it in a randomly chosen person."

At this testimony, Nikki leaned over to talk to Nina. "How accurate are those tests?" she asked.

"I believe the techniques for identifying blood are now very sophisticated and reliable."

"That's so bizarre," she said.

"What?"

"I never touched that sword."

Something was wrong with this witness, who came off as so poised and confident. Something was wrong with her evidence and Nina couldn't figure out what. Henry, keeping it brief and to the point, had put on his white kid gloves with Ditmar. What dirt were they both trying to avoid?

When Nina's turn came, she said, "Detective Ditmar. What evidence did you find that the defendant was at any time inside the study? Did you find any of her fingerprints?"

"None that we have identified at this time."

"Any hairs, fibers from her clothes? Skin under the victim's nails? Anything like that?"

"None of those types of evidence, no."

"No little muddy footprints?"

"No."

"No high school ID card dropped beside the body?"

"Asked and answered," Henry said. "Objection."

"Move on, Ms. Reilly," Flaherty said.

"So the only thing placing the defendant inside that study, inside that house, was this blood sample you sent out for special testing?"

"Right."

"You mention odds of fifteen thousand to one that the weak contaminating band that suggests the presence of a second person's blood would be found in a random person's blood. Another way of looking at it would be to say that this so-called unusual third allele could, in fact, be found in the blood of millions of people the world over?"

"Yes, but—"

"I notice you have not mentioned a definite DNA match between the blood found on the sword and the defendant's blood. Why not?"

"Unfortunately, the amount was quite limited and that limited the number of tests we could run on the sample."

"How many tests did you run?"

"Several."

"But only one showed contamination by another person's blood."

"That's right."

"You didn't bother to confirm your finding on that test with further testing?"

"As I think I explained," Ditmar said, seemingly unbothered by the pressure Nina was making an effort to generate, "there was a very low level of contamination, and generating a signal in the presence of massive amounts of victim DNA is iffy. This particular allele/primer pair combination showed a trace of the third allele was present and it matched the defendant's blood pattern."

"So you're saying there's no confirmation possible and no retesting available?"

"The test is accurate, Ms. Reilly. No retesting is necessary," Detective Ditmar said mildly.

"That's convenient, isn't it?" Nina asked the court. She felt frustrated. In spite of Ginger's priming and her preparation for the topic, she found listening to DNA evidence like listening to a senile relative repeating a joke for the thousandth time. She couldn't concentrate on the material and enjoy the twists, so urgently did she want it over. And in this case, the feeling of urgency was enhanced by a violent premonition that this witness was obfuscating, trying to lead her away from something. She had no idea what.

"Objection," Henry said. "Not a question."

"Sustained," Flaherty said. "Save the commentary, Ms. Reilly."

"So, in your opinion, as an expert, what did this single PCR test indicate?"

Jamie Ditmar looked very uncomfortable. "A strong probability that the sample from the murder weapon was a match with the defendant's sample."

"And what is your conclusion from that?"

"Well, I would say that it's more likely than not the defendant's blood."

"What's that mean? 'More likely than not'?"

Ginger was tugging at her arm. "Stop right where you are!" she hissed. Nina bent down so Ginger could whisper in her ear.

"You want me to stop?"

"Don't lead her into making any more pronouncements about it. No more conclusions. You'll have a harder time shaking her at trial if she commits to something more definite."

Nina straightened, facing the judge. "Nothing further at this time."

After the afternoon break, which Nina used up listening to Sandy tell her the crises narrowly averted in her absence, they reconvened.

A terrified young woman in a ruffled blouse came forward to be sworn. Alicia Diaz was from Happy Housemaids, and she and her partner had discovered Sykes's body on their regular day to clean, Sunday morning, just after eight A.M. Strangely, the front door had been open when they arrived.

"Describe the scene that you saw as you entered the study," Henry said.

"Blood everywhere. Dr. Sykes lying on his back in the middle of it, next to his big desk. His throat and face were all cut up. It was terrible."

"And he appeared to be dead?"

"His eyes were open but he wasn't moving at all. He just looked dead. I knew right away. I backed out and was screaming and ran into the kitchen."

"Did you notice anything else while you were looking into the study?"

"Not really. Oh, the desk chair was knocked over. And, you know, Dr. Sykes, he was naked. His face was all messed up." She swallowed. "His nose...it was mostly gone. There was a towel lying next to him, like he just got out of the tub or something. And I saw the cell phone on the floor too."

Nina's turn came. "Mrs. Diaz, had you ever seen the front door open like that at any other time when you arrived for work in the previous three years?"

"Not really."

"Not at all?"

"No. Dr. Sykes and Mrs. Sykes were always careful about locking the front door."

"No further questions." Ginger, sitting next to Nikki at the end of the counsel table, looked a little surprised at Nina's brevity. Nina was drawing an open door next to the witness's name on her legal pad, her eyes narrow. The open front door was the kind of surprise that occasionally falls casually into a hearing—it hadn't been mentioned in the witness statement, or in the witness summary Henry had provided before the trial. An open front door! It was as if the case was inviting her, saying, walk right in.

Nikki had said she heard the front door bell. Of course, she was the only one who could testify about that, and chances were she never would. But Nina hugged the testimony to herself, feeling energized. It meant there was objective, third-party evidence that someone else might have come to the house that night. It also meant, on this point at least, Nikki had told Nina the truth about what happened that night. And it suggested more, given what Paul had told her...

Henry didn't care. The open front door wasn't part of his case, so it didn't impinge on his consciousness except as a vague loose end. Ginger was nodding. She got it.

Barbara Banning called Nikki's mother.

Dressed in white slacks and high heels, looking every inch the showgirl, Daria stepped like a dancer, toe to heel across the courtroom, riveting the attention of a few strays in the audience. Nina tensed and told herself to listen.

"You were home on the night of May eighth?"

"Yes."

"Doing what?"

"Well, we had dinner at around six. Spaghetti. Nikki sat with me, but she wouldn't eat much because she said she wasn't hungry, so she ate a little salad and helped with cleanup. About six-thirty she went to her room and I set up the living room, moved things around so I could dance. That's what I do, I'm a dancer. That night, I was learning a new routine."

"Where was your daughter during this time?"

"In her room, listening to music."

"For how long?"

"I don't know," she said, any brightness in her voice waning.

"You told Lieutenant Potts that your daughter was not home that evening."

"I don't remember what I told him. I was upset."

"When did you discover she had gone out?"

Daria looked at Nikki, who was picking dark polish off her fingernails and did not look up.

"I knocked on her door at about ten-fifteen. When she didn't answer, I went in."

"Is it your practice to put your daughter to bed at a certain time?"

"Not really. No. She puts herself to bed."

"Is it something you frequently do, knock on her door in the evenings after dinner?"

"No," she almost whispered. "She's holed up in there doing homework, talking on the phone, playing music, doing whatever it is she likes to do on the computer. She's always busy. I usually leave her alone."

"But that night, you went to her room."

"I did. I was looking for some new hand cream she bought..."

"And she was gone."

"She could have been in the backyard. She could have been next door!"

"That's all."

"Any cross-examination?"

"No, Your Honor." Thinking, Nina watched Daria walk gracefully back to her seat.

Louise Garibaldi was called. Paul had prepped Nina on his interview with her. She seemed quite relaxed, sunny and secure. Her eyes twinkled.

"I was filling the wild bird feeder," she said. Though age cracked her voice, her words came out steady and clear. "I do it at night, after the birds are asleep so that I won't disturb them."

"And from your front porch you can see William Sykes's yard?" Barbara asked.

"Most of it. Including the pool."

"Tell us what you saw happening on the night of May eighth at that house."

"He went skinny-dipping again. You know I spoke to that man several times about how I could see him out there. He didn't care. Maybe it gave him a kick, imagining me watching him in the buff, lusting after him."

She got a snicker out of the sparse audience.

"You saw him go swimming?"

"Yes. Odd sort of swimming. Diving. Bobbing."

"What happened then?"

"He came up with a little box in his hand. Don't know where that came from. He got out and sat there playing with it. I couldn't see what he was lookin' at. Then he jumped back in and when he came out this time, no box. Then he went into the house."

"And what did you see then?"

"That little girl right there," she said.

"Let the record reflect the witness is pointing at the defendant, Nicole Zack. Where was she when you first saw her?"

"Coming out of the bushes by the pool."

"You could see clearly, even though it was dark?" Nina asked.

"The pool light was on."

"And what happened next?"

"Well, she took her sweatshirt off and dove in there herself."

"Did you see her again?"

"I saw her take the box and get out of the pool but my teakettle was whistling so I went back into the kitchen to turn it off."

"I note that you have stated you did not call the police, Mrs. Garibaldi. Is there some reason?"

"Well. I wouldn't violate someone's privacy like that. I keep my nose out of other people's affairs." Nina repressed a smile at this.

"And she was such a little thing. Just a child. I guess I just didn't know what to make of it. I finally went to bed."

Nina made an instant decision to end her questions right there. Since Henry hadn't brought it up, she would not ask Louise about the car she had told Paul she had seen on the street that night.

Nina knew Louise had called the police with her recollection sometime that morning, and that the police had undoubtedly passed it along to Henry, but why would he care? As far as he was concerned, the car was a red herring which interfered with his preconceptions about the case.

Good, because that gave Nina a little time to consider the host of issues the information raised.

Because she knew that car. She had seen it often enough around town lately, the battle-scarred, silver VW convertible belonging to Daria Zack.

The standards of evidence in a preliminary hearing were much laxer than they were during a trial. Nina did her best, pointing out that "trace" amounts of blood did not make for much of anything; that no real proof existed that Nikki had been present on that evening aside from some dubious blood results and eye-witness testimony, which could be in error.

Though she put her heart into it, even Henry had moved on mentally, shuffling paperwork and conferring with Barbara at the table, considering the hearing over.

Flaherty ruled that Nicole was to be tried in Superior Court on a charge of murder, with a special circumstance of homicide while in the commission of a felony. Round three was over and they had lost again.

In the parking lot, Nikki worked at hardening her eyes and failed.

"Don't lose heart, Nikki. We're making progress," Nina said, closing the car door behind her.

"You call that progress!" Daria hissed as soon as Nikki was out of earshot. "They're trying her for murder with special circumstances! This is worse than a nightmare. It's the worst moment of our lives. My friend Kyle said I should have hired this other guy, Riesner. A guy like that, well, nothing against you, Nina, but he plays golf with the judges! That's what Kyle said. I don't think that judge likes you one bit..."

"Daria," Nina said, "I need to talk to you."

"Believe me, you don't want to talk to me right now! I'm too pissed off!"

"Oh, but I do..." Nina began.

Just then, a beefy boy with stubbles of black hair on an otherwise bare skull stepped up to the car and pounded on Nikki's door. "Hey, Nik! Long time no see."

Nikki glanced quickly toward her mother, then rolled the window down. "Scott! What are you doing here?"

"Heard this was your new place to hang and thought I'd stop by and bestow my blessing." He laughed, pulled her toward him by the hair, and planted a kiss on the struggling girl. Then he leaned in to whisper into her ear.

Daria, watching from a few feet away, apparently unrecognized by the boy, was galvanized. Catching him completely off guard, she roared up behind him, pulled his arms back, and shoved him aside. "Don't touch her, you bastard!"

"Daria, no!" Nikki said.

"Isn't this the boy they picked up for ripping off those lake houses?" her mother said grimly.

Scott, who had barely caught his balance

253

without falling, straightened the cuff of his jacket coolly, saying, "My fame spreads."

"Don't you ever come around us again," Daria said.

"You gonna let your mother talk to me that way, puss?" he asked Nikki. " 'Cause you really don't want to do that."

Her reply was to close her car window.

Turning her back to him with deliberate rudeness, Daria walked to her side of the car, got in, and drove off.

A small crowd that had gathered to take in the scene watched her drive away.

"Uppity bitches," Scott said, giving Daria's disappearing car the finger. "Fuck 'em. That's all they're good for anyway." He laughed unpleasantly and headed back toward the courthouse.

Nina walked over to her Bronco, wondering what Scott Cabano had said to Nikki. The girl had looked scared. And she had never seen Daria so angry before. In action, the dancer was stunning to watch, muscular and strong. Had she been this angry the night she went to Bill Sykes's house? Angry enough to kill him?

PART THREE

In his dream the man he is trying to kill breathes fire onto his hand and turns into a giant lizard.

He never was a man. He was a predator of men.

The creature grows a long tail.

He steps on this tail and the creature tries to scream, but he is still holding his burning hand over the awful lips of this lizard who is beginning to open its mouth and he snatches his hand away just in time and screams across the fiery breath:

"Rhapsody on a windy night, motherfucker."

He hopes this chant will kill the lizard. But the sound blows away on the wind. The lizard is beginning to move. And he drives the knife in up to the hilt, straining to get past the scales and gristle of the thing. While he pushes the knife in he chants:

"The last twist of the knife."

14

HOME SUPERVISION was what the Probation Department called it. House arrest was what it really was. Nikki had to stay home all the time.

Daria had gone out to run errands for Beth, although Nikki suspected she was happy to get out of the hovel. Nikki wanted more than anything to get the hell out with her even if Daria was just going to buy groceries, but the anklet did its job and held her back.

She went into the bathroom to regard her ugly face. Speaking of losers.

It didn't matter whom she admired or what bands she liked, did it? The System had her. She was going down. Her dad hadn't wanted them and that was when it all started, the whole snarl her life had become, the thing her mother had done. She tried not to think about the shock of that shadow she had seen coming into the study while she peeked through the French doors.

She had edged away as fast as she could and run like hell for the boat. When she finally got home, she climbed in through her bedroom window and threw herself under the covers and never saw Daria. And the next morning when she woke up and went in to find out what Daria had been up to, Daria was on the phone and got this wired look and said, My God That's Terrible, etcetera etcetera, and Nikki knew then and there that life would never be the same.

She had forced herself to act very natural around Daria ever since. Nobody else knew about her seeing that familiar shadow, and nobody ever would know.

Even if she went down.

She went into her room, ignored the text-books piled on the table, and picked up her electric guitar. For a while she just let her fingers walk around on the frets, plunking at random until she found a riff. She played it over and over, and then she started getting some of her fighting spirit back. Some lyrics appeared in her brain out of nowhere about a girl loser who makes a startling comeback.

She wrote down the lyrics in pencil on the back of a math worksheet so that she could read them while she played. Then she picked out the riff on her guitar and screamed the words in the general direction of the backyard, recording the whole thing into her computer and through headphones plugged into the mike jack of her bad box.

Afterward she played the bad box tape over and over and felt better. She had started a Web page a while back, although all it had at the moment was a picture of her with animated fire hair, a few poems she made up when she finished ahead of the slowpokes at school.

She designed a snapshot button for music, used a program to encode the computer version of music into MP3, and uploaded the song to her site, calling it "Comeback Girl." Then, studying how it looked, she prefaced "Comeback" with the word "Sexy" for marketing purposes, just to see if anybody was out there listening.

After sending out her musical beacon, she had one more thought. She dragged out an old recording on cassette of her dad's and uploaded it to her site. Afterward, she listened to it play, the tricky undercurrents of his bass runs, the sadness she thought she heard in his voice. She lay down on her bed, arms under her head, listening and waiting for Bob, who had promised to come by after school and maybe help her with something. Maybe she dozed for a few minutes, because when the phone rang, it surprised her. At first she thought it might be the officer that was supposed to call and check on her to make sure she was really at home. Then she got nervous Bob wanted to cancel on her.

"Bob?"

"Nicole Zack?"

Not Bob. This voice was nasal like somebody with sinus problems, older, with a really fake-sounding English accent. "Who is this?"

"Is this Nicole Zack?"

Well, it wasn't a wrong number. "Yes."

"You have something of mine."

"Who is this?"

"Says in the newspaper that a witness saw you take something out of Sykes's pool."

"She lied," Nikki said automatically.

"It's mine and I want it back."

A thought struck her. "Scott?" Could Scott

disguise his voice like that? It was so fake sounding.

"Listen up, little girl. You will give me what's mine. Return it now, and I won't lay a hand on you or on that hot mama of yours, even though the thought has crossed my mind more than once." He laughed, a nasty sound.

Jagged and fast as a flying spear, the idea ripped through her, lodging in her stomach. He had seen Daria. Was he following her? How could she get rid of him? She steadied herself and thought: He's shaking your cage, just like Scott. He won't really hurt you or Daria. He won't. Get rid of him. Make him believe you. "Look, I'm sorry I can't help, but I didn't take anything."

"Bullshit."

"I can't help you, mister," she repeated, allowing just a little of the desperation she felt into her voice. "So leave us alone."

"You have one chance and one chance only to make things right. Leave the stuff in the backseat of your mom's car tonight. Leave the doors unlocked. Or I'll cut on you. That's a promise. And then I'll cut on your mama's pretty, pretty face..."

"I'm not putting anything in that car, and if you come near us, I'll call the cops! I'm siccing my lawyer on you! She'll trace this call and they'll track you down and put you in jail where you belong! I'm not scared of you!"

"You dumb bitch," he said, and his voice dropped to a whisper that was way more disturbing than the threats, because it sneaked inside her. "You don't want to get in my way like this."

"Fuck you!" Nikki said. She hung up and looked at the phone.

She thought of the pouch buried in the woods. It *must* be valuable! Just her luck, if Uncle Bill stole the stuff from someone else. And the jerk had threatened her and Daria! She was really, really tired of being scared. And of having things taken away.

She went into the kitchen, where they kept a shillelagh that Daria had squandered money they didn't have on at an Irish fair. It hung on a cord behind the door to the yard. A cudgel with a thick knob on the end, it was varnished, hard and heavy as stone. An hour to go before Bob came. She spent the time sitting at the window looking out at the street holding the shillelagh, just in case. When she heard Daria fiddling at the door, Nikki ran to open it, struggling with a powerful impulse to tell her all about the threatening phone call. But she didn't need Daria hysterical. That would throw her plans off.

"Great news!" Daria said.

"They've dropped the charges. I'm never going back to jail. I'll graduate from Harvard and I'll get married and have a child with some nice guy," Nikki said.

Her mother winced slightly, then squared her shoulders. "I have a lead on a show!" she announced, dropping a brown bag of groceries on the kitchen table.

"Uh huh."

"Really, Nikki. This is going to help so much. Remember the magician?"

She remembered the magician, the juggler, the clown, the big-band leader...a whole circus of men who had led Daria on, promising the impossible. Still, there was always that moment, probably the same moment her mother felt, when her heart expanded at the thought, opening up to allow a flood of hope and dreams inside. No one would ever know, and Nikki would be acquitted. Her mother would get her big break, would get famous and rich. Their ship would come in, all due to Daria's exceptional talent and beauty... She looked hard at Daria, who pushed a gold wisp of hair out of eyes surrounded by a fine tangle of laugh lines.

Just for a second, she wanted to ask Daria why she had had to kill Uncle Bill, but she didn't. There were just too many reasons why that wasn't a good idea.

"He put me onto this friend, Kyle, who's getting a troupe together to revive *Music Man*. I ran into him at a couple of auditions and I think I really made an impression!"

Nikki thought back to a few of her mother's recent unexplained late evenings out and felt a small shiver of revulsion at the idea that the impression involved rumpled sheets in a casino hotel room.

"He says he's giving me a major part. I'll be Marian the Librarian. The love interest. The star!"

Nikki's heart sank back to its usual place, down in the dumps. "Daria, you can't sing," she said.

"He says they'll revamp the part. Make it more of a dancing role. Come on," said Daria impatiently. "Aren't you happy for us? This is so important. We need money! We can't rely on Beth for everything, you know. She's been such a doll. So generous, helping out with the rent and even paying for your defense."

"Too bad it took her so long. Then maybe we wouldn't be in this boat. And how come she never helped us before... ?"

"We never asked," Daria said.

"She knew how dead broke we were."

Her mother slipped out of her shoes and rubbed her feet. "In a marriage, you don't just throw money around to your relatives. Bill was thinking about letting go of his practice, according to Beth. He had to save for their retirement, don't you see?"

Daria tried to put her arm around Nikki but Nikki felt her shoulders hardening. Her mother noticed the resistance and gave up, dropping her arm.

"But we had the money you got from Uncle Bill when you sold him the land!"

Daria said slowly, "I told you, I paid bills with that."

"Daria, I've got time on my hands around here and I added those bills up. There should have been enough to keep the bank off our backs."

"Oh, all right. Rudy took it when he left."

"That cocksucker!"

"Nikki! Watch your language. I don't like hearing you talk like that about my friend."

Nikki picked up the phone. "Call the police, Daria. If you don't, I will. This has gone too far. You're too easy on these lying skunks! He's not going to get away with this. He can't just steal from us like that..."

"He didn't steal it, exactly. I mean, he's going to pay me back. It's a loan, honey."

"Oh, Daria. Oh, shit. You sold that land, the only thing we had and then you gave that cocksucker the money?"

"He was sick. Plus..."

"I don't want to hear it! I don't want to hear another stupid sob story by some lame dog jabroni! Why do you listen to them?"

Daria began to put groceries away. "I don't know why you always have to make such a drama out of everything, Nikki. We manage all right. And I don't want to live in a world where friends don't help friends in need."

Nikki was damned if she would start crying. She pushed a fist hard into one eye, then the other, a trick she had used as a child. It worked. "Daria, you told me you sold that land because we were desperate, remember? You didn't want to sell Grandpa's land. You always wanted to go back and live in the desert again, and someday we were going to move out there. You must have told me that a million times. I dreamed about those places you told me about, the hot summers, the wide open spaces, the little animals that came out only at night, the incredible sunsets. How could you just throw it away!"

Daria slammed a cupboard door shut. "I wish you wouldn't call me Daria," she said in a low voice. "I'm your mother."

Nikki sat down at the table and put her head in her hands. She thought, I'll get a job at the Wendy's, the car wash, anything. Then she remembered the house arrest and the charge against her. Her case was mentioned in the local newspaper almost every day, along with dire warnings from the fearmongers to the general public about rabid teens. Everyone in town knew about her and, even though some papers never mentioned her name, most people had figured out who she was by now like Scott had. Who'd hire her?

"Maybe you ought to tackle some of that homework the teacher sent home for you," Daria said, reverting to her traditional method of getting Nikki out of her face.

"Later," she said, slamming a cupboard door and sitting back down at the kitchen table. "Bob's stopping by with some worksheets," she lied.

"That's nice," said Daria, drifting out of the kitchen, holding her shoes in her hand. Nikki could see she was hurt. As if it was Nikki's fault! "I'll be in my room if you need me."

Nikki heard Bob's skateboard jumping a curb before she saw him. She flung open the door.

He handed her a bag. "Cookies. I'm starved." They went back into the kitchen. "Your mom here?"

265

"In her room."

"Are you okay?"

"Yeah."

" 'Cuz you look kind of funny." Tearing open the package, he looked down at her foot. "What is that thing?"

"My ball and chain. Like in the old days, when they used to put them on convicts to keep them from running away."

"What's it do, shock you? Like in a Bond movie?"

"No. Just snitches to somebody somewhere if I leave the house. I'm not supposed to do that."

"Can you take it off?"

"No, it's twenty-four seven." Twenty-four hours a day, seven days a week. She was in prison. The only real difference was the presence of her mother, not always necessarily a plus.

"That's whack." He pulled a cookie apart and licked the insides. "I bet you hate that."

This was the boy who was going to save her. She couldn't help smiling. "Yeah."

"So what's this thing you want me to help you with, Nik?"

"I need you to do some digging."

"You mean like research?"

"No. I mean like with a shovel. Bob, you can't tell anyone about this. Not the police. Not your mother."

"There's nothing illegal about it?"

"No." She didn't like to lie, but couldn't see that she had a choice anymore.

"What do you want me to dig up?"

"The less you know about that, the better." Pulling open a drawer, she grabbed a pad of lined yellow paper. "I'm going to draw you a map."

"A treasure map." He was on his eighth cookie, and had two more stuck in his hand.

"You're gonna make yourself sick," she said. "Daria got some food. How about a baloney sandwich?" She started to draw.

"No thanks, I have to be back home for dinner." He leaned over her shoulder.

"Move back, you're getting crumbs all over."

"Sorry." He sat back, finished his cookies, and rubbed his hands clean on his pants. "Milk?"

"Check the fridge." Thinking hard, she drew. She had buried it in the woods behind the house, behind a tree she knew very well. But how many layers of trees were there before he would get to that particular spot?

Bob drank an entire glass of milk without stopping, set the glass in the sink, and exhaled a burp.

"Grow up," she said.

"Will do," he said.

She handed him the map.

"It's behind your house."

"Right."

"In the woods."

"Uh huh."

"How deep?"

"Maybe a foot? Not very deep. I wrapped

267

it in one of those plastic bags that zips tight. Gallon size."

"So, not too big." He stuffed the map in his back pocket. "I gotta go. I didn't tell my mom I was coming here. She calls when I'm supposed to be home most days if she can."

"When are you going to do it?"

"Tonight. I'll come over after my mom's in bed."

"As soon as you can, okay?" She hadn't forgotten the voice on the phone. She couldn't. But she had told him she wasn't going to put anything in her mother's car, so he had no reason to be coming around. She had warned him off. "I'll be watching. Be careful." She walked Bob to the door.

He picked up the skateboard from where he had propped it on the porch. "I can't look inside when I dig it up?"

"Please don't, Bob."

"What will you do, once you have it? I mean, you can't leave the house."

"That's my business."

"I have a bad feeling about this."

"I know. I owe you."

"No, Nik. You don't owe me anything."

"Hey, I made a tape for you. I wrote a song. Here. It's a present." She smiled, and he smiled back.

"You did?" He took the cassette and stuck it in his pocket. "You sang on it and everything?"

"It was easy. I didn't need Scott. I put a song of my dad's on there, too."

"Cool." He jumped on his board and rode off down the street.

After straying out to light up the landscape outside a few times in brief flashes like a faulty lamp, the moon finally tucked itself permanently behind low streaks of black clouds, leaving blackness behind. Nikki stayed in the living room until eleven o'clock watching *The Matrix* with her mother for the third time, then encouraged her off to bed.

"I ought to practice," Daria said. "We have rehearsals starting next week." Even so, she yawned.

Nikki knew better. Rehearsals would be postponed indefinitely while the magician tested out his powers on her mother. If he couldn't get her to bed within a reasonable amount of time, he would do a final classic act of magic and disappear. "Get up early," she suggested.

"I say I will then I don't," said Daria. "I'm a night owl."

"I'll get you up." She wouldn't, but Daria wouldn't mind.

Once she could hear the even rhythms of her mother's breathing, she closed the door to Daria's bedroom and took up a post at the back window, watching for Bob. He said he would come, and he would.

A scratching at the back door awoke her. "Bob?"

"Let me in."

She opened the door and he entered. "You bring a shovel?"

"Yep."

"Got the map?"

Pulling the crumpled paper out of his back pocket to show her, he said, "I need to borrow a flashlight. This one's broken." He set a small plastic flashlight on the table beside her.

Nikki searched the hall closet, finding a hefty, industrial-sized one with a rubber hand-grip. Putting fresh batteries into it, flicking it on and off to test it, she ran back into the kitchen.

"Thanks, Nik. Oof," he said, playfully dropping his arm. "Weighs a ton."

"Now get going!"

He hung back, reluctant. "I hated sneaking out. My mom will combust if she notices I'm gone."

"That's why you've got to be quick!"

"Nik?"

"Uh huh."

"Don't ask me to do anything like this again, okay?"

"I won't, Bob. I promise." She felt sick. So many circumstances in her life lately made her stomach hurt.

Shining the light into the backyard, he grabbed the shovel and took off.

The huge pines and firs, so friendly in the daytime, shot black tendrils against the lighter navy of the sky. Where there were clouds, the stars evaporated. The yellow beam that was Bob grew feeble, oscillated between the trunks of the trees, and faded to nothing.

Nikki waited. Unable to sit still, she walked from the front of the house to the back quietly, nervous about waking her mother, but Daria slept on, oblivious. Checking a few times as she passed, Nikki reassured herself of this. Her mother must not know.

As she sat on the couch, stretching and unstretching her legs, a car pulled up across the street. She looked out.

One of those generic Tahoe pickups. Big. More than that, she really couldn't tell because their block had no streetlamps, which was basically a good thing, at least for tonight. She heard the car door slam, then nothing.

Then footsteps around the house.

She froze.

Tramp, tramp, tramp, but softly, muffled by the bed of pine needles, crunching when feet ran into leaves. The feet made an entire circuit, stopping briefly outside Daria's window, then moving on.

They climbed up the steps to the front door. But no knock came.

She tried to swallow. A dry throat, a desert in there. Who could it be? The magician, looking for Daria?

The voice?

She leaned around the window, craning to see who was standing at the door, but the windows were too close to provide a decent view if someone stood directly in front of the door.

Fright got her up. He might... "No!" she yelled. She stood in front of the door, but immobilized, she could not make her hand undo the latch.

Her hand moved. Her thumbs made contact with the cold brass of the knob, then her fingers. She willed her muscles to tighten, to get a grip. She opened the door.

But the man was running, running into the woods.

He had seen Bob with the shovel.

15

UNABLE TO SINK his crotchety bones and plaster cast into the hot tub at Caesars, Paul sublimated with chicken satay at Sato's, skipping the rice to devote himself entirely to the delicate peanutty flavor. Late on a week night, the restaurant was uncrowded. He sat at the table with his back to the wall, facing the doorway, as he always did, with the deeply inculcated paranoia of an ex-cop.

He was thinking about the pass he had come to and the sense that things were deteriorating on him, the business, the leg, Susan. Ah, well. Such things were all in a day's work for the Lone Ranger. He would get back on the horse and ride into another satisfying adventure any minute now.

Pushing his plate away, Paul finally wiped his lips with a napkin and consulted his watch. Late. Too late to go anywhere, except to a casino.

Back in his van, he turned right onto the highway, then swerved onto Pioneer Trail, continuing almost all the way up the dark road until the turnoff on Jicarilla Drive.

He parked across the street. Hmm. No porch light. That suggested Nina and Bob had gone to bed. Up in the second-story window, he thought he saw a glimmering. Pushing his crutches out before him, he worked his way out of the car and up the stairs to the front door in cool night air. Stars flooded the high-altitude sky.

He knocked, but there was no answer. He knocked louder. Wild barking ensued.

Within seconds, a sleepy-eyed Nina appeared. She held a bathrobe around her, silk, very soft, very lived-in looking, which parted somewhere below to reveal the white knobs of her knees. She was holding her big black dog by its collar, half choking it.

"What's the matter?" she asked, alarmed.

"I shouldn't have come so late. It's a school night. Sorry. There's nothing wrong. I just stopped by on my way back to the hotel." She was standing there, nailed like she'd been hit with a hammer, looking at him.

He looked behind him. Nobody was there.

"How come you keep calling me so late and coming over late?"

"Too busy during the day."

"Is that really it?"

"What else would it be?"

Then she saw his cast. She gasped and looked from the cast to his face.

"You're hurt! Why didn't you tell me..."

"Didn't want you getting any ideas about hiring someone else."

"Oh, Paul. What happened?"

"I hurt it skiing." He held out his hand to the dog and when it came over, began stroking its furry head.

"In summer?"

"That's my story and I'm sticking to it."

"Why didn't you tell me?"

"You were busy."

"How long with the crutches?"

"Doctors no longer prognosticate, did you know that? They give odds, they speak in tongues. Their language now resembles their handwriting."

"You don't know."

"No idea."

"Well, come in, come in. Can I help you?"

He waved her away and came stumping in and lowered himself onto the couch.

Nina went to the Swedish fireplace in the center of the room and opened the grate. Paul watched as she leaned over with the stick she used as a poker, stirring up the wood, which flared up and sent a heat wave toward him. She seemed uncomfortable.

"Thought I saw a light," he said to get the ball rolling.

"You did." Walking into the kitchen, she pulled two cups out of the cupboard. "Darjeeling okay?"

"Got anything stronger? I've been drinking tea all night." While she found a beer in the refrigerator and poured it into a cup, he made a decision of his own. He couldn't take the physical shock of seeing her. This would be the last case for him and Nina. Like a stupid bird, he kept flying into her glass door, hurting himself. He couldn't stand being close but not close, and he had no intention of revealing the things that would bring them together. Case closed on that front, he thought with a rush of feelings that included only a little relief.

She handed him the cup. "Sorry. I haven't run the dishwasher in a while."

She seemed to be taking his visit well, as if she might have been feeling the teeniest bit lonely herself. He ran his eyes around the familiar kitchen, enjoying the bits of painted pottery on the window above the sink and collection of unique cups that told him things about her. He hadn't ever seen much of her domestic side, and it was another side he liked.

"Sorry about the prelim," he said.

"Yeah."

"I went to the clinic and talked with people there, some new patients and some postsurgical ones hanging around waiting for checkups. Dr. Brett's got a lot of fans."

"What about his alibi?"

"After meeting his wife, who was as lovely as described, I could see Dylan Brett home cuddling with her that night. He certainly should have been."

"People that perfect irk me," Nina said. "A bad flaw in me, I know."

"Even more important, I found out he comes from money. He doesn't need the clinic financially. He just loves what he does. I can't see why he would off his partner who was about to retire."

"Is it possible he was involved with Beth?"

"Well, that's the interesting part. I did talk with one nurse who praised him to the skies, then admitted that our good doctor can be a real flirt, especially around Beth. All harmless fun, according to her, but the first scratch in his shiny exterior. So, I'll say it is possible he was involved in some way. I get the impression all was not right in the Sykes marriage. On the other hand, the Brett marriage appears solid. They grew up together, were high school sweethearts. They appear close."

"Hmm," Nina said. "It's strange how, even while you say that, you don't seem to believe it yourself."

"Maybe I find the concept of a perfect marriage difficult to buy," he said lightly. "My secret flaw."

"A scratch in your shine? That leg must really be bothering you."

He smiled a little and decided to leave it at that. "Tell me more about Linda Littlebear," he said.

She filled a teapot with water, turned on the gas, and sighed. "It's sad. She's trying to destroy herself." She told him about the conversation in more detail, and Paul said thoughtfully, "It's a decent description. We should be able to find the man with Sykes. I can't see how it could be Dave LeBlanc, if he sounded like a foreigner, but I'll keep that possibility open anyway."

"I know how Linda feels because I felt just like she does, Paul. I don't know what would have happened to me, except that I still had Bob and my work."

"What's happened is that you are stronger than ever," Paul said. "It's remarkable to watch."

"You think so? I hope that's true."

"You still worrying? Having those bad nights?"

"Oh…" She made a motion as if to brush the question away.

"Anyway, we have leads," Paul said. "I need more of Wish's time. Is it all right to put him on the payroll for a few extra hours?"

"How many?"

"About five hundred bucks' worth."

"I'll check it out with Beth Sykes, but I'm sure she'll okay it."

"I'm going to ask to see what's left of the plane early next week. The investigator postponed the appointment."

Nina said, "I suppose I'm dreaming up links that don't exist. The two deaths must be coincidence." She had her back to him, making her tea. In her kimono, her hair tousled, her hands making the graceful movements of pouring and stirring, she seemed so remote and self-contained that Paul felt a suffocating despair creep over him.

If only…he would have tried again with her, he could see that now, once she was over her husband's death…maybe she would have turned to him again.

But seven months before, after a moment that took no longer than it takes a lizard to leap toward the sun, he had cut himself off from her forever. She would never understand what he had done. She would shudder and turn from him in horror. She'd turn him in.

"No. This time I think you're right," he said, trying to strike an appropriately casual note in spite of what he was feeling. Good old lighthearted Paul.

"You actually agree with me on something?" She turned around and gave him a puzzled smile. She was wondering what the heck he was doing there. With her there was always a subtext.

Paul said, "I do agree. There's a link between the crash and the murder. Why is LeBlanc missing? It's a red flag. I talked to Connie Bailey on the phone again and she hasn't heard from him either. She's determined to prove Skip Bailey wasn't responsible. She'd be hiring me if you hadn't." They talked on for a while, gossiping about Matt and Andrea and the kids until Paul looked again at his watch. "I better let you get to the sandman." He got up.

"See you tomorrow." But the puzzlement never left her eyes. She couldn't place him here in her house or anywhere in her life.

Probably that thought was what compelled him to do one final supremely stupid thing before leaving. He intended only to touch her arm, offer a little physical nourishment.

"Nina," he said, and her name came out sounding like it tasted in his mouth, sweet and thick as butterscotch. He pulled her into his arms, slipped his hands inside the robe and around her back, felt her breasts pillow against his chest, breathed in her hair, and kissed her.

When he let her go, she closed her robe and handed him his crutches. "You stand up pretty well without them when you want to."

"Briefly," he said. "All too briefly."

"Is that why you came tonight?"

279

"No," he said.

"Good thing," she said, "or maybe I would fire you after all."

After Paul left, Nina took another compulsive walk around the house, snapping the windows and locks closed, making sure all was secure. She considered leaving Bob's room alone—sometimes he slept so lightly—but found she couldn't.

Tiptoeing in, she moved toward the window, twisting the lock just enough to make sure all was well. From Bob's window, she could see Paul's van. Acting in place of the moon, the truck's dome light illuminated his every awkward move. Paul had managed to open the van door, but had not managed to get himself inside yet.

His touch reminded her of how lonely she was. There was comfort in Paul. But, she thought, I never should have brought him back up here. It's finished. She began listing again all the reasons why: His anger sometimes blasted beyond all boundaries. He said he didn't want kids. He was too unpredictable.

Their liaison was knotty and emotional and full of trepidation on both sides. It bore no resemblance to the simple, unbridled love she had experienced first with Bob's father, Kurt, and later with her husband. With these thoughts rumbling around in her mind, she petted Hitchcock's head so vigorously the dog's eyes rolled back in ecstasy.

Paul's engine started up. His headlights

came on, and she heard his gears grind as he shifted into drive.

Turning back toward the door, which she had left open a sliver, she glanced down at Bob's bed intending to kiss him perhaps, intending to straighten his loose covers...ultimately it didn't matter what she had intended, because what she did was quite unplanned. She screamed.

"Bob!" She ran around the kitchen and bathroom, ran upstairs, scanned her room, and ran back into the living room. "Bob!" He had been sleepwalking lately, she told herself. He had to be here somewhere.

She cried out again, but there was no answer. The house, so small, did not have many places that might conceal a boy his size. Still screaming his name, she flung open the front door. Maybe she could catch Paul. Hitchcock ran outside, barking frantically.

She didn't have to worry. Paul had heard her, and was rushing along on the crutches back toward the house.

"He's not in his bed. He's gone! Just like before!"

"Come back inside," Paul said, taking her arm.

"No!" The empty house frightened her, because it was the only witness, and if it spoke, she didn't think she could bear listening.

Noting the lights coming on in the house across the way, Paul pushed her back inside. "Calm down. This isn't like last time. He can't have gone far. When did he go to bed?"

She struggled for a moment, grappling with the question, then felt her mind reengage. "When I did. About nine-thirty."

"Did he leave a note?"

She hadn't checked. Hurrying back to his room, she searched for one, tossing bedclothes on the floor, pushing papers off his desk and to the ground, and found nothing except his school notebook. Bringing it back with her into the living room, feeling the cold creeping up her bare legs, she set it on the table and began leafing frantically through. "There's got to be something..."

"Think," Paul said, an oasis of calm in a world that had suddenly fallen into wreckage. "Where would he go? You have to think."

Closing her eyes, she tried to reach inside the deep well of her mind. Bob had seemed happy lately. He and Troy spent weekends messing around on the computer or riding around on skateboards and playing hockey. He talked about school very little, but talked incessantly about joining a band.

Nikki's band. She opened her eyes, slamming the notebook shut. "He's at Nikki Zack's. Yes, that's where he is."

"Nikki's?"

Nina let her robe slip to the floor, pulled a sweater and a pair of jeans out of the dirty clothes basket and pulled them on, while Paul watched.

"Will you come get him?"

"We could call over there."

"Of course." She ran for her address book and punched in the number. "No answer," she said. "But where else would he go?" She called Andrea and said a few words, then hung up. "When I find him, I'm going to—"

"Let's go over to the Zack house," Paul said.

She grabbed her keys and wallet. "I'll drive. You should be able to get that cast in the Bronco."

"Nina," Paul said, "excuse me for being so dense. But you say she's Bob's friend. Are you afraid she's dangerous to him?"

By now they were on the porch. Nina locked the door, trapping Hitchcock inside. "I don't know what to think. Listen, maybe it would be better if I went alone. I mean..."

Paul was already climbing in.

Nikki didn't wait to consider the consequences. She ran down the hall into Daria's bedroom, pulled the covers off her mother, and shook her. "Wake up, Mom! Get up!"

Daria's eyes opened. She blinked twice to clear her vision, then said, "Oh, now suddenly I'm 'Mom' again." Sitting up, she fluffed a pillow behind her back. "Why did you wake me, honey? What's going on?"

But Nikki had her mother's jacket in her hands and was shoving Daria's arms inside. "You've got to go outside. Bob's in trouble."

"Bob's here?"

"He's outside. We have to be quick. Listen to me." She stood by the bed, her attention

283

riveted on the black hole of window where she thought she saw a flashlight glowing. Two flashlights... "When I went to Uncle Bill's that night, I took something, something of his that I thought might be ours." The words spilled out all over the place. She didn't have time to plan what to say. She didn't have time to explain. "Oh, forget that! Doesn't matter." The impotence she felt at the moment, that was important. Telling her mother this thing she never meant to tell, that was important. "Damn it!" she said.

"You were really there that night. Oh, Nikki."

"You know I was!" Nikki shouted, noting her mother's lack of real surprise, but putting the information aside immediately. She couldn't deal with Daria or what she had done, not now, not ever. They had to move forward and not look back. "Anyway, so I took this thing from Uncle Bill's and buried it out back before they put this ankle thing on me. Tonight, about ten minutes ago, Bob went out there to dig it up for me because I couldn't leave. I couldn't do it myself. Then this man came."

All dullness left Daria's narrowing eyes. "What man?"

"That's just it! He's a total stranger! It must be the same one who called me. He—he knew about the bag and he wanted it. I told him I didn't have it. I never expected him to come here tonight! It must be him! He saw Bob out there!" Nikki couldn't help herself. Tears flowed. "I can't go out there. I can't do any-thing."

Daria leaped up. Pulling a pair of dark leg-gings up over her nightgown, she stepped into a pair of shoes and moved fast across the room to the closet. She reached up to the top shelf, flinging clothing down to the ground around her feet.

Nikki's shock at seeing her mother with a gun stopped her tears. "What's that?"

"Grandpa Logan's shotgun," said Daria grimly. "A twelve gauge. Sounds like a cannon, under the right circumstances. Ought to give someone an awful scare."

"Is there shot inside?"

"It's loaded, yeah," Daria said, checking by cracking the gun in half and peering into the breech. "Grandpa always called number four buckshot primo antipersonnel materiel." She rushed to the back door. Nikki was right behind her.

"Step aside, honey," Daria said, trying to push Nikki out of the doorway.

Nikki stood her ground, arms outstretched in front of the door. "Mom, wait. You know how to shoot? What if you hit Bob!"

"Don't worry. Bob's going to be all right. I'm an ace shot."

Nikki continued to block the door. "And what about the guy. What if it's Scott?"

Daria stared. "I thought you said it was a stranger. Is it Scott?"

"Maybe," Nikki said. "I know you're mad at him... Just don't shoot anybody, okay?"

"I'll be careful." Almost out the door she turned abruptly to her daughter and planted a kiss on her cheek. "I like it when you call me Mom, honey," she said, and swept into the night.

Nina pulled up vaguely near the curb, slammed on the brakes, and jumped out of the car. While Paul opened the door laboriously, she made her way up the path to the house and began pounding on the door.

"Who is it?" a quivering voice asked from inside.

Paul, reaching the porch, hobbled up the steps.

"It's Nina Reilly and Paul van Wagoner. Nikki, open up. Please."

The door opened slightly. Nikki's puffy eyes scrutinized them.

"Is Bob here?"

She appeared to be looking out at something beyond them. Nina turned her head to study the street but noticed nothing unusual. "What's the matter?"

"Everything."

"What's wrong?" Nina asked. "Nikki, please. Where's Bob?"

Nikki pointed behind her. "He's out back."

"Why is he out there?"

"He came because I needed him to come." Her teeth chattered. "Don't get mad at him. Blame me," she said. "It's all my fault."

At that moment, they heard the first shot, and in that split second, Paul had them all on the wood floor of the porch. Before Nina could raise her head from the dust, he was struggling up.

One of Paul's crutches fell. He held his gun in that hand. When had he found the time to get a gun out? Nina wondered. "Where are you going?" she cried.

"Who's out there?" Paul barked at Nikki. When she didn't answer, just opened flooding eyes to his, he grabbed her by the arm and pulled her up. "Speak up, girl!"

"She has the shotgun! But she knows Bob's out there. She won't shoot Bob!"

"Who?"

"My mom!"

"But who is she shooting at?" Nina asked.

"Somebody's out there," Nikki said. "A man. He's after Bob."

"You two, stay on the ground," Paul said. Before they could say another word, he took off.

He made the crackling pain in his leg his friend. The more pain he felt, the faster he whipped the single crutch he had left toward the still light of a flashlight on the ground ahead. Moving as quietly as he could, allowing his face to contort all it wanted as long as it screamed silently, he made quick work of the backyard, found his way into the pine woods, and lodged himself behind a tree, breathing hard.

All around him, the night sounds chorused. An owl hooted. A distant frog sang a mating song. Hard as he looked, he could see no one in the thicket of trees ahead. Then a movement. The moon flickered. A boy running. A man running after him. Then the moon disappeared for good.

He heard a scuffle. Something nearby. Grunts. Bob yelling. Maybe Bob going down. But where were they? He turned his head back and forth, squinting, hoping to see something. Black against black. The heavy night sky had lowered over the woods and absorbed them.

"Give me that, you little bastard!"

"Let go!"

Paul moved to his left, seemed no closer. The sounds continued, here, there, everywhere was thrashing, brush flying.

Then, a rush. Someone running away. Bob? Paul finally thought he had a lock on his direction. Oblivious to the noise he was making, he followed the sound.

Then, another tackle, loud as a truck crash, and Bob went down, crying out, his voice wobbly, weak, from somewhere farther away than Paul had thought he would be. Bob was afraid, and Paul, somewhere in the woods nearby, heard the sound and felt his blood chill.

"Hang on, Bob!" Paul called, pure reaction now, abandoning all discretion. "I'm on my way!" He gave himself one more second to listen, to find a path through the shadows, unable to remember ever feeling so powerless. Then, panting, feeling his own sweat shivering over his skin, uncertain about which way to turn, he shoved blindly forward, one hand tearing through the brush, first this way, then that, as the sounds of struggling reverberated off tree trunks and drifted around, an ambient swirl of violence and fear.

Another shot blasted, coming from somewhere ahead of him. Then, dead ahead, a crack and a howl of pain. Deeper. A man's cry. Not Bob's.

Someone running.

He heard someone running, getting closer, then someone coming up on him. He had to make an instant decision. In the darkness, he could not identify the runner, but logic told him it was Bob. He let the first figure, light and fleet of foot, pass by. From no more than a few steps behind, sounding heavy as a lumberjack, another runner rushed through the woods.

Paul stepped out from behind the tree and brought the base of his gun down on the passing runner's shoulders. They fell together, the gun falling away into the darkness.

A rain of curses. Rising onto his knees, wielding his crutch like a battle-ax, Paul pounded on the crouched figure before him.

Something flashed. A knife?

Paul hit hard.

"Bloody hell!" said the man. Rolling swiftly out of reach he jumped up, and Paul tried to stand, but he couldn't do it, the leg wasn't going to let him this time. He was at his mercy...

The figure hesitated, as if considering whether to attack Paul or catch up with Bob or cut his losses, and then moved on, slowly at first, picking up speed as he got farther away.

His shadow faded into the trees.

Then, appearing out of nowhere, another figure. Without the benefit of time to consider, Paul again wielded his crutch.

A shotgun flew through the air, landing nearby. A body flopped forward and stayed down. Sobs muffled by the earth came out of it.

Female, Paul thought, holding tightly onto his lame, useless leg, trying to hold the pain at bay. Must be Daria. But where was Bob now? He listened, hearing nothing but the skittering of night animals and grumbling in the sky over the mountains. Bob had been running fast. He was far away by now. He couldn't catch up with the boy now.

He couldn't save him.

Sucking air into his lungs, he cursed out loud and pulled himself up to lean against a tree.

Daria quieted. Suddenly she arched, sat up, and scrambled around for the shotgun. When her hands found it, they found Paul's good foot, too.

"Won't do you any good, you know," he said, foot fast on the gun. "You only have two shots with this thing."

"Who are you?" she said. "Where's Bob? If you hurt him, I'll kill you, you bastard!" Lashing out, furious as a trapped animal, she beat on his leg with her fists, her vigor not a bit abated by an accompanying flood of tears.

"Hey. Stop that now. I'm with Nina," Paul said. "I'm on your side."

"We've lost him," she said, almost incoherent, arms falling to her sides. "I should have shot the guy. I should have killed him."

"It was too dark. It was too dangerous. You did exactly right."

"You should have stopped him. He came right by here. I heard him come right by here!"

"Bob had a good head start. He's fast. He got away. Don't worry."

He was worried. Had it been enough, holding the man back? Had he given the boy enough time to get away? He was not at his best lately. He had a crick in his soul.

Gathering his crutch to his side, he searched the area all around, found his gun, and tucked it safely away in his shoulder holster. He could not locate a knife. Had there been a weapon at all?

"Bob!" Daria shouted into the sky, past the woods, out to the street, to the houses, to the birds sleeping in the trees. "Bob, where are you?"

Silence.

"Where are you?" only this time, her voice came out quiet, prayerlike.

A wind murmured through the treetops and across the clearing, gathering momentum, gusting, hitting Paul in the face, harsh as a slap in the face.

"C'mon. Get up. Let's go find him..." Paul said.

"Daria?" A voice from far away. Bob's voice. "Is that you?"

"Bob?" she called back, but her emotions got the best of her and the word came out choked.

Paul picked up the shotgun and moved away from her. "We're over here!" he shouted.

In the distance, they heard a crashing through the brush heading toward them, then a long silence.

Bob stumbled out of the woods into the clearing.

"Are you okay?" Daria said. "Did he hurt you?" She was on her knees now, attempting to stand.

Bob ran over to help her up. "I'm okay," he said, waving toward Paul, hardly even seeming out of breath. Then, as if he had not just fought off an attacker, he made a polite introduction. "Daria, you know Paul van Wagoner?"

"We met. He damn near broke my leg," Daria said tearfully.

"Sorry," Paul said. "Bob. The guy who was chasing you...?"

Way in the distance, up the long street, an engine burst to life. They turned their heads in unison toward the street, listening as a car roared away.

"There goes our man," said Paul.

"Thank God you're all right, honey," Daria said, smoothing the hair on Bob's forehead.

"I'm fast, and I know these woods. I ducked around in circles. He couldn't catch me."

"But he did," Daria protested. "Twice, Bob. I heard it. I just couldn't find you."

"I got away fast the first time. Then, he just flew at me, knocked me down. I think he had a gun or a knife..."

"Oh...!" Daria wailed.

"But he didn't get a chance to use it, because just when he was starting to pull something out, pow, you fired! He just about jumped out of his skin. So I hit him with a branch. But he was catching up with me again," he cleared his throat, gulping, "and then after that something slowed him down, because after that he quit chasing me."

Paul patted him on the arm. "Good going, champ." He let his hand linger long enough to feel the boy trembling. "Let's go inside, shall we? A few explanations are in order." Paul handed Daria the shotgun to carry and they hoofed it toward the house, Paul bringing up the rear, as he so often did these days.

Once inside with hot drinks on the table in front of them, Bob, Daria, and Nikki clammed up. No mention was made of any knife. Bob, with Daria and Paul's collusion, was protecting his mother, which was just as well because Paul wasn't sure about the knife, and involving a weapon upped the ante considerably. He would call the police right now, if he'd found a weapon. Instead, downing a couple of ibuprofen at the sink, he let Nina do the interrogating.

"I don't know who it was," Nikki insisted, arms crossed, the very picture of stubbornness following her temporary lapse into emotional fragility.

"He came to the door first, then went after Bob. We were scared to death. So I got Grandpa's gun..."

"Who was it? Why would he come here? Why was Bob out in the woods in the dark?" Nina asked.

"I asked him to take out the trash..." Daria said.

"He was moving his skateboard out around to the back..." Nikki said.

"I went out to see the moon," Bob said.

The lies tumbled over each other. "There was no moon tonight," Nina said.

"It went behind the clouds, Mom, I swear! It was out before!"

Paul asked the same questions plus one about what the man was trying to take from Bob, only presented in stronger language, but threats, arguments, and demands were deflected. Nothing disturbed the wall the three had built. They had said all they were going to say about the matter.

Nina drove Paul back to his car, not saying a word to Bob, who slouched in the backseat.

"What's with you and Daria?" Paul asked. "You were shooting daggers at her."

"I was?" Nina said, surprised. "I didn't know it showed."

"Well?"

"I need to clear something up with her."

"And you don't want to talk about that now."

"No. But, Paul, I do want to say I'm glad

you were there," she said. "Bob said if you and Daria hadn't been there... You're better on crutches than... I'm sorry I doubted it."

"No problemo," Paul said. He started up the car, allowing himself the first small, safe moan of pain as he watched Nina's door close.

He hoped he could make it to the ER at the hospital before the screaming started.

After fighting the impulse to no avail, Nina again made a circuit of the house with Hitchcock, this time touching Bob's face to assure herself that it was he and not some camouflage body breathing so regularly in his bed.

Troubled by the thought that tonight she had tripped over the biggest lie she could remember him telling, and wondering if it was the biggest lie or just the biggest one she had caught him at, she tossed in her bed, disturbing Hitchcock on his rug by the bed, who then decided to scratch at the door.

Two in the morning. She let him out. She was up anyway. She punched in Nikki's number.

Nikki answered, sounding wide awake. "Is Bob okay?"

"He's sleeping," Nina said. "And now I want you to tell me what it is he was digging up for you out there."

"Did he tell you?"

"No."

"Nothing."

"Nikki, listen carefully. If you don't tell me right now, I'm off this case. Go find yourself another lawyer."

"Isn't that unethical or something?" said Nikki, outraged.

"So sue me. You put my son in danger. I want to know why, and I want to know right now."

"Okay. I was going to tell you tomorrow. Only it's nothing. You'll see. Just a buncha nothing."

"That's hard to believe."

"Yeah, I don't get it either. I mean why would my uncle bother to hide something worthless in such a slammin' good place?"

"Tomorrow, then."

"I'll try to fit you in," Nikki said.

16

NINA WENT OVER to Nikki's at nine A.M.

The weather had turned. As she drove along the lake, black clouds scudded over the mountains, making for the basin. A couple of canoes battled their way into shore. The tops of the trees tossed and swayed, blurring to gray in the mist. As she turned toward Nikki's house a powerful wind buffeted the heavy Bronco. She kept her hands firmly on the wheel, correcting its sway.

Her client answered the door, dressed in a black T-shirt that hung down to her knees. As usual, the curtains were drawn tight over the front windows, blocking out all natural light in the living room. The place was so shabby and cold that Nina wondered if she had done the right thing requesting the home supervision. Anyone would be depressed being locked up here.

In a corner a Macintosh computer monitor showed some windows, and Nikki coughed violently, as if the blast of fresh air through the opened door had shocked a system grown accustomed only to the musty indoors.

Before closing the door, she looked up and down the street.

"There's nobody," Nina said.

"Of course there isn't," she said, pulling the door shut and locking it behind her. She led Nina through the living room and into the kitchen.

Dark paneled cupboards inside and trees out-side blocked most of the light that might have had a chance to squeeze through the window above the sink. The main illumination was pro-vided by a dim bulb shaded by a fake Tiffany glass shade. They sat down at a small break-fast nook in a dark corner of the room. Nina said, "Where's your mom today?"

"Aunt Beth called. She's not handling things very well. Daria went over to calm her down." Nikki felt around in the pocket of a loose sweatshirt she wore open over her long T.

Nina had hoped to see Daria but was coming to the conclusion that she would just have to chase her down, because she was never around.

"It's here somewhere," Nikki said.

"It better be," said Nina without thinking.

She got a glare in return. Nikki slapped a velvet bag onto the table and folded her arms. "That's it. Uncle Bill's big bad treasure. I took it from his house the night he was murdered and buried it in the woods. Then I couldn't get back out to dig them up, so I asked Bob for help. Bob got the bag and slipped it to me last night."

"What's inside?"

"Open it."

Nina opened the drawstrings and dumped the contents of the bag out onto a piece of news-paper.

"See what I mean?" Nikki said. "Freakin' rocks!"

It did indeed appear to be so. In a small pile of plain dirt about a dozen small chunks of rock had scattered. Nina picked one up. Black rock. Disappointment didn't begin to describe her reaction. "But what is this?"

"I'll tell you what I hoped. I hoped it was like silver or gold ore. You know how in the old days, people mined for gold and silver up in Nevada? And we owned this land…"

"I heard about the land. Your mother sold it to your uncle."

"That's bull. He conned it out of her! Anyway, it was my Grandpa Logan's and before that, it was his dad's. My grandpa mined it out a long time ago, or so they said, so, when I first saw these rocks, I thought maybe they had silver in them and that was why Uncle Bill…" She frowned. "Well, you know. But they're just…rocks! I showed them to Daria last night right here where we're sitting. We rubbed some of them to expose that black stuff that looks glassy. She actually knows a little about silver and gold ore. She says it isn't the right kind of rock. It looks like petrified wood or something, except for how dark it is."

The scenario Nikki had invented was falling apart. No treasure meant no con. Then she had gone to her uncle's house for nothing, and her uncle hadn't conned anybody.

How painful it must be for Nikki, realizing all her trouble had come out of a fool's errand. She seemed to be waiting for Nina to belabor the point in standard adult fashion but Nina didn't see any need to add to her misery.

Turning the largest stone over in her hand, Nina noted that the surface was brittle. Flakes came off readily in her hand, although the stone beneath remained intact. "Let's move into the light," she suggested. They did, but the lighting in the house was dim at best and a dark overhang of sky outside did not help matters.

"See here." Nikki pointed at a place in the stone where the gray outside had fallen away to reveal glossy black. "Obsidian, maybe? I tried looking it up on the Web."

"I don't know."

"It's not very valuable, obsidian, unless maybe you're a Native American a couple hundred years ago making arrowheads."

"No, I guess not, although we'll ask someone more knowledgeable about that." In the poor light, she couldn't see much, just the kind of thing Bob stuffed his pockets with when he was little, something with a little visual interest in the reflective sheen that peeked out of the rubble here and there, but nothing particularly exotic otherwise.

"It's just junk," Nikki said. She began collecting the rocks and putting them back into the fabric pouch.

"But why would he go to so much trouble to hide rocks?" Nina asked. "That's a really unusual hiding place."

Nikki shrugged. "I was sure they'd be something special, too, that's why I had Bob dig them up. Thought I must have missed something the first time I looked at them."

"But the man who chased Bob—he thought they were valuable."

"He was just guessing, like me. The newspaper article on the hearing said that neighbor saw me take something. Junk is what I took. I'm such a loser. I ruined everything going over there. I caused the whole—it's all over. I might as well..."

"Do you think you caused the whole thing?" Nina said.

"I didn't say that! Don't try to get me mixed up!"

"You might as well what?"

"Nothing. Don't cross-examine me, I'm not in the mood."

"Listen to me," Nina said. "We are in the middle of a process, Nikki, a hard process for you, unbearable sometimes. I know you feel scared and alone, but you're not alone. Besides your mother and aunt, you have me. I'm with you." She took Nikki's hand and looked intently into the girl's eyes. "You're going to have to start trusting me, or this will crush you."

"What do you want me to do?"

"Don't give up hope. Let me help you through this. All right?"

"Okay," Nikki said in a small voice.

"Promise me you won't do anything to harm yourself."

"I'll stick around for the bitter end."

"Good girl." Nina got up to leave. "You'd better give those to me."

Nikki was looking down at the floor. "I just wanted a fair price for the land," she said, "so we could pay the landlord and not have to live in the car or a tent. Daria spends money we don't have. She brought home the guitar and the amp. I can't imagine how she got that credit card. I came home one day and she had her boyfriend of the moment installing the computer in the back room. She wouldn't let me take it back. But the fact is, we can't make the payments, so it is going back, and so's my guitar, and it won't be long. The collection agencies call to threaten us every day."

"You had all that wrapped up in these little rocks?" Nina said gently.

No answer.

"Does your mother use the computer?"

"She can't even turn it on."

"So she bought it for you. And the guitar?"

"Yeah. For me. Without them, I wouldn't be—have, I mean—anything going on."

"It's complicated," Nina said.

"It sure is."

"That guitar looks to me like somebody's dream."

"Yeah. I want to be in a band. I've been writing songs and practicing a lot. Daria never complains, even late at night, just says, 'Follow your passion and everything else will follow.' Life's so easy for someone like her, just full of lucky charms and prayers that get answered. I wish it were that easy for me," Nikki went on, handing Nina the pouch. Childlike, she had moved to a new mood. "When do I get this thing off my ankle, anyway?" she asked. "It's a pain when I shower."

"After the trial, Nikki. Or sooner, if we win the next hearing."

"What's that?"

"It's called a 995 hearing, after the Penal Code section that describes it."

"When is that going to happen?"

"I'm thinking mid-July. I'll let you know as soon as the papers are filed."

"After we win my case," Nikki said, "I might leave Tahoe. Maybe go to the desert or maybe a big city."

They both looked at the bag on the table.

"Did your mother decide to call the police about last night?" Nina asked.

"Sure. Made sure they got a good look at Grandpa's unregistered, unlicensed firearm, oh, and of course rushed to tell them all about how it was shot recently. And pointed out the trail of blood out there in the woods to make 'em really jump for joy."

The trail of blood was an exaggeration. There had been some blood but Paul said the man might have cut himself on rough bark. "I see," Nina said.

"I'm like my father," Nikki said suddenly, and Nina felt the lurch as the girl took an awkward step toward her. She hardly breathed, waiting for her to come closer.

"After we win," Nikki repeated, and this time, Nina heard the hope embodied in the repetition, "I'll be in a band, too. He's a rocker like Steve Tyler. I have a tape of his music he gave to everybody one Christmas, and he's really good. He played in the house band at Harrah's here and in Vegas and all over. Maybe I'll see him on TV one day." She flung her hair forward onto her cheeks and hid behind the cascade of brown hair.

As she walked out the front door to her car, Nina stashed the bag in her jacket pocket. Once in the car, deciding rocks in her pocket would rapidly demote her new powder blue jacket to cheap-looking rag, she moved the bag into the so-called secret compartment hidden in the armrest between the driver's and passenger's seats and set off.

Of course, given the deserted neighborhood and deserted street, the one car for miles would start up immediately behind her. Looking for a place to pull over and let the roadhog hog on ahead, she slowed at the corner. The pickup pulled swiftly in front of her and came to a dead stop.

Stalled, probably, she thought, frustrated. She looked at her watch. She had an appointment in ten minutes. She unrolled the driver's side window and looked out, then gave a brief honk. When no engine started up and no one emerged from the truck after a minute, she tried to make it around, but the street proved too narrow.

Suspicion and fear rose up in her. She hadn't seen the pickup when she went in. She threw the gears into reverse, ready to haul out, then thought about Nikki alone in the house. She didn't want to leave her with a potential threat. So she reached for the hammer she kept under the seat with other important items, cautiously opened the door, and approached the silent vehicle from a safe distance, ready to run.

But it was empty. She walked around the front to make sure. Now she was very suspicious. Where had the driver gone? She put a hand up to shade the tinted window in the rear, but could see nothing inside except a clutter of clothing and tools.

Returning to the Bronco, she called Nikki. "Lock your doors," she said. "I'm about a block away, and there's an empty pickup blocking the road here that I don't like the looks of."

The driver seemed to have abandoned his wheels. He could be watching from the forest along the road. Nina put the Bronco in reverse and wound her way up another side road and away.

Rain splattered onto the window. She slowed down, cruising slowly through an area of National Forest that would eventually open out to the highway.

She was almost to Al Tahoe when she looked into the driver's mirror and saw the corner of a denim sleeve in the back seat.

The sleeve was moving, and before she could breathe, an arm clamped around her neck. "Keep driving," a man said. "You and I have some business."

Was it Him?

She drove because she had no choice and because her hands were on the wheel and her foot was on the accelerator. She let the adrenaline pump through her body, urging her to get away.

She didn't dare look in her rearview mirror, although the temptation was unbearable, but if she saw Him there what then? She might die of fear...

Not a good day to die.

She slammed on the brakes and the Bronco jerked into a skid. The arm loosed, pulling back from around her neck, and she felt a heavy body slam into the back of her seat as she herself was thrown forward into the seat belt. Holding tightly to the wheel, she ducked her head and steered straight for a gully full of water. The Bronco stopped cold.

She yanked the steel buckle of the seat belt and tumbled out of the driver's side. Scrambling to her feet, she ran across the empty slick road toward a driveway.

She heard a car door slam and despite herself turned her head back for one frantic look.

He had fallen out of the back door into the gully and her view was blocked by the Bronco, but she heard him grunt as he hit. She went down into a crouch behind a boulder guarding the driveway and saw feet in brown boots and heard splashing, then saw a figure rush into the woods across from her.

Silence. A duck quacked somewhere. A few last drops of rain fell on her forehead.

He was gone. Trembling, she walked back across the street to the Bronco, searching the back seat and the cargo area. Nothing that wasn't hers, but he had been hiding in the back seat as she drove, preparing to do—what? Her hammer lay ready on the front passenger seat, along with her purse. She jumped back into the driver's seat and locked the doors and rolled up the windows and sat huddled and shivering. After a moment, when her ability to move had returned, she gunned the Bronco out of there and drove like hell to the office.

Had it been him? Not the man who had chased Bob, but Him—the one who seemed always to be roaming around just at the edge of consciousness, not satisfied with having killed her husband, wanting to hurt her or Bob. Her personal devil, who everyone from the police on down said had cut and run many months ago, who never did the expected. He had assumed an almost supernatural aspect in her mind. She felt that he had linked himself to her and that he would be irresistibly drawn back. A devil!

Let it be anyone but Him.

She skidded into the parking lot, still breathing hard. She turned the engine off, unsnapped the gray plastic of the armchair compartment, and pulled out the pouch. So he hadn't gotten it!

It was not until she grabbed her briefcase and reached into the back seat for her jacket that she realized the jacket was missing.

Her expensive, brand-new Donna Karan jacket! Her first reaction was relief. It wasn't Him, it was the other one, the one who wanted the rocks. The case shrank to ordinary proportions again. The man in the woods had thought she put the pouch in the jacket. He had watched her on Nikki's porch, then.

Nikki's treasure, pebbles collected by a kid, worthless. He must not know. Maybe Sykes had switched pouches on him. She jumped down onto the pavement, leaned against the wet door, and poured the stones out into her hand again. Black and dirty little rocks, not gold, not silver, nothing to steal, terrorize, murder for...

The squall had blown through and bleached clouds made way for a sky the fresh rich blue of an oil painting. A ray of sun pierced through the blowing clouds to shine onto her palm. She picked one of the chunks up and twisted her hand in the light.

The glossy surface clarified into transparence. She looked inside the rock, through it really, and finally saw its secret: pale green, violet, pink flames shooting out sparks of rainbow light.

PART FOUR

In his dream, the giant lizard tries to say something. It staggers. He has delivered the death blow and is no longer afraid. Now the lizard is finally afraid. It cries out because it wants to live after all.

He looks down. The lizard is shrinking! It's shrinking and shrinking, and suddenly it runs up his pants leg. It can't be killed! It runs up his pants and under his belt and up his chest and he claps his hand to his own mouth but too late. The lizard has run into his mouth and is now lodged inside him.

17

"BLACK FIRE OPAL," said the bearded geologist, inspecting the rock with one eye to a jeweler's loupe. "Really large, too. Maybe ten carats uncut. Flawless, to my eye."

Nina had turned out of her office parking lot, driven straight to the local rock shop, then called Sandy on her cell phone to ask her to cancel her appointments for the early afternoon, and endured Sandy's ire. She couldn't wait to find someone who could tell her more about the rocks. Unfortunately, the shop was closed. Possessed by a passionate curiosity, she had driven over Spooner Pass, down to the high desert and around Washoe Lake to the brick buildings of the University of Nevada in Reno. There she had knocked on doors until somebody directed her to Tim Seisz's office. A professor of geology for twenty-seven years, Seisz specialized in mineralogy, and had a real passion for his work. Nina knew him from a previous case but had never seen his office.

The unpretentious room was cubicle sized with a brown metal chair on wheels and an overstuffed bookcase. All spare surfaces sported dusty rock samples in every color and size. Bald and heavyset, the professor was in his forties. Wild strands of gray and brown beard stuck out of his face like metallic bristles on a scrub brush. His rugged, multi-pocketed shorts revealed long brown legs. His dusty brown boots were crossed on a mottled oak desk, and as he leaned back in his chair examining the specimen with interest, the hinges squeaked.

Nina stood in front of the stuffed bookcase.

"Black fire opal?" she said. "What is that? I've never seen anything like it."

"It's rare," Seisz said, looking at the rock, holding it and turning it in the sunlight coming through his window.

"But...opal is white, isn't it?"

He nodded. "That's the background you most commonly see in jewelry. But the ground mass can be many colors. Honey-colored. Milky-white, gray, brown, orange, or red. Translucent to opaque. Of course the more transparent stones are preferred, because the light penetrates and you can see the light show on the surface better."

She was thinking about how she could turn the stones over to Henry McFarland without making Nikki appear guiltier than ever. They were hot in every sense of the word.

"What are you doing with these?" He showed slightly crooked teeth in a smile, a relief after Dylan Brett and his bionic crew. "You didn't even know it was opal."

She put aside the question. "Well, I first saw it in very dim light." She had spent much of the drive to Reno meditating over the stones sitting in the sunlight on her dash, but her meditations had nothing to do with their geologic origins. She had been seduced by the glitter of colors that shifted like rainbows. Closing her eyes at a stop sign, she had still seen the same brilliant flashing colors on the inside of her eyelid. They were covered with dirt and a crust of grayish-green rock, and they smelled like dirt. But inside they were beautiful, magical, precious. Whatever Seisz might say, or any expert, the stones had infected her with a strange fever.

"You can see the colors even in dim light if you get the angle right," Seisz was saying.

"We had no idea what we were looking at. Where do you find this kind of opal?"

"Where did you find these?"

"I asked first," Nina said. "And that's a long story. Don't want to bore you."

He picked through the collection of stones and found another one to study.

"Mostly in Australia," he said, pulling a book off the shelf nearby. He flipped to a double-page spread of a dry desert setting. In the foreground, a man's dirty hand held a collection of what appeared to be pebbles. They were very similar to Nikki's rocks. He thumped a finger on the picture. "Those come from a famous mining area called Coober Pedy. You've heard of it?"

"No."

"Mintbee Mine or Lightning Ridge...ring any bells?"

Nina shook her head. Experts in other fields often impressed her, but just imagine spending your life studying rocks, she thought. How deadly. On the other hand, she liked the little office and the big man with his tanned brown pate. This office held what her office never held, serenity and the implacable march to knowledge through pure science, as opposed to her office, which played host to some wild experiments in legal alchemy.

It's early, she told herself again, trying to incorporate this new information into the case. The plane crash, the plastic surgeon, the samurai sword, and now Australian opals. Wildly divergent elements. She could see no rational pattern emerging, and so far the usual trusty intuition wasn't kicking in to help her find one.

"Those places are well-known sources for black fire opal," Tim said. "It's rare. Found in only a few places in the world."

Nina picked up a stone and turned it to reveal the magical flash of colors.

"These are dry samples," he went on, "which is good. Shows they are relatively stable. Opal is mostly water. The black opal is a product of volcanism. At some point in time, a volcano erupted, and hot ash drifted over the surface, burning plants right down to the root, but not necessarily disturbing the soil where they grew, and leaving a hollow in the shape of the root or twig. Water and silicates mixed with volcanic by-products dripped in over a few million years and formed opaline deposits. At least, that's the common scientific explanation, that black opal is a kind of fossil."

Getting into it, the consummate professor now, eyes traveling to faraway places, he said,

"If you want, I'll tell you all about the clay you find opal in, bentonite, and how it's composed of a mineral called montmorillonite. But I've noticed people who don't share my...um...what my wife used to call my obsessions, glaze over when I talk in three syllables or more."

"What can you tell me about these particular samples?" Nina asked.

"I believe pieces this large are quite unusual. Of course, until you rub them, you won't know if they are crazed or cracked." Again, he looked through the loupe. "However, most of what I can see looks good."

"I'm not following."

"Rubbing is grinding down the outside of a rough opal to get a better picture of where the opal is, and how much there is in the rock. Crazed describes a superficial network of fine cracks that happen when opals dry. Crazing also happens spontaneously, or during the cutting process, which keeps things interesting, doesn't it? Might have a fabulous-looking stone that can't take the processing."

"You mean...one of these stones, even if it looks perfect right now..."

"After it's rubbed and you can check out its fire, the dominant color, its translucence..."

"Might get...crazed later?"

Tim laughed. "Right. You never know how long a stone may last. Obviously, the ones that have been dried and around for a while are going to do better. How long have these been dry?"

"I don't know. They were stored in a moist environment until some weeks ago. Then they were...er...buried. So, not dried completely yet."

He reacted to the burial concept with scientific neutrality, ignoring the irrelevant fact. "Store them in a dark place, in a zip bag with a paper towel or something to absorb moisture. Don't subject them to too much bright indoor or outdoor light for a few months."

"You said something about 'cracking.' Is that different from crazing?"

"A crack is a fracture. It's a deeper flaw."

"Okay," she said. "Can you evaluate these stones for their...uh...stability? I guess what I mean is, are they precious gems or worthless junk?"

"I could look into that for you. It's not something I know offhand. I'm not much involved in the market."

Someone knocked. Fortunately, the door opened out into the hall.

"Dr. Seisz?" With shoulder-length blond hair and abs of steel defining a tanned midriff, the girl waiting there had that trendy Britney Spears look. Seisz gave her the same polite regard he gave Nina. His ruling passion really was rocks.

"I'm having trouble studying for the midterm," said Britney's clone. "I wondered if..."

"I have a class to teach in just a few minutes, but if you want to come back here after, I'll be glad to go through your work with you."

"I knew I could count on you." The clone

316

batted her eyes, but Seisz had returned to the rocks on his desk. She left, and only Nina observed the casual swaying down the hall which was probably habitual but was surely wasted on this particular professor.

"So you're saying this is black fire opal from Australia," Nina went on. "Assuming it's not defective. Is it valuable?"

"No, no, no," said Seisz, shutting the Australia book. He smiled. "You've misunderstood. I never said this came from Australia. I said that's where you find almost all black fire opal."

"If you find it there, and it doesn't come from there... I'm confused."

"It could be Australian. However, there is one other place in the world where black fire opals are found and it's probably a much more likely source of your hoard."

"Which is..."

"The Virgin Valley."

"And the Virgin Valley is... ?"

"About a hundred miles from Winnemucca right here in Nevada. Oh, and maybe you don't know this. Black fire opal is the Nevada state gem."

"Really." She didn't even know the state gem of California, if it had one.

"Yes. If I were to hazard a guess, these opals come from the Virgin Valley, up in the Sheldon National Wildlife Preserve area. Opals found up there have a perhaps undeserved reputation of being more brittle than the Australian blacks. I think that's arguable. Depends on the water content. Some are, some aren't." He touched a stone in her hand. "This is big. Never saw one so large or so immaculate. There have been some incredible finds up there, so I've heard. One over ten thousand carats."

"Wow," said Nina.

"Yeah."

"Tell me something, Tim," Nina said. "How does someone become a geologist?"

"I take it you're not asking about my course of study at USC."

"No."

"I was born to it, maybe the same way you were born to practice law. I see it as a micro-philosophy versus macro. You deal with people and their everyday woes. I deal with the grand scheme. Daily events, people, their little worries, don't interest me much. I'm also a pilot. I love being up there, looking down at the Earth. Speculating about what formed those hills or why that river ran dry eons ago."

"But...it must be hard on a marriage." It just came out. She had no business...

He broke into a hearty chuckle. "Oh, yes. I should have said my ex-wife earlier. She grew tired of my everlasting field trips and took a hike of her own. So you see, I'm not excused from being human! Believe me, I come down to earth now and then, despite my godlike perspective."

She knew he was making fun of himself, and she appreciated it.

"I don't ignore the human links entirely," he

said. "In fact, I'm quite interested in the folklore associated with stones. I'm working on a book. Don't know if anyone will be interested besides me, but it amuses me to find connections between elemental Earth and ancient cultures."

"Do you know any stories about opals?"

"Oh yes. The stones have a long human history. Centuries ago, people called opal 'opthalmios.' "

"What's that?"

"Means eye-stone. It's a word they used in the Middle Ages. People then thought opals formed in the eyes of children."

Nina thought of Nikki.

"The stones were believed to have a magical power: anyone who wore opal became invisible. That's why they also called the opal the 'patron of thieves.' "

"Really? What an unfortunate name." Nikki again, the child-thief. If the samurai sword could hold souls, then opals could too, and Nikki's soul seemed to have attached itself to the dirty gems. Nina couldn't see how they could protect her, though.

"And as for the question you didn't ask, whether that secret vein of it you probably found somewhere up there in the Virgin Valley is quite a find, my best guess is yes." He lifted himself out of his chair, piled books into his arms and went toward the door. "Is it ever."

Back at the office after the eighty-mile-return drive, Sandy welcomed Nina with a grunt. The outer office was, for a change, empty.

319

"I said I'd be back by two," Nina said. "Nobody here?"

"I thought I'd save myself an afternoon round of cancellations," said Sandy. "In case you didn't make it."

"You canceled everyone?"

"Every mother-loving one."

"I got a speeding ticket coming back."

"I'm sure you deserved it."

Sandy squinted at her, and the way she looked straight through Nina to the molten core Nina took such care to hide made her feel uncomfortably exposed. Needing to deflect the focus from her emotional shortcomings to something else, Nina removed the bag from her briefcase, spilling the stones out on the desk. Under Sandy's decent halogen lamp, with more of the dirt rubbed off the surface of the stones, the opals glinted and flickered.

"Pretty," she said noncommittally, but Nina noticed she did not take her eyes off the stones as she spoke.

"They're called black fire opals."

"This is something to do with Nikki Zack, isn't it?" Her eyes dug into Nina's face.

Nina shrugged. She didn't know how she would handle the issue of Nikki's acquisition of the opals, and until she considered the ethical questions and made a decision about that, it was best to say nothing. She gathered up the stones.

"Joe took me mining for opals in the Virgin Valley years ago," Sandy said unexpectedly.

"Really? How'd you do that?"

"There are a couple of places up there that are open to fee mining. You pay by the day to pick through the tailings or even poke around in the bank. Use a pick and shovel. Spritz the chunks and you can see the lights inside."

"Did you come back with anything?"

"Rocks. No lights. It's not that easy."

"Where is the Virgin Valley anyway? I checked the map but couldn't really find it."

"Northwestern part of the state, almost in Oregon. It's something like twelve miles long and a couple miles wide." The phone rang and she picked up. "For you," she said, handing it to Nina. "It's Paul."

Nina handed the phone back. "I'll take it in my office. Say, Sandy, if I wanted to go up there and mine...are those places still open?"

"Every summer. I'll bring you a brochure."

"Thanks."

Sandy nodded.

"Uh, I have to apologize for leaving you in the lurch today. Sometimes I just..."

"Hmph."

"How's Linda doing?"

"Sobering up. She agreed to go into detox. We're driving her to Placerville tonight. Now, you better get in there and talk to that man," Sandy said.

"I'm waiting outside in the lot," Paul said on the phone. "Too hard to get in and get out and all that. I've got to show you something."

"I'm on my way."

· · ·

"Where's your van?" she said after hurrying outside. Paul was sitting inside an unfamiliar car, the motor growling, his blond hair striking against the bright color.

"Gone," he said. "This is what I wanted to show you."

"You bought this? A new car!"

"What do you think?"

He sounded like a little boy. She made an instant decision not to tell him what really flashed in her mind. You didn't put a damper on adolescent wet dreams. You politely overlooked them.

He had bought a cherry-red Mustang convertible with a white canvas top.

"Sensational," she said, placing her dusty shoe onto the pristine floorboard.

"V8," he said cheerfully. "Brand-new, even though it looks classic."

"What happened to the van?"

"I'm selling it to Wish," he said, stroking invisible dust off the dash with his left hand while he started the engine with his right. "Didn't even make a very good deal. I wanted this one too much to dicker."

"I'll miss the zebra-skin upholstery."

"You mean the leopard-skin bed." He looked at her out of the corner of his eye. "Maybe Wish will preserve it for posterity."

"This is...not exactly practical."

"Depends on what you use it for."

"Hard to picture you going off-road in this. If a case ever called for it."

"True. I considered a metallic-blue SUV, four-wheel drive, but I just couldn't get passionate about it."

"What's gotten into you, Paul?" she said. "You've got a broken leg you won't explain, an attitude that won't quit, and now, out of the blue, a brand-new car. So many changes. I'm thinking..."

"What?"

"Oh, never mind."

"I know what you're thinking."

"Oh?"

"And frankly, my dear, I don't give a damn."

They rode along with the tourist traffic on Lake Tahoe Boulevard in silence for a while. Paul turned into the McDonald's and bought them both coffee. Then he drove them back to Regan Beach and they sat in the car watching the kids wading in the lake.

Nina thought the choice of location was oddly appropriate. They weren't more than a few blocks from the house where William Sykes had been murdered. That was what they needed to be thinking about right now, not messing around with low leather seats. Nina didn't like the car. She didn't like any changes at all right now.

"Something disturbing has happened," she told Paul. She related the whole story about Nikki's rocks and the man who had climbed into the back seat of the Bronco.

"Did you call the cops?"

"I thought about it, but I can't even describe the guy. He didn't hurt me."

As Paul listened, his powerful body gave the impression of growing larger until he barely seemed to fit in the car.

"The worst thing was that I thought at first it was the other one," she said, and he understood immediately.

"No," he said. "Stop scaring yourself like this."

"I can't control it," she said. "I sense him around every corner. The only way I can protect myself and Bob is to put my head in the sand and hide. I do my work and then I just want to go home and lock the doors and check and check and check the locks, and then I still can't sleep."

"He's long gone. I told you that."

"You don't know he's gone. You only think he's gone. You don't know him like I do, Paul. How he thinks."

"You might be surprised."

"Anyway. Let's just drink coffee and watch the kids and the sky." They did that for a while, and Nina calmed down, but Paul seemed to have fallen into deep thought.

"What are you going to do about Bob?" Paul said eventually.

Startled, Nina didn't answer.

"How are his grades?"

"Sliding a little, but still okay."

"How's his mood?"

"Boomeranging from one extreme to another.

He sinks into moods. He's jumpy. I tried to put my hand on his cheek yesterday and he flinched. He has nightmares. And now— going over to Nikki's house—he knew better."

"How are you going to stop it?"

"I don't know. I think I'll call Kurt and talk to him about it."

"Kurt can't do much from Germany."

"No."

"If I was his dad, I'd take him out behind the woodshed. He thinks he can get around you on everything."

"So shall I beat the tar out of him?" Nina said, gloomy. "I'll tell you, Paul, I feel like it sometimes. Matt recommends it too. Beat his butt, he says."

"I like Bob," Paul said. "More now that he's older. I think he's going to be all right. Of course, I'm speaking of years from now."

Nina shook her head.

"When do I get to see the opals?" Paul said. In answer, she opened her purse and took out the pouch and handed it to him. She was keeping them with her. He took out a chunk of raw opal and went through the same double take she had when the sun hit it. When she told him they were probably from the Virgin Valley, Paul said, "Then they're not from Daria and Beth's claim."

She managed to get her coffee swallowed, barely. "Why not?"

"It's in my report. Their claim is eighty or ninety miles from the Virgin Valley. Nowhere near. Might as well be Australia."

"Not good, Paul. Speaking as Nikki's lawyer."

"Not good? Why?"

"Well, it could have been a main point in the 995 hearing coming up. If I could have established that the opals did come from that property, I could attack the felony-murder rule that's keeping her in the adult criminal system."

"And if you can't?"

"She'll go in as an adult."

"And that's not good."

"She might get out when she's in her forties," Nina said.

Paul was silent for a minute. Then he said, "Think she did it?"

"No."

"I don't think she did it either."

"Well, that's a first," Nina said, secretly thrilled. To have Paul on her side somehow added weight to her position. "I don't think I ever heard you say that about one of my clients. It's encouraging."

"Maybe, instead of worrying about legal shenanigans this time around, we should concentrate on finding out who killed the good doctor."

Nina folded her arms.

"Not that I don't highly esteem and honor your respectable, integrity-saturated profession," he added.

"So what's your plan?"

"Wish is over at Prize's right now trying to find out what he can about the man Linda saw.

If that doesn't work, we'll check the description with Daria and Beth and see if they know anything about him."

"You do that," Nina said. "I'll get to your reports right now, Paul. Then I'm going to take advantage of the client cancellations and go over to the law library and do a little research for the 995. Can I use your phone for a second?" She picked out Daria's number. Nikki answered. Daria was gone again. Nina hung up, frustrated. She was dying to hear an explanation of what Daria had been doing at Dr. Sykes's house that night. Why hadn't she told anyone? She hated knowing, hated what it probably meant.

Shutting the door with some care so as not to leave marks on the brand-spanking-new wax job on the Mustang, she waved good-bye to Paul. He revved up the car and tore out of the lot, showing off. She walked slowly back to her office, thinking, whatever gets you through the night. Wasn't that what John Lennon, keen philosopher of the twentieth century, had said? If a red Mustang did the trick, however temporarily, maybe she ought to be in the market.

18

IN ADDITION to a series of closely scheduled clients that she could not miss the next morning, Nina had a lot of catching up to do. She spent a harried half hour returning emergency phone calls. Pausing for a breath, she took a sip of her coffee and found it cold.

"What's the afternoon look like?" she said, passing Sandy's desk and heading for the drip coffeemaker in the conference room.

"Busy."

"Any holes at all?"

"One big one. Nothing scheduled between twelve-thirty and three."

"Perfect." Carrying her freshly brimming mug very carefully, Nina stopped in front of Sandy. "I want you to reserve tickets for the one o'clock magic show at Prize's. Want to come?" She took a sip, relishing the hot Kona coffee. Black, freshly ground. Heaven.

"You ever seen one of those shows?"

"No."

"I have. I'll pass. You should be working, shouldn't you?"

"I am working. I've been trying to reach Daria Zack. Nikki told me this morning she's on stage there today. I thought I might catch her before or after the show."

"It's so urgent you'll spend the afternoon with a bunch of tourists watching a man in a tuxedo torture a hat?"

"I have to talk to her. And I like magicians."

"You would."

She called Andrea on the off chance.

"Why aren't you at the shelter today?"

"I'm part-time, remember? That means I come home and think laundry, do laundry, fold laundry, and accumulate laundry."

"Well, I'm going to a magic-show matinee. You want to come to see the magician with me?"

"Can he make laundry disappear? No? Then I'd better not."

Calling Caesars, Nina was surprised to find Paul still in his room at eleven in the morning. "Wake up, sleepyhead," she said, intentionally using the gratingly cheerful phrase he had used on her, aware from the stickiness in his voice that he had been dozing. It made her jealous. Anyone who slept regularly made her jealous these days.

"What time is it?"

"Time to get a move on. You're coming with me to a magic show at Prize's this afternoon."

"Four is my appointment with the crash investigator," he said.

"The show will be long over," Nina said. "You all right?" She wondered about that leg of his. She had seen little improvement in his condition. She had given up trying to find out how he had injured himself in the first place. He sidestepped all questions coming from that direction.

"Yep."

"The matinee, twelve-forty-five at Prize's. Got it?"

She could hear him scribbling. "Got it."

The rest of the morning passed in a blur of turmoil and trouble. She left with only a few minutes to spare, too late to catch Daria before the show. Parking next to the casino, she made her way to the small theater.

The line snaked like a heavy boa through the casino. After making sure the line was for people with reserved tickets, she found her way to what looked like the end and waited for Paul.

Most of the audience consisted of two-parent families with kids, but she didn't feel odd alone. An older couple in line ahead of her engaged her in conversation while the couple behind her took turns standing in line and dropping coins into the nearby slots. The husband, a man in a red aloha shirt who appeared to have gambled through one night and into the next day, if his wrinkled clothing and ashen skin spoke the truth, hit a $250 jackpot just as the line began to move. Tossing the coins into his straw hat, he whooped and screamed, gathered up his wife into a hug, and let the kids begin the long count for him.

Paul arrived just before Nina and the line moved into the anteroom and out of sight. "I had my eye on that machine," she complained. "My slot muscles were twitching in anticipation. I probably missed out on two hundred fifty bucks because of you." She handed over his ticket.

"Stop grumbling. I probably saved you from dropping a bundle. Mind telling me why we're here, not that I philosophically oppose frequenting dens of iniquity in the afternoon, it just doesn't seem your style."

She told him about Daria's car. He rubbed his forehead and said, "Ah. So that explains why you seemed so upset at Daria Zack that night in the woods. She was there the night of the murder, and she's been lying about it."

"Let's see what she says now."

They sat on faux leather seats at the back of the small theater in a raised, semicircular booth surrounded by regal purple velvet drapery. A brass railing kept them from the riffraff below.

"How'd we rate the plush seating?" Paul asked.

"Your handicap," said Nina.

"You're kidding."

"No. They said you might have trouble at one of the tables below. I wasn't taking advantage, I promise."

The theater, though not jammed, held a respectable crowd for an afternoon show. A big screen in one corner of the stage, now blank, would reveal, presumably, the details of the magic tricks to come. Projected on the stage curtains were the words "Phantasm of Fantasy." A waitress wearing a tuxedo which ended more or less at her waist where the black stockings began, arrived at their table to take orders almost before they had a chance to settle into their booth. Given the earliness of the hour, they went for what Paul called the fuddy-duddy choice, soft drinks.

The permanent midnight effect of the casino was enhanced by twinkling lights that offered little to no illumination, and a black ceiling sucked up any stray beams. Small gold individual candles flickered murkily on the tables. Paul fumbled for his drink, accidentally touching Nina's hand.

"Oops," he said.

The juggler, dressed in an electric-orange jumpsuit, bounced five balls off a drum to a maniacally inventive medley that somehow melded the Hallelujah Chorus with the 1812 Overture. He then began with the rings, big silver rings which he put around his neck, then pulled off as others flew in the air.

"I am so fired," he said after he dropped one. "Wonder where I'll be workin' next week."

Mesmero, the magician, handsome in his tuxedo, put on a good show riddled with doves and knives and thrills galore for the kiddies. Daria showed up about halfway through his act for one of many finales, the girl jabbed by swords in a box, who emerges unscathed to great fanfare. From a distance, with stage makeup, she could pass for any one of the fresh-faced assistants, but Nina sensed desperation in her frantic gestures and bright smile. When Mesmero finally closed the box on her with malevolent enthusiasm, Nina had to wonder how long she would last in the role.

After the audience had thinned out, Nina and Paul spoke with the stage manager, who agreed to allow them backstage for a word with Daria.

They located her in a closet-sized dressing area, her sequins tossed aside, wearing a shabby robe. After a distracted greeting, she resumed a conversation with Mesmero, who stood in the corner, hands on hips, looking years older, smiles erased, all his staged insouciance mysteriously disappeared.

"You almost got yourself killed in there!" he shouted. "You know as well as I do, you've got to move yourself the hell into position and stay the hell out of my way."

"I had a cramp," she said in a small voice.

"That kind of fuckup could ruin me! Just imagine the looks on everybody's face when the girl pops up gashed and bleeding!" Suddenly noticing Nina and Paul gaping in the doorway, he stalked out, turning one last time. "I'm sorry, Daria. You'll have to find yourself another gig. I'll help you find something if I can."

Daria turned to her mirror and wiped a cloth across her face, rubbing gently below her eyes. "He's sleeping with Regina, now," she said. "He just felt he owed me one last bow since he's the one who introduced me to Kyle and my part in the show fell apart and everything. But I'm hoping the backers will change their minds about my singing. And one of the girls just turned me on to this terrific voice coach..."

"My apologies if this is a bad time," Nina said, "but it's been really difficult getting hold of you."

"I'm glad you came. Nina, I'm sorry I blew my top at you after court the other day..."

"Forget it," Nina said. "That was a really rough day."

"I got your messages. I didn't get a chance to call back sooner. Rehearsals," she said, "not that they did me any good." She shrugged, looking rueful. "Go on, heap it on me," said Daria. "I take it something's up with Nikki's case? News?"

"It isn't news, Daria. Just a question. What was your car doing parked outside the Sykes house the night William Sykes was murdered?"

"My car?"

"Your car."

"Someone says they saw it?"

"Yes."

She chewed over the information.

"Were you there that night?"

"I was hoping no one would ever know. Let me get dressed and we can talk at the bar."

So it was true. Nina felt grim. She couldn't stand another second in the dark casino. She wanted to get outside into the summertime, where she could see more clearly. "No," she said. "At my office."

After the dim nether realms inside, the sunlight stung her eyeballs like buckshot. Agreeing to meet at the Starlake Building, they caravaned west up the highway, Daria in the lead. Although a frowning client waited across from Sandy, they went directly into the conference room and closed the door.

Outside on the lake, sails billowed and snapped in the stiff afternoon breeze. Daria sat facing the window, the sun in her eyes. Nina and Paul sat in front of it in the classic interrogation stance, although Nina hadn't intended it. Taking out a yellow pad and pen, she uncapped the pen and dropped the lid on the table. They all watched it roll off.

"Tell us about the night Bill Sykes died," Nina said.

Daria pulled back from the table, closing her eyes against the sun then opening them slowly, adjusting to the shadows. "There are some things I haven't told you that I want to say first about Nikki. Can I do that?"

"Of course." Nina didn't look at her watch. Her other client would just have to wait.

"Losing her father was an awful blow. This was six years ago now. We adults...well, there are things we can do to recover from someone leaving like that but a child has nothing but memories that are fading every day. She asked about him constantly: where was he; why did he leave us; when would he be coming back. At first, I was patient. Then, I just couldn't stand the constant reminders. After a while, I quit answering. I quit making things up to console her. And it worked, too. She stopped asking about him. I thought she had gotten over it. Now I think I was dead wrong about that."

"What was it like for you before...before your husband left?" Nina asked.

"Oh, we had such a blast. Beth and Bill lived here in town, and we were very close. My husband and Bill played cards together. We hiked in the mountains, stayed in tents, burned marshmallows. Then, after Nikki was born, we spent more time up at their house on the lake. We would swim..." Her voice faded, and she looked up at the ceiling, remembering. "Let me tell you something. Those years, I was really happy. No woman in the world could be any happier."

"What was your husband like?" Nina asked.

"I met Nicholas at a concert down in Riverside. He played bass. After we had Nikki, he did carpentry to keep the money coming in and keep us all safe and happy. He fixed up the house. I used to put in bulbs every fall so we had pretty flowers in the spring, because I didn't work for a couple of years when Nikki was young. He was crazy about Nikki. Taught her to ride a bike like a pro, up and down steep mountain roads before she was eight years old. He worked hard at his day job, too, even though music was what he loved. He specialized in remodeling jobs on run-down motels. For months after he left, these foremen would call asking for him."

The low roar of traffic outside on the nearby highway migrated in and out of her words. "I know Nikki blames me for driving him away. Maybe she's right. I've thought, gee, maybe the two of us were too much for him to support. It's true, we had fights about money. Then I thought, okay, he wanted to really go for the music. But... I loved that, I wanted him to succeed. I suppose he went to LA where the music business is, unless you're country, then you go to Nashville. He must have done all right somewhere, since he did send us money a few times. Anyway, I've thought and I've thought and I can't understand why he didn't take us if he had to go. Sometimes they just go and you never know why.

"Anyway, after he left we didn't see much more of Bill and Beth. We lived different lives. Bill was a real local celebrity. He gave to all the right causes and came out to root for politicians he liked. He was on TV all the time. He had a reputation to protect. Nikki and I didn't fit in. We were scraping the bottom. I was lonely. I started dating a lot. I didn't think I'd be much use to Nikki moping around for the rest of my life, so it was my way of recovering. I'm afraid Bill didn't think much of my kind of medicine."

"Did Beth agree with her husband?"

"Oh, she called now and then. But Bill was the strong one in that relationship. He pretty much put us out of his mind and Beth went along."

"That must have hurt," Nina said.

"I could understand. Really. I mean, they couldn't exactly call me up to see if I wanted to go golfing or weekend on Maui. Our lifestyles were different, that's all. But we're here to talk about Nikki, right?" She looked at Nina with the question, who nodded, even though she only half agreed.

"I suppose it was a couple of years ago that Nikki began to withdraw. I chalked it up to being that age. But she didn't get over it. She read all the time in her room and started complaining that she hated school.

"Maybe while she was in that room stewing one time she suddenly decided that Bill was, I guess you might say, snubbing us because we were poor. She's young. She took it like a needle in her heart. She thought that meant there was really something wrong with us, that we would be snubbed like that. Also, sometimes I have a hard time paying bills and that kind of thing. I'm disorganized and my income isn't very steady. Bill and Beth were prosperous, and we weren't. It made her mad. I tried to teach her about how negative feelings bounce back on you, but she—oh, she was fourteen. Anyway, I think that's when she began to hate Bill.

"The past couple of years with Nikki have been hard. She's struggling, just like everybody. Trying to find which way happiness is." Staring at the table, she threaded her fingers together. "Then Bill offered to buy my one-half share of the land Grandpa Logan left Beth and me. I didn't tell Nikki about it beforehand because I knew she would be opposed on principle. When Nikki came across the paperwork she decided Bill had cheated us. She talked about nothing—and I mean nothing—else. Night and day. All we had sacrificed. Our paradise in the desert, wasted, gone, thrown away on that conniving Uncle Bill.

"So that night, the night Bill died, when I discovered she wasn't in her bed, I jumped in my car and I ran over to Bill and Beth's house. I can't tell you what a state I was in...the thoughts hopping around like jumping beans. Because...she had made some threats. But you don't have my permission to tell anyone about this," she said quickly. "I'll deny ever saying it."

"Relax," Nina said. "I'm her lawyer, remember? I don't want her hurt. Go on, Daria. Tell us about the threats."

"They aren't important," she said. "Pretend I never mentioned threats. It was kid stuff. She was so hurt. Holding a child her age responsible for shooting off her mouth is what's criminal. Anyway, I got there about ten-thirty, parked my car, the telltale VW, and went up to the house."

"The front door..." Nina said.

"Was open, yes," Daria finished. "Otherwise I wouldn't have walked in like I did. Beth had called a few days before to tell me she was taking a trip to visit Jan in Los Angeles, so I knew she wasn't there. I went looking for Bill. I looked in the living room and walked through there and the hall and then I went into the study and found him lying on the ground. My God, what a sight!"

"Was he dead?" Nina asked. "Did you check?"

"I checked. He was dead. Still warm, though." She shuddered.

"You touched him," Nina said.

"I took his wrist. I looked at his eyes." Her own flicked around the room, as if avoiding the sight. "I think that was the worst moment of my life. I dream about those open eyes. I could see the pain in them even though he wasn't there. And then I had a sudden thought that almost stopped my heart. I thought of Nikki. I thought, maybe whoever did this to Bill is still out there. Maybe he's hurting her right now! I dropped his wrist and pushed open the double doors that led to the pool. I ran through them. And that's when I saw it, her sweatshirt, her favorite, hanging on a bush."

"No fingerprints on the inside of the door," Paul said.

"I was wearing gloves," Daria said. "My hands get cold at night!"

"No sweatshirt found at the scene," said Paul, checking some notes.

"That's because I took it home with me. I washed and dried it and put it into her dresser drawer before the police came."

"Did Nikki ever mention it to you?"

"I think she must have forgotten all about it."

"How do you know she lost it that night?" Nina asked. "Couldn't she have left it there on some other visit?"

"No. Because I had washed clothes that morning, and it was in the load. Oh, Nina, you have to save her." Nina and Paul looked at each other.

"Daria, does Nikki know you saw her there?" Nina asked.

"No."

"Why not?"

"I didn't tell her."

"You took the sweatshirt to protect her, to hide evidence that she was there, and you never told her?"

Daria nodded and offered up some of her inimitable reasoning. "I've been pretending I didn't know she was there, so she'd get how I believe in her, no matter what she says or what it seems like she has done. The reality of what happened that night isn't as important as our perception of the reality, and I wanted her to get out of the experience that I'm always and forever one hundred percent behind her. That's also why I never told you. The fact of the shirt being there wasn't important. I knew it didn't mean Nikki had done anything, therefore, no one needed to know about it."

Nina couldn't help it. As a mother, she absolutely loved Daria. She loved her waving around a shotgun in defense of her daughter and Nina's son, she loved the crazy lioness stance. What a shame that as a lawyer, she couldn't believe a word she said. This superficially ditzy mother with an unusually intelligent child and unexpected skill with firearms and lies aroused deep-seated suspicion. "Did you hide anything else?"

"No. I took the sweatshirt, ran to my car, and left."

"Did you leave the front door open?" Paul asked.

She considered this. "I guess I did leave it open."

"Think about fingerprints?"

"Like I said, I had gloves on because of the cold, so I didn't give it a thought. There was blood on my pant leg. I rinsed it out with water as soon as I got home and tossed it in the washer later. And I swear, that's it."

"Tell me this," Nina said. "Did you ever tell Beth you went there that night?"

"Oh, no. I couldn't because of Nikki, but I felt so terrible leaving Bill there all curled up like a baby with the blood all around. I went over last week and I almost told her. Should I have? But I can't see how it would help her."

"The police are going to find you, Daria," Nina said. "Because of the eyewitness. Mrs. Garibaldi."

"I'll lie," Daria said. "I'll leave the sweatshirt out, okay?"

It was one of those moments. Nina wanted to shrug and let Daria do what she was going to do, but she had asked Nina if it was okay. Paul had a disgusted look on his face as if he could predict what Nina would say and thoroughly disapproved.

"You have to tell the truth if asked, Daria," Nina said. "Don't perjure yourself."

"I could leave town. But I can't. I can't leave Nikki."

"The thing is, you don't have to volunteer information."

"So—if they don't ask me directly..."

Now Nina could shrug, and she did.

"You do realize," Paul said, "that this puts an entirely different slant on things."

"I know it's more proof that Nikki was there," Daria said. "I know that's not good."

"And of course, it places you at the scene of the crime," he said.

"What?"

"You were there."

"I told you he was dead when I got there."

Nina tried to read her expression, but Daria had sunken further from the light. Her face wasn't easy to read. Was it really conceivable she had not considered that her presence at the dead man's side might implicate her?

"How do we know that, Daria?" Paul went on. "You lied about going to the house in the first place. You admit you stole evidence and conveniently wore gloves to a murder scene. You say you want to protect your daughter, yet you let it slip that she made threats against the murdered man."

"You also testified that Nikki wasn't home at the time of Sykes's death," Nina said. "It made you seem to be at home. You provided yourself with an alibi by burning Nikki."

"I never thought like that. Never. You're making it all ugly. All I want to do is protect my daughter!"

"You know what I think?" Paul said. "I think you're the one who hated seeing your rich brother-in-law snub Nikki and you. I think you felt such financial pressures, you were railroaded

343

into a decision you didn't want to make when you sold him the land. I think you were the one who envied their lifestyle. They lived like kings in a castle and ignored you. It rankled, didn't it?

"And speaking of your sister, well, without her husband around to tighten the purse strings, she's much more generous, isn't she? Getting close to you again, more like when you were kids. There to help out with money when you need it. Yes, you had more reasons than Nikki to kill Bill Sykes." He stood next to Daria, looming, intimidating. "Maybe you found out he had cheated you. Maybe you discovered the land was valuable after all. And you were there..."

Daria leaped from her chair and threw open the door to the reception room, startling the client who was still waiting patiently in his chair. She whirled around at the door.

"I told you the truth! You people have seen too many bad things. You're the ones who are evil. You can't even tell an honest person!"

"Whew," Nina said after Daria left. They had left the poor client gaping and closed the door to the conference room.

"Yes," Paul agreed.

"She's right. We have seen too many bad things."

"What? Are we supposed to feel guilty that we discovered what a liar she is?" Paul went over to the coffeemaker and poured himself some mud left over from early morning.

"Louise has already told the police about the car. Eventually, they'll work out that it's hers."

"What do you think?"

"If she's telling the truth she's been keeping critical information from you and everybody else. If she's lying, she killed Sykes and she's letting her daughter go through hell. I suppose it's even possible that Nikki saw her and is protecting her."

"I don't want it to be her, Paul."

"Better rethink that. She's not the client. I gotta go. It's two-thirty and I have to get down to Carson City to see a man about a plane."

He left and Sandy arrived to announce that the client had now officially completed all the stages of waiting, from annoyance to rage to hopelessness to passive dejection. Nina hardly had room for a thought for the rest of that afternoon, but one image leaked through, a vision of Daria and Nicholas and baby Nikki, before all this had started, before Daria's downhill slide into fecklessness and Nikki's growth into bitter resentment.

And she found herself hating Nicholas Zack, because it had all started with him, and it was too late to fix, really.

19

NIKKI USED UP ONE DAY of her home supervision searching the Net about minerals, but
she couldn't find any photos of rocks that
looked like her rocks. When Nina called for
the fifteenth time trying to find Daria, she asked
her flat out if she had found out anything. She
could tell Nina didn't want to get her upset
or anything but Nina wasn't going to lie.

So now she knew the rocks were opals.
What Nina wouldn't tell her was how much
they were worth. Again, the Net wasn't much
help. On eBay she found some Australian
opals for sale but they sure didn't look like her
dirt-colored rocks.

She logged onto her Web site. She had
spent the past few weeks making animations,
adding links and formatting the site and it now
looked unbelievably thrashed. Her MP3 clip
was up there for anyone to download. That was
exciting. She uploaded two more songs she had
taped as soon as Daria had left. They were awe-
somely powerful. She had screamed all her
misery into them, just her and her guitar.
Now she could hardly talk, but as always,
she felt better after letting the rage out. She
thought for a minute, then changed the html
headline on the Web site to "Girl, Arrested."

Log off. She shut down the computer, got
up, and realized she had to get out or go
crazy. She wanted to go out to the claim but

if she couldn't do that, at least she could find out what the opals were worth.

Problem was, she was so limited in what she could do. If she was a detective, she would not only know what to do, she would have wheels, fake ID, everything else that might be useful. Instead, she had a beeper on her leg blasting out her position to some disinterested bureaucrat who basically held the power of life or death over her.

In the phone book she found that South Lake Tahoe had its very own rock shop. She called the number and a girl answered. "I have some opals I want somebody to look at," Nikki said.

"The owner could do that. But he's out today."

"How about tomorrow?"

"Sure. Just bring them in. Ask for Digger."

Now she had to get rid of this damn electronic monitor.

Hamid knew a lot about electronics.

An hour passed uselessly on the telephone. Nikki couldn't raise Hamid. In desperation, she finally called Jane, who had techno-nerd tendencies, and her mother asked her very politely never to call or darken their door again. That made her feel shitty.

And infamous. Good band name. Infamous.

For another hour, she trolled the Net. Eating a peanut butter sandwich, she studied a Web site that explained all about how electronic monitoring worked. Try as she might, she could find nothing about people who had managed to foil the ankle monitor. Disgusted, she moved to the window with a soda and the telephone.

Bob ought to be out of school by now. She found him at his cousin's number.

"You have to come over," she said.

"Why?" He sounded busy, and the sound of his busyness drove her crazy. How could he have a life! She was so unbusy, so bored out of her brain, so up the wall!

"I'll explain when you get here."

A pause.

"Hey, it's important."

"If it's so important, I don't see why you can't tell me over the telephone."

She felt he had reached out through the phone and landed a punch on her nose.

"Did you get in a lot of trouble about the night you came over?"

"I can't touch a computer for a month. I can't go to San Francisco with my cousins next weekend. No TV until hell freezes over. Plus, my mom totally doesn't trust me anymore. If I come over to your house she'll probably put me in some Virginia military school."

"She hates me. Like everybody else does."

"Nah. She would stop representing you if she did."

Nikki was realizing that what she needed no longer counted. Any influence she once had with him, any feelings he had for her, had faded without the day-to-day stuff to keep it alive.

It hurt. "Okay," she said. "I'll tell you. Are you alone?"

"Yes."

"No one else could be listening in?"

"C'mon, Nik. Most people don't find my phone calls all that riveting."

"Well, some people aren't so eager to have their kids even talking with me. Has your mom said you shouldn't talk to me on the phone?"

"Not really."

He lied. She knew it; he knew she knew. Still, here he was talking to her anyway. That was something. "It's this monitoring thing they have on my ankle," she said.

"What about it?"

"Did you look at it?"

"No."

"It's a plastic strap with a transmitter about the size of hotel-sized soap. Maybe a little bigger. Anyway, here's the way it works. There's a computer hooked up that keeps track of me when I'm home. When I have an appointment, like to go to court or something, they program in a curfew, meaning, when I have to get back. You following this?"

"Ye-ah."

"When the computers figure out you've violated curfew, a notice of violation goes out, sometimes right away, sometimes a few hours later. Now, here's what I thought at first. I take the thing off, put it on my bed or somewhere, right? But it turns out even the strap is made out of a plastic that's impervious.

You just can't do anything with it at all. Next I thought, the easiest thing would be to just disconnect the power, right? But I read these things have a battery-backup system that stores and transmits information later. Anyway, I'm out of ideas. So I wondered if you, who are technical and so smart, might have some brainstorm..."

"You want to bust your monitor."

"Can you help me?"

"No."

"Listen, I'm desperate. I need to find some things out, and I can't do it from here. Please, just help me with this one little thing."

"You already checked out the Net?"

"Yeah. Nothing there."

"That's all I can think to do."

"Well, thanks a bunch. Bob, couldn't you come over just for a few minutes?"

"I just can't."

"So you're abandoning me too. The only friend I had left!" She hung up, breathing hard.

She would go crazy if she couldn't leave this house. She had to get out. Had to.

She called their family doctor. "I need an appointment right away. I'm so scared. I have these symptoms. I'm afraid I might have something bad..." She knew every symptom by heart. She ought to, after the way they yammered at them about it at school. "Oh, please. Don't make me talk about it. Well, VD, okay? Tomorrow at ten sounds good."

She hated blood tests, hated the needles coming at her, but she wanted a quick appointment, and whatever worked. She couldn't have VD. She had never even had sex yet.

When Big Brother called that afternoon, she asked for permission to see her doctor the next day. After some serious throat clearing and stalling and negotiating like Arafat and Barak, they compromised on three hours and he was not about to spring for a minute more. That gave her fifteen minutes at the doctor's to get an order for a blood test, a quick run to the clinic lab—maybe forty-five minutes to an hour, including travel time. Two hours left. Long enough to see Digger.

Back in her bedroom, she reached under her dresser and removed a Ziploc bag taped to the bottom.

To squirrel away the most precious of her treasures was an old, old trick. There she kept a photograph of herself sitting on her father's shoulders, pulling his hair, mouth wide open in a scream of delight, and one of her mother and father on their wedding day. Daria wore a brocade gown, with flowers twined in hair that was still light brown like hers. Her father, who always smiled like he was holding on to a lot more laughter inside, just waiting to spring a fun trick on someone, wore leather pants and a ruffled shirt. In lonely moments, she loved studying his wide nose and skin that looked fuzzy as a peach. Sometimes she thought she could remember his smell. Like nutmeg. Not sweet, not heavy. Just uniquely him.

Putting the photographs and other bits

aside for now, moving toward the window's shaft of sunlight, she thanked herself for what she had thought was a psycho move at the time, hiding away the largest rocks in her room instead of giving them to Nina. Pulling open the bag, she took out the largest one, a chunk the size of a small plum. She ran into the bathroom and dipped the stone into water, then rubbed it with a towel.

How it gleamed. "Opal," she said out loud.

She spent the rest of the hot afternoon at the kitchen sink sweating as the sun poured in, rubbing the rocks and picking out the little dirt bits with the ice pick. The System was trying to break her spirit. She was going to stand up for herself.

The little town of Carson City, capital of Nevada, was primarily a place of moping casinos and slumping antique stores housed in grizzled if sometimes venerable buildings. The federal building, a small gray replica of a Greek temple, stood out as a haven of unexpected beauty.

Paul sat down with the chief investigator from the NTSB in charge of the investigation of the crash of Skip Bailey's Beechcraft. Traffic rumbled by, so close Paul could almost feel the tires treading over his body, but Chuck Davis, the crash investigator, looked not at all concerned with the noise. He stroked a closely shaved jaw. "We have radar information from the FAA. The pilot was right on track with his flight plan. He wasn't lost."

"Any sign of equipment failure?"

"Not so far. We have checked the maintenance records. One thing you must say for the pilot, he was meticulous. Never missed an overhaul. Met or exceeded all recommended service."

Confident in his facts and opinions, Davis spoke under the proud aegis of big government.

"Did he know he was going down?"

"His flaps were up and the landing gear was down, which makes it appear that he was trying to land, but in that mountainous country he didn't have a chance. So he did know at some point before the crash."

"The Reno paper said this morning that the working theory is pilot error."

Davis said, "It's a process of elimination. You familiar with how many things can go wrong for a pilot?" He swiveled in his faux leather chair, frisky as a kid on a merry-go-round.

"Aside from mechanically, you mean."

"Yes."

"Are you talking about physical problems?" Paul said. "Because there must be a million." Paul's chair did not swivel, he determined. "I've heard about some that can affect pilots. Oxygen deficiency, ear block, sinus block, hyperventilation, carbon monoxide poisoning..."

"Bailey had seen a doctor two days before. He was in perfect health. He was flying well below twelve thousand feet, which almost rules out hypoxia. There's no information to suggest that this was anything other than a routine charter flight like hundreds he had flown before and therefore, hyperventilation as a result of stress also seems unlikely. So we are looking at some sort of perceptual problem."

"By a process of elimination."

"Exactly. We are used to relying on our senses for information. Under most conditions, pilots are trained to be responsive to the normal information gleaned from sensory data. However, many times that information can lead to false conclusions when you're flying. Ever heard of illusions in flight?"

Paul had read all about them. He had figured this would be the road they would have to take, since no evidence existed to suggest anything more easily proven. "No," he said, eager to hear more.

"Well, they rank among the most commonly cited factors that contribute to fatal aircraft accidents."

"No kidding."

"One category of illusions causes spatial disorientation. Another arises during landing maneuvers. Since Bailey was not trying to land the aircraft, we think he was affected by one of the former. In these, the motions and forces of the plane give a false sense of position. The pilot needs to reorient by referring to reliable fixed points on the ground, or use flight instruments. If he corrects instead based on what his senses are telling him...it can be fatal."

Paul pictured the small plane, the two people inside, gliding through the night.

"Just for an example, say Bailey entered a banked attitude slowly, too slowly to arouse the motion sensors in the inner ear. He corrects quickly. That gives him the illusion that he's banking in the opposite direction. We call that 'the leans.' Then he rolls the plane back into its original dangerous position or may lean in the perceived vertical plane."

The two men in Paul's mind rocked back and forth. "Witnesses did not report anything of that nature happening before the crash," he said.

"Or there's the graveyard spin. If a pilot's spinning and recovers properly, he may suddenly feel that he's spinning in the opposite direction, so he returns to his original spin."

The picture returned to level. "Ditto. There was no spin."

Davis ignored him. "Then there's the false horizon..."

"It was a clear night."

"But it was night. A tricky time to be in the air, actually. Then there is autokinesis..."

By now, Davis had to know Paul was no innocent in these matters, but he went on anyway. "Then there's the inversion illusion, where a sudden change from climbing to straight and level flight creates an impression that the aircraft is falling backward. The pilot pushes into a nose-low attitude, which increases the illusion and causes an accident." He waited for Paul's refutation, and gave a satisfied grunt when none came.

"There's the elevator illusion, where an

355

updraft causes abrupt upward vertical acceleration. Again, the pilot goes nose low... Anyway, you get the idea. There are a number of possibilities."

"Possibilities."

But in the tradition of all storytellers, Davis had saved the punch line.

"What happened in this case, I would speculate, is something called a somatogravic illusion. If a pilot reduces the throttles quickly, the plane decelerates rapidly. The pilot's disoriented, and he pushes the aircraft into a nose-up attitude. That causes a stall."

The face at the window turned toward the pilot, mouth open in a silent scream. The pilot never took his hands from the controls as the plane swooped down, soundless as a bird in flight until the last instant. Annihilation.

Davis shrugged. "It could happen to the most skilled pilot. He had logged thousands of flight hours. But sometimes our instincts are too compelling to ignore."

"Speculation, like you said," Paul said.

Davis said, "It sounds to me as though you're looking for some other cause, Mr. van Wagoner. Is there an insurance connection?"

"No," Paul said.

"What, precisely, is your interest in this case?"

"It may be connected to a murder in South Lake Tahoe."

"You mean the passenger's father? You have some evidence of a connection?"

"Not yet," Paul admitted. "That's why I'm

here. Look, Mr. Davis. I've been looking into situations like this for many years, logging my own flight hours. I know there's a connection."

Davis had lost interest. "Well, if and when you have something hard, let me know," he said. "We've seen hundreds of these accidents. We do not reach conclusions without confirmation in the form of witness statements, documentation of the physical state of the plane, and collateral proofs."

And the old process of elimination. That piles and piles of scut work appeared to support that position, Paul did not doubt. So that would be their explanation, henceforth writ in stone, if Davis had anything to say about it. "Are you personally convinced that's what happened?" Paul said. "If Skip Bailey was, say, your father, would that explanation satisfy you?"

"We interviewed witnesses who saw the plane gliding before landing, indicating that the engine was not engaged. And then, of course, you must remember this pilot was implicated in another near incident some years ago."

"Let me get this straight. Your office has reached the conclusion that Bailey went down because, in spite of twenty years of experience, he made a novice's error in judgment."

"Our final report will be some time in coming, of course..."

Yes, they had those months of paper to generate, sign, and copy a dozen times before dead filing.

"...But yes, I believe that's a fair prediction

of our analysis." Davis stood up and stuck out his hand.

Paul shook the dry, steady hand. "Oh. One more thing," he said on his way out the door, and Davis looked up with an expression of long-suffering patience. "Just to satisfy Mrs. Bailey and the lawyer in the Zack case. Could save us all a lot of trouble. I'd like to have a peek at the plane."

"Not during the investigation."

"But your investigation won't be concluded for a year. It could avert a lawsuit. Let me help you out with the relatives. You know?"

"Well, maybe I could arrange something," Davis said.

20

"SHE'S CLEANING a friend's house," Nikki told Nina. "Forty bucks for four hours." She sat in a puddle of morning sun on the porch steps wearing cutoffs and a buttoned-up brown shirt that hung like a burlap bag. Her elbows rested on her knees, and her chin rested on her hands. It was eight-thirty in the morning. "What now?"

"Didn't your mother tell you?"

"We don't talk to each other. We coexist. I want a peanut butter sandwich, she hands me the bread. She wants to watch a soap opera and gives me a couple of bucks, I let her."

Nikki could be funny. Realizing that an invitation into the house would not be forthcoming, Nina leaned against the railing. The street was quiet, all the neighbors scratching out a living somewhere. She wondered if Nikki was keeping up with the independent study she was supposed to be doing since she couldn't go to school, but she decided not to ask. She didn't want to get involved in anything unessential to her case, and she had a painful topic to discuss today.

How to bring this up? She took a deep breath and decided she might as well just come out with it. "I came to talk to you about your mother. She came to my office yesterday and said she was at the house the night your uncle was killed."

"Really? I'm not surprised. Why are you? She

was full of shit when you met her, and she's bursting by now."

It was a nice lying job for a sixteen-year-old. Nikki actually didn't seem surprised. Her blasé manner made Nina very suspicious.

"So you don't know anything about that?"

"No."

"I want to remind you about something before I ask you again. When you confessed to the police that you were there that night, you thought the worst that could happen to you would be a stint in a juvenile facility. I've told you that's not true. You watch cop dramas on TV?"

"Sometimes," she said grudgingly.

"Ever seen a prison scene?"

She tsked impatiently. "Of course."

Nina leaned down and spoke very softly. "It's really like that, Nikki. People behind bars. Shouting...the noise is incredible. No privacy, and constant monitoring. Nowhere to go, nobody to see, nothing to do. Just you and a couple of roommates you will not like, fear, and loneliness."

"But I'm not going to prison," Nikki said, shifting her pose. She put hands down and made a triangle on the step with her body at the center of it, as if trying to firm up her position. Nina could see fear moving around inside her like the flecks of gold in her eyes. "I didn't do anything but take the rocks, and they're ours."

It can't happen to me. Nina remembered the salve of that belief. A few deaths of people you loved taught you differently. "I told you before, there are no sure things in law. I'll do my best. What I want from you is the truth."

"Okay."

"You've kept things from me. The opals..."

"I didn't know they were valuable!" All cool departed. "I didn't know they were important. They're freaking rocks!"

"Tell me what happened that night. I mean everything. Include what you know about your mother."

"I don't know anything about my mother. What do you mean?"

"Then just tell me about that night."

"I'm sick of talking about it," she said, but reconsidered. "Oh, okay. Let's return to that windy night in May, when the stars were bright and Nik went out hunting in her little boat..."

The basic story remained the same, although a few new details emerged. Nina made notes, unsure what might be important at this point.

"It's major cold and windy, a cruddy night to go out. I'm paddling in a kayak we have from one of my mom's former lovers, I can't remember which. I don't want to make any noise...mega hassle.

"When I get there, I pull the boat behind a bush. See lights on a wall next to the pool. He's got a gate, of course. Doesn't want anyone in that pool except him and maybe when he's feeling generous, his wife and son."

"You were never in the pool before?" asked Nina. "You never saw the hiding place before?"

"I was in the pool before but for some

reason he never pointed out his stash to me. Anyway, by luck, the gate is unlocked, so I slip inside. That's when he blows out from his study with the bottle in his hand. Boom! Stark naked! I have just enough time to dive bomb behind a bush."

Nikki described again how Sykes dove in and how she ran for the study.

"What were you looking for?"

"Nothing special. Anything useful. Papers? Information about our land? Something that would hurt him?"

"Money?" Nina said.

"Maybe. Why don't we ask the parole counselor guy who keeps track of me? Maybe he's scoped me out. I'm too deep into my own headset rap to say."

"How did you get the idea to go there in the first place?"

"My ex-friend Scott. Scott Cabano. Well, you saw him that day after court."

"The one with the shaved head that they picked up for stealing from the houses on the lake."

"Yeah. He used to always talk about how lakeside people never lock anything on that side of the house."

Nina said, "Did you know Scott has been arrested again? They revoked his bail."

"No! So that's why—he wouldn't leave me alone otherwise. Will he get out again?"

"I don't think so. He's eighteen. I hear from a friend in the public defender's office that he's going to plead guilty to a single burglary charge and wants to stay in jail so he can get out earlier. He's looking at almost another year in County."

"Good," Nikki said, her brown eyes showing naked relief. "I lucked out there."

"Nikki, what did he say to you that day after court?"

"The usual garbage. How he was going to get me if I didn't give him his share of what I took from Uncle Bill's house. He came here a while back saying he figured out I had taken something. He wanted a share. He almost beat me up that day. I think he wanted to."

"When was this?"

"Couple of weeks ago."

"Why didn't you tell me?"

"It was my business."

"He threatened you?"

"I handled it."

The truculent pride reminded Nina so much of herself in youth. Innocence made her brave. "You're only sixteen. You don't have to handle things like this yourself. You act as though..."

"Don't criticize me."

"I'm not..."

"Like hell."

"Take it easy, Nikki," Nina said, adding a rough edge to her voice she would never use with Bob, but that Nikki needed.

"Hey," Nikki said, "you started it." But this was said in a conciliatory tone so Nina forged on, wondering what else Nikki hadn't told her.

"I was wondering, could Scott have been the

guy in the woods? No, wait," Nina said, reconsidering. "He was arrested before that. It couldn't have been him."

Nikki said, "I guess not. I was hoping it was him. Well, it's really clear the decks day. I'm going to tell you something else you don't know. The night Bob came over to dig up the rocks, a man called me. He had a funny way of talking, like he was from England or something, and his nose was all stopped up. It didn't sound real. I thought it might be Scott at first, or somebody trying to disguise his voice. Somehow this guy knew I had the rocks. He wanted me to give them to him, and he threatened me too. So it must have been him in the woods."

Nina held her hand up. "Wait," she said. "I just don't understand this. Why didn't you tell me about Scott and the man who called you before? I could have done something to protect you. That must have scared you, no matter what you say. Did you tell your mother about all this?"

"No," Nikki said. "I can protect myself." She bit her lip.

"Why are you so afraid of letting adults help you?" Nina asked, trying to keep her voice gentle because the girl would react strongly to any authoritarian manner.

"They have their own problems."

"What about me?"

"I'm telling you all this, aren't I? Even though you're Bob's mom and you must really hate me for dragging him into it."

Nina shook her head and said, "I was angry about that. But it doesn't change our relationship."

"Sure."

"I'm your lawyer. I'm not quite sure how to make you understand what that means."

"What does it mean?"

"That I help you in spite of my problems. I help you if you lie to me, are rude to me, if I don't like you, and I help you even when you don't want help." She reached over to touch Nikki's thin shoulder. "It's a sacred trust," she said.

"First one I ever had of those," Nikki said, but a smile sneaked around her mouth. "Sounds awesome."

"It is. Now let's get back to it, all right? I want to go back to your uncle. He had dropped the phone and fallen to the floor." Nina was trying to understand this.

"Crying. Kind of moaning."

"From something he heard on the phone." Could someone have called him to tell him that his son's plane was down? But who would know that? Could Beth have called him with some bad news? Or Dylan Brett? "Think hard, Nikki. Did anything at all that he said on the phone give you an idea who was on the other line?"

Nikki was shaking her head. "Just, he was friendly and laughing and happy, then he was having a fit. Really strange. I should have left, but I just kept my eyes glued to him. Then..."

Nina waited.

"The doorbell rang. And he went to answer it." She paused. "And that's when I finally took off."

"You didn't wait to see who arrived."

Again, there was the merest hesitation. "No."

Such a tiny hesitation, gossamer, nothing to hang your hat on.

Nina let it go. If she had seen Daria then, she wasn't going to admit it. That would mean Daria had gone there when Sykes was still alive...and probably was the one who killed him. "You had taken the rocks and run almost to the beach, then come back to get your sweatshirt, and that's when you saw all this."

"Right."

"And you grabbed your sweatshirt?"

Nikki's eyes widened.

"You forgot all about it until this moment, didn't you?"

"Why do you say that?"

"Your mom took it," Nina said. "She was there, and she saw it by the pool hanging on a bush, and she took it home and washed it."

"Now I get it. I should have known. That's what all this was leading up to. Daria."

"The doorbell rang, and someone came into the study with your Uncle Bill."

"Someone sure did. But I wasn't there anymore, and I didn't see anything." Nikki closed her eyes and leaned back against a post, trying to look relaxed. Nina didn't say anything, and after a minute her eyes opened again.

"Ding-dong, you're dead. But it wasn't Daria. She's just pulling one of her stupid moves to try to help."

"How do you know it wasn't your mother, if you didn't see anything?"

"I just know!"

"Listen, Nikki," Nina said. "The neighbor saw your mother's car parked on the street. Your mother admits it. She was there."

Nikki's face convulsed. "Leave me alone! And leave my mother alone!"

"Did you see her? Tell me!"

"No!" She started to jump up, but Nina had taken her arm.

"All right, Nikki. Your mother says that Dr. Sykes was already dead when she got there. But I had to know if you had seen something different."

"You should have told me that right away!" Nikki cried, throwing off Nina's hand. "You tried to trick me!"

"Sorry, Nikki. C'mon, calm down. I'm sorry I had to do that. Sit back down."

" 'Trust me,' " Nikki said, and laughed, not a happy laugh. She stood on the porch looking down the street. "That's what you said. What a joke. Don't even try to ask me any more questions. And besides, I've got to split. I've got a doctor's appointment this morning."

"You have permission to leave?"

"I called my guardian angel. He gave me three hours. Okay? I'm going to be late. Where's Daria? I told her I needed a ride. I can't be late..."

"Let me give you a lift."

"No more questions. I am completely done with you pushing stuff on me."

"All right."

"I'll get my bag." She returned almost immediately with a tattered backpack covered with slogans about shark finning and saving Tibet.

"What's in there?" Nina asked lightly, as they drove away. "The kitchen sink?"

"Schoolbooks for the waiting room," said Nikki promptly.

"Let's see. Open it up."

"*Jawohl*, Adolf." She opened it up and Nina saw schoolbooks.

"Are you ill? Is that why you're going to the doctor?"

"I said no questions!"

Nina pulled over. "Sorry, the deal's off."

"You broke the deal! Asking questions!"

"So sue me."

"You're not funny!"

"And you're not going anywhere," Nina said, "until you speak to me respectfully and until you explain where you're going and how you got permission."

Two minutes of black silence. Then Nikki sighed and apologized and said she was going to the doctor and why.

Nina started up again. Nikki didn't say another word. She stared straight ahead, clutching the backpack on her lap. Nina thought, what is she really up to? And after she let her out at the doctor's office, she drove the car around the clinic buildings until she found a convenient spot hidden behind a semi that gave her a decent view of the entrance. She punched her cell phone.

"Sandy? I want you to..."

"Cancel appointments for the foreseeable future," Sandy finished.

"I'm sorry. It's just that Nikki had a doctor's appointment this morning so she's away from her house."

"You gonna follow her?"

"For a little. Until I'm sure..."

"She's monitored, isn't she?"

"Yes, but I'm not interested in after-the-fact analyses."

"You have court at eleven."

"I won't forget."

She waited for Nikki, watching the stream of patients enter and exit the clinic, thinking about Nikki and her mother. Nikki was still lying to her. She would lie to protect her mother. If so, if Sykes was still alive when Nikki saw Daria, Daria had killed him.

She didn't think for a moment that Daria would murder her brother-in-law in cold blood, but hot blood and access to weapons could have led to Sykes's death.

And yet she didn't want it to end with Daria Zack. New information was still coming at her fast. She decided to wait a few days before deciding whether to go after Daria. She wanted to find the man who had chased Bob, and the mechanic, Dave LeBlanc, who seemed to have disappeared in LA. And talk to Ginger some more about that blood.

Correction, Paul would have to do most of that for her, because what she had to do was practice some law. She had very little time left before a crucial motion in the case had to go on file. She checked her diary. The 995 hearing was twenty-four days away. She had three days left to file the paperwork and still allow the prosecution twenty-one days notice of her arguments.

Back to the law library this afternoon.

It was getting late, she had a divorce trial in a few minutes, and she was sitting in the Bronco spying on her sixteen-year-old client.

She called Paul.

"I was on my way out the door," he said. "Just eating a final bite of oatmeal."

"Could you stop over at the Sykes house and pick up something from Beth today?"

"What do you want me to pick up?"

"Any phone bills that include the night Sykes died."

"Sure. Good thought. I've been wanting to talk to her anyway. About the marriage and about her son."

"And ask her if Daria has told her about going to the house that night."

"Don't give her time to think about it. I hear you. Anything else?"

"Has Dave LeBlanc been located yet?"

"It's a missing-persons case now. No word from my buddy at the LAPD. The crash investigators in Carson City are still insisting that there's no sign of sabotage so far. So we have no grounds to assume that his disappearance is linked to the crash. He had just been fired. Maybe he just rode the 'Hound to some more welcoming state, like Alabama."

"And maybe Aerosmith will retire one day."

They both had a good laugh over that one.

"I'll call LA again and see if I can build a fire."

Nina saw Nikki leave the medical building and walk over to an adjacent building in the trees where there was a lab.

"I have to go now, Paul. I was wondering. Matt and Andrea and I and the kids are going over to Sand Harbor to edify ourselves with Shakespeare tonight. They're doing a preview performance of the festival coming later this summer. Want to come?"

"Sorry. I have to get back to Carmel for the weekend. Business."

Back to Susan with the shiny black hair, Nina thought. It was just as well.

"My local doc's coming in on a Saturday to take my cast off," he added.

And Susan could take off the rest. "That's great, Paul. When will you be back?"

"Sunday night. Late."

Nikki came out of the lab and headed east, crossing the strip of parklike woods that led to the street. She stopped at the bus stop, standing back in the shadow of a building as if she didn't want to be seen.

"Uh, Paul. How soon could you get to the

371

corner across from the consignment store? Nikki's about to hop a bus for points unknown."

"I'm on my way."

Nina was out of time. She had to get to court. With a strong feeling of uneasiness, she shifted gears and pulled out of the parking lot, watching Nikki out of the corner of her eye as she hung in the shadows at the bus stop, her pack swinging against her side, looking as resolute as a missionary in search of a convert.

21

SANDY SAID ON THE PHONE, "Paul called while you were in trial."

"What did he report?"

"He followed Nikki to a rock shop over by the factory outlets." Sandy gave her the address. "He's waiting for her around the corner."

Nina called Paul and ten minutes later parked beside him in the Raley's parking lot. He sat about two feet below her in the Mustang as they talked through their open car windows. "She still hasn't come out," he said, pointing to the sign over the hole-in-the-wall shop called Diggers.

"I'll take it from here," Nina said.

"Just in the nick. Beth Sykes is waiting for me. I assumed you didn't want me to alert Nikki that I was following her. So the little monkey's doing a little research of her own."

"I'll catch her on the way out," Nina said, "and have a talk with her."

"Walk softly, and dump the big stick before you go. I don't think I've ever seen you so mad."

Paul stopped up the block to park in an extra-wide spot on the street that looked like it would keep his new car safe from passing traffic. He approached the Sykes's house on foot. Two cushioned chairs were next to each other on a porch on the private side of the house facing away from Louise's. In them, in one of them, two people squeezed together. As Paul got closer, the woman hauled off and slapped the man.

"Dylan, no!" said Beth Sykes. She pulled herself up and out, dislodging her companion in the process. He lurched to his feet also, struggling to right himself. Paul, who found himself conveniently near a cluster of red-berried hawthorn bushes, ducked down to take in the scenery. "You have to go now," she said. "I'm expecting somebody." She looked up the block, straight at Paul's bush and through him, and turned back without seeing him.

"Beth, I've always wanted you. Didn't you know that? You're holding on to a past that's over. You can't go on loving someone that's dead and gone," Dr. Dylan Brett said, with an expression Paul pegged as calculatingly winsome and charming. To Paul's eyes, Brett looked too standard issue. Eyebrows not too bushy, lips not too fleshy, forehead not too broad. His negatives never quite added up to a positive. He blended well into the scene, however, in a romantically casual outfit of brilliant white, the perfect contrast to emphasize his dark hair. "You're alive," Brett continued, in a voice unappealingly close to a coo. "And this is our chance to be together. It can be the way we always wanted it to be..."

"Have I ever said anything to encourage you? Done anything to make you think I..."

"You're so sad," he said. "I can make you happy."

"Dylan, go."

His response was to pull her close into a kiss. At first, she did not resist. She lolled like a soft doll in his arms. The languorous moves that followed gave Paul time to position himself to maximize his viewing pleasure. He didn't get off on watching other people make love, but he didn't object to the show, and he found Beth's face, when it came into view occasionally, so interesting. She did not look like a woman in love should look. She looked tortured.

After a while, inflamed, Dylan pushed for more. The gentle kisses heated up. Beth, now mashed against the side of the house, skirt rising in Brett's well-groomed hands, began to struggle.

Brett ignored her protests and pressed on.

Which Paul did find objectionable. Strolling out from behind the bushes, he pretended to tie his shoe, allowing them one second to unclench, and another second for Beth's skirt to adjust itself, and walked up to introduce himself.

"I'm glad you came," Beth Sykes told Paul after the guilty-looking Brett took an abrupt leave. "I should explain about Dylan."

"No need."

"I want to explain. He and I have been friends for a long time. I'm afraid I've cried on his shoulder once or twice lately, aroused the white knight in him. He sees me unhappy— well, you know, some men think love solves everything. He's a junkie for love, the poor guy.

And it was nice to be kissed again, nice to remember what it was like, getting swept away..."

"You mean love doesn't solve everything?" Paul said lightly. "News to me."

She laughed, loosening slightly. "If you hadn't come along, he would have stopped, you know. He really loves his wife. He can't resist taking liberties when they're offered— he was an ugly duckling and he jokes around about being female-deprived growing up—but he never goes too far."

Paul wondered if that was true. Maybe this latest incarnation of the perfect doctor was just as false as the last one. Maybe Dylan loved her, not his wife. Maybe Dylan's alibi was a lie and he was a murderer.

"Come in. There's something I want to show you." Ushering him briskly inside, she led him straight into the living room, where a large photo of Christopher Sykes hung above a brocade couch next to a smaller one of his father. Paul had passed right by it on his previous visit with Wish.

"My son," she said. "An incredible, fantastic human being. In the middle of all this, somehow I feel he's been forgotten."

"It's a terrible loss," Paul said, wondering if she would be suing Connie Bailey after the final NTSB report came in, heaping pain on pain.

They stood for a moment looking at the photograph, Paul covertly checking her out. She stood next to him, a pale woman, small-bodied, beautiful in that immaculate way of some women, her curly blond hair falling softly over her shoulders. He imagined that she looked damn good in a tailored suit or an expensive tennis outfit. She looked good enough in the loose skirt and bare feet, her face blushing pink from Brett's whiskers.

She seemed to nod at the boy in the photograph, a fleeting conflict wrecking the serenity of her features. He thought she probably spent a lot of time gazing at it. Observing her face as she looked at the boy, he felt a tingle of recognition at her expression. He knew how she felt. He knew the anarchy of losing someone you loved and how you scrambled afterward for a direction, diverted by obstacles that rose as turbulent as volcanoes between you and some kind of peace. The kid looked like her, not too tall, close-cropped hair, intelligent and calm-looking, the kind who never goes through that stage of resistance and rebellion that makes growing up and away so hard.

Another reason never to have children, Paul thought, feeling the pain passing through the woman next to him like a current. He couldn't see opening yourself up to that kind of experience voluntarily.

The air was still. He heard a cat meow somewhere in the back of the house. He was very conscious of the door into the study, which he could see a few feet away. It was closed tight. No wonder she had put the place up for sale.

She saw where he was looking and said, "Let's go back outside."

To Paul's surprise, Jan Sapitto, curves

clasped by a blue bikini, lay on a lounger at the far side of the pool. She pulled her sunglasses down and called out a greeting to them, then took up some oil and began to rub her tan arms. Paul and Beth continued on, finally settling on the back side of the house under a purple-and-white-striped canvas umbrella on a slight rise between the lake and the house. Paul admired the streaky blue of the lake beyond the bushes. He hadn't had time to look at the view on his first trip here.

"I used to love this view," she said. "That's why we bought this house."

"You have a lot of space too. Plenty of room for visitors."

"Yes. Jan loves spending time up here when the weather's good. She's been here a lot this summer."

Paul took that to mean she had visited more this year than usual. Apparently, Bill Sykes had made her feel slightly less at home than Beth did.

"I can't help thinking about that hiding place your husband built down there in the pool," Paul said. "Did you know about it?"

She shook her head. "Bill was secretive. He had a safe deposit box I didn't know about either, with old coins he had collected over the years. That collection turned out to be worth almost twenty thousand dollars."

"Hope you checked under the mattress, then."

"Nothing there," she said. "I suppose when I move we'll find something else."

"So he hid things from you?"

"Not from me especially. It was just his way. Bill grew up very poor in a little farming town in Indiana. His parents went bankrupt, so he worried about money, although we had all we needed." She motioned toward the cup in her hand. "Would you like some coffee?" Her long-fingered left hand still flashed with a diamond that was at least a couple of carats.

"No, thanks. How was his business going?"

"Well enough, especially since he hired Dylan Brett, but he was winding down. I think he loved what he could do for people, but he had learned his job a long time ago and he was getting out of date. He never took to the less invasive techniques, the skin peels and collagen injections. He was a surgeon, first and foremost. He didn't care to retrain. I think he would have retired soon. He was in his late sixties, you know. And he hated getting sued. He would tell me it was part of being a physician nowadays, but I think he had hoped he'd make it all the way through his years of practicing medicine without legal problems. He practiced for twenty-five years without a single malpractice claim, and then they started coming. Two in six years. The malpractice insurer was having a fit."

Paul said, "Robin Littlebear and Stan Foster?"

Beth said, "That's right. You probably know more about those lawsuits than I do at this point. Paul, could it have been one of them? I keep thinking about Linda Littlebear."

"I understand she attacked your husband."

She nodded. "That was awful. She jumped him one night, and came around here another time. She really hated Bill for what happened to her daughter. She suffered. I know..." she said, and swallowed at the thought of how much she knew before she continued. "That's why Bill didn't have her thrown in jail. I wanted him to press charges, and his attorney was particularly gung-ho..."

"Jeffrey Riesner?"

"Right. You know him?"

"I gave him a shampoo once."

She frowned, puzzled.

Paul smiled to show her he was making a little joke even though he wasn't. "Your husband refused to go after her."

"He didn't want the publicity," she admitted.

"So you think Linda Littlebear might have killed him?"

"Yes," she said slowly, "I do."

"You say she came to the house one night..." Paul prompted.

"She climbed the fence and came around the back, found Bill in his study. This was several months ago. I was in the bedroom getting ready for bed."

"What happened?"

"All Bill would tell me is that they argued and he prevailed. He wouldn't discuss it. Do you know...have you checked to see if she has an alibi?"

"Word is she was drinking with some people at a bar near the Round Hill Mall."

380

"Do you believe everything you hear?" Beth asked.

Beth's alibi was also based on the testimony of a friend, but Paul wasn't ready to get into that until he got a chance to talk with Jan Sapitto in LA again. "It might not stand up," he conceded. "I think I can imagine how you must feel, with your niece accused of killing your husband, but I have to ask, what makes you so sure it wasn't Nikki?"

"It wasn't Nikki!"

"Because she's family?"

"Because I don't believe it. Okay, maybe she came here to take something. She's mixed up right now, growing up. You have to make allowances for her age and the kind of person she is. She has her own integrity, you know, and that's one reason I won't—I just don't believe she had anything to do with hurting Bill. That's why I brought in Nina and you, to prove that to everybody else. What kind of world is this, where we believe such terrible things of children?"

He had no ready answer for her, except that this kind of world was the real world. "What about that restraining order your husband got against Linda Littlebear?"

She lifted one shoulder in a half shrug. "I imagine Bill threatened her with legal action that time she came into his study. That would be his style. He had given her a break, but she had blown it. Bill expected her to feel grateful to him for being easy on her, even for forgiving her. For someone who worked so closely with people and their psyches, he didn't really understand people that well. I think I understand her better. She blamed him for killing her child. Her emotions got the best of her..." She said this sadly. "She went on a rampage."

"You think that meeting set her off?"

"Maybe. What I do know is that she's more likely to have killed him than Nikki. Nikki is a child, not a vicious one, either. Just picture Linda, a strong, young, strapping woman, picking up that sword and striking him with it. It seems possible to me."

"Why do you suppose the police didn't arrest her?"

"I know they considered Linda. They asked me a lot of questions about her, and I understand they questioned her. But Nikki's a whole lot easier, that's all. That's why we have to push back hard."

"Linda's depressed and mentally disorganized. It's hard to see her..."

"I imagine you've seen plenty of drunks in your job?" Beth asked. "Because she's a major alcoholic. And I don't care how nice someone is sober, drunk they're something else."

"It's true. An awful lot of violent crime is fueled by alcohol."

Having made her point, Beth moved on to another theory. "And then, there's the casino announcer, Stan Foster," she said. "Bill said he was unbalanced and angry. Told me he threatened him too... I don't know how far it went with him, but I know Bill took his threats seriously."

"Stan Foster is dead."

"No!"

"He died in a car wreck in March." And from what Nina had said about the man, his death could be called a blessing. The quest for beauty was an equal opportunity destroyer. No amount of plastic surgery would have made that man like himself.

"I didn't know," she said, frowning. "That's a shame."

"Did you know him well?" She looked rather stricken for someone that didn't.

"No. I only met him once. He was a terribly troubled person."

"Okay, let's look at this from another point of view," Paul said, moving on. "Two malpractice lawsuits in six years. Was there anything in your husband's behavior that changed during that time in particular? I mean, he had a real stretch before where everything went remarkably well."

"A change? Well, he got older," she said lightly, not liking the question, which Paul saw in the way she avoided it. "What are you getting at? If you're thinking he had some neurological problems or something that caused him to make mistakes in his work, I have to tell you I think you are wrong. Bill was an accomplished surgeon always, and always in control."

"Was there any change in your relationship?"

Beth shook her head.

"None?"

"I'm sorry, Paul, but I'm not used to sharing such personal matters with people. I've lost the habit."

That made Paul wonder when she'd had the habit and when she'd lost it, because she didn't give the impression that this was a recent change, one that had occurred due to her husband's or son's death.

"I guess I'd like to keep whatever shrouds— I mean shreds—of privacy I still have wrapped around me," she said. "For myself, as well as for Bill."

"My apologies," Paul said. "I didn't mean to add to your troubles today."

"You're just doing your job," she said, "being thorough."

She had that right, and unfortunately for her, it meant he could not let this meaty bone lie. "So, a couple of lawsuits...and an implication of changes...were you happy he was retiring?"

He caught it, the tiny tension in the way she held her cup. "I don't follow," she said. "I didn't say anything about changes."

No, but everything about her suggested otherwise. "Something to do with Chris?"

"Chris? Not at all. Chris never caused us any pain. He was an angel."

"I don't mean to attack Chris," he said.

"You couldn't, anyway," Beth said. "I really believe Chris would eventually have come around to a medical career. He was a wonderful son."

"Did Bill want him to be a surgeon?"

"Yes, but Chris had his own mind. He was still exploring. If he had gone that way, I know he would have made a wonderful doctor and helped so many people."

She was openly grieving for Chris, but elusive about her husband. Maybe it was as simple as her being a very private person. He saw depths and surprises in Beth that he knew he'd have to explore. It didn't hurt that she was a very pretty woman. Was he developing a thing about grieving young widows?

"Do you have anything new on the plane crash?" she asked.

"No evidence of anything but pilot error, according to the crash investigators."

Beth nodded again, started to say something, then stopped.

"Nina and I feel there must be a link," Paul said.

"Maybe we'll never know," Beth said. "I don't even care what happened. All I want to know is that it happened fast. He saw a bright light, and then he was in a new place in a new phase of the life process." It was an echo of what Connie Bailey had said about Skip.

"It happened fast," Paul said. They were both silent. Paul's mind was still stuck on what might have happened to change Sykes a few years before. It hurt like a hangnail.

He said, "You're in a position to know better than anyone. How did your husband feel about Nikki?"

There was a long silence. Then Beth said, "You've met her. She can be insufferable, and Bill never had any tolerance for that adolescent phase."

Paul nodded. "What are you going to do now?"

"I suppose I'll move to Los Angeles. Jan wants me to live with her. I might even help her in her business. I used to be in marketing."

"That sounds positive," Paul said, allowing a passing thought that Jan popped up suspiciously often in these investigations but unable to figure out how that was important at the moment.

"But before I leave," Beth said, "I want to be sure Daria and Nikki are all right. I have to see this through with them. What happens next in the case?"

"A hearing's coming up in less than three weeks. You should talk to Nina about it."

"Paul?"

"Yeah."

"Is Nikki going to be convicted? You must have some idea by now."

"I don't have any idea. None at all," Paul said. "I wonder if you could do me a favor? I need to look at your phone bills for May."

"Why?"

"Just part of the investigation."

"Well, of course," she said. She left him outside for a while, leaving him to fantasize about taking a dip in the aqua blue waters of the pool with her, and returning only after a significant amount of time had passed.

"I'm so sorry," she said. "I can't find any bills at all. I've been forgetting everything lately. I keep locking myself out of the house and forgetting to feed the cat."

"You don't keep your paid bills?"

"Of course. The police might have them. They took a lot from the house, I don't know what all. Do you want me to check the receipt they gave me?"

He did. She went through a list and found that the police had taken the phone bills for the house's two lines and just about every other record in the house. Nina was supposed to get copies. Paul made a note. They were at the front door again.

"By the way, did you know that your husband had bought Daria's share of the mine?" Beth looked shocked, and he wondered why.

"Am I a suspect, Paul?" she said. "Your questions are so pointed, and your eyes—I don't feel that you're a kind person like I did before. No, I never knew until Daria told me after Bill's death."

Ignoring the many issues she had raised, Paul pressed on. "You must have gone to your grandfather's claim many times."

"Not for years. I had no interest at all in the claim. We all knew it was just tumbleweeds and rock."

Paul paused. Beth looked very frail and alone as she leaned against her door, and he didn't want to add to her burden of sorrow, but Nina wanted to know, so he had to ask. "Beth, Nina needs a straight answer from you on this question I'm about to ask you. For Nikki. The truth. You understand?"

"You're scaring me. But—just ask, will you?"

"We need to know if Daria ever told you that she came here the night your husband died. Wait—don't start protesting. Don't be angry. Just answer, please."

"Daria was here that night? Oh, no," Beth said. "No, no, no."

"Get in," Nina snapped out the window as she skidded to a stop in front of the bus stop.

Nikki got in. "Guess you were watching me."

"Seat belt."

"I was going to. Look, I've only got fifteen minutes before I miss the curfew and explode or something."

"What? They'll put you back in jail!" Nina sped up quite a bit. They drove in silence. Nikki polished off the ice cream in a sugar cone she had bought at the mall as they took turns at top speed.

"Don't you want to know what I was doing?" she asked finally.

"Tell me after we get you home."

Shooting through intersections, racking up misdemeanors, they made it with seconds to spare. Nikki got out and ran for the house, where the phone was ringing. A few moments later she returned to the front porch, panting, her face riveted with dirt.

"They're sure on the button," she said. "They wanted to know why I didn't come home right after my doctor's appointment. Did you know they can tell exactly where you are?"

"No. I never had cause before to wonder," Nina said. "But electronics are pretty sophisticated these days. What did you tell them?"

"Told 'em I got my period unexpectedly and I had to go over to the Raley's at the Y for Tampax. They asked why I didn't go somewhere closer, can you believe that? I said my mother had an account at the Raley's and I had no money." She looked just like Bob when he told a whopper. Her eyes shifted around and she opened them uncommonly wide in a childish effort to appear innocent, exposing her mendacious core.

"Which was all a pack of lies, right? You're good at inventing things," Nina said.

That shut her up momentarily.

"Did you go to Raley's across from the movie theater?"

"I was hoping if they got an address, this place was close enough to pass. I did go right close to there, to the rock shop in the same strip mall."

Nina sat down on the stoop and put her head in her hands. "If it's not too much trouble," she said, "maybe you could tell me why you took a huge risk that almost landed you in jail."

"I wanted to ask the guy there about the rocks. About what they were worth. Obviously, I didn't have any to show him," she said hurriedly.

"Give me the backpack. Let's see them."

"I was going to give them to you as soon as

I had them looked at." Six more chunks of the incredible glistening rock fell into her hand.

"I'm really..." Nina began.

"You're going to forget all about this when you hear what I found out," Nikki interrupted.

"I doubt that. But go on."

"The owner was there. His name is Digger. The name of the shop is Diggers. Shouldn't that have an apostrophe?" she said thoughtfully. "Anyway, Digger said a guy came in who had some stones just like these a few weeks ago! So there!" She looked breathless with triumph.

"A few weeks ago? When?"

"I asked him but he couldn't remember exactly."

"Nikki, you shouldn't have done it, any of it. But... I think you've learned something really helpful," Nina said.

Nikki smiled broadly. She sat down next to Nina, and Nina got a look at her under the hair, her face streaked with dirt, dried blood under her nose.

"What's that in your hair?" Nina asked. "You're bleeding!"

"I tripped while I was running."

The mama in her kicked in, and Nina forced the girl into the bathroom. There, she washed and poured disinfectant over the cut while Nikki yelped. Nina couldn't help allowing a small tingle of satisfaction at her discomfort. Served her right for her general attitude. "It's not too bad," she said, "but that lump must be sore."

"Duh," said Nikki, reaching a tentative finger up to poke at the bandage.

After eliciting a firm promise from Nikki never, ever on pain of extreme measures, to fool around with the monitoring system again, Nina followed her into the kitchen. Nikki opened the refrigerator, which was as barren as a Martian crater, not even a carton of milk in there. Then she opened the cabinet. Some rice in a half-opened bag, some canned corn. Nikki put water in a pan and measured some rice into a cup, then started the stove. "Sorry," she said. "Hunger attack."

"This is all you have to eat at home?"

"Daria's supposed to get paid for the magic show today." Evidently Nikki didn't know Daria had been fired.

"I'll be back in five minutes," Nina said. She went to the Safeway on Al Tahoe and brought back several sacks of groceries. Nikki was lounging on the porch like an old Appalachian lady when she came back. She took the bags in and started unpacking them.

"Wow," she said. "Christmas." She turned off the rice and made a thick turkey sandwich for herself. They went outside again and she began wolfing it down.

"Where is Daria?" Nina said. "She's never here when I see you."

"She auditions. She has afternoon quickies with guys in the band at the cocktail show. She hangs around the shows. She goes to Aunt Beth's. She actually can't stand the hovel," Nikki said, her mouth full. "I can't blame her."

"But you're too young—"

"You still don't get it? She's the one who's too young."

"This is something extra for food," Nina said, handing her some cash.

"Forget it. I mean, thanks for the groceries. But I won't take your money."

"Don't make me mad," Nina said. "I'll screw up your case if I spend all my time worrying about whether you're eating enough."

Her mouth still full of turkey, Nikki let Nina push the money into her pocket.

"Now," Nina said. "Let's talk about this man Digger remembers."

"He's a supplier who comes in now and then. His name is Dennis Rankin. He's out working one of his claims," Nikki said. "Gone for the next ten days."

"Digger hasn't seen the stones again?"

"Only that one time."

"We need to talk to this character Rankin," Nina said.

"Well, get ready. I know where he is. Digger told me where the claim is, not that he wanted to. He warned me off." She shrugged. "Said you don't want to get involved with this guy. Called him a wild man not fit for human company and a mean desert rat that'll bite your head off before you say hello."

"Sounds lovely. Where is his claim?"

Nikki finished the last of the sandwich and smiled again. "Right next to my Great Grandpa Logan's claim. Got a map of Nevada? I'll show you."

PART FIVE

He's in the dream and wants to wake up but when he does he has this giant lizard inside him, and he stumbles off the porch into the snow and tries to roll it away, but it won't go. It's rapidly taking over and he is growing scales and he feels his tailbone begin to extend until there is a long beating thing behind him.

He turns his head this way and that. He opens his mouth and the tongue flicks out. He moves awkwardly toward the shelter of the forest. If he is surprised by an enemy, he will kill. If he is disturbed, he will kill.

He is the lizard.

22

COOL AIR DRIFTED over the mountains and leaked down over Shakespeare's audience that June night, but the Reillys arrived prepared with jackets and warm snacks.

Sand Harbor, a unique area of the lake where large granite boulders lay strewn by glaciers, reminded the man sitting next to Nina of Virgin Gorda, an island in the Caribbean he had visited the summer before.

"Of course the boulders are smaller here," he said, "but it's the same effect. This is a place where a kid can dream up forts and pirate caves and secret hideaways."

Behind the stage the lake glowed purple and the moon gleamed through the glaze of sunset like a spotlight in the sky.

Andrea had packed blankets. Cocooned together in pairs, Nina with Bob, Matt with Brianna, and Andrea with Troy, they stayed warm and enjoyed the performance and each other's company.

As the faeries and mortals of a midsummer night cavorted on the stage, Nina allowed her gaze to roam over the lake and beyond, all the way to her husband, now asleep in a cold dark place, his life with her as swift as a shadow, short as any dream. He was truly gone, devoured by the jaws of darkness. These thoughts, which once would have strangled her pleasure in the moment, affected her differently now. Time had wound a soft cushion around her pain. Visions of him danced over her like the reflections on the water of the lake, changing the color of her skin but painlessly, without penetration. Now, remembering his gray eyes, his rare, terrific smile, his voice, she pulled her knees in close and hugged them tightly, to keep him with her as long as she could.

She realized that she was recovering from her grief and moving on. The realization made her a little sad, but she knew the time had come, not just for Bob's sake but for her own.

She would need all her strength for this case, and even more to resist what felt like a yearning for Paul. She did not want to fall back into a relationship with him out of loneliness and weakness. Paul was a violent man, a strong arm, a dominator, as she had seen over the two years they had worked together. Their time together had been troubled, and they had broken up for all the right reasons. There were things she couldn't understand about Paul, a philosophy she didn't share. Still there was such a connection between them she could not imagine life without him. Despite the confusion of his presence, she was glad to have him to lean on again.

Shaking herself out of her reverie, she watched the stage again, half of her mind engaged, as it always was, on pressing problems. Daria and Dennis Rankin. The mysterious phone call to Bill Sykes on the night he died. The man in the back seat. The role of the opals. The plastic surgery patients.

Paul would be gone for the weekend, so she would work at home on the 995 motion. The desert would have to wait until Monday.

"All better," the Carmel doctor said, giving Paul's hairy leg a pat. "Now you do have to take it easy for a while."

"Oh, I will," Paul said, ever the good patient, at least for as long as it would take him to get out of the doctor's office and back in the saddle.

"You need to build that leg up slowly..."

He and his nurse went on for quite a while. Paul tried to listen, but found himself admiring the nurse, thinking about Susan and Nina, and his two wives, along with other miscellaneous girlfriends. All these women, beautiful, mostly, great fun in bed, all. Some relationships that cut deep.

Susan wasn't cutting deep. The night before had been a romp, and they both had had a good time. That was it.

Once again, because of Nina, he was in trouble. He'd gone back up to Tahoe supposedly because he needed the money, then blew most of it on a down payment for his new car. Stupid, stupid, stupid. A psychologist could have some fun with this pretense, and would rapidly conclude he had not gone up to Tahoe for the money at all, but had gone up to Tahoe vainly hoping for a resumption of relations between him and Nina. Nothing he did ever moved the pointed chin and piercing brown eyes very far from his mind.

Sitting there getting his cast off, he had to face it. He was still in love with her.

He had to get away from her for good. He had sacrificed any chance of her loving him, unless he lied and went on lying to her, and he didn't think he could be close to her and keep up the lie forever. And if the truth was told, she would—what? Turn him in, maybe. Turn away from him forever, certainly.

As the doc shook his hand good-bye, he thought, after this case, I'm gone. He'd stay strictly away from her and away from Tahoe.

And Susan? Two days in a row was too much Susan. Susan bored him. Bored him stiff, he thought and had to smile, because that was exactly how the relationship had gone, good sex, no relationship. Tonight she wanted to make dinner for him, probably already had the greens out and washed and ready to go. He would call her and tell her it was over.

Forgetting everything the doctor said, he took a hard step forward and cursed. The nurse ordered a wheelchair and insisted he sit in it until they could dump him at the door.

The nurse hung over him. "Where's your ride?" she asked, not about to let him just get up and walk away, although he was perfectly capable. She might even call the police on him if he tried to drive. Half-registered words had warned against it, earlier.

He got up. "Right here," he said, pointing

toward a Buick driven by an older man that was parked at the curb. He walked gingerly over, grabbed the door handle on the passenger side, and waved her off.

Whipping the wheelchair around, she turned away.

"Who the hell are you?" said the man. "Get your hands off that door or I'll blow 'em off."

"My mistake," Paul said, backing away. He took his time getting to his car, then drove straight to what was left of his office in Carmel.

Same scene, getting musty. Deano hadn't been back. Deano's techno-industrial furniture wore a dusting of cigar ash here and there.

Paul descended carefully into his chair, which bore unfamiliar indentations from Dean's ass. Okay, he needed a new chair anyway.

The mail had been coming through the slot for a long time unattended. He had to get up again and pick it up off the floor. He made a stack on his desk and looked at it for a while. The bills-to-checks ratio was about ten to one. Finally he picked up the phone.

"Ez? Don't hang up."

Good old Ez said, "Don't bother me again. You are terminated long since."

"So's Deano," Paul said. "He's been spreading some mighty nasty rumors about me around town, trying to get my business away from me."

"Like hell. Dean showed me the papers. I know all about you."

Now they were getting somewhere. Ez was talking.

"So he showed you the papers?"

"The letter from your probation officer."

Paul couldn't help it. He burst out laughing.

"What'd I do?" he said. "Which crime was it?"

"I'd prefer not to talk about it." Ez's voice went down to a whisper. "I'm as liberal as the next guy, but...I never would have guessed... you seemed so...You go have that operation if you have to. Maybe that will calm you down, keep you out of trouble in public restrooms, but don't expect me ever to call you Paula."

Paul enjoyed the afternoon. Now that he knew what had happened, he made a few more calls.

Paula!

Good old Dean. He wasn't quite finished with Deano yet.

Along with paying the down on the car, he had paid bills and sent money to the folks with the first good check from Nina. He was broke again, but the business was wobbling to its feet like a newborn calf.

Before he left, he called Deano's Monterey number. A disconnect. He was thinking about whether to hunt him down like a dog through his investigator's license when his eye fell on an emergency number Dean had once given him. Dean's mother in Atascadero. He nodded slowly. And called the number.

"Hello?" An elderly lady.

"Mrs. Trumbo?"

"Yes?"

"This is Rod Stricker with the Internal Revenue Service."

"Oh, my God."

"I'm trying to locate a Dean Jay Trumbo."

"Dean doesn't live here."

"You're a relative?"

"Yes. No."

"Do you know where Mr. Trumbo is?"

"I have no idea," said Mrs. Trumbo stoutly.

"Well, we are trying to find Mr. Trumbo. We have sent a number of letters to his Carmel office and his apartment since he missed his audit appointment."

"Oh, God!"

"We are going back to 1995, and there are serious problems. I mean, serious. If you have any contact with Mr. Trumbo in the future, would you please give him this audit number and tell him to come into our Los Angeles office to avoid further proceedings."

"Yes, of course. What is the number?" He heard scrambling.

"ZXCVBNM3347," Paul said.

"I can't find a pen! What was that again?"

"ZSFJRTX3347." He hung up. It really was sweet.

Late that night after tossing and turning for a few hours, Paul packed a duffel and got on the road for Tahoe. The empty gray highway soothed him in a way his bed could not. He liked going somewhere. Action in any direction was enough to silence those bothersome night goblins.

His first stop was the casino. He hit the tables with a furious, frantic energy, and because his leg ached and his mind felt uncommonly disgruntled, he hit the bottle of Louise's red elixir a few more times than was probably judicious. He lost steadily, and it was only after he found himself tossing four-of-a-kind down without a bet that he realized the atmosphere had undergone a subtle metamorphosis. What started off as the usual night-owl crowd, pasty-faced and determined, was suddenly looking greener. He checked out the overhead lights, and sure enough, more green. Turning back to the dealer, he opened his mouth to comment on the strange cost-cutting measures of the casino, but shut it again as her scaly hair crawled wildly over her shoulders and down to the table, separated from her scalp and scampered over the table, now changed into small, mean lizards, red tongues flicking at the flying cards.

Holy shit, he thought, feeling bubbles of laughter bursting inside. Didn't something like this happen to Hunter Thompson in Vegas?

As he turned to remark upon it to the man seated next to him, he stopped himself with a fist to his mouth, stifling what would have been a startled shout. The man's face was swelling—his eyes rolled over into opaque marbles, his teeth grew spear sharp, and from beneath his white T-shirt, like a dinosaur hatching from an egg, a tail began to emerge, glinting in the turmoil of green light that now shined down in distinct beams, alien light on a reptilian hell...

The whole thing was so damned funny! He nearly busted a gut laughing, until the pit boss stood him up and firmly but gently steered him out of the room, inviting him to leave.

Ducking the man's bulging eyes, which were making a beeline across the heads of the patrons toward him, Paul staggered to the nearest rest room giggling hysterically, and, not entirely without regret, forced himself to upchuck. Pulling himself to the sink a few minutes later, he was afraid to look in the mirror, but he did, and what he saw did not surprise him. A sweating man. A grinning, gib-bering idiot.

Sitting on a stool, door closed, he gave himself a long time to recover, unhappily monitoring the nocturnal comings and goings of his fellow gamblers. Coming out later, he rinsed his face, entered the casino gingerly, and found things restored to the more usual bright lights and pleasant amusements.

Cursing himself, he headed straight out to his car and drove to Nina's house on Kulow. One light knock and Bob answered the door.

"It's Sunday morning," Bob said, squinting into the darkness to see. "And really early, isn't it?" In spite of the hour, he looked combed and unrumpled.

"Right," Paul said. "Sorry. Your mom home?"

"She's sleeping." He bent down to pet Hitchcock. "She worked late writing a motion."

"Any idea when she'll get up?"

"Not really. But you can come in and wait."

"Thanks."

"I'll make coffee," Bob said dubiously, leading the way toward the table. Around a cardboard cereal box, small o's were arranged into an elaborately layered rectangle. An empty milk container lay on its side nearby.

"That's okay," Paul said. "Allow me." He opened cupboards until he lined up Nina's equipment, asking, "You want some?"

Bob's eyes opened ever so slightly. "Sure," he said, voice casual.

After measuring the coffee with a table-spoon, Paul sprinkled it into the filter basket, loving the smell of hot water soaking through ground beans. He searched farther to come up with sugar. Ladling some into Bob's cup along with some half-and-half he found in the refrigerator, he said, "You've been up a while."

Bob nodded.

"Couldn't sleep?"

He shook his head.

"Neither could I," said Paul. "Nightmares. Things that go bump in the night." He laughed, and after a minute, Bob contributed his own dry chuckle to the thought.

"Me too," he said.

With his back turned, Paul added instant chocolate to Bob's cup along with a dab of coffee. He handed it over. Bob took a tentative sip, then another. "Mmm," he said, surprised. "I didn't know coffee was so good."

"Secret recipe," said Paul.

They drank their coffee in companionable peace for a few minutes while the dark outside paled toward morning.

"What's your nightmare?" Bob asked. "You don't have to tell me but...do you have one that really scares you, the same one over and over?"

"My nightmare," Paul said, thinking. "I turn into a lizard."

"Sounds funny."

"Trust me, it isn't."

"I didn't know adults had bad dreams like that."

"We do."

Bob put a finger in the bottom of his cup and came up with sticky black goo, which he licked. "In my dream," he said, "there's someone trying to get into the house. Someone who wants to kill me and kill my mom. I know he's out there, out in the woods. I can hear him, but I can't see him. I hunt for him and I feel like he's right behind me all the time. He's got a knife. I can hear him getting closer. I get scared, really scared, and I try to shout but nothing comes out. He gets closer...and then I wake up and it's like I died or something, I feel so bad."

"Sounds awful."

"It is." He nodded. "Yep."

"So that's why you were up so early on a Sunday."

"Right."

"You don't have to answer this either, but...are these dreams something recent?"

"Yeah."

"Did they start after that night at Nikki's? You know, the night that man chased you."

Bob looked startled. "No, not then. Before. Last fall. After...you know. That's when the dreams started, right after he died."

Son of a gun. But why was he surprised at the notion that Bob hadn't forgotten what was probably the most horrible experience of his young life? Just because Nina managed to erect stone wall defenses didn't mean her son had the same talent. "You tell your mom?"

"What's she gonna do about it? That guy killed her husband. It's worse for her. She gets up in the middle of the night and I hear her walking around in circles upstairs."

"She does, eh? And you wake up at dawn. So you just get up and build cities out of cereal."

Bob flicked a Cheerio across the table with his fingers. "I can't watch TV. That would wake Mom up. They never caught him, and they never will. Someday he'll come back and try to hurt us. So Hitchcock and me keep a lookout."

Paul got up and poured himself another cup of coffee. The Tahoe birds, more musical than the seagulls near his condo, were waking up and beginning the morning chorus. Better than any choir, he thought. Out there, just singing and praying louder than Baptists this

Sunday morning. "There's something I want to tell you, Bob, only you can't tell anyone else, understand?"

"What?"

"Can you keep a secret?"

"My mom says I'm getting to be an expert."

Paul let that go by. "That guy...the one outside the door. The bad guy. You know who I mean. The real one."

Bob hesitated, and his features went to war against each other, the vulnerable boy and the invincible teen vying for equal time. The boy won. "Yes," Bob said, so softly Paul could barely hear him. Then louder, committed, he said, "The one that did it. The one who tried to kill us all. That's who I dream about."

"Here's what I want you to know and this is what you can't tell anyone, not Uncle Matt, not Aunt Andrea, not Troy...nobody, ever, okay?"

"My mom?"

"Definitely not your mom."

"I don't like keeping secrets from her."

"She can't know this. Ever."

"Why not?"

"Because...your mom is an officer of the court. She might feel obliged to do something. It might hurt me. Keeping her out of this protects her from involvement."

Curiosity broke through his doubt. "All right," Bob agreed. "I won't tell anyone."

"You promise me?"

"I swear."

"Okay. Listen up, Bob. The bad guy is gone. He'll never, ever come back. I'm not saying this just to comfort you. I am not shitting you," Paul said, using the language intentionally, knowing Bob would understand he was being treated like an adult entrusted with serious information. "He'll never come back. He isn't out in these woods waiting to get you and your mom. He isn't hiding somewhere else and waiting for his chance to come forward. You're safe. Don't waste another second worrying about that bastard coming after you. He won't. He can't. Got that? He can't. You have my word."

Bob looked directly into his eyes, and Paul saw belief beginning to dawn in the face that was lit by the foggy light now pouring through the window. "You sound like you know what you're talking about," Bob said.

"I do."

Holding his cup out for a refill, Bob gave voice to a final, loitering suspicion. "Well, but if he isn't anywhere, where is he?"

"Which piece?" Paul said. Then he picked up his cup and started some eggs.

And on the stairway above, now past enjoying the songs of the birds and the comforting murmur of Bob and Paul in the kitchen, Nina pulled her robe tight around her and reeled back against the bannister. Paul said what he said to comfort Bob as he had comforted her once, but somehow the assurance in his voice, the sheer arrogant confidence, hit her differently this time. He sounded so absolutely certain.

She went back to her room and lay down on the bed, putting her thoughts together.

Ten minutes later, she went down to the kitchen in her kimono. She acted surprised to see Paul, ate the eggs he set before her, and told him all about the rock shop owner and Dennis Rankin, with the claim next to Nikki's. Paul was at loose ends and agreed right away to go out to the desert, although he insisted they make a quick stop to drop something in the box at the Post Office on the way out of town. Bob said he had homework and opted to stay behind.

Nina dressed and packed water and sandwiches. They stopped in Zephyr Cove for gas, and as they were leaving the mountains, rushing down toward the flat desert floor on the twisting freeway, she allowed herself to take one swift look at Paul, sitting beside her rubbing his leg and wearing his sunglasses.

And it seemed to her that she had met the real Paul for the first time when she heard him talking to Bob in the kitchen, the real Paul who was an utter mystery, masking himself with joking and pranks and systematic underachievement. He was as unreadable as a—what was that mythical lizardlike animal who could kill with a look?—a basilisk! And having seen the mystery in him, she was filled with horror and wonder and unable to speak of it.

23

WHILE THEY SAT stuck in traffic on McCarran in Reno, Nina took time out from her driving to observe how Paul massaged his leg. He seemed much better, but the leg must still be a bother. She puzzled over his urgent insistence that she rush Louise's red "mixture" to Ginger for immediate analysis before they could leave town.

"But why?" she had asked.

"Let's just say, nothing that much fun is ever innocent," he had said wryly.

She turned her mind away from that and back to traffic while passing between trucks. Paul broke into her thoughts. "You got hold of Dr. Seisz?"

"Yes," she answered, "but call him that and he'll probably die of surprise. I warned Tim we were coming. He was a big help in my last—my last murder case. He's expecting us and a fat check for his time, too. I hope this isn't pointless," Nina said. "We may never find Rankin."

"We won't if we don't look," said Paul.

Nina found an opening in the traffic and went for it, passing on the right of a stalled car and skipping through a yellow light to get across the next big intersection. "Nikki gave us a good idea where to look—"

"Within eighty acres."

"We've got to find him. He'll probably stay near a road or track."

"Get a lot of work done on your motion yesterday?" Paul asked.

"Uh huh. I'm going to attack the preliminary hearing testimony in two ways."

"I'd like to hear about it."

"You will. I'm calling a meeting for tomorrow at eleven A.M. You, Sandy and Wish, and Ginger, who's coming up from Sacramento. I'll give you all a copy of the points and authorities setting out the arguments I'll be making at the hearing and we'll go over everything. Are you available?"

"Yeah. Then I have to come right back down to Carson City in the afternoon and look at plane parts with Chuck Davis. By the way, any word on the phone bills from the Sykes house?"

"I got the copies from the D.A.'s office and reviewed an entire year's worth," Nina said. "Sykes also had a cell phone that he used mostly for work. Several bills showed that he made regular calls to another cell phone number which has since been disconnected. I called Beth to check the number and she said that was her phone. She didn't have those bills handy. She said her husband paid the bills and she was having trouble finding things but if she found them, she'd call me. She also said she lost the phone in the confusion of returning from LA after hearing about the plane crash and the murder."

"I'm very interested in the phone call Sykes received on the night of his death," Paul said.

"Nikki's description of his reaction to it is puzzling. From a big smile to awful distress.

I'd think the call was a notification of Chris's death if I didn't know the plane was still in the air around the time Nikki was watching him there at the house."

"It won't show up on Sykes's phone records since he received the call. It won't be easy to follow up on."

"It seems that way," Nina said. "How did it go with Beth? I don't have your writeup yet."

He filled her in on the scene he had witnessed between Beth and Dylan Brett.

"I knew he was too good to be true."

"Hey, at least he's human. I was beginning to wonder."

"Think he had it in for Sykes?"

"I just don't know. He's so Gatsby, sort of ethereal and false, I can't imagine him mustering up the depth of feeling that motivated someone to take a sword and kill. If you believe Beth, he's all talk anyway."

"What did you think of Beth?"

"I like her, but I have a credibility bone to pick with that entire group of women," Paul said. "Beth seems smarter than Daria, deeper, and even though she's grieving she's very careful about what she says. She says Daria didn't tell her she was at the house the night of the murder. She won't say much about the marriage but I'm pretty sure she wasn't close to Sykes. But man, did she love the boy."

"How are you feeling? Leg better?"

"I'm on the cane for another month. Have to do some exercises and have it looked at then. But the pain's down to a dull roar."

"Good. You came back earlier than expected. I thought you said you'd be back on Monday."

"Uh huh."

"Paul?"

"Yeah?"

"Nothing."

"Is something wrong?"

She didn't answer.

"Why are you looking at me like that?" Paul asked. "Did I do something?"

"Forget it."

"You know that's the worst thing you can do, getting me hot with anticipation and then letting me down."

"Sorry. I'm just feeling the stress of...all this."

"Why don't you just chill? Enjoy the scenery," said Paul, turning on the radio.

"So we're going somewhere north of Winnemucca?" Tim Seisz said, climbing into the back seat of the Bronco. He had been standing beside his pickup in the main UN parking lot, dressed for prospecting in a straw hat, leather boots, and jeans, and toting a long heavy pack.

As Nina zipped across 80 to 395, Paul explained. "We're looking for a certain piece of property owned by a fellow named Dennis Rankin, an antisocial character, by all reports. We want to talk to him. We have a geological map to guide us to his claim, which we can read, although unreliably. We need your help to find it."

"Simple enough."

"We're also hoping that you can tell us if someone might have made a strike of black fire opals on the claim next door."

"I knew it wouldn't be that simple. What do you mean, the claim next door?"

"His claim is contiguous with a forty-acre property in which we have a strong interest," Nina said briefly.

"And we have permission to be on this second property with a pick and shovel?"

"The adjoining property, yes," Nina said. Daria had granted permission, saying her sister wouldn't mind, and she would speak with her about it. "Rankin's property, no. I don't expect him to be friendly. He may actually be dangerous."

Tim raised his eyebrows at this. "But I told you before, Nina, that color of opal has only been found in the Virgin Valley, north toward the borders of Oregon and Idaho, unless you go to Australia. These stones are incredibly rare. The geologic conditions that produce them don't happen just anywhere."

"Then we won't find any," Paul said.

Tim unfolded the map and studied it. "This claim is nearly a hundred miles from the Virgin Valley."

"Well, this is just an off chance. You're not going to say the whole state has been so thoroughly prospected that it's impossible, are you? We have black fire opals, and we have a pair of mining claims back-to-back, and this fellow Rankin, who has one of the claims, may also

414

have had the opals at one time." In truth, Nina had absolutely no idea how the opals fit into her case. She desperately wished to know. She thought Rankin had some idea, though, and thought having an expert along couldn't hurt when they finally did talk with him.

They settled into the ride, Nina driving, Tim and Paul chatting about airplanes. Paul seemed pleased to learn that Tim was a licensed private pilot and had a million questions.

Time passed. Nina concentrated on the scenery. Caught by her eye like perfectly rendered animals in a painting of nineteenth-century bucolia, cows browsed a narrow strip of green alongside the Humboldt River. Brown and black hills with scruffy vegetation lined the horizons, and the occasional distant antlike hiker recalled images of Humphrey Bogart and his crew squabbling over gold in a similar two-toned desert. Witch's water mirages formed and disappeared in the small hills of the road. "I love it here. I love everything about it," she said.

Tim, hacking away on a hand-sized electronic organizer in the back seat, said, " 'The stars speak of man's insignificance in the long eternity of time; the desert speaks of his insignificance right now.' Or so a man named Teale said once. Anyway, it's ninety-four out there. Just pray the air-conditioning doesn't fail."

At Winnemucca they stopped for more gas and a pit stop. The river town rose out of the desert like another mirage and just as quickly fell behind them as they headed north.

This part of Nevada was empty except for the occasional ranch homestead. Now and then they passed a sign directing them to some old mining town that hadn't survived when the silver and gold ran out. As they rolled toward the distant Idaho border, down blacktop so hot they could smell it, the landscape shifted from blowing tumbleweed to low green brush on sand surrounded by hills and mountains painted with blue and purple.

After an hour and a half of hard driving, they turned onto a side road. The pavement narrowed, dropping off on both sides into gravel slopes. Eventually they came to the end of that too. Wind shook the SUV. All around, the bare and silent sands stretched far away.

"Is this the place?" Nina asked.

Tim consulted the map. "No." He got out of the car and walked around. Finally, he pointed. "That way."

Nina and Paul followed him. "But...where's the road?" Nina asked, looking down a narrow, rutted path that seemed to go straight uphill.

"That's it. Typical for a mining claim."

"No way," she said. "Too steep."

"We could walk," Tim suggested. "It looks like it's only four or five more miles. I brought plenty of water." He gestured toward his backpack on the back seat.

But Paul had pulled himself into the driver's seat of the Bronco, shifted into four wheel drive, and lunged forward. "That's what these cars live for. Not your perfectly flat freeways and groomed mountain roads. Hop in."

Pulling the car door shut behind her, Nina said, "I'll bet they never saw a road like this in Detroit." Once Tim was in and securely belted, Paul pushed on.

The pathway up was so narrow that grasses and brush screeched as they passed by, scratching tiny gouges along the sides of the Bronco. So pitted was the road, Nina kept her tongue firmly in her mouth, afraid she would bite it. On the steepest parts, she leaned back in her seat and closed her eyes, unwilling to look, only half-trusting Paul and her faithful Bronco to keep them alive. Five miles on a normal road didn't take long. Five miles up and down harrowing mountain roads took forever.

Finally, Paul pulled the Bronco to a halt. They had gradually climbed along a high valley to the foot of a moderate mountain range. From this close, Nina could see wind-eroded passages into the rocks that led to tiny higher isolated valleys. There would be caves and box canyons. Nothing was moving anywhere except a restless breeze which had sprung up and was protecting them from the worst of the heat.

They got out and looked back toward where they had come from. The valley was like a long narrow plateau, its edge visible in the dry air, half the state of Nevada spread below it like a satellite picture. Nina smeared sun-block all over her face and hands and covered her hair with a bandanna. Paul threw a couple of pills down his throat and squirted water into his mouth. Tim shouldered his bag.

"Onward," he said.

．　　　．　　　．

They had been walking about fifteen minutes into the mountains following the opening Tim indicated, when they came to a shanty with a tin roof. An old Jeep sat out front. All around they saw the desiderata of the prospector: empty plastic water jugs, wood stacked against the wall, rusting metal equipment and tools. A card table had been set up a few feet away, under a large bush which provided a modicum of shade, and Nina could see that it was covered with plastic trays of small rocks in various stages of sorting. Nearby was a wheelbarrow and a pile of dirt and rocks about five feet high, covered with white dust. "Nobody here," Paul said, peering inside through a flapping screen.

"This way," Tim said.

They set off down a well-worn trail which led to a set of switchbacks, trooping silently, Paul in front using the cane as a walking stick, Tim bringing up the rear. Suddenly, Paul stopped. Nina grabbed his arm so that she wouldn't fall off the trail and looked ahead. Paul had his finger against his mouth and was motioning toward a gully on the left.

Now that they had stopped, she could hear what he had heard: the rhythmic thud of a pickax against rock.

They crept forward and looked down into the gully.

A man stood with his back to them, about a hundred yards away and down, swinging a large pickax against the other side of the gully, raising a cloud of dirt. After each ten or fifteen strikes against the rock he would stop, lean over, and examine the rocks he had pried from the rock face. With a slovenly beard and hair clumping down to his shoulders, both thick with dust, he was sweating brown streaks. His torso was powerful, the shoulders twice as wide as the hips, the straining arms huge. He hadn't heard them.

Nina nodded. They got up and started down the gully. He heard them now, and turned around, pickax in hand, red-faced, coughing, wiping the sweat off with the tail of his shirt.

"You must be Dennis Rankin," Paul called out pleasantly. "What luck."

"And you must be trespassing," said Rankin. The big man wore jeans caked black and a striped shirt with one sleeve rolled up, exposing a fat, filthy bandage around his elbow. Next to him on the ground sat several metal buckets laden with rocks and several more containers of water. The rock face had been wetted down and Nina smelled damp earth.

"We came a long way to talk with you," Paul said.

"Why?"

"We're interested in black fire opals."

"I'm interested in getting you the fuck off my property," Rankin said. He stood his ground, his dark eyes focusing on them hard enough to pierce skin.

Tim let out a yell. He held his foot in one

hand, face contorting with pain and fear. "Something bit me!"

"What's out here?" Paul asked. "Scorpions?"

"I think it was a snake!" Tim cried. "Omigod. Omigod. Omigod."

"Tim, don't panic," Nina ordered. "It's probably an insect bite." Just to make sure, she surveyed the ground near him. Seeing no sign of any crawling things, she took him by the hand, leading him toward the rock face, stepping right past Rankin, who swayed but made no move toward them. Pulling a canteen out of Tim's backpack, she lifted his pant leg.

"See," he said. "Right there. Shit!"

"Cool it," Nina said. "Don't get hysterical. I don't think it's a snakebite. Now, do you have a first-aid kit in there?" She poured water over a spot Tim indicated while he mewed like a kitten, then unzipped the canvas pack and began feeling around inside.

"I'll give you ten seconds to put a Band-Aid on the kiddie and get the hell out. This is my claim." Bending over Tim, Nina finally recognized the accent. Australian. Agitated, she continued ministering to Tim, her back to Rankin, blocking Tim from Rankin's view.

"This lady, Nina Reilly, represents Nicole Zack, a young woman who is charged with the murder of Dr. William Sykes," Paul said. "My name is Paul van Wagoner."

"Never heard of him. Never heard of any of you."

"You and Dr. Sykes were seen together at

Prize's, arguing, a few days before his death," Paul said. "So that's kind of unlikely."

"No law against hoisting a few with a fellow in a bar, last I heard," Rankin said.

"What was the bag on the table? Was it opals? What was your business with Sykes?"

Rankin answered by raising the pickax. "You a little slow, mate? Let me make it easy on you. I want you gone. Go or be damned."

He spoke through his nose, Nina noticed. Nikki had described that nasal voice, that accent.

He was Nikki's phone caller, which meant—

"Just give me a second to clear this," Nina said, gesturing with a plastic jar of antiseptic she had discovered in Tim's well-stocked backpack. "He's bleeding."

"That was you in the woods behind Nikki Zack's house a few nights ago, wasn't it?" Paul asked Rankin. "I mean, otherwise there's another Australian prospector in Tahoe with a ferocious interest in opals, which I find far-fetched, don't you?"

While he talked, Nina, ostensibly taking care of Tim, was fighting an interior battle. All she could think was: Rankin might have hurt Bob. Anger welled up, so thick and opaque, it temporarily blinded her to Tim, to Paul, to her surroundings. Hot, sweating, she busied herself with Tim's leg, trying to subdue her fury.

Paul went on, "That arm of yours is looking pretty nasty, Rankin. Did the woman with the shotgun nick you? That must have hurt."

Keeping the pickax raised and steady, Rankin reflexively drew his arm closer to his body.

Paul placed his hands in his pockets. Nina had noticed this ploy before. He used it to reduce his power superficially while maintaining absolute control. When Rankin spoke, Paul leaned slightly toward him, looking friendly and interested, as innocuous as an applicant hoping to hear something positive from the loan officer of a bank.

But Rankin didn't underestimate Paul. "Hands out where I can see 'em," he commanded.

Paul complied, spreading his arms palms up so that Rankin could see he wasn't looking for a fight. "You went there to steal the opals, didn't you?"

"I'm no thief!" he snarled. "If I go after something, it's mine in the first place."

"How could the opals be yours? Did you dig them up yourself?"

"Maybe I did. And maybe they were owed me."

"Sykes owed them to you? And then you read that he was dead and Nikki Zack was there that night. Figured she had them, didn't you?"

"I never hurt anyone," he said, taking furtive pleasure in this literal interpretation of the truth. "That wood behind the house is public property and that woman with the shotgun should be locked up."

Paul passed over this. "And for that matter, where did Sykes get opals in the first place? He's no prospector." Paul shook a rock out of his shoe. "But you are. So, let's say, for the sake of argument, you discovered the opals. They belonged to Sykes because you found them on what you thought was his property. Let's put aside for a moment what you were doing on the claim next door. You brought them to him. That's the act of an honest man," he said, and Rankin responded with a nod, following along with some curiosity. "And then, you say, he promised to give them back to you," Paul continued. "In payment for something? To manage the opal strike on his claim?"

Rankin frowned. "Not even close. Not the deal at all."

Paul waved a fly away. "So what was the deal?"

Rankin looked at Paul, Nina, and then Tim. Apparently appeased by the sight of three blundering city folk out for a walk in the vicious sun, with no visible weaponry and unthreatening manners...whatever it was he saw, he decided to answer. "The deal was that I *wouldn't* mine the opals."

Paul seemed momentarily taken aback. "You *wouldn't* mine the opals?"

"He paid me to stay off the claim and keep my mouth shut about it."

"So he refused to pay you, and you had an argument at Prize's."

"Wrong again. He was holding the opals for a few months to make sure I didn't tell anyone about the strike. He just got sidetracked by a sword before he had a chance to get them back to me."

"But that doesn't make any sense," Paul said. "Help me out here. You were arguing."

"That was after I found out..."

"What?"

"Nothing. I didn't kill the doc, and I didn't break any laws. Which concludes our business here today, in my view."

"But you were fighting," Paul persisted. "And you won't say why. That leaves a huge question hanging out there."

Nina moved. She got up to stand in front of Rankin, hands on her hips.

"Nina," Paul said, his voice warning her.

She ignored him. "You chased my son in the woods," she said, aware only of Dennis Rankin. "You scared him to death. And you would have hurt him, too." She remembered that night, the smell of the moist clumps of leaves on the ground, how hard Bob's heart had pounded when she finally got to hug him again. The thought of him running in the dark woods so afraid blinded her momentarily to the brightness all around them. All she could see was Bob's face when they got back to the house, the new dark place in his eyes that resided there all the time now.

Rankin stared at her, then let out a laugh like a bark. "That was your son? Nimble little bugger."

She could see every clogged pore on his face, the wild hairs on his eyebrows, the dirt streaming down his neck. "This is for you," Nina said. She handed him a subpoena.

He took it.

"And so's this." Nina's arm went back and swung forward before Paul could stop it. Her palm connected with Rankin's filthy face so hard that he reeled back a step. Fast as a scorpion, he jumped toward her, jerking the pickax up over his shoulder, getting ready to let loose...

Paul grabbed her and pulled her out of reach.

"How dare you," she said to Rankin, rubbing her stinging hand. "You were the one in my truck, too, you bastard!"

Tim sprang to his feet and took a position next to Nina and Paul.

Just in time, because Rankin raised his ax and charged, swinging wildly as they scattered. Screaming curses, he followed Nina, who was running pell-mell down the hill, slipping on clods and gravel, falling and picking herself up, with the big man rumbling down after her, heavy as a truck. Paul managed to get between them, and ducked out of the way as Rankin swung. "Run!" he said to Nina and Tim. Nina paused just long enough to notice the mark of her hand across Rankin's fleshy cheek. Then she ran after Tim, who had put a jackrabbit's distance between himself and the fight.

Paul, not moving fast, used strategy. He got Rankin running fast down a steep slope behind him, then shifted direction suddenly and watched with satisfaction as the huge man lost his balance and fell. "We'll be going now," Paul said before Rankin had time to shake his brain back into place and come after them.

He climbed as quickly as he could to join Nina and Tim, who were waiting for him uphill on the trail. Accompanied by a steady stream of threats and invective from the gully below, they headed back, Tim grabbing his pack on the way. After they got out of visual reach, Tim started to whistle softly.

"You move surprisingly well for a guy who was freaking out a minute ago over a snakebite," Paul observed, panting.

Tim pushed his pant leg firmly over the spot Nina had neatly cleaned. "I'm tougher than I act," he said.

"There was no snake. There was no bite," Nina said.

Paul's eyebrows shot up.

"He faked it."

"Got a real good look in those buckets," said Tim. "Got a good look at the rock wall. That's what you wanted, wasn't it, Nina?"

"That's what I wanted, Tim. Did you see anything?"

"Bentonite. The right kind of clay. But no opals. He's not finding anything but low-grade opals he couldn't sell for a couple of bucks to the rock store. You practically took his jaw off, Nina. I thought lawyers were—"

"Bare-handed, she takes on Charlie Manson and his pickax," Paul said.

"I never did anything like that before," Nina said, feeling the contact with Rankin's grizzled, stinking skin on her hand again. She wiped it on her leg, trying to remove all traces of the encounter. "I don't know what came over me."

Paul said nothing, but he put a hand on her shoulder and squeezed.

When they got back to the Bronco, Tim pulled out a small sample he had filched from one of the buckets while Nina had been playing nurse, and examined it. "No. He's not working a strike. He's looking, but he's not finding anything."

"The opals must be on the Logan claim. Rankin started out prospecting his own land," Paul speculated. "He found inferior opals there and checked out some nearby properties, maybe without permission. That's where he found the really good opals Sykes had, that Nikki took."

"The geology in this area is under-examined." Tim shuffled the map. "But it seems impossible that black fire opals would be discovered so far from the Virgin Valley. The adjoining claim would have had to have the volcanic action plus the right minerals. I want to see the claim. It's due east of here, but we have to go all the way out to the main road first."

"Tim, we don't have enough time to look at Grandpa Logan's claim today," Nina said. "I have to get back to Tahoe tonight. It's a five-hour drive."

"Fine," Tim said from the back seat. "I'll show you where to drop me. I've got a tent, water, supplies, and a phone in the bag. I'll camp out on the claim tonight, and call one of the T.A.'s from the university to come and pick me up when I'm finished."

"Your phone might not work this far out," Nina said.

"I've got a satellite phone. I do lots of work in remote places. Now, don't you worry about old Tim."

"You're a good man, for an expert witness," Paul said. "Tim, those opals Nina showed you in your office, you thought they were valuable, right?"

"They were larger and more stable than any I've seen."

"If another half dozen existed, even larger, the real cream of the collection, would you say they were extraordinarily valuable?"

"Hmm," Tim said. "Depends on your context. The largest rock she showed me *might*— and highlight that word in your mind with a bright yellow marker—might just fetch a few thousand. So take a dozen, half of them even larger than the ones I saw..." A dreamy look came into his eyes. "I'd say that entire stash was worth over $100,000, sold to the right bidders. Maybe more. That's if they are uncut. Cut and polished by the right expert, much more."

"It's a lot," Nina said. But it was really just money. She felt tired. Was that what this case came down to, another brawl over money?

"Hitchcock's MacGuffin," Paul said.

"What?" Nina said. She thought he was referring to a dog toy.

"In every movie of his, there's some impor-

428

tant object everyone's chasing. Only it isn't really important what it is. It's the story that comes out of how much people want it that is important. Remember in *Pulp Fiction* they opened the attaché case and you never even got to see what was this shining thing they'd all been struggling to get through the whole movie?"

"That wasn't Hitchcock," Tim protested. "That was Elmore Leonard, wasn't it? No, wait. The Italian guy."

"You think the opals are at the heart of this?" Nina asked.

"No," Paul said. "That's what I'm saying. They're just objects. The heart of the case is inside someone, beating fast."

"Poetic," Nina said. "Who?"

"And the suspects, they go round and round," Paul said. "Or maybe the opals have nothing to do with this, and our original theory, that Sykes's murder was connected with a malpractice case, is the more likely one." They continued their discussion until they reached the end of the dirt road. Relaxing his hands on the wheel as they hit smooth asphalt, Paul said, "At least we know one thing. We know who was calling Nikki, who came after you, and who chased Bob through the woods that night. And who argued over something with Sykes at the casino a week before he was murdered. Are you going to sic the police on him, Nina?"

"I think...we can use him in our case somehow. So I guess not. And he's right. He never did hurt any of us, just used scare tactics. I don't think he's a danger to us, now his story's out."

"He knows we know who he is," Paul agreed.

They fell into thought. In the back seat, Tim, who had been marking their map with a highlighter, said, "Stop here."

They all got out and stretched. Late afternoon had brought the long blue-green shadows out. Buzzards circled overhead. A faint track led off across a scrubby meadow with the same line of mountains behind it. A wooden post beside the track was marked with a couple of black stripes. The Logan claim.

"You sure you want to do this?" Paul said.

"I've never been so thrilled in my entire professional life," Tim said. He shook hands with them. "I'll report in when I get back."

"Take it easy," Nina said. Climbing into the driver's seat, she looked down the dusty track toward the barren hills.

"Maybe there's a claim I can stake myself nearby," Tim said.

"I have the feeling all the relevant land is taken," said Paul.

"Oh, well," Tim said philosophically. He tucked the map into his bag along with his stolen rock. "There's still the glory of scientific publication."

24

PAUL, NINA, SANDY, WISH, and Dr. Ginger Hirabayashi sat around Nina's conference table on Monday morning in postures that to Nina's eyes perfectly exemplified their roles. Paul, the sly spy, lolled innocently on the chair, his leg hanging over its arm as if he were sitting at home watching a ball game, but the eyes in his sunburned face were sharp on Nina. Sandy, the sentry, was parked like a Humvee near the door. Wish, the disciple, listened eagerly, his big ears pricked, eyes wide as he took in everything. And Ginger was the resident skeptic, arms folded, buzz-cut head cocked to the side, scanning for defects in Nina's train of thinking.

"The worst thing about this whole case is that Henry McFarland is buying into the current hysteria surrounding juvenile violence and has decided to try Nikki as an adult," Nina said. "I've practically gone down on my knees to him..."

"You mean, as in groveling, or as in pulling a Monica?" Paul interjected.

Nina looked at him, at his silly smile, at his powerful shoulders, at his capable hands, most of all at his hazel eyes flecked with yellow which caught everything, and she thought again, a basilisk, checking the word against the man she thought she knew. Inhumanly cold on the inside. A killer.

He noticed the look. "Sorry. Lousy joke," he said.

With an effort, she went on. "But the prosecutor has a lot of discretion in making that decision, and no prosecutor or judge is going to go against the tide of public opinion. The whole country is paranoid about kids her age right now. So she's charged with murder in the first degree. It can't be a death penalty case, but there is a possibility of a life sentence." She shook her head, looking down at her coffee cup. "It's incredible. It's all wrong in light of the factors cited in the *Kent* case, and..."

"How come she's charged with first-degree murder?" Sandy said. "It'll have to look like a crime of passion to a jury. Not cold-blooded. No plan and all."

"You mean no premeditation, Mom," Wish told Sandy. Wish was studying law enforcement at the community college and getting much savvier. Sandy slitted her eyes very slightly and Wish said, "Uh oh."

"I know what I mean," Sandy said.

"Sure you do, Mom."

"Damn right she does," Paul said.

"You stay out of this," Sandy warned.

"Wish is just trying to be helpful, aren't you, Wish?" Paul said.

Wish nodded.

"He's got a lot on his mind," Paul added.

"That would be a first," said Sandy.

"What do you have on your mind, Wish?" Ginger asked him. "Now I'm just dying to know."

Wish said, "I'm buying Paul's van. I'm getting some work done on it. A ring job, new brake pads, new CD player, and new upholstery in back."

Paul said, "You're replacing my upholstery?"

"Well, I mean, leopard skin? Pretty dated. Like the hippies or something."

"What will you put back there?"

"Industrial carpeting. I'll have my bike back there a lot and my friends won't have to wipe their shoes."

"I just happen to have some surplus industrial carpeting," Paul said. "Come down to Carmel with me when the hearing's over and I'll give it to you. I might even have a job or two to keep you busy until school starts up again."

"Excellent concept!"

"Excuse me. Can we get back to Sandy's important question?" Nina asked. "Why is Nikki charged with first-degree murder? With her usual discernment, Sandy has zeroed in on a crucial point in this case. First of all, Sandy, there doesn't have to be premeditation for someone to be charged with first-degree murder. The charge in this case is based on something called the felony-murder rule."

"A homicide that occurs during the commission of another crime," Wish announced, looking sideways at Sandy. She made no sign she had heard.

"That's right," Nina said. "The theory is that Nikki was committing, or at least attempting to commit, a burglary at the time of the death. Burglary's a felony. That's why we face a first-degree charge. Now, we have to try to get Nikki back into the juvenile system. I think I could manage that if we could convince Judge Flaherty to throw out the burglary portion of the charge. Then the case would become a second-degree murder case and Flaherty would be much more likely to let Juvenile Court take over. That's going to be the main strategy at this hearing."

"What would happen to her there?" Wish asked.

"She'd be out at age twenty-five," Nina said. "At worst."

"Nine long years from now," Wish said. "That's the best we're hoping for?"

For the length of time it took to adjust a few cramped limbs and take a sip or two of coffee, they all looked at Nina. They would take their cue from her.

"No," Nina said. "That's not the best we can hope for her, but it's all we can do right now. I think we have an innocent client. The problem is, we can't prove it. It's too early. We have leads that go all over the place. At this point, I don't have any way of getting the entire case thrown out. So I'm attacking on a technical point that will substantially lessen our burden at trial."

"So it's sort of an intermediate motion. You're trying to get her into the juvenile system. You're not trying to prove the girl is innocent," Ginger said.

"I would if I could."

"What are the main leads you're working?"

Paul answered Ginger, counting them off on his fingers. "One. The girl's mother did it. She was there that night. The girl may be protecting her, or she may be protecting the girl. Two: For several years, Dr. Sykes had been running into trouble with his practice. He made some serious professional blunders that may have generated a motive for murder. I'm thinking of Linda Littlebear in particular."

Sandy stirred but said nothing.

"Three: Dennis Rankin had an argument with the good doctor over opals soon before his death. Four: Could have been a robbery. A kid named Scott Cabano was making a career of robbing houses along the lake. Maybe he came along after Nikki. Five: Persons unknown wanted both Dr. Sykes and his son dead, and sabotaged his son's plane flight. And that's just for starters."

They thought about this, drinking from their cups, drumming fingers, and in Wish's case, tapping his heel against the floor until his mother smacked the table and insisted he stop.

"Okay," Nina said. "We are filing the paperwork this morning to move to strike portions of the testimony that was taken at the preliminary hearing. Does everyone understand that?"

More nods all around.

"I am requesting what's called a 995 hearing. That's a hearing based on Penal Code section

995 to review whether, based on the testimony and evidence at the prelim, there was probable cause to bind Nikki over on the first-degree charge. In this hearing, I'm going to move to strike the felony portion of the complaint.

"To do that, I'll attack two things: all the prosecution testimony about Nikki's blood being on the sword, and Louise Garibaldi's testimony.

"There is a problem. A 995 hearing is usually based only on the transcript of the prelim—it isn't usually an evidentiary hearing. And we need to get Detective Ditmar and Louise Garibaldi on the stand."

"So?" Ginger said. "How do you get around that and make the judge accept new testimony?"

"Well, there's this seldom-used subsection I found..."

Ginger broke into a broad smile, and Nina smiled back. "Section 995b. Essentially, if we can convince the judge that there is some sort of minor error in the written charges against Nikki, Henry can ask the judge to allow new testimony to correct the error so the Information can stand. I can't ask for it myself. I have to make Henry do it. So I'll try to make Henry nervous enough about the motion to strike that he asks to bring in some more testimony from Detective Ditmar, his blood expert, and Louise. That will open the door for me to cross-examine them and maybe even put on Ginger in rebuttal."

"So you have the setup," Ginger said.

"Then what? How, exactly, do you use it to persuade the judge to strike the felony charge?"

"Like this. First, move to strike all testimony placing Nikki in the study. Show the judge that Detective Ditmar, who testified that Nikki's blood was on the sword, didn't really conclude that the blood was Nikki's. Detective Ditmar waffled at the prelim, Paul.

"Without testimony that the blood matches Nikki's blood, there isn't any evidence putting Nikki inside Dr. Sykes's study. It isn't a felony just to trespass on her uncle's property, or to jump in his pool, or to look into the study from the outside. None of that is enough to show an intent to burglarize."

"But she took something out of a box she got in the swimming pool," Ginger said. "The neighbor—what's her name... ?"

"Louise Garibaldi," Sandy said.

"Louise testified that she saw her take it! How do you get around that?"

"Claim that Louise is an incompetent witness, so her testimony should be stricken," Nina said. "We're going to strike out half the prelim evidence if we can."

"Incompetent? How?" said Wish.

Nina said, "I'm waiting to hear from Ginger on that, Wish." Paul had finally consented to fill her in on his experience without going into too much detail. "Let's just say that Louise is amazingly cheerful for this hard world we live in." She smiled and ignored the puzzlement of Sandy and Wish.

"If all that was stricken, nothing would

place Nikki at the scene," Paul said. "Wait! What about the blood on the wall outside the study? And what about her statement to the cops?"

Nina nodded. "Can't do much about that at this hearing, Paul. I can't get the whole case dismissed because of that remaining evidence. That's why I'm just trying to knock out the felony allegation at this stage."

"Sounds like a plan," Paul said.

"No plan comes without a glitch," Nina said. "Here's the glitch. I am sitting on what may be some very valuable opals that I know were taken from Sykes's house that night. I may have to give them to Henry."

"But then—then it'll be clear that she did take valuable items, even if she took them from outside, so it's a felony, right?" Wish asked.

"Except for one thing. You can't steal your own property," Nina said. "I've done some research on this and I'm going to run with that idea. If I can manage to show they came from Nikki's family's claim…maybe we can find a way to put on Tim Seisz to testify that he found black fire opals on the Logan claim…"

"Your secret plan behind your secret plan," Paul said. He reached over and patted her knee. "That's my girl." His eyebrows drew together as he felt her draw back from him.

Wish pulled on his long chin, saying, "Whoa." Everybody else looked dubious.

"And how do we prove that?" Sandy asked from behind her notepad.

"Are you sure she's telling the truth? Has she told you what she took?" Ginger asked.

Nina nodded. "She took a bag of opals given to Dr. Sykes in late March by Dennis Rankin, who thought Sykes owned the property where he found them. Well, Sykes didn't own the property. The property was owned jointly by Daria Zack and Beth Sykes. So Sykes had no right to take the opals, but he took them anyway. And within days he had persuaded Daria to sell him her share." She filled in some details of Nikki's story for them.

When Nina was finished, Ginger ran her hand over her scalp and said, "I have a question."

"Fire away," Nina said. She had been thinking about the move to strike for one solid week now, always with trepidation that she might have a blind spot somewhere or was missing something. The whole structure was so convoluted. She tensed, waiting for Ginger to blow it all away.

"Sykes's wife—Beth—she owned half the opals. So what about community property? Didn't that make Sykes a part owner too?"

"Good question," Nina said, relieved. "The answer is that the opals weren't community property. Under California law, property that is inherited is separate property until the heir expressly or by implication decides to change its character, by using it to buy a joint asset, for instance.

"I talked to Beth again last night. She said that she'll testify that there was never any intent on her part to convert the claim to community property. She'll also testify that she has no problem with Nikki retrieving the opals."

"Well, well, well," Ginger said. "That's quite an edifice of legal thought you've built. I'm so glad I went into science so I don't have to build these skyscrapers out of air."

"It's like high-school geometry," Nina said. "You start out knowing what you want to prove, then you work backwards until you find the steps that add up to the answer you already want."

"What are the chances Tim's going to find opals on that claim, though?" Paul said. "They shouldn't be there."

"But they are."

"What's that?" Paul said. "Did Tim call?"

"Twenty minutes ago," Nina said, sitting back, preparing to enjoy the reaction she was about to get. "You should have heard him, Paul. He says it's the biggest black fire opal strike since 1972, when an immense gemstone was found in the Virgin Valley. He found the wall where Rankin had been working almost immediately, before dark last night. There were signs of a recent landslide that must have exposed the vein. He took samples back to UN this morning, and he says it's big."

In spite of her confusion about him, she found herself offering up a big smile. Paul was grinning too. "Vindication," he said. "Go on."

"Okay, where was I? Right. Let's say the judge lets me run rampant in this hearing. Flaherty has his moments. We'll see. If he allows it, Tim will testify, then Rankin can confirm where he got the opals and testify that he gave them to Dr. Sykes. Then I'll put on Daria and Beth and public records to confirm that Sykes had no ownership interest in the Logan claim at the time Rankin gave him the opals. Eh *voilà!* Like magic! Out goes the burglary charge on a lack of probable cause. What's left?"

"All that work and it's still a homicide," Sandy said. "But you have a lot more room."

"And we have a much more sympathetic-looking kid in trouble," Ginger said. "I wish you luck. I really do."

"Ginger, I know you are still working with the DNA findings. Dig deeper. We need you to prepare the attack on the blood testimony. And the sooner I get that chemical analysis on the Louise Garibaldi issue the better. We don't have much time."

"There's a guy in Sacramento I work with now and then. He's been busy busting inmates out of state prisons based on DNA evidence with Barry Scheck's group, but he's back in town now. He's good. I'll consult with him."

"Great. Paul, you and Wish have to be sure that Rankin shows up for the hearing. He won't want to be involved, but he's been sub-poenaed."

"I served him yesterday and put the proof of service in the file," Nina said in an aside to Sandy, who made a note.

"She served him all right," Paul said.

"And Paul, we need the Nevada records of ownership of the property. Also, the registration of the claim."

"Check. I'll get on that tomorrow. I'm looking at plane parts this afternoon."

"I'll prepare Daria and Beth to testify," Nina said. "And figure out how to make this thing work."

"What date do you want to set the hearing for?" Sandy said.

"We have to give twenty-one days' notice. Plus three days to pull the motion to strike together. So…" Sandy already had her calendar out.

"Earliest is July sixteenth," she announced.

"July sixteenth it is."

The door was open to the NTSB digs. Paul entered without knocking and found Chuck Davis inside, editing paperwork, a red pen slashing across a section as he read. The place was piled with files and papers. He tucked the pen into a ceramic cup, gave his notebook a flick to shut it, and offered Paul a chair. "We've concluded our field investigation," he said. "The Go Team is heading back to Washington tomorrow."

"Any change from your initial conclusions? You still thinking pilot error?"

"We're thorough," he said, not answering. He took his notebook and filed it carefully in a drawer of his desk. "Let me walk you through this process a little better than I did the first time we spoke. When a plane goes down, even if there's a fatality, there is not automatically an investigation by the NTSB."

"I didn't know that."

"Everything costs, and not all accidents are suspicious. Most causes are relatively straightforward. In this case, our investigation is being paid for by the plane manufacturer's insurance company."

"Not the government?"

"That's right. But believe me, despite what you may infer from that," here he beamed a light ray out of his black beady eyes toward Paul, "we are disinterested observers, not insurance company shills. We are looking for the truth, that's all."

"The insurance company has a stake, though."

Davis smiled. "They don't want to have to pay out on a faulty airplane, obviously, if the machine's not faulty."

"Obviously," said Paul.

"And they are satisfied that there is evidence for a conclusion of pilot error in this case."

"So you're not going to try to put the plane back together?"

"No. The parts will be stored for now at the Reno airport." Paul was catching Davis's drift. Davis wasn't necessarily equally satisfied.

Having hinted at his misgivings, Davis moved back to the investigation. "We have pretty thoroughly picked over the Beechcraft's engines, hydraulic and avionic systems. We looked for something in the meltdown which was all that was left of the cockpit gauges. We reviewed the FAA radar images and interviewed the examiner who last tested Skip

Bailey. The plane was a model 18, built in the sixties, but completely rebuilt. The engine was only a couple of years old. All the other parts had been completely refurbished or replaced within the past few years. And," he said, forestalling a question he apparently saw Paul formulating, "the work that's been done was done well. We checked that wreck down to the rivets." He pulled out and opened a sandwich wrapped in waxed paper. "Will you pardon me? I missed my lunch."

"So, you found nothing new."

"I'll take you through some of our thinking on this." Davis seemed determined to parade the entire length and breadth of the investigation before releasing his captive audience back into the wild. He leaned back into his chair, as if settling in for a cozy fireside chat. Paul followed his lead, stretching his recuperating leg out on a second chair.

"Our exam of the engines and fuel-system components, what was left of them anyway"—he was nibbling at his sandwich—"indicated no preimpact failure."

"This is what the final report will say?"

Davis said, "Over the next year all this information will be very carefully reviewed. I can only give you some preliminary information. Data from the last radar return recorded showed the airplane was holding steady at about six thousand feet—much too low in an area where eight-thousand–foot peaks are common. No distress calls or communications to ATC were received. We conclude that the pilot continued VFR flight into instrument meteorological conditions. His failure to maintain sufficient altitude and/or clearance from the mountainous terrain, which may or may not have been precipitated by one of the illusory events I described to you earlier, caused the crash."

Paul tapped his foot restlessly. "What about what the witnesses said?"

"...and a possible engine stall, cause unknown."

"So, the original mistakes Bailey supposedly made are compounded in your report. In spite of all his experience, you've decided he, one, had some kind of muddled reaction to wind, and two, didn't pay close enough attention to atmospheric conditions," Paul said. "I find it harder than you to ignore the engine crapping out on them."

"We didn't ignore the reported stall. When you gas up a plane, a good pilot checks the fuel for contamination. Sometimes it's mixed with a little water."

"It's delivered that way?"

"Not normally, but it occurs. Now what happened up there, the stall you mentioned that was reported by witnesses, made us wonder if the fuel was compromised, because what you get when you have a certain amount of water in a tank is you get a sputter, and maybe, if you're unlucky and there's a quantity of water, you get a stall. The engine quits. You don't want your plane to stall, so you check your fuel whenever you fuel up."

"How much water would it take, say if you wanted to make sure the engine would stall?"

"You mean, if you were trying to cause the engine to fail?"

"Right."

Davis scrutinized his face. "Do you have anything that suggests that's the case here?"

"Not a thing."

"Well, I'd say a cup would cause major problems for certain."

"Did the pilot check his fuel?"

"His mechanic swore both he and the pilot checked it. Because we're suspicious devils, we checked with two other customers that bought fuel from the same supplier that day. The fuel was good. There was no water."

"What did you find in looking at the fuel tank?"

"You'll recall there was a fire."

"So there's no evidence of water."

"That's right. But if, and I'm just giving you an if because you seem skeptical in the face of all the evidence we have compiled. If someone wanted that plane to go down, the suicidal pilot, his greedy wife, his childhood enemy, someone...if that evil person wanted the plane to stall and crash, water in the fuel tank would cause the symptoms noted by witnesses before that plane crashed."

Paul tried not to let his surprise show on his face. So Davis had taken his doubts seriously and had looked for evidence to repudiate them. He wasn't as hardass about his conclusions as Paul had originally thought. "Was there any fuel left in the tank?" Paul asked.

"The tank's mangled and cracked open, plus it caught fire. Even if we had some fuel left, there's not much point in doing chemical testing unless you suspect contamination." He folded his arms. "As I said, our investigation indicates that the fuel was pure."

"All right," Paul said. "I can see the team has done a thorough job. I don't have any problem with your work. But I came here to look at the plane parts, so I may as well finish my job, too."

"I'll drive you there." Balling his sandwich paper up, he threw it toward a can and stood. They walked outside together into bright sun and quadraphonic traffic.

Half an hour later they were in Reno at the beginning of the rush-hour traffic. An old building adjacent to the Reno Air hangars leaned precariously to the right, but inside it was dry and scrupulously clean, down to its concrete floor. Skip Bailey's pride and joy lay disemboweled in a thousand labeled, mutilated pieces on a table covered with pristine white paper on the far left of the room. Larger pieces, such as the charred wings, sat on paper on the floor in the center of the shed. They walked along, hands in pockets, until Paul got to the fuel tank, or what was left of it.

"You can see it's in bad shape," Davis remarked.

"What's this?" Paul held up a twisted piece.

"The fuel screen."

"That would be responsible for keeping out..."

"Bits and pieces of things that shouldn't make it into the fuel line."

"Huh," said Paul, setting it carefully back in its place. "And this over here?" He motioned toward another piece.

Davis had much to say about this second object, which had some arcane purpose in steering, so he stayed engaged and happy while Paul palmed the fuel screen.

After a long look at all the pieces, and lectures as long-winded and forbidding as a few he had had to endure back at Northeastern, Paul was ready to leave. As they walked out, he noticed an object lying by itself near one of the seats, remarkably undamaged. "What's this?" He could see what it was at a glance. He turned the object around. White, about the size and heft of a Ping-Pong ball, it appeared to be solid Styrofoam. Familiar. He had seen something like it recently...

Davis lifted an eyebrow, then a bell must have donged in his head. Things fell back into place on his face. "It's nothing. We found it under the seat Christopher Sykes was sitting in."

"Didn't burn up in the fire?"

"The fire was concentrated elsewhere. That part stayed cool enough so this item survived."

"What's it for?"

"It serves no useful purpose in flying, that I can tell you."

"So why did they have it on the plane?"

"A little game of catch?" Davis shrugged, clearly bugged. He didn't like the stall, cause unknown, and he didn't like Paul finding the one thing that didn't fit into his reenactment. "The interior of the plane had been thoroughly cleaned preflight. The only other loose things clearly belonged to Christopher Sykes— his bag, cell phone, sunglasses, baseball cap. We never did figure out what the ball was doing there under his passenger seat. You find out, you give me a call."

So, Davis rated among the truth seekers after all.

"Thanks," Paul said. "I've seen enough."

As he pulled back into the parking lot in Carson City, Davis turned to Paul. "When you actually see the pieces, you realize two people died," he said. "When you see how it all turned out, you keep thinking you have to do something to prevent it from happening again. And then you go back to Washington and go back on rotation, and in a few weeks you get another midnight call. I'm not here to snow anybody. You and your experts find something we didn't, I want you to call me immediately." He gave Paul his card and shook his hand.

A pay phone back in Carson City took his calling card number. It suited his current financial purposes to go easy on running up charges on his cell phone. "Ginger? It's Paul van Wagoner."

"Hey, Paul. I just walked into the lab back here in Sac."

"I'm sending you some items Air Express. Two items. One's metal. It's a filtering screen for an airplane fuel line. Do every chemical test known to woman on this sucker. I'm looking for contamination."

"What kind of contamination?"

"No idea."

"You have to give me a hint. A direction. Otherwise I have too many miles to go before I sleep."

"I can't help much...except maybe you should look for some evidence of water."

"Water? You'll be stopping by in five minutes then?"

"I know, I know. This filtering screen was in a plane crash during which the plane went up in flames. It's totally thrashed."

"So, hunt for evidence of water on a mangled-up, dry screen, check," she said. "What other small miracles do you pray for?"

"I have a little ball. Make it speak and tell you its origins and purpose." He remembered where he had seen several like it, in Dave LeBlanc's living room collection of junk. Maybe Christopher saw one at the hangar the day they took off and picked it up, as Davis had suggested, just because it was something to pick up and play with.

"Where'd you find it?"

"Under someone's seat on the crashed plane. I want to know why. You're the forensic expert. You find out, you give me a call."

"I can't do this instantly, Paul. You understand? You're asking me to test for everything."

"I know that. And you probably won't find a thing," Paul said.

"If anything is there, I will find it. Anything else?"

"One thing. Ginger—do you know what's wrong with Nina?"

"Huh?"

"She's been acting a little strange the last couple of days. As though she's upset with me."

"I can't imagine why you're asking me for advice about your love life. All I can say is, before the meeting started, we were in the little girl's room and she was brushing her hair. She said something about you."

"What?"

"She looked so sad and I asked her if she was thinking about her husband. And she said no, that she was thinking about you."

"I see."

"I have to go."

He felt it like a blow. Paul thought, the kid told her. I never should have said a word to him. As he considered what that meant, snapshots of Nina assailed him: curling up in that bed of hers; propping bare feet on her desk; walking, face pink in the wind; swimming, her long hair spread like a lily pad around her.

It was over with her, every possibility, every potential future.

He felt relief, in a way.

Now all he could do was wait for her to speak.

25

"THE COURT OF THE COUNTY of El Dorado is now in session, the Honorable Judge Flaherty presiding," Deputy Kimura, who was substituting for Flaherty's usual bailiff, announced.

"State your appearances, Counsel," Flaherty said. Lightly tanned over his usual ruddiness, he had an unceremonious, mellow summer air about him. Although he frequently began proceedings that way, his speedy mood changes were famous, taking him and everyone in court from zero to *Sturm und Drang* in sixty seconds, or so the D.A.'s joked. White-haired and rotund, he was a right jolly old elf on this warm July morning, an effect Nina suspected he cultivated.

"Henry McFarland, representing the People, Your Honor." Henry looked like a cat that had swallowed something a whole lot bigger than a canary. What was he up to? He wasn't known for his subtlety. It made her even more nervous.

Barbara Banning hadn't come in with him. As cocounsel, she should be here.

Something was going on.

"Nina Reilly, representing the defendant, Nicole Zack, Your Honor." Out in the echoing hallway, Tim, Daria, and Beth waited, potential witnesses Nina wanted to keep in the wings. Rankin hadn't shown up yet, although Paul had promised they would bring him in. Sitting next to Nina at the counsel table,

Nikki could not have dreamed up a more contrary courtroom demeanor. Her newly tinted flaming orange hair, gelled into careful tangles, broadcasted frenzied instability. Her jeans had torn-out knees, her tatty red sweater an elongated droop, and her face sagged into its habitual sulk.

Oh, well. At least she hadn't painted her skin purple or tattooed her face or studded her tongue for the occasion. In spite of the shabby teenage chic and the stubby black fingernails thrumming the table in front of them both, Nina could feel the girl trembling. She was afraid, and the trembling she couldn't control gave her away.

I can relate, Nina thought, but they couldn't both sit there quaking like aspens in a spring wind in front of Henry, so she stilled herself all over except for what she couldn't stop.

"Let's start at the beginning. So you don't like the way the prosecution's blood expert testified at the prelim, is that right, Counsel?" Flaherty said to her. He didn't seem to be taking the motion too seriously. He had read a thousand motions that were filed *pro forma* by defense lawyers in criminal cases, because they were expected. Only one in a hundred 995 hearings resulted in any change in the case. But you never could tell what Flaherty was really thinking, until he blew.

"I don't like it at all, Judge. As you can see from the portions of the preliminary hearing transcript attached to my motion, the witness never did conclude that the defendant's blood was found on the murder weapon. She danced around it a lot, but she never said it. Without that conclusion, Your Honor, there isn't a scintilla of evidence..."

"Neither a mote nor an iota," Flaherty said.

His facetiousness heated her blood. "This sixteen-year-old child has been committed without probable cause on a charge of murder of the first degree," she said in a strong clear voice. "There is no first degree if she wasn't in the process of committing a felony, Your Honor. And as matters stand there is no evidence that she ever took a step inside that house or attempted to do so."

"Can't one find probable cause she intended to commit a burglary from the mere fact that she was on the property at night, skulking around?" said Flaherty. He leaned to the side as his clerk whispered something to him.

Nina waited until he returned his full attention to her. "This isn't the situation of a complete stranger going on to a property at night," she said. "Dr. Sykes was her uncle. She had been on the property before, even swum in the pool before. You can't conclude she went there to burglarize the property from that."

"If I may, Your Honor."

"Go ahead, Henry."

Now in charge of the floor, Henry took his time, flipping through paperwork and clearing his throat before speaking. "The defendant's mother testified that the girl was angry about some sort of fancied wrong she thought her uncle had done her. Without telling her mother where she was going, she sneaked out of the house, appropriated a kayak, and prowled onto the Sykes property from the back. These actions are hardly as innocent as Counsel would have you believe. Her prints are all over the glass doors..."

"Not on the door handles," Nina interrupted. "So there's no indication of intent..."

"Wait your turn, Counsel. Teenagers do like to sneak around," Flaherty said. "I recall that in my own youth in the Paleozoic era"—he paused for appreciative chuckles from the news reporters and his own court staff—"I used to row over to a house where a girl I had a crush on lived. I'd sit in her bushes and look at the light on the second story and dream under the moon, then go home. It was only years later that I learned she lived in the next house over." More chuckles.

Henry said, "And we have an eyewitness who saw the girl steal something from a box in the swimming pool. Louise Garibaldi."

"But I'm making a motion, Your Honor. I move to strike all her testimony," Nina answered, "on foundational grounds that she didn't have the ability to perceive what the defendant was doing down there."

"We'll get to that. But let's talk about this blood evidence," Flaherty said. "Henry, you state in your responsive papers that you have placed the defendant inside the house, the proof being that the blood of the defendant was found on the murder weapon."

"That's right, Your Honor," Henry said. "I spent an hour with Detective Ditmar on the stand at the preliminary hearing examining her methods, her qualifications, every step she took in coming to her conclusion."

"And what conclusion was that?" Flaherty said, in his most benevolent tone, practically beaming.

"I beg your pardon?"

"Where, precisely, in this transcript of court proceedings which I have gone through several times, with no help from your paperwork, I might add, do you ask the witness whether she can state with any degree of certainty that the second set of blood markers on the murder weapon match the blood samples provided by the defendant?"

Henry began flailing at his papers. "It's all over Detective Ditmar's testimony, Your Honor. It's implied by the cumulative total of the testimony. She testified that there was the reasonable probability, 'a strong probability,' of a match at page seventy-seven, lines twelve to twenty of the transcript."

"So she did. But where did she say that probability is enough to conclude it was the defendant's blood?"

"All we need is probable cause, Your Honor. And 'strong probability' translates easily into probable cause."

"Why's that? Because it's more than a weak probability? Is it sort of like a preponderance of the evidence test we're inventing here? We seem to have a whole lot of research provided by Ms. Reilly here, indicating that 'strong probability' constitutes an iffy match, Counsel. I do feel obligated to take judicial notice of this research as she requests. Apparently a 'match' is ordinarily along the lines of ninety-eight percent probability or higher. And upon looking back at the transcript carefully, I sense a definite reluctance on the part of your blood expert to derive any conclusion. That's what *I* think is implied by the cumulative total of the testimony."

"Your Honor, if the rare blood found on the sword belongs to someone other than Nicole Zack, we're looking at a fifteen thousand to one coincidence," Henry said with calm logic. "That was the testimony. Those are pretty long odds even at Tahoe. In fact, the vast majority of people in this world would not match that blood as closely as the defendant does. This scientific method is somewhat new and there's the occasional error, but our blood expert has provided evidence that this girl's blood was on the sword. Hard evidence that doesn't go away. It may not be dispositive, but it's certainly not speculative. And the standard of proof in a prelim is only probable cause to believe under *all* the circumstances that a burglary was intended. In addition to the blood evidence, she was seen taking something from that box, just steps from Dr. Sykes's study. Her fingerprints are on the wall right next to the study. The court must also consider her sneaking around, the secrecy of the entry onto the property, the testimony her mother gave regarding her motives, and so on."

"I see," Flaherty said, not sounding like he did.

Nina saw what was coming and kept her mouth shut. "I think you made a little misstep here, Henry," Flaherty went on. "You didn't quite get that conclusion from Detective Ditmar, your expert, and it's about all I had to go on in making the determination that the defendant broke into the home. Now this presents a bit of a problem in the Complaint you have filed, because the charge of first-degree murder doesn't stand without probable cause to show a felony was committed."

"I can get Detective Ditmar in here to give additional testimony on ten minutes' notice, Your Honor," Henry said. "This is a minor problem that we can fix with a little extra testimony." He was recovering quickly, moving toward his Plan B, doing exactly what Nina had hoped he would do.

"But the evidence is already in," she said. "This is a 995 hearing, based on the transcript only."

"Oh, no," Henry said quickly. "I have a right to produce additional evidence to correct a minor problem with the Information, Your Honor. Section 995b allows that. If counsel doesn't know that, she hasn't done her research."

Nina nodded her head. "I bow to your superior knowledge," she said.

Henry gave her a suspicious look.

"I think it's worth another half hour," Flaherty said, looking to his clerk, who nodded to indicate he had time for that.

"The defense may need a little time too," Nina said. "For cross-examination. And so forth. Depending on the testimony."

"Naturally," Henry agreed stiffly, since he had no choice.

"All right," Flaherty said, "if that's what you want to do, Henry. We'll adjourn until after lunch and pick it up then."

Out in the hall, Daria came up to Nina. Sobriety had prevailed today in her choice of clothing, as though Beth or someone else had taken her to her closet and shown her what to do. She wore a skirt slinking only a few inches above the knee and delicate beige heels. "Mr. McFarland looked mad," she said, her voice full of doubt. "Did it go well?"

"Fine so far."

"So far." The words slipped out of Daria's mouth, took shape and hung like a toxic cloud over them. She clamped her hand over pale pink lips. "Sorry," she said. "Of course you can do it. I'm just so worried."

"Daria... Daria, will you do me a favor?" Nina said.

"What?"

"Look me in the eyes, right now, and swear to me that it wasn't you who killed your brother-in-law. That you went there and he was already dead. Will you do that for me?"

"You think I would let my daughter go

through this just to save myself? I swear it! I swear it!"

"She's not trying to protect you? She didn't see you do it? She's not relying on my getting her a reduced sentence because she's a juvenile?"

"I told you! No!"

Nina's frown remained on her face.

Frantic, Daria said, "You think I'm an idiot. Flaky. Can't keep a job. A hopeless no-talent dreamer and a lousy mother."

Nina started to speak. Daria raised a hand. "Maybe I am all those things. But that doesn't mean I don't love Nikki. It doesn't mean I would let her go to jail for me, for God's sake. You can't believe I would sink so low. Can you? It's just that I was there, and Bill was dead, and that sweatshirt was hanging off the bush in the back. Who else could it be?"

Nina didn't answer that. She gave Nikki, who had just come up to join them, an encouraging smile, saying, "Think you could keep the hair that color at least through the afternoon?"

One-thirty rolled around too soon, and as Nina took her place at the defense table, she had a new worry—Dennis Rankin still hadn't shown up or called the court with an excuse in spite of being subpoenaed.

She needed Rankin! Should she ask for a continuance? Flaherty would be pissed when he realized she had lined up three new witnesses. He could easily refuse to hear them on grounds of general exasperation. She had to keep a very low profile if she was going to get the testimony in. She had to trust that Paul would find Rankin and bring him in somehow.

She watched Detective Ditmar approach the witness box.

The detective must not help Henry. And if Detective Ditmar tried, Nina was prepared, with the help of the preparation Ginger had given her, to take her out.

Paul made the mistake of letting Wish test drive his new Mustang, a decision he regretted instantly the first time they skidded through a wet intersection.

"This is so great," Wish said, giving the wheel a brisk turn. Paul put up an arm to prevent banging his head on the window. "Real receptive steering, tight brakes," Wish continued. "Man, if you weren't selling me your van I think I'd be going into hock for one of these."

They rolled along Upper Truckee Court toward Meyers. In addition to being a prospector, Dennis Rankin was a certified gemologist and Paul had obtained his home address easily. Although he apparently spent much of his time in the desert, he lived near the California agricultural inspection station in the townlet of Meyers, a few miles inland from Lake Tahoe on the road that led through Echo Pass.

"Right or left," Wish said, as they approached an intersection.

"Er..." Paul said, one eye on the map, the other on the street signs. "Here we are. Take a right on Grizzly Mountain Court."

They swerved into a ninety-degree turn. Wish pulled up smartly in front of the house and turned the keys. "They just keep making cars better and better..."

Paul got out. "You stay in front. If he comes out that door, grab him. But remember. He's big, and he's probably armed. I know he doesn't want to testify, so he may fight. Don't take any unnecessary risks with this guy. I'm serious."

"How about if I shout and you grab him?"

Paul didn't answer. He saw no sign of a car and no garage in front of the modest cottage that apparently housed Dennis Rankin. After opening a creaking wood gate very slowly to make sure a Doberman didn't make a silent rush for him, he went around the side of the house and tried the kitchen door. It opened easily. Up here, people didn't worry so much about strangers coming around and trying their doors, which worked for Paul.

He entered silently, pulling the door almost shut behind him. Other than a stack of receipts on a metal spike sticking up from a dusty Formica counter, and a mountain of dishes that had never seen soap, he could have been in any kitchen in any motel. Listening for a television or radio or an electric razor or anything that might indicate an inhabitant somewhere else in the house, he took a step and froze. He heard something.

He then put his head into the living room, hand on his gun, but there was no one there. In the bedroom, he found the source of the noise, a radio playing softly. The only other room was closet-sized and furnished with an exposed mattress, torn comforter in a heap, and two pillows without cases. A wooden desk in the corner was covered with rock samples. They would have to wait for another day, because he had to find Rankin. Paul gently pulled the door shut until he heard it click.

Outside, Wish stood behind the car. Paul transferred the stack of receipts to his pocket. "Drive back to Highway 50. There's a convenience store near the corner."

They drove out, turning right again toward the highway for about a mile. Wish pulled into the asphalt parking lot. "Why are we stopping here?" Wish asked. "You hungry?"

"This is Rankin's favorite restaurant."

"The food in those places was wrapped in China and shipped by slow boat," Wish said, his nose crinkling.

"Ah, but it has the virtue of being a mere two blocks away. That's the way guys like Rankin"—and guys like Paul in certain moods— "select their dining venues." They parked to one side of the low wooden building. Paul stepped up to the door and peered inside. "Damn!" he said, kicking his foot against the building in frustration. Rankin could be anywhere, drunk in a casino in Reno, off to Santa Fe on a rock hound's dream holiday, lying low in any one of a thousand motels along the highway.

He pulled the kitchen receipts out of his pocket and began to study them.

Detective Ditmar was trying to explain the "strong" probability finding, and this time Henry was leaning on her, and she was trying to help, but unwilling to stretch the truth. "If the blood found on the sword was not the blood of the defendant, what other findings might the tests you were able to run show?"

"Ordinarily, we can completely exclude the defendant as a possibility."

"Meaning, you could state a probability figure of zero?"

"Well, not zero. But infinitesimal."

"And you made this determination after testing blood that was taken from the sword that caused Mr. Sykes's death?"

"Yes."

"And according to your best professional judgment, that finding of a third allele in one test provides strong and convincing evidence that, in addition to the blood of the victim, Nikki Zack's blood was found on that sword."

"Yes," she said eagerly. "It is strong evidence."

"Is it possible the testing is somehow in error?"

"There's always a small possibility, of course, but the fact that there's a match of this unusual third allele which is also found in the defendant's blood tells us there's nothing wrong with the testing. I'm willing to stake my reputation that that test was an accurate one. Our lab was very careful."

"So, in your expert judgment, there's a match?"

She hedged. "We wouldn't ordinarily declare a match based on one test..."

Nina stood up, saying, "You know, Your Honor, the last time I checked, you weren't supposed to lead your own witness. Or cross-examine her, or browbeat her, or put words into her mouth. Or..."

"Rephrase the question," Flaherty said. Henry tried again, but all the detective would say was that the blood indicated the strong probability of a match.

"So you are saying that the sample *probably* came from the defendant?" Henry asked.

"Your Honor," Nina said. "I have to object. He's trying to get the witness to give us a conclusion of law, not a conclusion of fact."

"Using the word 'probably' over and over again isn't going to make this finding add up to probable cause, Henry," Flaherty said. "It's beginning to grate on my nerves a little, I must admit. Can you wrap this up?"

If Henry's rigidly set shoulders were any indication, he had finally admitted to himself that this particular skirmish was lost. Returning to his table, he moved around some more papers, giving himself time to think.

He's not as good as Collier was at the job, Nina thought to herself. He's more predictable. These thoughts that should have buoyed her up instead left her even more nervous. It left a void for Flaherty, and she knew from experience Flaherty had unpredictability in abundance, enough for all of them.

Henry was saying, "I have nothing further for

this witness, but I would like to have the opportunity to cure any defect in the Information as to the felony-murder charge by bringing Mrs. Louise Garibaldi back to the stand.

"Defense counsel claims that we did not in the prelim establish a foundational fact, namely, that Mrs. Garibaldi could see the pool area of the Sykes house. Well, that'll take about thirty seconds to cure. She is waiting outside."

Me and Machiavelli, Nina thought. Henry had volunteered to bring in Louise. It was too perfect.

Louise marched in, chipper, quite chipper in spite of her own arthritis. Although she wore street clothes, there would always be an indefinable essence of gardener about her. She was like a dandelion herself with her head of white hair and the good cheer she emanated.

Too much good cheer by half.

Henry spent five minutes with her. He cured the foundational objection Nina had made in her paperwork right away by establishing that Louise could in fact see the area of the pool. Then he let her expand a little on her testimony. She added more details about Nikki's furtive manner as she watched Sykes from the bushes that night, added that Nikki waited for Sykes to go in the study before dashing out to steal the box, and clarified that she saw Nikki moving toward the study door before her sightline was cut off.

"Thank you," Henry said, satisfied. He thought he had it made.

Nina picked up the chemical analysis Ginger

had given her the day before, based on the small amount of red elixir Paul had provided her. She had followed up with a conversation with Beth Sykes, who had told her a very interesting story about her neighbor's habits every night before bed.

"Hello, Mrs. Garibaldi," she said.

"Hello."

"Having a good day?"

"Always do."

"Tell me, Mrs. Garibaldi, what were you doing just before you looked out the window that night?"

"Well now, let me think. Along about nine I always settle down in my armchair and read a bit."

"I understand you have a touch of arthritis."

"Yes, I've had it for years. But I keep it under control. I'm an herbalist and I know how to take care of that."

"You have quite a—what would you call it, a laboratory?—set up for your work with herbs in your basement, don't you?"

Louise nodded, smiling. "So your investigator mentioned it?"

"Indeed he did. Now, let's recap. About nine you settled into your armchair? With your book? Did you eat or drink anything?"

"No, just took my usual infusion. Some herbs I take every night to help me get to sleep."

"What do you call that infusion you take?"

"Why, my red elixir. I take it every night at nine like clockwork." It was exactly as Beth had said. She had met Louise one night the year before walking down the street in her pajamas, singing a merry tune. Louise had explained that she had taken a double dose of elixir that night because her arthritis was acting up, and Beth had led her home and made sure she was tucked in. Beth claimed that Louise had never once stopped smiling.

"What exactly is all this talk of herbs and elixirs about, Your Honor?" Henry demanded. "What's it got to do with what this lady saw?"

"It has everything to do with what this lady thought she saw," Nina said.

"I'm afraid I agree with the District Attorney on this," Flaherty said.

"May I approach the bench?" Nina said. She and Henry came around to the side of Flaherty's dais and Nina whispered, "I have moved to strike the testimony of this witness for lack of foundation and I need some latitude for a minute or two."

"But we've made clear that she could see—" Henry began.

"The defect in this testimony is more serious than that."

"We haven't had notice of any other defect!"

"But I have laid adequate legal grounds to question her further about her perceptions on the night of the murder."

"I object," Henry said. "She saw what she saw."

"Her perceptions weren't the usual perceptions," Nina said. "Judge, I just need a minute or two."

Flaherty said, "Well, she looks pretty darn smart and emotionally positive to me. But go ahead for a few more questions."

Henry sat down, shaking his head, and Nina said to Louise, who continued to smile, "You mentioned my investigator, Mr. van Wagoner."

"Yes."

"He came to your home to talk to you and you took him downstairs, right?"

"Why, yes."

"Why did you take him downstairs?"

"I thought I'd help him out. He was in bad pain from his leg, and he asked me for help. I don't think we were put here on this Earth to turn our backs on people in pain if we can help them."

"Did you give him something for his pain?"

"I think I did, yes."

"Some red elixir, right?"

"Could have, I suppose."

"You did, am I correct?"

"Just a little. A few days' worth."

"What's in this red elixir that you take each night at nine, Mrs. Garibaldi?"

"Oh, just a few herbs I get from all around."

"I want to remind you that you have sworn to tell the truth, and, by the way, I want to inform you that we have had that red elixir analyzed," Nina said.

Louise heaved a sigh. "He seemed like such a nice man," she said. "That's what I get for helping out."

"What's in that red elixir?"

"I don't care to say."

Nina looked down at Ginger's report. "Kava root?"

"A bit, yes."

"Saint-John's-wort?"

"Uh huh."

"Not to mention cocaine, morphine, and jimsonweed?"

Henry jumped to his feet, boiling. "Objection! This witness—"

But Louise was smiling. "My, my," she said. "What modern science can do. I never thought you'd be able to identify the jimsonweed."

There was a short burst of shocked laughter. Deputy Kimura's eyebrows went clear up to his hairline.

"Let's take a five-minute break," Flaherty said.

Nina went out into the hall, happy, stretching her back and smoothing back her hair as she went. Daria and Beth were sitting next to each other on the bench outside the courtroom, and Tim was talking on the phone down the hall, but there was still no sign of the prospector.

"Paul said to call him as soon as you come out," Daria told her. "And Sandy's trying to reach you."

"But I don't have time—all right."

She skipped down to the phone downstairs and called Paul's cell phone number. He answered on the first ring.

"We have a line on him, I think," Paul said.

470

"He eats regularly at the Cantina on Emerald Bay Road."

"How far away are you?"

"A couple of miles."

"What's the traffic like?"

"Relax, Nina. We'll get there as fast as we can."

She had to think. There was no time to call Sandy. She looked at her watch. She had two minutes.

Louise's testimony would be stricken. Ditmar's testimony would be stricken. She was riding high and had already accomplished her purpose in calling the hearing. The felony allegation would be dismissed.

The rest of it had been a house of cards to cover the fact that Nikki had the opals. Did she still have an obligation as an officer of the court to turn over those opals? They would incriminate Nikki! Were they still relevant evidence, when there was no longer any competent evidence that Nikki was actually at the Sykes house the night of the murder?

She didn't know. She had talked to a legal ethics expert, who had suggested handing the opals over would be the wisest course. After running her strategy by the expert, she got a yes, it could be okay to hold on to them if they belonged to the defendant's mother, and a no, it might not be okay at all, depending upon how the judge saw things. So she had decided to produce them with a flourish in court today, explaining them away at the same time.

But now—now what? Open the can of vermicelli?

Hard plans laid in advance of court had a way of melting into a puddle as a hearing progressed. Things changed, and she needed to be responsive to the need to change, too.

She straightened up, tucked her blouse in, licked her lips. She wouldn't tell the judge that she had the opals in her office. She wouldn't bring in Rankin, Tim, all the rest to try to show Nikki had a right to them. She would be silent.

Her primary obligation was to protect her client. Nikki might be hurt if she turned the opals over.

Let sleeping opals lie.

26

DEPUTY KIMURA MOTIONED them back into the courtroom. Flaherty had just taken the bench. Flaherty looked at the clock on the wall. It was three-ten.

"Your Honor," Henry began. He should have been flabbergasted, overwhelmed, desperate. Why did he still have that pregnant look? What was he about to deliver?

"Well, Counselor?"

"The prosecution has been unfairly surprised by Mrs. Garibaldi's testimony."

"Maybe, but counsel for the defense has performed a valuable service bringing the defect in her testimony to the Court's attention."

"Yes, but—"

Barbara Banning walked in, up the aisle, to Henry. Handing him some papers, she looked over her shoulder at Nina. It was a good thing human beings couldn't be incinerated by a look.

Henry grabbed them and read the top paper. An expression of hot triumph mottled his features. Nina thought, uh oh, here we go.

"If it please the court," Henry said. "We have had a new development. At about three o'clock today a search warrant was served on the law offices of Nina Reilly, based on information provided by an informant named Dennis Rankin. According to this informant, Ms. Reilly had come into possession of certain valuable gemstones which Mr. Rankin had given to William Sykes a few days before his murder.

473

Furthermore, these gems had been provided to Ms. Reilly, according to the informant, by the defendant, Nicole Zack."

"What?" She had to stay calm, had to think—

A uniformed cop came in right behind Barbara and handed Henry a small velvet bag. He promptly upended it on the counsel table. The courtroom lighting actually did a rather good job of making the stones shine.

Blue, lavender, red, purple, addictive and magical light. Flaherty leaned over on the bench to have a look.

"Bring those up here," he commanded. He looked at them for a long time.

His complexion began to change and as Nina watched in sick anticipation, Flaherty went into ballistic red-button mode.

"You took these from Ms. Reilly's office safe?" he yelled at the cop.

"Yes, sir!"

"Ms. Reilly! Get up here!"

She went. So did Henry, and so did Barbara.

"Where did you get these?" Flaherty demanded.

"From the defendant, Your Honor."

"When?"

"Two and a half weeks ago."

"Impeding an official investigation!" Henry said.

"Why didn't you turn them over as evidence?"

"I didn't consider them evidence."

Flaherty scowled, a scowl from a god about

to melt the ice caps and make the earth flood forever. He was awful to behold now, a beetling, bristling, ferocious presence. She had heard about this but never seen it. She took a step back.

"You are going to jail," he said. Barbara's mouth twitched.

"I can prove that the opals belong to the defendant."

"You are going to jail," Flaherty reiterated. It was hard to respond to the absolute decision in that voice.

"I can prove it. I have witnesses."

Flaherty regarded her as he would something that had crawled onto his blanket at night. He looked at the clock.

"It is three-fifteen," he said. "At four-thirty you will be remanded to the custody of the bailiff for contempt of court."

"Pull over, Wish. Let me drive," Paul said.

"I thought you said we were in a hurry! Anyway, there's nowhere good to pull over so just let me keep going, I'll make it through the Y without having to spend a half hour waiting for the signal to change."

It was true. Traffic on 89 was heavy approaching the Y, and they didn't want to get stuck in a right-turn lane and end up going the wrong way.

"Anyway," Wish said, "you don't even know the guy's going to be there. Three receipts. That's nothing."

"He'll be there." He hoped that was true.

"If I were him," Wish said, swooping around a slow-moving RV in the left lane and breaking seventeen or eighteen road rules in the process, "I'd be at the beach today."

Paul thought he might prefer Wish at the beach too, but now they were stuck with Wish driving and he would have to sit back and be patient and call on all the universe owed him to make this thing happen right. Opening one eye, he saw that they were nearly there.

"You're getting good, Wish," he said, getting ready to hop out.

The unexpected praise threw Wish off his stride momentarily. A big rig moved in front of him and slowed to a crawl.

Up to now, out of consideration for Paul, Wish had driven with assurance but without great speed. Apparently, the challenge to his dominance proved too much for him, just as it had for Paul down in LA. He floored it. "Eat my dust, wanker!" For the next few thousand feet they flew, coming to a landing in the parking area in front of the Cantina.

"Wanker?" Paul said, throwing his door open.

"At the end of the summer last year these guys I know on the west shore hosted an end-of-tourists party. They put up a big sign: 'See Ya, Wankers.' Sounds bad. Wonder what it means?"

Paul thought the insult was humorous but harsh, considering that the tourists made it possible for locals to make a living up here, but didn't take the time to update Wish. Running up to the restaurant door, he threw it open and looked inside.

Bless him, bless Wish, bless 'em all. There sat Dennis Rankin, mid-bite, his fork interrupted while attempting to carry an unwieldy, beefy bite of enchilada toward his mouth.

"One of the witnesses subpoenaed to testify at this time has—has…"

"Speak up, Counsel," Flaherty bellowed. "We all want to hear this."

"Has—" Nina said, but her sentence was interrupted by the arrival of Paul, with Dennis Rankin in tow.

"…arrived," she finished. "Call Dennis Rankin to the stand."

Looking decidedly unprepared, Rankin made his way to the front of the court to the witness stand.

"Your name for the record?" the court clerk asked.

Rankin gave his name. He pulled out a kerchief, pointedly dabbing at a stain on his khaki-colored shirt, making it clear how much he resented being there.

"You're not here voluntarily today, are you, Mr. Rankin?" she started.

"Lucky someone showed up to remind me of the subpoena. It somehow slipped my mind."

"Do you consider yourself something of an expert in opals and the geology of opal mining?" Rankin looked surprised. She was asking a reasonable question in a reasonable

477

tone of voice. Maybe he had thought she'd back-hand him again. She would have enjoyed it, since he had just caused the cops to ransack her office.

"Mined Coober-Pedy for more years than I can count. Grew up around miners. I'm also a certified gemologist. Read a lot, but listen more. I reckon I know more than anyone else in this room about it."

"Tell us, Mr. Rankin," Nina said, crossing her arms and pacing a little in front of the counsel table, "about your prospecting activities in northern Nevada. How long have you been prospecting for valuable minerals there?"

"Eight years."

"Your land adjoined land you thought was owned by William Sykes, is that right?"

"Yes," Rankin said. "There was a sign on the property with the name Sykes and an address right up here in South Lake Tahoe."

"You recently contacted William Sykes about that land, didn't you?"

"Yes. I drove up to that address at the lake one day last spring and Sykes opened the door. We started talking. He said he owned the property with his wife and sister-in-law and he could make deals for all of them."

"What kind of deal did you discuss?"

"I wanted to buy some mining rights. Or maybe form a joint venture to mine it."

"What happened then?"

"He put me off."

"Why did you want these rights?"

Rankin looked more sullen than Nikki.

"It was because you had found black fire opals on that property, isn't that right?"

"I never..."

Nina hurried on, "Without realizing you had strayed from your own property boundaries. Right?"

Rankin's spirits improved. "Right."

"Can you be more specific about when this discussion happened?"

"Early May. A week before he died."

"Why wouldn't Dr. Sykes sell the land to you?"

"Calls for hearsay." Henry spat it out. He was tired, hot, and bored. He had what he wanted. Now he wanted to go home, after making sure, of course, that Nina wasn't going home.

"Sustained."

"Did you tell him about the opals?"

"Took eighteen of them to him and handed them over."

"And you told him their value?"

"Roughly." He smiled, and a metal tooth glinted. "I'm not stupid. These black opals aren't the usual found in Nevada. It was my opinion they were uniformly less brittle and therefore very valuable, but I had no hard and fast information on that when I went to him. I just brought the opals and suggested they might be worth something."

"And did Dr. Sykes then or thereafter make an agreement with you regarding the opals?"

"Yeah. But it wasn't the agreement I wanted. The agreement was that I would keep quiet about the opal strike for at least a couple of months and stay off the land. He said he would give the opals to me in a couple of months if I did that."

At last Nina was making some progress. She had struggled desperately to get here. She felt as if she'd been swimming under-water under thick ice and finally found a hole back to the air. Now to climb out. She took a deep breath.

"And did you leave the opals with him?"

"I did. Then he got himself killed. And I don't have my opals."

Nina brought him the cloth bag, freshly bedecked with its exhibit tags, and they all watched him take out the stones, one by one.

"And are those the opals you brought Dr. Sykes?" Nina asked.

He looked at them, exhaled, and said sourly, "Those are most of them."

She paused and studied Rankin. She had him on the stand. He had threatened Nikki, chased Bob; he had never been cooperative. She felt that he knew more, but what?

He looked back at her. And showed his teeth in a grin. He just couldn't help himself. And she knew, was absolutely positive now, that he had snowed her and Paul, had made himself a little hard to find, had let her pull a few things out of him.

"Anything further?" Flaherty asked.

"Just a moment, Your Honor." She was mentally trying to make him for the murder. He knew the house; Sykes had his opals; who knew what else was true? What if he had come to the house after Nikki, rung the doorbell, gone into the study, and killed Sykes with the sword? Then left when he heard Daria?

But there was no physical evidence, no fingerprints, no blood—the blood on the sword was probably Nikki's...

She had no more time. She had to get Daria on the stand but the thing that had been fulminating in her mind had reached a critical mass. Daria and Rankin came together in a mental explosion, leaving a cloudy but seductive thought.

What if Rankin was Nikki's father? That was the thought, and she was definitely losing her concentration and everything else—what was the even crazier thought? That if he was her father, wouldn't his blood exhibit the third allele?

"Mr. Rankin," she said, "do you know, or have you ever known, Daria Zack, the mother of the defendant?" Rankin looked very surprised at this.

She waited.

"Never had the pleasure," Rankin said. And she nodded urgently at Paul, who got up and went out to the hall where Daria was and came back in a second shaking his head. So Daria denied it too. She was on the wrong track. What had she expected?

So she was crazy.

But what about the allele?

From Rankin and Daria to the allele—

"Nothing further," she said.

"No cross," Henry said, affecting extreme boredom.

It was four o'clock. "Call Tim Seisz."

Deputy Kimura walked down the empty aisle to the door, opened it, and called out the name. Tim followed him back in, looking like a lean gray wolf in professor's clothing, wearing his hiking boots.

"You are a full professor at the University of Nevada in the Department of Geology, am I correct?"

"That is correct."

"How long have you been a professor there?" Nina took him through his education and experience, which was impeccable. The best thing about Tim's background, and the reason Nina had gone to him originally, was that Tim had been awarded his Ph.D. from the University of Southern California, where Flaherty had gone to law school. At this point, though, she doubted anything would help.

"On June twenty-fourth, did you accompany me and Paul van Wagoner on a trip to a mining claim in the Nevada desert?"

"I did. I confirmed our location with a United States Geological Map and I have also obtained copies of the claim registrations in the area, indicating names of the registrants." Nina had both items marked as exhibits and after a few more questions and a shrug from Henry had them admitted as evidence.

"Where did we go at that time?"

"To this particular claim, located about a hundred miles northwest of Winnemucca. The sole claim holder is named Dennis Rankin."

"And what did you do there, at my instruction?"

"Examined the contents of several buckets of rock samples Mr. Rankin was collecting from one of the rock walls on his property."

"Were you able to identify those samples?"

"Yes. They were low-grade opaline rocks."

"Did you observe at that time any example of rocks which might be gem quality?"

"No."

"What did you do then, again at my direction?"

"Traveled to an adjoining claim." Tim pointed to the map again, showing Grandpa Logan's claim, and went on, "That land was originally owned by Beth Sykes and her sister Daria Zack, who have an undivided interest as tenants in common. My instructions were to examine the claim for evidence of high-grade opal rock. I did that, and within an hour located a ledge of bentonite beneath a volcanic extrusion which showed evidence of an ancient lava flow and a more recent landslide. I must say I was quite surprised. It was an entirely localized phenomenon and I have not been able to find any report of any prior examination of this area by a qualified geologist."

"What else, if anything, did you find?"

"Evidence of recent digging in one of the walls. I chipped at the wall in the same area and found that the entire ledge at a depth about three feet above ground level and running horizontal for about seventy-five feet was rich in very high-grade rock. Because of the unusual geologic history of the rocks in that area, the opal rock that I was collecting had a rare feature."

"Which was?"

"The color. It was a very rare color with a very rare quality of fire, known among gemologists as black fire opal. It has been found in Australia, and it has been found in a small valley about ninety miles from the claim I was examining called the Virgin Valley. Other than that, there has never been a major strike of black opals anywhere. Gem-quality black fire opals are incredibly rare. They are—"

Henry broke in. "I really have to object on grounds of relevancy, Your Honor. I'm certainly learning interesting things from the professor's rock lesson, but how is it going to keep counsel for the defense out of jail?"

Before Flaherty could say anything, Nina said, "Just a few more questions, Your Honor." Flaherty waved at her to go ahead, and she turned back to Tim and asked, "Professor Seisz, did I subsequently ask you to compare rock samples taken from the Zack claim with certain other rock samples I provided to you?"

"You did."

"And you made that comparison?"

"Yes."

"And do you have that second set of rock samples I gave you with you today?"

Tim reached into the chest pocket of his sport coat and answered, "Right here. I've kept them with me ever since you gave them to me." He pulled out the velvet bag Nikki had given Nina, enjoying the undivided attention he was getting, and shook the bag so that the rocks spilled into his hand. Flaherty leaned far to his right to look down on the rocks and the rest of them were craning their necks too.

"Did you come to any conclusions with regard to the similarity or lack of similarity between the two samples in question?" Nina asked.

"I did. I concluded that the rock samples are identical mineralogically. These opal rocks in the velvet bag you handed me come from the property in question. No doubt about it."

"Thank you. No further questions. Your witness."

"What would I ask him?" Henry said. "I have no idea why he's even up there." Tim left the stand and winked on his way out.

"I will demonstrate the relevance of that testimony with the next witness," Nina said. "I call myself."

Henry snorted and shook his head pityingly.

Deputy Kimura made her raise her right hand and swear to tell the truth, the whole truth and nothing but the truth, so help her God or be found in contempt. Barbara gave her the stinkeye. Flaherty continued shaking his head as if he couldn't believe the squirming he was witnessing.

Nina stepped into the witness box and sat

down. It was the first time she had ever testified in any proceeding. The courtroom from this vantage was quite different, ominous: everyone seemed to be facing her with accusatory eyes except for the judge above her and to the side, whom she couldn't see at all. She was appalled at how nervous she felt.

"My name is Nina Fox Reilly," she said. "I am an attorney at law licensed to practice in the State of California with my primary offices located in the Starlake Building, South Lake Tahoe, California. I am attorney of record for Nikki Zack, the defendant in this case. On or about June twenty-second, my client handed me the velvet bag previously admitted into evidence as defendant's exhibit two, containing the same stones which have just been shown to the court. I kept the bag with the stones on my person at all times until June twenty-four, when I placed them in the possession and custody of Professor Tim Seisz.

"At the time she gave me these stones, my client advised that she had taken the bag with the stones from a box hidden in the swimming pool of the decedent, William Sykes, on May eighth, the night of his death, without his permission. As an officer of the court, and mindful of the current criminal investigation, I duly took pains to preserve the chain of evidence should they ever become evidence."

"Duly? Duly?! Stop right there!" said Henry. "You withheld evidence! And that's pure hearsay, what the defendant told you!"

"You're free to object, Counsel," Nina said. She sat back and waited to let Henry think about this. Nina had just testified that Nikki was at Sykes's house on the night of the murder and had taken the opals from his swimming pool. It was a dazzling windfall for Henry. She hoped it was so dazzling that Henry wouldn't see the point she was working toward, and wouldn't object to bringing in Nikki's hearsay statement.

A couple of minutes went by, a couple of minutes she no longer had. Barbara was whispering with him and bringing him around. She was smarter than Henry. Maybe, by the time Nina got out of jail, they would be married with a couple of whippets for children.

Henry folded his arms and said, "Well, I'm not going to object to the hearsay statement. It's actually an admission. Withdraw my objection."

"Do you have any further testimony, Counsel?" This was said with chilling formality.

"No, Your Honor."

"Then you may cross-examine," Flaherty told Henry.

"Your client advised that she had taken the bag from William Sykes's pool, is that right?"

"That is right." Nina had never been so nervous. If she had committed a crime she would have confessed immediately. Hold the line, she told herself.

"What, if anything, did she say regarding why she took the bag?"

"Any such statement falls under the attorney-client privilege, which my client has chosen to exercise. Therefore I can't answer."

"Oh, no," Henry said. "Oh, no you don't. You've opened the door. I have a right..."

"I will answer questions regarding where my client obtained the opals. Other subjects are beyond the scope of the direct testimony and the privilege still applies," Nina said. She was thinking, I sound like a robot. Good robot. Keep it up.

"I request that the witness be instructed to answer the question," Henry said, turning to Flaherty.

"You don't waive the privilege entirely by testifying with regard to one carefully circumscribed matter," Nina said. "Henry can't root around in all my communications with my client because I have made an essential and narrow disclosure as an officer of the court."

"Do you have some case precedent to aid me on this?" Flaherty said to both of them. He was thumbing through Jefferson's Bench Book, the red bible used by all California judges and kept on the bench for reference. "Ah. The question is whether a significant portion of the communication has been disclosed."

"It certainly has," said Henry.

"But what does 'significant' signify?" Flaherty went on, still reading but apparently not finding out what he wanted to know, talking to himself. "We are now entering a dangerous side path without a map."

"But, Your Honor—" Nina said, half-standing in the box, but Flaherty steamrolled right over her.

"The court will now rule on the privilege objection. The court rules that as to the particular conversation in which the defendant handed her counsel the evidence that has just been admitted, the attorney-client privilege has been waived. A significant portion of the conversation has been disclosed." Flaherty pressed his lips together.

"What?" Nina said. She couldn't believe it. The whole conversation? What had Nikki said to her in that conversation? She had just reviewed all those notes, and it came at her in a rush. Nikki had said she was leaving Tahoe when the case was over, had talked about the scene in the woods and the decision not to notify the police—which dragged Bob in!— had talked about her grandfather's claim, her financial problems, had said—what had she said?—"It was supposed to be fair pay for the land."

All the things she didn't want Henry to know about were in that conversation. She felt as if she had walked out into a crosswalk on a green light and been hit without warning by a semi.

Henry said, "Let's have the reporter read back the pending question."

"What if anything did she say with regard to why she took the bag," the reporter read in a monotone.

"You are instructed to answer the question," Flaherty said.

"I can't do that. My client asserts the attorney-client privilege as to the remainder of the conversation."

"Answer the question!" Flaherty barked, all hints of jolliness now buried under his naked anger.

"I can't do that, Your Honor. It wouldn't be ethical."

Flaherty actually stood up and said, "You want to think about it overnight at the County Jail? Because you're in contempt, do you hear, Counselor? I have made my ruling and you had better abide by it. This is my courtroom and I have made a ruling!"

"I must respectfully submit that your ruling is wrong, Your Honor."

"I am citing you for contempt! Appeal it! But now, answer the question!" Flaherty shouted. He gripped the edge of the bench and his eyes blazed down at her and his voice was the voice of doom, but if she answered the question, Nikki's defense would be hopelessly compromised.

"Judge," Nina said. "Find me in contempt if that's what the Court is going to do, but the issues that brought us into court today are still pending. I request a separate hearing on the contempt citation. I request to argue the matters before the court today."

Flaherty seated himself again. "You're right," he said. "Argue your 995 motion. You have three minutes."

Three minutes! "Very well. The testimony regarding blood evidence on the sword must be stricken. There is no scientific conclusion that the blood sample matches that of the defendant. The testimony of Louise Garibaldi must be stricken in its entirety. She is incompetent due to her ingestion of controlled substances within one hour of observing the events about which she testified. Finally, although the defendant did go to the Sykes home on the night of the murder, the only thing missing from that property is the bag of opals, and it is clear from the testimony today that Dr. Sykes had no right of possession to those opals.

"Therefore, there is no evidence of a burglary or attempted burglary or any other linked felony, Your Honor. The 995 motion should be granted."

Flaherty said, "Henry?"

"If I may, Your Honor." It was Barbara who stood up and obtained an answering nod from Flaherty.

Barbara turned almost lazily to look at Nikki. "We now have an admission from the defendant's counsel that the defendant went to the property on the night of the murder. She acted furtively, she took something, no matter who owned it. She spied on Dr. Sykes. She left prints right outside the room where he was murdered. She hadn't been invited, that's for sure. She hadn't established any right to those gems. Her mother had sold her rights to the decedent, and her aunt had no idea she was there. So how is it that she had the right to take them?

"It's a sad thing to see, Your Honor. This defendant has just been sold down the river by her lawyer in a vain attempt to save her own hide."

"Just a minute!" Nina said.

"Siddown!" That was Flaherty.

Barbara looked at the clock and said, "It's exactly four-thirty, Your Honor." She sat down.

"The Court has heard and considered all the evidence, including the new testimony brought forth in this hearing," Flaherty said. "The Court finds that there is probable cause to find that the blood sample on the murder weapon is that of the defendant. The Court finds that the testimony of Louise Garibaldi is competent. The defense motions to strike all such testimony are denied. The Court finds that there is probable cause to believe that the defendant went to the Sykes home to commit a felony, and attempted to or did commit a felony. Therefore, the Court finds that the 995 motion is denied. In its entirety."

"You can't find that, Your Honor," Nina said. "I object to all the findings and conclusions of the Court on grounds that the judge herein is biased and affected by a strong prejudice against the counsel for defendant. The Court should recuse itself. The Court is unable to objectively—"

"The contempt hearing will be held on Monday morning at eight o'clock," Flaherty interrupted.

"Let me finish—"

"Court is adjourned!"

"You're trying to punish me by punishing my client—"

"Bailiff, arrest her!" Deputy Kimura came out from behind his desk. He liked her, and he didn't want to do it, but he was about to arrest her.

Nina showed her palms. "Eight o'clock Monday morning it is." There was a long, strained moment while everyone waited to see what Flaherty would do.

She would never know what stopped him. "Court is adjourned," he said again. She fell back in her chair, saved for the moment, as he left the bench. The deputy cleared the courtroom.

Nina didn't want to talk to anybody, but Paul caught up to her at her car. Boosting herself into the seat, she turned on the ignition.

"Let me buy you dinner," he said.

"No, thanks. I need to hurry home and shoot myself."

"Now, now. You couldn't have known Rankin would go to the D.A. We'll think of something."

"It's all my fault. All I had to do was bring the opals to Court and hand them over. Now— I feel like a jackass."

"I'll still eat dinner with you."

"No." Putting the Bronco in reverse, she backed away. She drove fast until the specter of him, hands in pockets, eyes full of concern, shrank to a speck in her rearview mirror.

27

For a real change, Paul had the rock-grotto spa at Caesars to himself. Sinking into the hot water, he had one thought, that he hoped Nina had poured herself a really stiff drink and gone to bed.

A few minutes later, his muscles now as soft as pudding, his pain a memory, he stepped out and dried himself off just as the attendant was locking the door and turning off the lights around the tub.

"Nobody else here?" the attendant, a smooth-cheeked fellow, said in surprise.

"No."

"Amazing, on a Friday night. This must be your lucky night."

That being so, Paul flexed his poker hand, promising himself an hour at the table before bed to take advantage. Waste no time crying. Always get back on the horse at first opportunity. Back in his room, he changed back into his clothes and counted his cash on hand, finding enough there to make him smile. He stepped toward the door.

The phone rang. He decided to ignore it, but it rang again and again. Turning back, he pressed the receiver to his ear. "Yes," he said. The "s" extended into a sibilant hiss.

"What's got you so pissed?" Ginger said. "On a losing streak?"

"Exactly the opposite," Paul said. "That is,

until you called and interrupted a certain aura I had going that was shepherding me downstairs toward a mind-boggling jackpot."

"I won't apologize. It's been a hairy day. I've got something for you on the airplane parts. Sorry it took so long. Here's what we've got. That fuel screen you gave me? I discovered a trace substance on it."

Yes! So, tonight was indeed a lucky one, and the stars had steered him here, to this phone call with Ginger. Here came the culmination to every chase sequence, the crash and denouement that explained all. "You found water," he said, full of hope.

"No," she said.

Leading him to a different sort of crash, then. His own. No water, no deliberate stall, no sabotage. Shit.

"Something remarkable. Something I bet you never expected. I found...well, I won't go into the chemistry. Or would you like me to?"

"Just tell me what you found."

"Okay. Styrofoam."

"Like the ball I gave you?" he said. Like the ones he had seen in LeBlanc's apartment.

"Exactly. Like the little white ball that was under the seat."

"Styrofoam. Uh...could you see it on the screen? I mean..." What did he mean? He took his old hypothesis out of the fire, shook the ashes off, and looked for something new. "Is it possible this Styrofoam was somehow used to plug the fuel line so that the fuel from the tank couldn't make it into the line?"

"No. Because I found only traces. Styrofoam degrades in airplane fuel."

"Huh. Ginger, why would someone put that into the fuel? Can you think of any reason... ?"

"There's more. Finding it on the fuel screen did make me fussy about inspecting the ball. After looking at it and taking some pictures, I was going to cut it into thin slices so that I could do three-D imaging on the computer...and by the way, that takes me for-effing-ever...but before I got to that point, I took a look at the ball under the microscope. Guess what I found!" she said triumphantly. "Something that didn't belong. An alien invasion. A solvent-based glue."

He knew from the sound of her voice that he should be excited. He just didn't know why. "Go on," he said cautiously.

"The ball had been cut in half and glued back together."

He still didn't get it.

"And hollowed out," she went on, almost gleeful. "And injected..."

"With water!" he hollered. "Hot damn!"

"Well," she said, "that's theoretical. I can't find evidence of water except the hollow in the center of the ball that might have contained it. It's long gone, if it ever existed. The injection site was fairly large. Probably used a turkey baster. Then your perp stopped up the hole with more glue."

"But..." Paul said, picturing the turkey baster on the floor in LeBlanc's living room, "why, Ginger? If someone wanted to put

496

water in the tank and force a stall, why not just pour some water into the fuel?"

"The time factor," Ginger said. "I tested an exact match of this Styrofoam, same density, same glue type, etcetera. Popped it into some fuel. Not airplane fuel, just gasoline, but it would give similar results. It took a long time, over an hour, for the Styrofoam ball to deteriorate to invisibility. How soon enough water might come out of several balls to cause engine failure, I couldn't say for sure. But various factors within the tank might mean the balls would degrade at a different rate. Enough of the water would have to accumulate to cause more than just sputtering, according to my friend the pilot. Also, the balls alone, if there were enough of them, might displace enough fuel to mean the pilot would have the added problem of not enough gas to make it to his destination, but the fuel gauge would show sufficient amounts."

"So the plane wouldn't stall immediately and the crash would happen sometime after the sabotage," Paul said. "How many balls would it take to make, say, a cup of water?"

"Quite a few, but the tank would hold plenty."

"The size of the Styrofoam ball was probably dictated by the size of the opening to the fuel tank," Paul said.

"That's right. I'm told the opening to the fuel tank on that Beechcraft is about two and one half inches. That would severely limit the size ball that could be inserted."

"Someone went to a lot of trouble to make sure that plane went down."

Ginger had been thinking. "What I want to know is what kind of person knows that Styrofoam degrades in fuel?"

"Any mechanic," Paul said promptly, his memory jogged. "I worked in a car repair shop during a summer in high school and I'm sure I heard it mentioned there. And any mechanic would certainly know sufficient water in the fuel tank will bring a plane down."

And the Beechcraft's mechanic, Dave LeBlanc, not only knew, he had foam balls and a baster lying around in the stuff in his apartment. Jackpot!

"You sound like you have someone in mind."

He wondered how soon he could get a plane to LA. He had heard there was a new service operating regular flights out of Tahoe. Maybe he would try them first, save himself a trip to Reno. "I wonder," Paul said, "how that ball ended up under Christopher Sykes's seat and not in the tank."

"What I think? We'll probably never know, but I think that boy saw a pile of them somewhere, and picked one up before he got on the plane. So many boys find balls irresistible. Can't imagine why."

Ginger was making a little joke.

"He was kind of old for that. He was in college," Paul said.

"And your point?" she said.

"He left something behind for us to find,"

Paul said, grappling with the lamentable truth that all the insight in the world could not bring back Skip Bailey or Christopher Sykes. "Without that ball, we would never have known what caused that plane to crash."

"He didn't leave you a clue on purpose," Ginger said, "but if you believe in a just universe once in a while, it has spoken." She paused. "How old was he, the boy that died?"

"Nineteen," Paul said. "The pilot, Skip Bailey, was in his fifties. He had a wife that loved him."

"Sad," Ginger said.

"At least his reputation won't go down with him. I have to call the airport. And LA. And the NTSB investigator. I have to call Nina."

Nina sat in front of the fire eating take-out pizza with Bob, hardly hearing what he was saying. Something about school. The shock was wearing off by now and she was furious at Flaherty for taking his anger at her out on Nikki. He had looked right at her as he denied every motion, letting her know why he was doing it. She had liked Flaherty, but he was a rotten old—and he wasn't done with her, either. Her head reeled. She would have to spend the weekend trying to save her own hide, as Barbara so elegantly put it. Right now she was so tired she just wanted to fall into unconsciousness and never have to move her brain again.

She woke up in bed with a vague recollection of Bob guiding her upstairs. Nine P.M. Charming. She must have fallen asleep by eight. She was so far beyond screwed this time—next stop, the El Dorado County Jail. Awake again, the kind of awake where her eyes were popping out of her head with fatigue, she trudged downstairs, seeing the light under Bob's door, and stood at the kitchen window looking out, Hitchcock at her side.

She looked out onto the summer night, at the end of some kind of line. It struck her then that she could look out now, go out now, live now, without worrying every second about Him. Even jail didn't seem so important when she finally and thoroughly realized this. She spent some time basking in the relief and almost fell asleep standing there. She mumbled a few words in the direction of the moon toward her husband, words like, he's gone, we'll be all right.

Leaving the window, she stopped at the kitchen cabinet on her way back up to bed and opened it up to get a vitamin. Vitamins made her think of Ginger and chemistry, which made her think about that funny little word which she'd never heard before this case, an almost unpronounceable word.

Allele. And it was so simple. She thought she knew where the blood on the sword had come from. But she couldn't do any more, sleep was stealing her consciousness away, the sweet dreamless sleep she'd been denied so long, and she unplugged the phone and tumbled into bed.

Paul arrived in LA at 10 P.M. after a dash to the Reno airport. He rented a car and drove directly to LeBlanc's apartment building in Newport and rang the manager's doorbell.

The apartment building looked exactly the same. Eddie opened up, wide awake and holding a beer, the TV mumbling behind him, and Paul said, "Has he been back?"

"Hey, man, I was gonna call you. He came back a couple days ago. He wouldn't tell me nothing, just handed me a check for the rent plus the damages and went into his place. Said he had a major windfall and was up on his luck. I asked was he gambling but he laughed and said 'Hope not.' "

"That's so good," Paul said. "So fine."

Stopping at the grungy green door of Apartment 108, he knocked. LeBlanc didn't answer. Big surprise. With Paul outside waiting for him, no wonder he was scurrying for cover like a bunny rabbit caught with prime radishes between his blunt little teeth.

Checking to ascertain that Eddie had indeed retreated back to his TV, he set the cane down, pulled himself back, and gave the door a hard shove. To his surprise, it sprang open immediately. Cruddy hardware; it figured.

Nobody sat on the mud-colored, ripped futon. The television, tuned to an old movie on TNT, but muted, infected the background with a low-level radiation buzz. Just like before, the galley kitchen smelled of old beef, with cupboards a matching color. The only bathroom had been crying for Mr. Clean since the days when his jingle jangled into the minds of all America.

The bedroom door was closed. Paul stayed to one side, turned the handle silently, flung it open, and jumped inside, his gun ready.

Dave LeBlanc lay on the bed. He was dead. He had bled all over the nasty brown comforter that matched the torn futon, the kitchen cupboards, and the stinking beef.

28

"GINGER?" NINA SAID into the phone. "Me again." It was Saturday morning. She had slept, slept endlessly, and realized in the morning that she had not even turned in her sleep all night.

Paul had just called from LA to grump about her turning off the phone for once in her entire life, and to tell her about Dave LeBlanc's murder. Working the LA connection, he was on his way to Connie Bailey's house in Redondo. Then, he told her, he wanted to see Jan Sapitto, the plastic food maker, to ask her some more about the Sykes marriage, saying that the alibis in this case were all too shaky and needed a good kick.

She was upstairs in the attic bedroom with its sloping ceiling, holding the phone to her ear, feeling very tense, very excited.

The case was breaking, shattering soundlessly, like a bright light going off. She almost had it, but not quite.

"Hi, doll," Ginger said.

Nina said, "You know, Ginger, there's nothing like a good night's sleep."

"Uh huh," Ginger said warily.

"I was too close to the case, preparing for this hearing. You can't process new information that comes out in court until later—you're much too busy making sure that you get your planned evidence in. So it's only now that I come to a conclusion that is obvious if you think about it. Nikki's father. You mentioned him. He permeates this case with his absence. He's ignored in all the equations, and I think that's why we're not getting our answers. So I put it to you: if Nikki inherited the third allele, and it's not Nikki, and it's not her mother, then doesn't it make sense that it's her father?"

"You said he's been out of the picture for years."

"Yes, he has. But you see, I'm unwilling to accept that the blood is Nikki's. That only leaves her father."

"Then where is he?"

"I had Paul check into it early on, but other than some scribbled postcards that are almost illegible, the trail's been cold for a long time. I just called Daria Zack. I believe she really doesn't know where he is. She tried to help. Said he was a musician, loved mountain biking, played in local clubs until he settled down and started trying to make a living for his family. He left six years ago, and no one seems to know where he might have gone. Ginger, in the lab report...they didn't note any degradation."

"Correct."

"Would a sample degrade if it was old?"

"Well, sometimes. It would depend on how old, conditions, etcetera."

"Tell me," Nina said. "Is it remotely conceivable this blood could have gotten on that sword, say, five years ago, or six, or even sixty?"

"It's much more likely to be five years than

five hundred, if that's what you want to know."

"So it could be from six years ago, when the father disappeared," Nina said.

"I'm liking this. If the blood on the sword belonged to Nikki's father, does that mean he attacked Sykes a long time ago?"

"Or Sykes attacked him," said Nina. "Maybe Sykes killed him."

"Why?"

"I don't know. But it has to be the father's blood. I believe Nikki."

"Gives me the shivers," Ginger said. "The two souls in the sword. The same sword used twice, and kept hanging on his wall as a gruesome memento. Only you would come up with this."

"It has to be," Nina persisted.

"Maybe, but nobody else would be crazy enough to imagine it," Ginger said. "That's your strength as well as your downfall, baby."

Nina went downstairs with her coffee cup and poured some more. "Bob? You need to get dressed," she called.

"I'm taping something," he called back. "Later."

Fine, she thought. Wear your little plaid boxers all day if you want. The fabric between her and him ripped a little more, painlessly, and she experienced the secret working of Nature that would help her let Bob go when the time came. She went out with Hitchcock onto the deck that overlooked the backyard. Around her, a peaceful neighborhood hummed with the sounds of dogs and a drift of music and Bob's drums thumping behind her.

Why? Why would Sykes attack Nikki's father? She knew so little about him; that he was a musician, charming, and he had been somewhat on the outs with Daria. He must share some of her flakiness. Apparently, he was the kind of man who could leave his family without a word, and the people around him wouldn't report it to the police, wouldn't even think about foul play.

She didn't know enough to say why Sykes might have attacked him. She didn't know if Nikki's father was alive or dead or had come back to revenge himself on Sykes and Sykes's son. She began reviewing the testimony at the 995 hearing. Louise. Tim. Rankin. Rankin—

The thought came, why had Sykes insisted that Dennis Rankin wait a few months before mining the opals?

She picked the thought up gently and turned it over and over as gently as she had turned over the opals. Rankin had said it on the stand—something about an agreement Sykes had made with him. Sykes offered to give Rankin the opals if he stayed quiet about the opal strike and kept off the property for a few months. She hadn't pursued that—she had been after something else—and only now had she remembered this odd agreement.

Sykes had bought Daria's share. He had wanted the land. She had assumed he wanted the opal strike kept quiet only until he owned the land.

But maybe he just wanted the opal strike kept quiet because...

Pulling her sweater around her, she thought about Bill Sykes. He had killed Nikki's father with that damned samurai sword, faked the postcards, and sent money to Daria. She felt certain he had. And he hadn't wanted anybody messing around on that land, the land Nikki and her father and mother had once walked on weekends...

She ran for the phone.

She saw Paul walk toward her from the little commuter plane in Reno, baggy-eyed, limping, relying on the cane. He wore blue jeans and loafers and a blue work shirt. The clock above the gates said that it was just after noon. He didn't grab her in a bear hug or even smile, as though he understood what she was thinking about him as he came through the gate toward her.

Good. She didn't want him to touch her. They picked up coffee at a kiosk, and he followed her to the parking lot and got into the Bronco.

"You look tired," she said. "I'm sorry."

"I'm too old to be flying back and forth across California every twelve seconds."

"I called Daria again. She didn't have a detailed map, but she went there often as a child and later with her family. She said there was an old mine shaft her father warned them away from all the time. Said of course she and all her friends made a beeline for it when he wasn't looking. It was blocked, but they could easily remove the wood and crawl inside. I didn't explain anything."

"Daria's husband was named Nicholas Zack, isn't that right?"

"Yes. Nikki is named after him. He was thirty-three when he left. And I called Tim Seisz. I asked him if he'd seen any place on the claim where a body could be buried. He said he'd seen the old silver mine shaft too. He didn't go inside. The opal vein was easy to spot on an exposed hill that had experienced a fairly recent landslide."

She waited for a smile, a nod, anything, but Paul just looked straight ahead at the sun, which had just risen over the hills in front of them. They would be heading east all the way back to Winnemucca, then turn north.

"I couldn't do this alone. I needed you, Paul."

"Yes," he said. "So you said."

"Look, I know you didn't like having to drop everything down there. And I know that even if Nicholas Zack was killed with that sword six years ago, it doesn't necessarily explain why Sykes and his son were murdered. But I feel the connection."

"You feel. Well, I don't feel it. This could have waited. Jan Sapitto is mixed up in this. I needed to talk to her." He was very different from the Paul she knew, hard and distant. She could see the violence she had always sensed inside him in the hard jaw, the narrowed eyes.

She had to keep that separate for now. She couldn't think about Paul and still function.

"And here's a crazier idea I just thought of," she said.

"I can't wait."

"What if Nicholas is living out there in the desert? Maybe he...cracked up and is in hiding there. Daria said he used to love going out there."

"Cracked up," Paul said thoughtfully. "You know, Sandy uses that word about you now and then. How would that explain the blood?"

"Sykes hurt him but didn't kill him? Did some neurological damage. And now Nicholas is out to pasture, living in the desert."

Paul didn't even deign to reply, just gripped the wheel, frowning. They drove on in silence until they had reached Grandpa Logan's property in the long rays of late-afternoon sun.

"Hey," Paul said. Fresh tracks in front of them showed that someone had been there before them, might still be there.

But there was no sign of a vehicle where they parked. They had come to a rocky ridge with a narrow crack in it.

"Through there," she said. "Then to the right about a hundred yards." She consulted the notes she had taken when Daria talked to her.

"Watch it!" Paul said, grabbing her. "You just about stepped in that hole. Anybody ever tell you you hike like a drunk on a lost weekend?"

"Anybody tell you lately you're about as charming?" She pulled her arm back to herself and rubbed it. For a moment, they locked eyes. Paul looked away first. They went back to scrambling. The rocks led to a scrub-covered hill.

"I think we've found our shaft."

She found herself unable to move. "You go."

He looked at the opening for a minute. It was just a hole in the side of a hill, partially obscured by brush and rocks. A thick piece of wood partially blocked it to within about twenty inches from the top. Paul positioned himself in front of it and tried to tear the wood away.

"I left my leather gloves in the car," Nina said. "Oh, no. And my flashlight. I'll go get them."

"Wait," Paul said. "Somebody's been here recently."

Nina was immersed in concerns that undercut the certainty she had felt the night before. "I shouldn't have brought you up here. It's a sickness, this imagination of mine. I let it run away with me; I let it make us do things sensible people..."

"Be quiet. Come help me." It was rude but effective. She shut up and began enlarging the opening with him. They finally had a bigger, safer opening.

"Flashlight," Paul said, a surgeon ready to operate. Like a good nurse, she slapped his flashlight into his hand.

They looked down. "The shaft goes straight down then breaks off into two passages, but there's a ladder," he said.

"I'll go," Nina said. "It's okay. Your leg..."

"I'll go," he said, placing the leg inside the

shaft and tucking his sunglasses into his pocket. "Wait up here. One of us has to go for help if something goes wrong."

"Should I get my flashlight from the car?"

"Yeah. We might need it. Go on."

"Be careful," she called after him.

Eddies of wind raised the dust and the tumbleweeds were on the move. A hawk wheeled above in private flight. Nina walked away, back toward the car.

29

PAUL SHONE THE FLASHLIGHT inside and sniffed. Dust motes floated on the yellow beam. As he left the bright desert outside he felt like he was clambering into a tomb, the tons of earth above insulating the tunnel air into a stifling coolness, the dust he was raising as he shuffled along the dirt floor moldy smelling, the pitted walls naked and ugly. Above and beside him, hand-hewn timbers kept the dirt walls from collapsing. The shaft, only about six feet at the widest, appeared to be long.

Someone had dug this thing using God knew what kind of equipment under the hard sun, worked like a fool for a dream that led to nothing but failure and dashed hopes, that had wasted months or years and probably ruined his health. The tunnel was the tomb of a dream. It had lasted much longer already than its maker.

The tunnel branched. His light disappeared down one of the passages. He went left, the sinister direction, the way he always went at the movies when there was a choice. Hunching to avoid touching the lowering ceiling, he made his way forward tentatively, not wanting to upset a delicate equilibrium that had lasted for a hundred years or more. Almost immediately, he jumped as he stumbled over a pile of something that clattered dully. His hand reached for the gun in his shoulder holster.

Bending down, he picked up tin cans and an old metal spoon, moving the light over them. The labels, if there ever were any, were long gone. The spoon was crude, dented and bent. Tucking it into his knapsack, he moved on a few more steps, then stopped, pointing his light ahead. The tunnel continued at a slightly downward slope, and after about thirty feet, split into two more sections. Again he went left.

He looked back toward the light. The tunnel entrance could have been the spot on the retina when a flashbulb goes off and the eyes close, tiny, insistent, and brilliant.

Stepping around small cave-ins where ceiling and side timbers had fallen and lay in splinters and dirt, he walked around a bend. If he continued, he would lose sight of the light entirely.

Another bend. So be it. He followed the tunnel a long way until it narrowed and both side walls brushed his skin as he walked, all the time thinking about turning back. Why would anyone immure himself any farther into this place? Whoever had made those tracks must be long gone.

The queasiness in his stomach was getting worse. He hated enclosed spaces. He poked at a timber above him with the flashlight, stupidly, and wood flakes showered down.

Stopping once more, he turned the light toward the walls of the shaft, and ran it over the ceiling. If there was something else Bill Sykes had been hiding besides what they suspected, he might see it there. The cold air and darkness began to work on him. Who knew how long the rotten support timbers would hold? In spite of the almost frigid air inside, he was sweating, a cold edgy sweat, and breathing shallowly.

He was about to give up and go back when the tunnel branched once more. To his amazement there seemed to be a little light coming in from above in this new, wider shaft, but he saw nothing in the dimness.

What was that? A sound! The hair on his arms stood up. He pressed himself against the wall, hardly breathing, and flicked off the flashlight.

A guitar? Someone was ahead of him, underground in the uncertain dimness, playing a guitar. He couldn't see anything, though his eyes squinted and blinked.

Over the music, he heard another sound. Rustling.

Nicholas?

30

A MAN BEGAN SINGING with the guitar. His voice was light and young. Paul could hear perfectly.

"Summers have passed since you caught my eye, You were too beautiful to pass by, I never believed I could hunger like this..."

Paul heard a moan. A voice, moaning in the background.

"Obsessed with your face, obsessed with your kiss..."

Another moan, ripped from a woman's lungs.

"Nothing else mattered. Emptiness..."

He had been edging forward, his gun in hand. What was the man doing to the woman? Her moan was a chronic sound, like they had been doing whatever they were doing for a while, not the cry of active distress, so Paul could stay cautious and reconnoiter a little longer. The tunnel was widening into a sort of chamber, and now he saw the amorphous shadows at the far end coalescing into an outline, and he saw...

In the dim, cold cavern beyond, a huge figure sitting on the floor of the cave. No, no, two figures, one propped against the wall, one leaning on a large rock away from the wall, his back to Paul, holding a guitar. So the woman was against the wall in that intent posture, leaning forward.

The man sang on, but now the woman was talking as he sang. They were at least fifty feet ahead of him and didn't seem to have heard him.

Her voice repeated the lyrics softly, and each syllable was clear. "Oh, it's very true, it's all emptiness..."

But the man didn't answer her. He sang on.

"You took me right out of myself, Yes you made me into somebody else, Took me right out of myself..."

Was it possible Nina's incredible theory had been right, and the man had chosen this hole in the ground as a hideout of some sort? All sorts of clammy thoughts struck him as his brain struggled to understand. Nicholas Zack must be insane. Had Sykes injured him terribly six years before? Had Nicholas avenged himself with the same sword?

Was it Zack? Was Daria with him?

His neck ached from holding it rigid for so long. He pulled back and rubbed it with one hand. What now? he asked them silently. Why do you meet here in this dead place?

The man stopped singing abruptly. His fingers made a clicking sound. Paul heard the woman murmur softly, "It's such a miracle to find you again," she said. His eyes caught a flash of blond hair.

Jan? Was Jan in there with Daria's husband?

The whole thing was making him damn nervous and a lot more emotional than he should be.

"I don't have much time, my love. She's coming soon to look for you. She thought of this place, not me."

The woman must be talking about Nina. Nina

had called Daria to ask her about the property just before she called Paul.

He waited for the man to answer. Nothing.

"Obsessed with your face, obsessed with your kiss—my love. My lying darling. Emptiness and more emptiness. You made love to me, but it was all a lie," the woman said in that half-crying voice. "You brought it out. You made it so nothing else mattered. It wasn't my fault. You brought out the monster."

Paul stiffened as an image from his dream intruded itself into the blackness in front of him. The lizard, leaping into the air.

"I'm s-sorry," she cried.

Oh, Christ, Paul thought. Painfully, his emotions in a twisting dark place and resisting all the way, he got himself off the ground and into a crouch, ready to move.

Why didn't the man answer? Working hypothesis: he was angry, he wasn't going to accept the woman's apology, he was drugged, or mentally ill. Maybe all three. But the woman was still talking, and something still kept Paul from going out there where she could see him. He squinted, trying to see them better.

He wanted to hear more about her monster. Instead she moved toward the man and he let the guitar fall to the side, but there was something passive, weird about the way the man let her move to him and embrace him, that same weird indifference. Now she had her arms around him, and was sobbing into his chest.

Gently, she separated from him. The man seemed to have something in his hand. She was holding his arm; she seemed to be helping him to raise his arm and there was definitely something in his hand—it was raised toward her head—a gun...

Reacting instantly, Paul ran forward in a crouch. Somewhere down there his bum leg was on fire. His own gun raised, he ran toward them. "Freeze!" he shouted. "Drop the gun!"

He halted uncertainly, both hands outstretched, standing now about ten feet away, holding his gun directly on them.

The gun dropped from the man's hand and the woman caught it in her lap. The man's head fell forward. He toppled over at an odd angle. Paul drew closer, closer.

A grunt of shock escaped from his mouth. Involuntarily, he stepped back.

It was a body, dead for a long time.

"Daria," he said, about to tell her to toss that gun out of harm's way. But then he saw it wasn't Daria, and this second shock made him stagger.

It was Beth Sykes, sitting there quietly with a portable boom box next to her. Her face was very dirty, and her eyes...

Emptiness.

Paul glanced quickly to the heap in the dirt, face-up, legs akimbo. Shreds of denim and bone, hanks of hair, and a desiccated head with skin still stretched tightly over it. He who once had had a wife and a daughter now had nothing but a big, gaping smile for no one. For the first time in Paul's professional life that he could recall, he felt paralyzed by indecision.

She had been embracing this mummified corpse. She had pressed her gun into the dead hand, raised it.

His skin crawled.

"Beth," he said. "The gun. Toss it toward me. Please."

A pause. "Go on, shoot," she said. "Please."

"No. I don't want to do that. It's me. Paul. I work with Nina, remember?"

"Shoot me. Shoot me!" He listened as the air eddied up the passageways and swirled around Nicholas Zack, and felt its fingers chill his arms.

"The gun, Beth."

She just sat there, her hands in her lap with the gun. This was a very dangerous situation. Paul thought she could probably shoot herself before he could stop her. His gun was useless since she wanted to die.

"The gun?" He tried again, gently. He moved toward her and she jumped. She had a tight grip on her gun there in her lap. He stopped again. Now about six feet separated them. If she moved it too high, pointed it at him—it was too dark in there to shoot to wound her. He'd have to kill her.

A voice inside him said, self-preservation, buddy, don't think twice. He recognized that voice.

"I need it," she said. "I'm sorry you came."

"It's Nicholas Zack, isn't it? Can I see him?"

Following a hesitation, a small gesture from her seemed to make it okay. She got on her knees and crawled just out of his reach.

Watching her carefully and still holding his own gun on her, he touched the torso. Mummified. The air down here would preserve a body well. Easier for the forensics people to check out the cause of death, although he had a pretty good idea about that. Whereas the skin on the rest of the body was stretched tight or had fallen away, the shriveled neck remained somewhat intact, except for a long, black, gaping wound.

Next to the huddled figure, a Spanish guitar. Where Beth had sat, the boom box. "His voice was on a recording?" he said.

"He wrote that song for me."

"How did he get here?" Paul asked, moving back from the body, favoring his leg.

"Bill put him here with his guitar, so everyone would think he just went away. Never even buried him. Bill didn't like to do anything that might harm his hands."

Beth raised the gun and took a shot at the ceiling. The blast in the enclosed space was deafening, and Paul almost rushed her. But she was holding her own gun very firmly. Dirt rained down on them for a few seconds. "What the hell are you doing?" he shouted.

"Shoot me! Or maybe I can make us both die."

"I don't want to die."

"Then go away. We don't want you here." She was unrecognizable now, both of them were covered with a layer of dirt and some of the small stones had hit him hard when they'd rained down. Now he heard some ominous shifting above that made him even more nervous.

"Come with me, Beth."

"Leave me alone!"

"Okay, okay. Look. Take it easy now. Listen. Let's take a minute here and calm down." Even as he said it, though, a sharp piece of timber fell onto his shoulder. He had never felt less calm. Talk to her, get her attention diverted, rush her...

"Did Bill kill him, Beth?"

"I killed him," Beth said. She just said it, no fuss, no emotion. She brushed dirt out of her hair with one hand. He kept the flashlight off her face and on her hands, where the gun was.

"That's a surprise," Paul said. "I hadn't thought of you. Tell me what happened, Beth. Why?"

She thought about whether she wanted to talk to him. Then she shrugged a little.

"Nicholas had decided to go back to Daria. He had an attack of conscience. He took my soul and smashed it and tore me to pieces, and I was supposed to wish him luck. He came to my house one night when Bill was gone and told me...we were in the study... I...this great angry hatred rose up in me and took over. The sword was right behind me. Nicholas never had a chance. He never saw it coming.

"I sat there with him for a long time. When

Bill found us, he doped me up. Much later he told me that he buried Nicholas out in the desert. I never realized where until Nina asked Daria about this mine. Bill kept my secret. Even faked postcards from Nicholas and sent money to fool Daria. But I paid, oh, I paid. He had me now. He could have taken Chris from me, I knew that every second of every day. He had me, and he wouldn't let me go, but he couldn't forgive me. He was punishing me the whole time."

"So you had to kill him? To free yourself?"

She breathed in deeply, and looked down at her gun. "Oh, no. It wasn't like that at all. I just accepted my fate. Six years of hell went by. Daria and Nikki's life destroyed—I couldn't bear to see them. Six years of Bill's tight lips, his hand squeezing my shoulder, the bed.

"Then Chris turned eighteen and started college. I had kept everything from him. He thought his parents had a happy marriage. You can't imagine how hard that was. I gave that child a good stable home and he was wonderful, he was everything to me. When he left, I finally told Bill I was leaving him." She shook her head as if she couldn't believe what she was saying. "And I lost Chris forever because of it."

He had to keep her talking. He had to get that gun. "Tell me what happened then, Beth. I'm trying to understand."

"No one can understand."

"I can."

"You're not a killer. Like me."

522

He almost told her she was wrong but kept his mouth shut.

Her white arm rose through the murk to push hair off her forehead. She stared at Nicholas Zack's body now and almost seemed to be talking only to him.

"I told Bill I was leaving him. He could have called the police and had me arrested right then and there if he wanted but he didn't. The scandal would ruin his practice and he would probably be arrested, too. He knew that. So he let me go without a fight. I went to LA to talk to a lawyer about a divorce. I planned to move south to be closer to Chris."

Paul's eyes flicked back to Nicholas Zack's frozen face. The vacant eye sockets seemed to look back at him, bearing silent witness.

"Bill called me in LA." She paused. "He said he would sign the settlement agreement my lawyer was drafting if I would come up right away on a plane he'd chartered for me."

Paul was edging toward her again, not breathing, taking only an inch at a time. There were definite cracking sounds overhead. Although Beth's hand gripped the gun, he could see the wavering ripple of nerves moving through her and down into her fingers. She was shaky, unstable. He didn't know what to expect.

"Beth, please. I think we should get out of here," he said.

"Go if you want."

"Not if you're going to shoot yourself as soon as I leave."

Beth made a sound that he couldn't quite distinguish, halfway between a sob and a laugh. "Then stay a little longer, Paul," she said. "It's good to talk. I've held it in for so long."

He almost left right then. He really wanted to go. The chances of saving her didn't look good. But he said, "I'm still listening. I'm not leaving."

"The night before I was scheduled to fly," she said, "Dennis Rankin tracked me down. He wanted to talk to me about an opal strike on Grandpa's land. That's when I found out Bill wanted to cheat me."

Paul was focusing all his energy on moving in minuscule increments. He watched for her hand to falter, to loosen, but all her vitality was concentrated in her right hand and on the gun.

She sighed. "I'm feeling quite tired, Paul," she said, "but nobody knows yet what Bill did. I want someone to know."

"You can rest outside, Beth. You can talk to me just as well where it's safe. Just give me..."

"No. I don't think I will. But I'll tell you the rest of it. You're a nice man, Paul. I'm glad you're here with me."

"That's good, Beth."

"I wanted to talk to Rankin without Bill knowing so instead of taking the charter I flew to Reno on a shuttle flight and drove up to Tahoe to meet him. When Rankin learned that I owned part of the land, he wanted to make a deal, so I said he could manage the strike. I was furious, I admit that. Bill was cheating me to keep me poor and weak. That was the only way he could keep me. I was so disgusted, so tired of living with a man who was my jailer. I decided to go home right then and pack a few boxes and leave for good.

"When I got home, I was so rattled I couldn't find my house key in my bag, so I just gave up and rang the doorbell. Bill came to the door in a towel. He seemed completely confused to see me, but before I could find out if Chris had already gotten in, the phone rang in the study. Bill answered and I went into the kitchen to get some plastic bags for packing small things. I could hear him talking. I thought it must be Chris on the phone. After he talked for a minute or two, he—I didn't understand what was going on. I'd never heard him like that before, not even when he lost a patient. I thought he was having a heart attack. He was screaming into the phone and I ran back in and he was writhing on the floor.

"You see"—she made a dry, rasping sound as she drew in her breath—"Chris had a few days off from college and I—I had said, 'Why don't you go to Tahoe? Take that flight your dad arranged for me. You'll be up there tonight.'

"I didn't know Bill had decided to kill me."

"Kill you?"

She nodded. "Because I was leaving him. He paid a mechanic a lot of money to sabotage that plane."

"Jesus!" Paul said. "He killed his son

525

instead!" He was shocked to the core, filled with the unspeakable horror of it.

"And the hell of it is, he loved Chris too, more than anything in the world," Beth said. "That's the hell of it. Nothing else mattered to either of us by then, it was all emptiness."

Paul just shook his head. He couldn't think of a word to say.

"Chris had called Bill to tell his dad he was on his way home. Bill didn't realize at first Chris was on the plane. But then—the engine quit. When I heard Bill sounding so strange, I came running from the kitchen. Bill was out of his mind. Hysterical. He told me that was Chris on the phone, and he had heard everything. Chris had shouted for help. He had cried. My poor, poor baby. The one thing left in my life. Such a fearful death, time to know that he would die, time for terror—it took a minute before I believed what Bill was telling me. That the plane had crashed. That the phone was dead. That Chris was dead."

"It came back, what I'd felt in that same room the night I killed Nicholas. A terrible anger, so powerful it was unreal, like living a nightmare. I grabbed the sword and brought it down on the back of Bill's neck. Then I slashed him again. So much blood everywhere. Just like it must be every day in Bill's operating room, that's what I kept thinking."

She stopped, then said, "It didn't show on me, did it, Paul? You never know with people, do you? Would you believe I could slash his face then, so some patient like Stan Foster would get blamed, and wipe the handle of the sword? It was easier the second time. I never saw Daria. She must have come after I left. And then Nikki got blamed."

Paul said nothing.

"I tried to help. I paid her legal fees."

"What if she'd been convicted?"

"I would never have told the truth," Beth said. "But it feels good to tell you, Paul."

"Come with me now," Paul said. "I'll help you get legal counsel. I still want to help you. Don't give up completely. Let's start with the gun, okay?"

"The gun." She seemed to be nodding. "I used it to kill the mechanic."

"I thought maybe you did."

"Three murders—but I was cold when I killed him. It was simple to fly down there and get in. Because he killed Chris. For money! So I avenged my son. But coldly, Paul. I didn't feel a thing. Then I started thinking that Rankin knew too much, and I thought maybe I should kill him, too. And now, you know, part of me wants to die, but what can I say, the monster wants to live, and you're here..."

He saw the movement of her hand, the movement he'd been dreading. "Don't do it!"

But she was raising the gun—

Toward him? Toward herself?

He launched himself the rest of the way across the cavern and, at the same time, heard the shot.

31

NINA HAD ALREADY rushed forward. She chopped viciously upward with her hand and Beth's gun flew up to the ceiling and fell to the dirt a few feet away in the gloom. Beth let out a scream and pulled Nina down and seemed to try to bite her. There were scuffling sounds and dirt and wood and stones were coming down on them. Paul couldn't tell them apart. He yanked on a loose arm. It was Beth. She screamed.

He pulled her away from Nina roughly and to her feet. He had his gun and for a millisecond his finger was tight on the trigger. Instead he flung her away, against the stone wall. She sank down next to the sightless, mummified witness to all this.

Nina got up, crying, "She shot herself in the arm! She's bleeding!"

"Are you hurt?" He checked her over, wiping her cheeks with his fingers. "The timbers overhead..."

"I'm fine. Really. You?" A big, too big, timber thudded into the dirt, accompanied by a stream of stones, and they all started coughing.

They both looked at Beth. She hadn't moved. The dirt was piling around her legs and hips.

"I got worried and decided to find you," Nina said. "I heard voices. When I saw her point the gun I..."

"She wouldn't have killed me. She was trying to kill herself."

"Maybe," Nina said. "Maybe not." She was pulling herself together rapidly. Her voice was hard.

Beth began rocking back and forth. The shower of stones was increasing. "We have to get out of here right now," Nina said.

"Okay, Beth," Paul said. "Beth?" No response. He turned to Nina. "Let's get her up and out."

Paul helped Beth to her feet. A stream of blood ran down her arm. He and Nina backed toward the tunnel, choking in the dust, blind, half-dragging Beth, and the noise increased as larger stones began to fall.

"Hurry! Damnit, Beth, help us or we're not going to get out of here!"

Paul gave up, picking her up and hunching into the tunnel, Nina right behind. A thunderous noise and a choking cloud of dirt came from behind them, and they stumbled and fell and crawled somehow beyond it.

Then there came a great silence. They fell into the dirt, breathing like locomotives in the blackness. Paul flashed the light behind them, toward the cavern. The entry was completely blocked.

"Nicholas," Beth said. But Nicholas made no reply. The body of Nicholas Zack had been buried by nature, for good this time.

They put her into the Bronco. Nina jumped into the front seat and started it up. Paul sat

529

in back with Beth, his gun handy. She held her forearm, where the bullet had grazed her as Nina knocked into her, but the blood had stopped.

Beth let out a short, bitter laugh. Nina stepped on it and they roared up the dirt road.

About twenty minutes later, as they finally turned onto the highway, Beth said to Paul, "It was all a lie. Bill killed him. I was out of my mind back there. The sight of Nicholas made me crazy! I can't be held responsible!"

"Shut up, Beth!" Paul ordered. "Don't tell me any more. I'm already a witness."

"I'll deny everything. Paul, I need you. You'll help me, won't you?"

"I'll help you, Beth," Paul said. "I'll help you get a good lawyer. And it won't be Nina."

Nikki was sitting at the computer in the hovel wearing her ball and chain. She had been reading her e-mail, starting with one from Scott in jail. He was doing a lot of reading on his case. He thought he might want to go into the legal field after all this was over. His attorney, Jeffrey Riesner, had told him he would be out soon. He was learning a lot from the dude, and could see it was the kind of profession that would really appeal to him.

She didn't know what to make of that. The less she saw of the inside of a courtroom, the better.

With the clicking of her mouse, three spams went straight into the trash. Then...Nikki stared at the screen, at the blue underlined letters. Could it be true? Did she have a message from Krigshot, the greatest, most hard-core band in Sweden? These guys weren't sellouts. They were better than HellNation, even better than Destroy! She clicked on the message line, holding her breath, and the message came up.

Hey Nikki, your songs are crusty...we down-loaded the screamers from MP3 web site...you deep, girl...your web site is thrashed and we never seen anything so hard core...

Nikki thought, oh, boy, this is it, they're asking me to join the band!

So we were thinkin maybe youd do a web site for us cuz we're just asswipe musicians not artists like you so how bout it Nikki? Is five grand enuf?

What? She scrolled back up to read again, starting from the beginning. The words made her blood jump, then:

youd do a web site for us

They didn't want her in the band, they wanted her to do a *web site?* But that was so easy, you just had to be obsessive and pissed off and throw stuff up there! She read it again.

Is five grand enuf?

Wow!

"Mom!" she screamed. "Mom!"

Daria dropped a basket of laundry, rushed through the doorway, and ran to her daughter's side. "Nikki, what's the matter? What is it? You called me 'Mom!' " Her eyes were wide with fear.

Nikki pointed at the screen.

Daria squinted at the monitor. "Well," she said and squatted down on the floor beside Nikki. "This is just so spectacular! We may or may not have opals, but here's the real proof we have a talented person here. That's so much more important." She tapped her chin. "Hmm," she said thoughtfully.

"Don't even start thinking about using that money for anything but bills, Mom. There's this notice that just came from the electric company…"

"Congratulations," Daria said. She was looking at her proudly. It made Nikki want to laugh, they were in such a mess, but for Daria, talent was the thing, and it always would be.

It was her own joy, her relief, that broke Nikki's resolve, made her open her mouth and say the thing that had been making her sick for months now. It just sort of crept out of her mouth. "Mom, you came into the study. Uncle Bill was still alive. I saw you."

"Saw what, baby?" She didn't get it at first.

"I saw you. Your shadow. It looked exactly like you. Exactly."

"No, honey. Whoever you saw, it wasn't me. You were gone already, and he was dead on the floor when I got there. Did you think I killed your uncle? You've been protecting me!"

"Mom, don't lie to me! Not now!"

But then the phone rang, and it was Nina Reilly, calling from some hospital in Winnemucca, calling to tell them about Aunt Beth, and to explain about her father, why he left without saying goodbye.

When Beth began talking again at the hospital, Nina went into legal mode, not allowing her to say anything. She recommended a lawyer, Karyn Sheveland, an experienced criminal attorney in Reno, and called her for Beth.

Then she called the Winnemucca police.

Paul left a card with Sheveland. He planned to keep track of Beth. He felt an obscure sense of obligation to her. Something had happened to him during those final moments down in the cavern with her, something important. He had felt the difference between them. Beth had let the lizard out of a crack in her soul. And that place—that place where it was all emptiness—that crack was still open in his own soul, and might never close.

He would be vigilant. He would guard himself. He would remember her eyes when she said that it had been easy to kill the mechanic.

She had helped him discover that he would have to be vigilant for the rest of his life.

Back at the hotel, Connie Bailey had left a message on his voice mail. She had finally gotten around to looking over Skip's papers and noticed that the passenger manifest Paul had read as "Mr. Sykes," said "Mrs. Sykes." Nobody could read Skip's handwriting like she could. Did that help him?

Thanks, Connie.

Well, at least Beth wouldn't be suing Skip Bailey's estate for the wrongful death of her son. Connie had lost her husband, but she wouldn't be losing everything.

Paul went to bed and woke up Sunday afternoon. Beth was in custody and Nina was meeting with Nikki and her mother and didn't seem to want to talk on the phone.

The knock on the door came at eleven Sunday night.

He had been lying in the hotel bed with the light off, his arms behind his head, thinking about his leg. This led him to roam more deeply than he had ever done into his private places. All this being bothered, the accident, the problem with Susan, had to do with the burden of carrying around a secret about himself. He understood what he had done. He didn't think anyone else could, but that wasn't a problem anymore, because his secret was out. Nina and Bob knew what he had done. Just as well. He was done pretending.

"It's me," Nina said through the door. "Let's talk, Paul."

He jumped at the sound of her voice. There was only one reason she would show up at this hour, after a day like this.

Confrontation time.

But he wasn't ready. He envisioned the talk ahead, laid out starkly as a walk from death row to the site of lethal injection. They would start with the wrong he had done and move into what he had to do to right it, such as turning himself in. She would say, "You have to do the right thing," just like she had told Daria that day. She was a lawyer, an officer of the court. She would tell him to have faith in the judicial system. And what would he say in response?

"Paul?" she said from the hall. "Are you there?"

He feared what was coming. He feared her, and he had thought he feared nobody.

"Paul?"

"I'm coming," he mumbled. He got up in his shorts and answered the door. She was all wrapped up in a long wool coat, holding it shut although it wasn't that cold outside. She probably didn't want him to get any ideas. She smelled like gardenias.

She came straight in and sat down on one of the chairs by the window. "May I?" she said, indicating the pint of Jack Daniel's he had been working on. He couldn't read her face.

Bringing her a plastic glass, he poured a finger of bourbon for her. She tossed it off as though she needed it.

Avoiding his eyes, she poured one for him. Handing the glass to him, at last, she looked up. She took a sip from her glass, then another, brown eyes locked on his face.

Paul couldn't drink. He had never cottoned to the Irish habit of celebrating with booze at wakes. "Dutch courage for an Irish lass?" he said finally.

Still focused on his face, she set her glass down. "So you killed him," she said.

There it was, the big moment. He could lie or he could tell the truth, allow the break to happen, as it inevitably would. He felt his whole vision of the future slipping away. She had been in his vision. He felt overwhelmed.

"He was breaking into your house," he said. "He'd jimmied the lock. But yes, I came up on him from behind. I could have taken him in. I just didn't think he should be alive anymore."

"He had come to kill me, hadn't he?" Strong, steady brown eyes looked into him.

"Yes, after he was through with you."

He watched the brutal thought sink into her and settle.

"The police looked everywhere," she said eventually. "Everyone thought he had left Tahoe. How did you know he would come to my house?"

"I put myself into his mind. He wasn't afraid of getting caught, and he wasn't finished, so I started watching. It didn't take long. Then I waited to make my move until he had made his."

"You were going to do this thing and go your whole life, and never tell me."

"That was the plan." He shrugged. "I probably would have kept breaking my leg until I told somebody, though. I'm not good at hiding things about myself."

"You didn't feel you could trust me by telling me?"

"The last time I confided in you about anything, when I punched out that jerk Riesner, you fired me. I thought you just might think this was worse. Plus I knew I could be quiet about it. I wasn't sure about you. But then

Bob... I couldn't let that kid go through his whole life having those dreams, being afraid."

"I know that you did it for me. I just don't know how you could do it, with your police background, knowing the risks."

"I took out the garbage."

That said exactly how he felt about it. He wasn't going to show any false remorse. If he couldn't fix it, if he couldn't make her understand, at least he could be honest.

She was silent.

"I'm stronger than Beth."

"Are you?"

"Yes. But I'm not going to lie to you and promise anything. I acted on instinct. It happened."

"Why did you do it?"

"For you. Because I love you."

She pulled him toward her, pulled him in until they stood body to body, her head resting on his chest. He made no move to put his arms around her. It was her show.

She was going to be classy to the end. No recriminations, no guilt trips, no demand that he tell anyone else. She was treating him as an old friend deserved to be treated, resting her head on his shoulder so sweetly one last time as her way of saying good-bye. He raised a hand to her long hair, pulling the band out that held it at her neck, stroking it softly.

She had closed her eyes.

"You always talk so much better than me," Paul said. "Talk to me. Just another minute. Don't say good-bye yet."

Still she didn't speak. He turned her head up toward him but her eyes were closed. "It's a crying shame," he said.

Putting both hands up around his head, she brought him closer, turning his head slightly, bringing his head down. She put her lips to his ear.

Gardenias. He felt her warm breath for the last time. He had lost her. He could do nothing to change it now.

Running a finger along the lobe of his ear, she whispered something. Too softly. He couldn't hear. "What?" he said. "What did you say?"

"Thank you," she whispered. "Thank you."

"Wh-what?"

"From the bottom of my heart."

And as she pulled off her coat, the light from his bedside lamp played over the long expanse of her naked skin, as mysterious and radiant as opals.

With heartfelt thanks to our agent, Nancy Yost, for her infinite good cheer and caring, and our fine editor, Maggie Crawford, who works so hard to keep our work tight and on track and to keep us mostly out of trouble. And to all the people at Delacorte Press/Bantam Dell, who have been so committed to making our novels a success.

Thanks to the folks at the Royal Peacock Mine in the Virgin Valley of Nevada for a wonderful day getting dirty—and for finding at least one opal, and to the ladies with a card table full of dusty gems at the Bonanza Mine for getting us hooked on the real things. For opal facts and lore, among other sources we consulted Allan W. Eckert's *The World of Opals*, John Wiley & Sons, Inc, 1997. For tips on natural healing, we delved into *100 Great Natural Remedies* by Penelope Ody, Kyle Cathie Limited, 1997. Some information on flying came from *The Student Pilot's Flight Manual* by William K. Kershner, Iowa State University Press, 1993.

Warm personal thanks to: Pat Lewis, who takes our whimsical speculations so seriously; Alan Penticoff, the insurance whiz who is just full of tricky ideas, and is definitely the man to consult in Illinois when you are investigating small plane sabotage; Arlo Reeves, pilot and dreamer, man of a million facts, who, strangely, really got into how to take a plane down, too; the real Zack family, who put on a great reunion; Sherry Jenks, great friend and fellow writer; and especially Sylvia Walker, our intrepid traveling companion, singer, and raconteur.

And, always, hugs to Patrick O'Shaughnessy and Brad Snedecor, bold heroes who actually read the first draft and offered shrewd but kindly worded suggestions on how we might make the next one better.

All errors are ours, unfortunately.